Acclaim for Carmel's deb

'A bittersweet, quietly brilliant novel that will make you
cry, laugh and cry all over again.' *Female First*

'Funny, poignant and bursting with heartfelt humour.'
I Heart… Chick Lit

'A remarkable read full of love, family and courage.'
BestChickLit

'A story filled with love, friendship, sorrow, forgiveness and
above all hope… a wonderful, unforgettable story that will
stay with me for a long time.' *What Danielle Did Next*

'A remarkable story about a truly remarkable woman that
will leave you desperate to make every last second of your
life count.' *She Loves to Read*

'You will laugh, you will cry, you might even get angry.
One thing is for sure – this, thanks to the warmth of
writing and the level of feeling Harrington obviously
has for her characters, is a story you will never forget.'
AfterTheFinalChapters.com

CARMEL HARRINGTON

With her husband Roger and two beautiful children Amelia and Nate, Carmel Harrington lives a pretty idyllic life in Ireland, full of stories, songs, hide and seek, Mickey Mouse, walks on the beach, tickles, kisses, chocolate treats and most of all abundant love. To make life even more perfect, she has now fulfilled a lifetime ambition to be a writer as she is both a published author and a playwright. Her debut novel, *Beyond Grace's Rainbow*, was awarded Romantic eBook of the Year 2013 at the Festival of Romance.

For more information on Carmel, her writing, books and events, follow her on Twitter @happymrsh, join her on Facebook.com/happymrsh or visit her blog http://carmelharrington.com/.

The Life You Left

CARMEL HARRINGTON

A division of HarperCollins*Publishers*
www.harpercollins.co.uk

Harper*Impulse* an imprint of
HarperCollins*Publishers* Ltd
77–85 Fulham Palace Road
Hammersmith, London W6 8JB

www.harpercollins.co.uk

A Paperback Original 2014

First published in Great Britain in ebook format by HarperImpulse 2014

A catalogue record for this book
is available from the British Library

ISBN: 9780007594405

This novel is entirely a work of fiction.
The names, characters and incidents portrayed in it are
the work of the author's imagination. Any resemblance to
actual persons, living or dead, events or localities is
entirely coincidental.

Set in Minion by FMG using Atomik ePublisher from Easypress

This book is dedicated to my parents, Christina and Michael O'Grady. They taught me how powerful words can be - both in written and oral form.

When I was a little girl, my mother introduced me to the magical world of libraries, and always used to read to us until we could read ourselves. I have no doubt in my mind that my vivid imagination comes directly from my father, who is one in a long line of Irish storytellers. To this day he can tell a story like no other I know. For their love and support this book is for them.

I always say that I couldn't do this, nor would I want to do this, without my husband Roger. His unfaltering belief in me sustains me and along with my children, Amelia and Nate, and my stepdaughter Eva, I am reminded every day how lucky I am to both love and be loved.

Thank you also to my mother-in-law Evelyn Harrington, who can always make me smile when she posts a letter to me, addressing it grandly to 'Carmel Harrington, Author & Playwright' and my siblings, Fiona & Michael, John & Fiona, Michelle & Anthony, Adrienne & George, Evelyn & Seamus and Leah, and all the nieces and nephews, Sheryl, Amy, Louis, Patrick & Matilda, who make our family wonderfully crazy and quite perfect!

To all my friends, I know how lucky I am to have you. I have too many to list, but special mention must be made to Tanya and Annie who helped with the early edits of The Life You Left. And Annie, my oldest friend, thanks for being 'my person.'

Special thanks to all at Harper Impulse, Harper Collins and Harper 360, who work Trojan hours for their authors and I'm blessed to be one of them. I'd like to give a special mention to my editor Charlotte Ledger and Publishing Director Kimberly Young, who rumour has it, don't sleep! I appreciate all the time you have given me and will always be grateful for your belief in me and know that I am in safe hands with you both. To my agent Tracy Brennan, of Trace Literary Agency, thank you for not only taking such good care of me, but for your friendship too. I look forward to many more 'Thelma & Louise' moments over the years.

A few months ago I ran a competition and the winner – Michelle McGuirk – won the chance to have a character in #TLYL named after her. I gave her the choice of whether she would like to be a goody or a baddie and I love that she chose to be bad to the bone! I hope you enjoy reading your namesake Michelle, it was a lot of fun writing her!

Finally, my last words here go to friends, readers & book reviewers who are all such loyal supporters of me and my writing. Because of all of you, I get to follow my dream and I'll always be grateful.

Prologue

Ballyaislinn, Co. Wexford

<Inbox (2)

To: sarahlawlor0902@yahoo.ie

From: paul.lawlor@cgqh.ie

Subject: Sorry

Sarah, I'm not coming home tonight. Don't try to find me or call my office, I'm taking some time out to get my head sorted. If I don't get away, I'm not sure what I'll do.

If you love me, you will give me the space I need.

Tell the children I love them and I'll be in touch when I can.

Paul

Sarah blinked back tears, confused and disorientated by the email she had just opened. She didn't understand. Those meagre sentences made absolutely no sense to her and mocked her by their cruelty.

She struggled to let the words sink in but no matter how many times she re-read the email, she could not fathom what was happening. She quickly hit re-dial on her husband's mobile, knowing that it was a futile exercise. Yes, damn it, still going to voicemail. She checked the time; it was getting close to 10pm. She hadn't worried at first when Paul didn't appear home for dinner. She figured that he had a late meeting and had forgotten to tell her about it. But by 8pm she was worried and started to call him. His phone kept repeating the same infuriating message.

She ran through the mornings events once again in her mind. Paul had gotten up for work at his usual time, showered and dressed himself, whilst she got the children ready for school. Mornings were always frantic in their house with Sarah making the children their breakfast and school lunches and then dressing them in their uniforms. At some point in the mayhem, Paul would leave for the office, with a quick goodbye kiss for them all if they were lucky.

She supposed he had been quiet this morning, she didn't recall him saying one word to her really, but then again he rarely did these days. She felt scared once again. What had she missed? Their lives had become so frantic – Sarah with the three children and Paul with work, it often felt like they were ships that passed in the night.

A flash of guilt overwhelmed her, almost suffocating her. How could she have been so blind to her husband's distress? Had they drifted so far apart that she, his wife, would not notice her husband falling apart at the seams? So bad that he was having a breakdown of such magnitude that he needed to stay away from his family. An image of Paul in a psych ward popped into her head and she reeled from it, as it evoked a memory so painful it pierced her heart. She quickly threw that image from her mind and went back to this morning. Had he seemed any different when he kissed them all goodbye? She tried to be objective but no matter how much analysis she gave to their humdrum movements, she couldn't pinpoint anything that should have alerted her to this email.

Paul had been his usual slightly moody self but nothing new there. Her stomach started to flip again and she started to pace the living room floor, feeling that somehow or other she was to blame for all of this.

She pondered his request that she not try to find him, but decided that it was impossible to obey. She had to at least try to talk to him, so she began ringing likely candidates that he might have confided in. She started with the obvious, his mother Rita.

'Sarah here. Is Paul with you?'

'No, I haven't seen Paul since last Sunday when you all came for lunch.' Rita replied. 'What's wrong?'

Sarah wasn't sure how to answer that. She glanced at the email again and quickly decided it wasn't fair to worry Rita – yet.

'He's not home, that's all.' Sarah replied, trying hard to disguise her anguish. 'Just a bit worried, as he's not normally this late. I thought he might have popped into you on his way home. I'm sure he'll walk in the door any minute.'

She could hear Rita sigh with relief in response. 'Course he will love. Sure, Paul has always been a workaholic. He's probably on his way home right now.'

Sarah doubted that. A feeling of foreboding overcame her and somehow or other she knew life was never going to be the same again.

Chapter One

'Time for the big finale,' James thought to himself. With a dramatic sigh he put his hand over his face and said, 'and as the sun set, I held her in my arms and she died. I just feel honoured that I was with her when she breathed her last breath. And maybe in some small way I gave her some comfort at the end.'

He wiped an imaginary tear from the corner of his eye and sneaked a peak at his date. Had he overdone it this time? Maybe the tears were too much. Nope, hang on; she had bought his story, hook, line and sinker.

'God she is beautiful,' James thought.

She stifled back a sob and leaned in close to James. 'Oh James,' She whispered, 'You were so brave.' She then touched him on his leg and he knew he'd be getting lucky tonight. Result! The hero story never failed him.

His date was clearly mesmerised by him. At 6 2 with blonde wavy hair, worn slightly long, James had always had plenty of attention. His blue eyes normally sparkled with mischief but sometimes would show hints of hidden depths that made women desperate to be the one to unlock their secrets. He was one of those lucky people that were born with a natural charisma that attracted both men and women. Men wanted to be his friend and women in the main had more than friendship on their minds when they met him.

The sound of his mobile phone blaring out Eliza Doolittle's *Pack Up* interrupted his daydream of how the night was likely to end. Glancing at the handset, he saw that it was Sarah. He ignored the phone and said to the blonde, 'Let them leave a message, nothing is more important than this, right now, with you.' She really seemed to like the cheesy lines. She was practically purring – some girls were just too easy to play.

Momentarily he felt a wave of guilt assuage him. He knew that after a few dates he wouldn't be interested in seeing her again. He just wanted some fun and had no intention of settling down with anyone, just yet. He'd grown up in a house with parents who at best were polite to each other, but on a daily basis made it quite obvious that whatever love had drawn them towards each other at the beginning had long since died. In his career as a private detective, he'd also seen more unfaithful marriages than he'd had chicken curries. From his experience there weren't very many happy ever afters anymore, any excuse and one or the other of the couple was jumping into bed with someone else.

And what about his sister, Sarah? Sure he'd watched her fall apart these past few weeks since Paul had done his vanishing act.

What he wouldn't give for five minutes with that man!

A hand gently touching his shoulder brought him back to his present situation and the hot blonde seated in front of him. He brushed aside any guilt he may have felt; after all they were both adults and he never promised any of the girls he dated anything more than they got. He had a firm rule that he always detangled himself before the fourth date. In his experience it was after this dating milestone that most girls started humming the wedding march.

He could see Sarah's disapproving face in his mind's eye and once again felt a slight twinge of guilt. But one look at his date's long bronzed legs and that guilt disappeared. He was just about to make a suggestion of a nightcap back at his house when his phone beeped with a new text message. It was Sarah again. He clicked open the message on his phone. Two words glared back at him.

Edward's back.

This was bad. Even though Sarah had not mentioned Edward in years, James knew immediately to whom she was referring. The aftermath of Edwardgate still left a mark on both of them.

'Sorry, I've got to go.' James leaned in with genuine regret and kissed the blonde on the cheek, slightly amused by the look of astonishment on her face.

James could see his date beginning to panic at the sudden realisation that James really was leaving. He smiled at her with genuine regret, she did seem like a nice girl, but he was needed at Sarah's and that came first.

'What's wrong?' She asked.

'Edward's back.' James replied.

'Edward?' She asked puzzled. 'Who's Edward?'

'Trouble, that's who Edward is, a whole lot of trouble.' James replied and with that ran to his car, texting Sarah as he went that he was on his way.

Chapter Two

'OK kids, bedtime,' Sarah said to her children. 'You've already had an extra five minutes, Tommy, so don't even think about asking for any more!'

Tommy made a face; he had just been about to ask for more time, how did his mother do that? She always seemed to know what he was about to say before he opened his mouth. At 8 years old, Tommy was already a heartbreaker; big brown eyes with a mop of brown curly hair. He was the image of his Daddy, getting more like him every day. Her son was a bundle of mischief, with unlimited energy that always amazed his parents. He never sat still for even a second. Lately though, he was a lot quieter than normal. Sarah knew that he missed having his Daddy around; she could see the effect of Paul's absence on Tommy's face more than with her two girls.

Ruffling his hair, she gently guided him to the door where Katie was already waiting for them, a mock stern frown on her little face as she confronted her big brother.

'Come on Tommy. We did promise Mammy we'd go to bed in five minutes.' This was said in a voice that sounded very like her own, Sarah realised with a smile. Her little girl had always been her shadow, mimicking her. She sometimes felt sorry for Tommy as he often had two Mammy's to deal with, but he seemed amused rather than irritated by his sisters stance. At seven, one year younger than Tommy, Sarah marvelled at how grown up her little girl had become. If Tommy was the image of his Daddy, then Katie was a miniature version of her. Both Sarah and Katie had straight, thick sandy blonde hair, blue eyes and sallow skin. Sarah said a quick prayer that Katie wouldn't inherit her big hips and thighs too. She'd always hoped that Paul's fast metabolism and ability to never to put on an ounce of fat would be bestowed on all of her children, rather than her own 'glance at an éclair and go up 2lbs' one. Time would tell.

'Teeth, face, hands, you know the drill,' Sarah said gently to them both as they walked up to their bedroom. 'I'll be there in five minutes to read your bedtime story.'

While Tommy and Katie got ready for bed, Sarah went to check on Ella, her eight month old baby daughter. She felt her heart contract with emotion as she gazed down at her little angel fast asleep. As normal, she had managed to do a full 180 degree spin and was at the bottom of the cot pressed right to the edge. Sarah gently moved her back to the middle, caressing her baby's cheek as she whispered to her, 'Mammy loves you Ella, always remember that.' Ella was dark and looked just like Tommy did at that age, already with masses of dark curly hair framing perfect round little cheeks and a rose bud mouth. Not for the first time Sarah wondered how on earth Paul could stay away from his children? Surely, no matter what was going on with him, being with his family, his children should be the best place to be? How could he just leave this life behind? Creeping away carefully avoiding the creaky floorboard in the middle of the floor, she walked next door to read the children their bed time story.

'Right, where are we kids? Did we stop on Chapter five last night?' Sarah asked picking up the storybook.

'Yes, Chapter five Mammy! Start it quickly!' Katie squealed, excitement flushing her face. Sarah was reading the Roald Dahl classic *Charlie and the Chocolate Factory* every night. She would read them one chapter per night and on a Saturday and Sunday night they got two chapters. It was one of the first books that Sarah had read as a child by herself and she loved reliving the excitement of Charlie Bucket and Willie Wonka with her own children now. The chocolate factory and the golden ticket had been an escape for Sarah as a child, when things were out of control and scary. Her parents disapproving faces flashed into her mind, but she quickly pushed that image away and started to read.

'"You mean people are actually going to be allowed inside the factory? Cried Grandpa Joe"', Sarah began. She looked at her children, their eyes wide with wonder at the words Roald Dahl had created. She knew that both Tommy and Katie were wishing they were Charlie Bucket, just as millions of other children had done for decades before them, Sarah herself included. Ten minutes later she finished the chapter and smiled as she noted the children's eyes heavy with sleep.

'See you in my dreams, my darlings.' Sarah said to them both. 'Where will we meet tonight?'

'Chocolate Land,' Katie said excitedly.

'You want to go there every night.' Tommy said disdainfully.

'Please,' Katie begged. 'And you love Chocolate Land!'

'OK, Chocolate Land again.' Tommy said quickly, giving in with a grin.

Smiling at them both, Sarah said, 'Ok, Chocolate Land it is. I'll meet you by the big Toblerone oak tree!'

'And we'll go swimming in the Dairy Milk pool!' Katie added.

'And eat the marshmallow clouds!' Tommy piped in.

'And pick Jelly Tot flowers!' Sarah said smiling as she turned to go. 'Night night both of you. Close your eyes and get dreaming. We've lots of chocolate to eat in our dreams tonight!'

Sarah walked to the kitchen and grabbed a bottle of wine, her favourite Pinot Noir. It was only €4.99 and really pretty decent for that price. 'Thank God for German retailers and their cheap wine', she thought to herself. She rarely had a drink anymore, as she couldn't justify the cost. But tonight, dwindling bank account or not, she needed something to help take the edge off. Glancing at her kitchen clock she realised James would be here any minute and right on cue, the doorbell rang. Opening the door, she looked at him and felt her lip begin to quiver, tears about to fall, so he pulled her tightly into his arms.

'I'm so glad you came.' Sarah said to him relief enveloping her immediately as she relaxed into his embrace. She always felt safe when James was with her.

'Of course I came.' James said tenderly. He loved her so much it was agony to see her so upset. He pulled back and looked at her closely.

'OK, shoot. When did Edward come back?'

Sarah looked at her twin brother and wondered where to start. At first she thought it was her imagination that someone was watching her. But the sense had gotten stronger this past week.

'It started after Paul left.' Sarah said. 'You know that feeling like someone has walked over your grave?'

James nodded, shuddering despite himself.

'Well it's kind of like that. I knew I was being watched but no matter how quickly I'd turn to check, there was never anyone there.'

'You've been under a lot of pressure lately. Between money worries, being on your own with three kids and working crazy hours, it's enough to put anyone on their last nerve.' James said.

Sarah acknowledged this with a nod. 'It's more than that though. It's such a strange feeling, it's not too bad when I'm working, or when the kids are with me. But when they are all asleep and I'm in this house on my own, well it can get a bit scary….'

'When did you suspect it was Edward?' James asked, feeling a little ashamed that he'd nearly switched his phone off earlier.

'It's weird, I've had a sense of déjà vu for weeks, but I couldn't quite place why. Now I can't believe that Edward didn't cross my mind. How stupid was I not to even think of him? But what with everything going on these past few weeks, I've not been sleeping well.'

James looked closely at her and could see fear etched on her face. The last time Edward was around resulted in Sarah being committed to a psych ward and James had to watch, helpless as his sister was dragged away from him kicking and screaming. There was no way on this earth he was going to let that happen again. He hadn't heard Sarah mention Edward's name in nearly two decades. But the impact he had made on both their lives ensured he'd never forgotten him and although Sarah didn't talk about that time anymore, he would have bet his house that she remembered every detail of that time clearly too.

'I'm not crazy, James.' Sarah said suddenly with tears in her eyes. 'I wasn't then and I'm not now.'

'I know that. You don't need to say that to me Saz; I never believed you were crazy back then and you are one of the sanest people I know today.'

'You haven't called me Saz since we were kids.' Sarah said smiling at her brother.

'Ah, you'll always be Saz to me.' He said affectionately.

Sarah sighed and continued. 'But Mam and Dad thought I was crazy didn't they? They had me committed. They still look at me like I'm a raving lunatic even now. Like I'm going to have a *One Flew Over the Cuckoo's Nest* episode any minute. I always feel that Mam would use any excuse to get her hands on the kids. She has something negative to say every single time she comes into this house.'

Sarah looked around her living room. It was lived in but pretty tidy, considering she had three children. 'I don't know how she does it, but she always seems to arrive on the one day that the house is messy and I've no food in! If she thought I was having one of my 'episodes' again as she called them, that would be it, she'd be onto Child Protection and looking for custody!'

'That would be over my dead body, Sarah. You're a fantastic mother and even Mam and Dad would have to agree to that. Forget about the folks for now, they are not important. Sure, how often do they visit, once or twice a year? Get back to Edward.' James reassured her quickly.

She took a large gulp of her wine; the alcohol helped to relax her.

'When the kids went to bed last night I was tidying up the sitting room. I was putting their toys away in the toy box and I had that feeling again. I looked up, but this time somebody was there, standing in the corner of the room. Over there.' Sarah pointed to the area.

James looked, half expecting to see Edward there right now. 'It was him.' Sarah said. 'The craziest thing though, he hasn't changed in the slightest. Three decades later, I'm unrecognisable, but him, he's the same.'

'You must have gotten such a fright. What did he say?' James replied.

'Nothing at all, at least he said nothing last night. He just smiled at me. It was the most beautiful smile and I got lost in it for a few minutes. I'd forgotten how his smile could make me feel like I was a child again. I closed my eyes for a moment and when I opened them again, he was gone. It all happened so quickly, I actually thought I'd imagined the whole thing.'

This time it was James who took a large gulp of wine. They sat in silence. Each in their own thoughts.

'You said he didn't say anything last night; can I assume he's been back again?' James eventually asked.

'Yep, he was here this morning, after the kids went to school. Ella was having her nap. And when I came downstairs from her room, he was sitting at the kitchen table.'

'Cosy.' James said wryly. 'What does he want, why come back after all this time?'

'Exactly what I thought. Why now? I mean life couldn't be more hectic for me; I haven't time to wash my hair some days, never mind deal with all this. These days I'm running around so much I swear one day I'll meet myself coming backwards!'

They both smiled at that. Gathering herself, Sarah continued. 'At first he just sat there. I joined him and he smiled at me again. It was very peaceful, very quiet just sitting there together. I felt like in that moment we were both reconnecting, catching up with each other, without the need for words. Oh, it's hard to explain.' Sarah ended with a sigh.

James reached over and grabbed his sister's hand. As hard as it was for Sarah to explain, it was very hard for him to take in too. Somehow it had been easier to understand Sarah and Edward when he was a child.

'Eventually he spoke and he simply said "It's time."' Sarah said.

'It's time for what?' James spluttered.

'He said that he knew that seeing him again after all this time was a shock. He knew I'd need to adjust to having him around again, but I need to believe in myself and acknowledge my gift. And after I acknowledged it I need to start using it!'

Sarah glanced at James. He looked a bit shell-shocked. He was the one person who had always believed in her, but she knew he was struggling to take all this in right now. Taking a deep breath she continued. 'He just kept saying over and over that I've been ignoring this gift for far too long and now the time has come for me to step forward and start helping others.'

'What gift is he talking about?'

'Oh you haven't heard the best bit. It gets better.' Sarah said with a sigh. 'He told me that there was a young girl who needed my help. That she'd been murdered... And that I could help bring her murderer to justice.' Sarah shivered at just the thought.

'For feck's sake Sarah.' James replied.

'Pretty much my reaction too.' Sarah replied. 'I'm no Sherlock Holmes; I'm a shop assistant for heaven's sake! If anyone around here is going to solve a murder that would be you.'

'Thankfully not many murders around here for me or anyone else to solve,' James replied. As a private investigator, with his own business, he did a lot of freelance work for insurance agencies, sifting out the fraudsters looking for big claims. Not to mention the considerable amount of clients who booked him to investigate their spouses and see if they were having an affair. All pretty mundane stuff.

'Well I hope Edward has gotten it wrong.' Sarah said. 'The thought of me even being slightly involved in a murder makes me feel sick.'

James topped her glass up with some more wine as he couldn't think of anything useful to say.

'Apparently I'm to go see a woman who lives in Arklow and have a chat with her. He told me to write down her name and address.' She continued, as she showed the piece of paper to James where she had written her name down.

'Mary Donegan. 5 Riverside Apartments, Arklow.' James read. 'Why do you have to go there? Some random woman you have to go knock on the door to, will she be expecting us? Is she even real?'

'I know it sounds crazy, doesn't it?' Sarah answered. 'But I've looked her up online. She lives there alright. She exists.'

Her head was banging with a growing headache that felt like it was about to explode. Over the years she had thought about Edward and the impact he had on her life when she was a child. Life was so hectic with the kids, she just didn't have time to worry about something that had happened nearly thirty years ago and, as far as she knew, would never happen again.

She glanced at James who was frowning. She'd had a few hours to digest the news that Edward was back; James had just had a few minutes. Plus, to be fair to her brother, James had never actually met Edward; he only ever had her word that he even existed. The fact that he always believed her left her in grateful awe. Sarah knew that it was extremely difficult for most people to understand and believe in something that they couldn't see or touch. That was why she had kept Edward's existence a secret for so long, not even sharing with Paul. Would he have believed her? Her instinct was no. He would have reacted the same way as her parents. They all thought she was crazy, and if she was honest who could really blame them? How could you expect people to believe that your best friend was in fact, a guardian angel?

Chapter Three

Sarah sat up with a start. A line of perspiration glistened on her forehead. She was shivering, despite the heavy duvet covering her body.

She leaned over and flicked on her bedside lamp, checking her watch as she did. It was 3.06 a.m. She knew there was no point in trying to go back to sleep. From experience, it would be at least an hour before that would happen, if at all. She had just awoken from a particularly bad nightmare. Already, as is often the way with dreams, the details of it were beginning to get murky. Unfortunately one image kept flashing into her mind, one she would have been happy to lose.

A young woman lying on the beach. Naked. Covered in blood.

'You look tired.' James said to Sarah when he was round at the house later that day.

'I had a nightmare last night, didn't get a huge amount of sleep. Thanks for coming with me by the way.' Sarah said to her brother.

'No worries. Sure this one could be a complete nut-job. There's no way you are doing this on your own!' James said emphatically.

'She could be a nut-job just like me, you mean?' Sarah asked playfully.

James replied in kind, 'You? Nut-job? No! But for the craic let's just summarise. An angel called Edward, who used to be your best friend

15

when you were a child, has casually rocked up into your kitchen. Incidentally because of your insistence that Edward was real and not a figment of your imagination, you were committed by Mam and Dad for psychiatric assessment, thereafter you spent years in and out of therapy. Now the bold Eddy, enigmatic as ever is saying very little, except that you have a gift. As yet we don't know what this is. I'd have put money on that it's your finesse at baking, but not sure that's what Eddy is talking about! Now that doesn't make you sound like a Cadbury's Fruit and Nut bar in the slightest!'

Sarah laughed at this, thank god for James; he was making this so much easier.

'And to top it all off, this ability of yours is expected to help solve a murder of which we know nothing about. Eddy reckons we need to speak to some lady called Mary Donegan. So here we are outside some random woman's home, about to knock on her door and say hello.' James took an imaginary bow.

'Why Watson, thank you for that summary.' Sarah said with a smile. 'Think that just about covers it! As much as I'm enjoying listening to you, I suppose we better get this show on the road. I've got to get back to collect the kids from Rita's house by tea time.'

Sarah knew a lot of people didn't have time for their mothers-in-law, but for Sarah it was the opposite. Rita was a godsend to her.

'She heard anything from that loser of a son of hers?' James asked.

'He has a name, James.' Sarah said with a sigh. 'And no, she hasn't heard anything from Paul in weeks either.'

'He doesn't deserve to be called by his first name, in my opinion.' James retorted. He could feel himself getting angry again, as he always did whenever Paul came into his mind. 'How can he leave a wife with three children, one only a small baby? What kind of man does that?'

Sarah could feel her head thumping again. 'Please James, not now. I can't deal with Paul on top of all this. I know you're right. It's not fair, but there's extenuating circumstances. He says he's having a breakdown. He can't help himself.'

'That's a load of bullsh…' Seeing Sarah's face, he stopped himself. 'Ok, I'll leave it, but he just gets me so wound up.'

She was close to tears, as she often was whenever her wayward husband's name came up.

'Hey Sarah, don't cry. I'll zip it about Paul, promise. Come on, let's go meet this Mary one and see what she has to say! Wonder what age she is?' James wondered out loud. 'She could be hot! Hey!' James yelped as his sister punched him on his arm. 'What was that for?'

'We're not here for you to get your next victim lined up!' Sarah said with a laugh. 'Come on, behave. I don't care if she looks like Angelina Jolie; keep your hands to yourself!'

'Hey, less of the victim, if you please. I'll have you know that all my girlfriends are very well looked after by me. Hey!' He yelped again. 'Leave out the hitting. You have some right hook on you! I promise I'll behave. There will be no chatting up of anyone. But if she's anything like Angelina, all bets are off!'

They rang the doorbell and waited with nervous anticipation. Sarah had no idea who or what to expect.

With that the door opened and a tiny woman, no more than five feet peeped out. She was middle aged but hard to determine what side of fifty she was on. Her face was lined, not from frowning but with what Sarah guessed were laughter lines. She was plump and exuded warmth, and Sarah felt the urge to throw herself into her arms for a hug. Pulling herself together, she simply smiled at her. Mary smiled back, an expectant look on her face.

'Hello' Sarah stammered. 'My name is Sarah Lawler. This is my brother, James. Are you Mary Donegan?'

'Yes, I am.' Mary replied with a friendly smile. 'How can I help you?'

Sarah wasn't sure where to start. 'Erm, it's a bit tricky this. I'm not really sure why I'm here. I was told to come and see you.'

'Who told you to come see me, pet?' Mary answered smiling, like it was the most normal thing in the world to have such a conversation.

17

'Edward did.'

'And who is that? Is he a friend of yours?' Mary continued.

'Well this is the tricky bit. You'll probably not believe me, not sure I would believe me either. Edward is a friend of mine. But most people can't see him.' Sarah blurted out quickly reddening up to her ears. She held her breath, never taking her eyes of Mary, wondering what the response was going to be. She half expected the door to be slammed in their faces.

Mary continued smiling and then opened her door fully, 'Oh that explains it! You should have said so sooner dear. Come on in so, both of you.'

They walked into the apartment and Sarah was surprised at what she saw. The apartment was ultra-modern and chic. It was clutter free and was decorated in varying shades of white and cream, the only splashes of colour on the wall were the art, which were contemporary. It seemed to contradict the first impression Sarah had formed of Mary, which was a mother earth type.

'What a beautiful apartment.' Sarah complimented.

'Thank you.' Mary nodded and smiled again. 'It suits me very well. One of the advantages of being on one's own is that you get to decorate your home to exactly your own tastes. No need to take into account anyone else's requirements!'

'Well it's very chic.' Sarah replied a little in awe. Her mind flitted to her chaotic house that always looked cluttered no matter how much she tidied up.

Mary indicated that they should sit down in the big open plan living space. 'So, you have met your guardian angel, Edward, you said?' Mary asked. 'How lovely.'

'You believe me? You know he's an angel?' Sarah asked incredulously.

'Of course. Why wouldn't I? Sure we all have a guardian angel.'

'Even me?' James said startled.

'Yes, even you.' Mary replied with a laugh. 'Your angel is called Lorna.'

'A girl! I might have known!' Sarah said with a laugh.

'What's she look like?' James asked Mary excitedly.

'She's very beautiful, tall with long blonde hair. All angels are beautiful. She has a message for you actually.' Mary said dramatically, winking to Sarah as she turned to him.

James nearly fell off the edge of the 18th century white chaise longue he was perched on. 'What message?' He whispered. He was feeling excited now.

'She asked would you mind changing your chat-up story, she's getting a bit bored of the dying children in the orphanage tale.'

James paled at this. Sarah yelped with laughter. 'Please tell me you're not still using that line – 'I held a dying child in my arms as she breathed her last breath!' story? You are unbelievable.'

James went from white to red. 'How on earth does she know that?' He spluttered.

Mary just smiled at him.

'In my defence I send money to Chernobyl every month.' James added lamely.

'Shame on you.' Sarah added, shaking her head.

Mary smiled herself. 'Your angel is with you whenever you need her. But angels have a good sense of humour you know. I have a feeling that Lorna is having a little joke here, teasing you about your love life!'

'Well you can assure her I'll not use that line again.' James replied with a slight sniff. 'I'll come up with something new to keep her amused!'

Making a face at James, Sarah whispered, 'Calm down, focus on why we're here.'

'Mary, do you know why Edward sent me to see you?' Sarah asked. 'Have you spoken to him too?'

'No. But he's here now, alongside my own guardian angel, Diana. Look, see for yourself.'

Sarah turned around and sure enough Edward was standing there, smiling at her.

'Hi Edward,' Sarah said with a smile. 'How come I can see Edward but not the other two angels? Yet you can see all of them?'

'Oh but you could see them if you wanted to, Sarah.' Mary replied. 'You just need to open your eyes and really look. All in good time.'

Sarah looked again. No, still only Edward. Frustrated, she turned to Mary. 'Why am I here?'

Mary walked over and sat close beside Sarah on the couch. She took her two hands in hers. 'Well, pet, I have a feeling that you and I are going to be great friends. You're going to need someone to help you understand and come to terms with your gift. And as I have that gift too, I know how much of a curse and a blessing it can be.

'What gift?' Both James and Sarah said at the same time.

'Why, you have the gift of being psychic, pet. You just have to believe in the power that is within you.'

Chapter Four

Mary felt sorry for the young woman sitting in front of her. Her revelation was clearly a big shock. For her it had been very different. There wasn't a memory for Mary that didn't include Diana. Every night while she slept as a child, Diana would exude a soft white glow that covered Mary in a blanket of safety and security. Her parents never questioned Mary's relationship with Diana. In fact they welcomed it; saw it as a gift from God. It didn't take her psychic powers to work out that it was a very different story for Sarah. She wondered what traumas Sarah had endured as a child, what lay beneath that façade she had created for herself. She'd find all that out in time she figured. For now, she needed to help Sarah understand the role of angels, help her come to terms with her revelation.

'What do you know about angels?' Mary asked. She'd made them all a pot of tea. She served it in a beautiful silver tea service, with pretty china tea cups and saucers, with such a delicate pattern of pale green and pink flowers. She also produced a cake stand filled with cupcakes with a pistachio green frosting on top.

'Wowsers.' James whispered, as he grabbed a cupcake.

'I don't really know much about them at all.' Sarah admitted. 'After Edward disappeared when I was a child, I tried my very best to block any reference to them I came across. I suppose that probably seems strange to you.'

'Not strange at all. I look forward to hearing your story about how you met Edward, but first of all let me tell you what I've learned over the past fifty years or so about them.' Taking a bite of one of the cupcakes, she mumbled, 'My one vice, pet. I can't get enough of cupcakes. Little pieces of heaven these are.'

James was happily munching on his second one and grunted his agreement.

Putting down her tea, Mary started, 'Well, let me see, what can I tell you? Let's start at the beginning; guardian angels have been popping up in literature for over 4000 years now. Some believe that angels are sent by God to bring messages to people who are in critical situations. These messages from God can be either a warning or a comfort in times of danger and fear.'

Mary couldn't help but notice the look that James threw in Sarah's direction.

'I'm wondering, if it's not too personal, is that why Edward is here right now for you? Have things been difficult for you lately? Are you in need of comfort?'

Sarah smiled wryly. 'I suppose you could say that. I'm on my own at the moment. My husband disappeared a few weeks ago without any warning that something was wrong. He's having a breakdown of some kind and needs to be on his own. But I'm coping the best I can. I have no other choice but to. You have to with three children.' Her voice cracked at the end.

'Don't put a brave face on it!' James exploded. 'He left with nothing but a weak cowardly email saying I'm sorry! It's been horrendous for you and the children. Especially the older two, Tommy and Katie, sure they don't know why their Daddy has disappeared.'

Sarah turned to Edward, looking into his black eyes. 'Is that why you've come back, Edward?' She asked him. 'Because my life is a complete mess?'

Edward walked over to Sarah and gently said, 'I've never left you, I've always been here right by your side – through every magical and wondrous time of your life to date. On your wedding day.

For each of your children's births. I was with you the whole time. But in answer to your question, yes, part of the reason why I've shown myself again to you is because I want to help you now. I want to give you solace and guide you.'

'What did he say?' James asked. 'This is so annoying, not being able to hear both sides of a conversation!'

Sarah smiled at her brother's irritation. 'He said yes, in part he's here to comfort me because things are hard.' She turned to Mary and asked, 'Can you tell me more about them – our guardians? Help me understand.'

'Of course I can. We mere mortals don't see everything. We only see what we want to. So angels are here to point out what our careless eyes can't take in.'

'Why doesn't God just tell us himself, cut out the middle man?' James asked.

Mary smiled as she said, 'You have a wonderful way of seeing things, James. But I think that God would be way too much for most of us to take in. Think of guardian angels as diplomatic envoys if you like.'

'Diplomatic envoys. I like that.' James said with a smile. 'That's kind of cool, sis.'

Sarah smiled and continued. 'Edward hasn't aged at all since I last saw him, Mary. Do they have a lifespan like humans?'

'That's a good question, Sarah. But no, angels don't decay or die, they are spiritual beings. They can think and hold conversations with us. They each have their own identities. And truth be told we are learning continuously about them and their powers, with more and more people believing in them.'

'I had a girlfriend once who had lots of angel figurines all over her house.' James interjected. 'She got them from a shop that sells angel stuff in Wexford.'

Mary smiled at this. 'Yes, the concept of angels is becoming popular. I think some people need to believe in something bigger than themselves. Especially right now with the way things are in Ireland.'

They all nodded in agreement to this. The recent recession of the past few years affected so many.

'Everybody has a guardian angel.' Mary continued. 'At some point or other everyone has had contact from their angel, even if they didn't recognise it as that. Have you ever had days where you kept finding pennies?'

Both James and Sarah nodded yes.

'I found one this morning!' James said in awe. 'A cent was on the doorstep when I was leaving to head to work.'

'That was Lorna letting you know she was with you today. I call those Pennies from Heaven. Often if you look at the penny you found and take a note of the date on it, it will have some significance. Other gifts from angels are white feathers. These are the most common form of angel communication. When we unconsciously ask for guidance from angels, they will often send us signs with the answers we seek.'

Mary stopped speaking for a few minutes. Sarah and James needed time to digest all the information she'd thrown at them.

'Drink up, pet.' Mary said to James. 'It's a blend of Monkey Picked Oolong and Silver Needle White tea. It's quite delicious.'

James couldn't help but agree. It was the nicest cuppa albeit the strangest afternoon tea he'd ever experienced. He half expected Alice to come running in followed by the Mad Hatter.

Turning to Sarah again, Mary continued, 'Every person has some innate psychic medium skill within them, and all of us are capable of seeing, communicating, and even working with our guardian angels. But most of us just ignore that side of ourselves. And then for some of us, pet, we have extraordinary psychic skills.'

'Psychic powers?' Sarah repeated, looking more and more bemused.

James put down his tea too. Taking a deep breath, he said. 'So basically all of us could see and communicate with our guardian angels if we wanted to?'

Mary nodded her confirmation to this so James continued. 'How come I can't then? I'm open to it. I've watched my sister talk to her angel for years as a kid. Yet never did I see either Eddy or Lorna. Why's that?'

'It's not as simple as just wanting to see our angel.' Mary responded. 'We have to trust in our inborn psychic potential to link up with these divine entities. And that's not something that most of us have the ability to do. Sarah however, she's different.'

Sarah was reeling. 'It's a lot to take in, Mary.' She stated. 'I'm feeling a bit overwhelmed. What exactly am I supposed to do?'

'You need to start working with Edward. Open your mind to him, talk to him, and allow him to guide you. Some of today's most powerful psychic mediums work with guardian angels. You're probably going to start having some new and different experiences. For now go home, try to come to terms with Edward's presence. And start looking at life with a fresh pair of eyes. You may start to see and feel things that will shock you.'

Sarah and James got up to leave. This time Sarah followed her first instinct and gave Mary a huge hug. She felt instinctively close to her, an immediate bond had formed between them and quite happily stayed in the embrace.

Walking to the car with James, he whispered, 'Don't you dare begin to see my angel! 'I can just about get my head around Edward, but I'll not cope with a disapproving angel who can tell tales to my sister!'

Sarah laughed as she got in the car thanking her lucky stars once again that she had James with her. He never let her down and was there for her. She thought of Paul and how it should really be him beside her right now, helping get through this revelation she had just received from Mary. But somehow or other, even if Paul hadn't left home, she doubted he would have been sitting beside her. The thought sobered her.

At what point in her marriage had it become normal that Paul wouldn't be with her either emotionally or physically when she needed him most? She felt a single tear fall onto her lap and felt a now familiar surge of panic overtake her, her breath becoming shallow again. It was all too much. She'd been putting off so many things lately, her AWOL husband and her financial crisis at the top of the list. She knew it was time to sit down and take a good look at how bad things were.

Once the children were in bed, Sarah sat down with a cup of tea and opened her laptop to check her online bank account. She needed to do an immediate assessment of her current financial situation.

Every day she woke up and the first thought she had was, is it today that Paul comes home? She repeated to herself over and over throughout the day, it will be ok once Paul is back, he'll know what to do. But as the days became weeks, the hope for his return was replaced treble fold with despair. Surely whatever mental state he was in wasn't so bad that he would forget about his responsibilities? She massaged her temples, a blinding headache beginning. She was getting a lot of them lately.

She looked down at the ever increasing pile of brown envelopes in front of her. Taking a deep breath she started to organise them into three piles – First request, Second Request and Final Demand. The pile for Final Demand with big, ugly, red lettering over them was the biggest; no surprise really.

She took out her calculator and started to add up how much she owed in each pile. As the sum got higher and higher, the more overwhelmed she felt. Her wages from the boutique didn't even make a small dent in how much she owed, plus she still had to pay their mortgage and feed them all.

Nervous breakdown or not, Paul was going to have to come home and answer some questions. She couldn't do this on her own. Closing her eyes she leaned back into the soft cushion on her sofa. She felt herself drifting off and soon was fast asleep.

An hour later she awoke, feeling cold. She'd stopped putting the fire on in the sitting room, to save on fuel costs, but the room had gotten quite chilly. Pulling her cardigan around her more tightly, she shivered as she remembered the dream she'd just had.

A woman loads a dishwasher. A man walks into the kitchen and looks at this woman. Evil exudes from his every pore. His disdain for the woman is impossible to ignore. Whoever this lady is, she's in danger.

Chapter Five

'Come on, lazy bones,' Molly shouted to her husband, Pat.

'I'm on my way, woman,' he answered good-naturedly. 'I must be mad agreeing to a walk at this ungodly hour!'

It was 7.30 a.m. on a bright October morning and the elderly couple had arrived at Ballyaislinn beach, ready to have an early morning stroll.

'You heard what the doctor told you,' Molly continued, getting ready to go into full monologue. 'Exercise and a healthy diet are very important for a man in your condition.'

Shaking his head, Pat knew there was no point arguing with his wife. Plus, he knew she was right. He had gotten pretty lazy since his retirement the year before. The most exercise he managed to get these days was switching the TV channels.

Catching his wife by her hand, the couple started their walk, chatting amicably about their grandchildren's forthcoming visit that weekend.

After a few minutes, Molly paused as she heard a noise.

'Did you hear that, Pat?' she asked her husband.

He stopped beside his wife and listened, ready to tease her about hearing things. But he did hear something. 'Yes. You're right. Sounds like a baby crying, almost.'

They stood for another minute trying to work out the direction of the noise and then together walked from the shore towards the dune in front of them, where they felt the noise was coming from.

'That's definitely not a baby,' Molly said suddenly. 'That's an animal of some kind. It sounds like a dog keening.'

Walking up the dune, Molly and Pat started to have a poke around the green dune grasses.

Molly stopped and grabbed her husband by the arm.

'Let's go home, Pat.' She shivered despite the warm anorak she was wearing. Somehow she knew that whatever was over to her left would not be good.

'You stay here, love.' Pat said. 'I'll go check out this noise.'

Shaking her head, Molly indicated that she would be going with her husband if there was any investigating to do.

The couple ran over to the area where the noise was originating and then stopped suddenly. Never in their lives had they ever witnessed anything so terrible. Lying in the dunes, naked and bloodied beyond recognition was a body of a woman. Beside the woman almost as if keeping guard was a dog, also injured, with a large bloody gash across its body. It was the dog that was making the keening noise. Even without checking, Pat and Molly knew that the woman was dead. Had been for quite a while it seemed.

'Molly, go call the Gardaí. Go on now, love.' Pat shouted at his immobile wife.

'I'm not leaving you here. What if whoever did this is still around?' she asked in a terrified voice.

'Whoever did this is long gone.' He answered. He, of course, didn't know this, but taking in the scene it looked to him like this had happened hours before.

'Go get help, Molly.' He finished more gently. He walked over to the body of the woman and carefully felt for a pulse. He didn't expect to find one but he had to look.

He took no delight in being correct in his assumption. The poor woman was dead. He automatically crossed himself.

Shaking his head, Pat turned to the dog. 'Here, boy.' Pat said gently patting the dog's head. 'You hang in there.'

The dog looked up at Pat and he swore he saw tears in its eyes. He wasn't sure what to do, but wait for Molly and help. Taking off his jacket he laid it gently over the dog and the woman. He didn't think the dog was going to last much longer.

Sarah felt like her whole body was reeling. She had arrived at school to pick the kids up and the Principal, Art O'Leary was at the gate greeting the parents. Sarah liked Art and more importantly the children loved him. Surprisingly she noted there was no sign of any of the children coming out.

As she got closer to Art, she realised that something was very wrong. He looked awful, his eyes puffy and red. 'I've some bad news I'm afraid. I've just been telling some of the other parents.' He said to Sarah gently.

'I'm sorry Sarah; there is no easy way to say this. Ms Finch, Rachel Finch, our 2nd class teacher has been found dead on Ballyaislinn beach this morning.' He paused, and then added. 'She – she was murdered,' the normally articulate Art stammered. He was obviously deeply distressed.

The dream of the bloodied body on the beach flashed back into Sarah's mind. Was that Rachel Finch? She felt the blood drain from her face and held onto Ella's pram for support.

'Ms Finch? That's Katie's teacher.' Sarah eventually managed to say. 'When, what happened?' She felt sick. This was just awful. This was the kind of news you see on RTE news. You don't expect to come face to face with it at the school gates.

'Molly and Pat Donovan were out for a walk and found her yesterday morning. She's been identified by her parents.' Art continued. 'There's no doubt I'm afraid.'

'I can't take it in. That poor girl and her parents. God help them.' Sarah said tears glistening in her eyes.

Art moved towards Sarah and reached over to touch her hand, before he continued, 'She didn't turn in for work this morning. Which

I thought in itself was strange. She's never off sick, extremely diligent. When she didn't call in I phoned her and got no answer. Her parents were at the hospital when I called, identifying her body.' He finished.

Sarah looked around, there were groups of parents all gathered together, some crying, all looking completely shocked.

'I can't believe it, Sarah. She was only twenty four, beautiful, her whole life ahead of her.' Art finished. 'I'm sorry. I just can't get my head around it all. She was my friend.'

'That's understandable.' Sarah said with sympathy, wiping her own tears and this time, she moved to him and gently patted his arm in reassurance. 'Do the kids know?' The thought of Tommy and Katie having to deal with this was unbearable to her.

'Not yet. We're going to have an assembly in the morning to talk to them all. But we wanted to give the parents the option of telling them at home tonight first of all. It might be better if they are with you when they hear of it. We'll have counsellors in the school all day tomorrow, it's all organised. They can help the kids talk through how they feel.'

She couldn't take it in. A murder in her village and not only that, it was Katie's teacher. This had to be the murder that Edward told her to prepare for. She needed to lean on Ella's buggy for support once again.

When the kids came out she gave them both an extra big hug. 'Come on you two, let's go home.' Pushing Ella in her buggy, the four of them set off. When they arrived at home, James's car was outside the house.

'Hey you guys!' he shouted to them all. Tommy practically knocked him down as he jumped into his arms. He hero-worshipped his Uncle James.

'You've heard?' James asked quietly.

Sarah nodded and quickly glanced at the kids, letting James know that they didn't know anything yet.

James squeezed his sister's shoulder. 'Come on, kids, let's go in and grab some juice.'

Sarah went up to her bedroom to splash some water on her face. She needed to compose herself before she spoke to the children. How do you tell young children that their teacher has been murdered?

Looking into her bedroom mirror, she felt like she'd aged decades in the past month, but her reflection hadn't changed. She still looked the same old Sarah, sandy blonde hair with blue eyes. Edward appeared in the mirror, standing right behind her. A few days ago this would have made her scream with fright. Now, she welcomed his calming presence.

'So Rachel is the young woman you talked about?' Sarah said to him. He nodded in response, the pain she felt reflected in his eyes.

'You never said it would be someone I knew. She was only twenty-four for God's sake, a mere child herself!'

'I know.' Edward replied.

'Where was her guardian angel? Why didn't they save her?' Sarah hissed at Edward.

'It doesn't work like that. We can't stop that kind of force. We can't stop death. Her angel did her best to warn her. She tried to make Rachel listen to her intuition that something wasn't right. But she ignored it. But I promise you she was with Rachel right up till she died. And she's still watching over her now.' Edward had tears in his eyes.

'How can I tell Katie? She loved Ms Finch. She's making her Holy Communion this year and Ms Finch was helping her prepare for it. She'll be devastated. Only last night she was practising her Communion walk.' Sarah smiled sadly at the memory. Katie with her hands clasped in prayer, walking solemnly from one end of the hall to other.

'Give me strength Edward, help me tell the children.' Sarah pleaded.

'They will be fine, as long as they have you Sarah. I'll be right here by your side. Always am and always will be.'

Sarah took a deep breath, trying to stop the tears from flowing that were prickling her eyes. 'I still don't know what I'm supposed

32

to do to help. I don't feel any different than I did a few days ago, except I can see and talk to you again.'

'Just be prepared Sarah, take note of any strange things you can see in your mind's eye. Trust your instincts because you have a great gift. You will see things that others won't and I'm certain you will be able to help with Rachel Finch's murder.'

Sarah thought for a second about the dreams she'd been having lately. Were they the start of her gift? They didn't make any sense and she really couldn't see how she was supposed to help based on what she had dreamt. But she didn't have the time to look into it now. Her priority right this minute was her children. Only they weren't just hers; she needed her husband more than ever right now.

She picked up her phone and quickly dialled Paul's number. It went straight to voicemail. She took a deep breath and left a message.

'I need you. The children need you. Please baby, call me. I'm begging you. Whatever is wrong, I can help make it better. Together we can get through anything. Remember? That's what we always said. Once we are together, we can do anything. I love you...' She hit end on the phone call quickly, before the tears overtook her. Lying down on their bed, she pulled the covers over herself, suddenly cold, her eyes never leaving the phone, willing it to ring.

James was making Spaghetti Bolognese for their dinner when Sarah came downstairs ten minutes later. Ella was in her highchair, swinging her dolly by its leg around in the air, giggling at how clever she was. Every now and then she'd let out a high pitched scream which resulted in everyone around her laughing. The children were watching SpongeBob on TV.

'Thanks James. You are a starbar!' She shouted to her brother, as she walked through the kitchen. 'Thought you had a date tonight?'

'I do, but I've cancelled. This is more important. When I heard on the grapevine that a schoolteacher from here had been murdered, I thought I'd better get here quick.'

'This is losing-my-fecking-mind-freaky.'

James nodded in return. He knew the feeling; he felt the exact same way.

'You know when Art first told me about Rachel, I got such a shock I didn't think about Edward's prophecy at all. And then it struck me and I nearly passed out. It was one thing having Edward telling me something would happen, but to actually be faced with it, it's too much.

James squeezed his sister's hand. He didn't know what to say.

'Try not to think about that yet.' James said. 'I was talking to one of the lads in Wexford Gardaí station and they will be doing an autopsy today, so we'll know more after that. No word on forensics yet either.'

'How's her dog?' Sarah asked.

'What dog?' James answered in surprise.

'I don't know.' Sarah answered looking confused. 'A dog just popped into my mind. He looked pretty sick. I think he was Rachel's dog.'

They were both silent for a few minutes.

'Ok. It's going to take a while for me to get used to this.' James said quietly. 'I'm going to call my mate in the station and see if there was a dog.' He punched a number into his iPhone and walked away.

A few minutes later he was back. 'Well, there was a dog.' He said with his eyes nearly popping out of his head.

'Oh feck.' Sarah said.

'Yep, feck.' He echoed.

'All I know so far about the murder is that she was on Ballyaislinn beach. The fact that her dog was with her indicates to me that she was taking him for a walk probably. Whether it was a random act of violence or premeditated they don't know yet. Remember Roger, my mate from school, the guard? Well he's on the case and will keep me posted.'

'You never said how the dog was?' Sarah asked again.

'He died a few hours ago.'

They both were silent again.

The sound of the Bolognese sauce bubbling broke the silence. 'Oh, you doing a Jamie Oliver?' Sarah said nodding at James and the chopping board.

James bowed as he answered, 'But of course. No chance of a bit of parmesan lurking in that fridge of yours?' James answered. 'Then I'd really pep this baby up for you!'

'Not a hope!' Sarah responded. 'Cutbacks, its only essentials these days, no luxuries.'

'Thing's that tight?' James said with a frown.

'Yep, things are "squeezed into a pair of too small spanx" tight. I've been going through my savings like crazy, what little we have anyhow. Tommy and Katie both outgrew their trainers this week. And it's coming into winter again, they'll be needing boots. They both were asking me about Halloween costumes yesterday. All their friends are getting new ones from Woodies apparently. I went in to have a look this morning, but they're nearly €30 each. I just can't afford it. Then next thing it's going to be Santa. It never ends. I've asked for more shifts at the boutique, hopefully I'll get a few more for Christmas.' Looking at James face, Sarah felt guilty suddenly. 'You don't need to be listening to me moaning about money. Ignore me. I'll make it work.'

'You can't keep going like this. You need to track Paul down. Or let me do it for you, I can do some digging, find out where he is. It's just not good enough him sending you the odd email telling you he needs time to sort himself out. He's got responsibilities. He had enough wits about him to empty your bank account, he's not that bad.' James ended sarcastically.

'I've got to go talk to the children.' Sarah said, ignoring James last comment, because she knew he was right. No matter how much she tried to rationalise Paul's behaviour, the fact that he took most of their money with him, made her break out in a cold sweat of fear.

'You can't keep dodging that bullet,' James shouted at her as she walked into the living room. She stuck her tongue out at him. She knew she had to face up to the fact that her husband had walked out on her, but there was a bigger crisis to deal with. Taking a deep breath she turned the TV off.

'Tommy, Katie, I need to have a chat with you.'

'I didn't do anything!' Katie quickly shouted.

'I know, nobody is in trouble!' Sarah reassured them gently.

Gathering the kids both close to her, she gently told them that Ms Finch had been hurt badly and was now in heaven. They were both confused and scared. They'd not really had to deal with a death before; this was a first for them. And Sarah knew that there was little point in lying about how it had happened, as they would get all sorts of stories in the school yard tomorrow. She needed to prepare them for some of the things that they might hear.

'Who hurt her?' Tommy wanted to know.

'Will he come and hurt us too?' Katie added, her big eyes round with fright.

'No, darling, nobody is going to hurt any of us. The guards will find the person who did this to Ms Finch and they will be locked up for a very long time.' Sarah replied firmly, pulling them in even closer to her.

'Uncle James will catch the bad person.' Tommy said quickly. He really believed that his Uncle was a superhero.

'Maybe, or one of Uncle James's friends in the Gardaí. Don't you worry; they will catch whoever did this. Bad people go to jail for a very long time, and that's where the person who did this will go.' Sarah promised.

'Mammy does that mean I won't have a teacher anymore?' Katie asked with big tears in her eyes. 'Do I have to stay at home now forever, and never go to school again?'

'No, darling. Of course not. You will have a new teacher soon. I bet that one has already been picked especially for you and your class. Mr O'Leary will explain it all tomorrow when you have assembly.'

36

'But who will help me make my Communion? Ms Finch said she had lots to teach us this year.' Katie started to cry and within seconds Tommy joined in. Sarah held them close and let them stay there crying their pain out. James was in the doorway rubbing his eyes with a tea towel.

'Onions.' He said gruffly, not wanting to admit that the scene before him had deeply moved him.

Ella, who had up to that moment been intently playing with two plastic balls, sensed that something was going on and wanted to get in on the act. So she started to scream. James walked over to her and picked her up, quickly laying her on the floor, tickling her and blowing bubbles on her tummy. This trick always worked and very quickly she replaced her tears with giggles. The sound of Ella's giggling was too irresistible for Katie and Tommy and both of them peeped up from their mother's embrace, watching their Uncle James tickle their baby sister. Sniffing away her tears, Katie wandered over to join in the tickling, Tommy following within seconds. And with that the house was filled with the sound of giggles again as James tickled each of the children one by one.

Sarah smiled through her own tears and watched her family, marvelling at how resilient children were. Their world can be pulled apart in a snap of the fingers, but they just picked themselves up and found joy in their baby sister's laughter in the next. They weren't moping about like she had been for the past couple of weeks since Paul had left. She could learn a lot from her children.

The time had come to find her husband. Yes, he was having some kind of mental health crisis. But by walking out of their life, he had in effect given up on his parental responsibilities. He didn't have the right to walk away from those or indeed his financial responsibilities too without at least a conversation about it all. He'd only sent a couple of hundred euros that he supposedly sent via his mother about a week after he left. Only Sarah felt it was a safe bet that Rita had used her pension to give her that money, out of embarrassment for her wayward son.

Watching her children deal with yet another blow, she realised that it was time she regained control of her life that had been spiralling out of control these past few weeks. She felt a hand on her shoulder, and looking up saw it was Edward.

'Good girl,' Edward said to her. 'That's the fighting spirit I remember when you were a child.'

Smiling, she vowed that tomorrow she would start her search for Paul. But right now there was a tickle fight to be won!

Chapter Six

Sarah woke with a start, her heart thumping so hard she felt like it was going to burst through her chest. She'd just had the weirdest dream about her postman Joey. If she had to guess all day who she might dream about, she didn't think that Joey would have ever been on her list. He had been her postman for years and although she saw him most mornings through her sitting room window, she only spoke to him the odd time, when a parcel or registered letter would arrive. She really didn't know anything about him on any level, other than he was punctual and very kind to the children if they did get to speak to him. Joey was in his mid-fifties she reckoned, and had a really pleasant manner. Always cheerful and if the children were around, he had a little joke or story to tell them. Sarah instinctively liked him, but if she was honest, other than when he came to her door delivering, he would never cross her mind from one day to the next.

Sarah shivered at just the mere memory of the dream.

The desperation. The poor man fumbling with a rope. A noose.

It was so vivid it felt real. But that was ridiculous, surely? She closed her eyes and tried to remember the details of the dream. Maybe it had happened in his house? She had no clue as to why he had done it, but she had felt an overwhelming wave of sadness and despair. It was incredibly unnerving.

A thought popped into her head, maybe she was losing it, and maybe she was really going mad this time. Was she having a nervous breakdown of some sort? First seeing angels and now dreaming of her postman's suicide. She barely knew him, for goodness sake.

She looked at her mobile phone, it was 6am. Damn it, it was early but at the same time too late to go back to sleep. She crept into Ella's nursery and straightened her up. She was as always scrunched up against the corner of the cot, blankets awry. She then peeped in at Tommy and Katie and they were both peaceful. They had to be tired because it had taken her a long time to get them to sleep last night. They were scared, worried that the 'bad man' who murdered Ms Finch might somehow come into their house and kill them.

James was asleep on their sofa. It was the only way that they agreed to go to bed, knowing that he was there keeping guard. He had left shortly after she told the kids about Rachel Finch, to go into the office. She wasn't sure what time he came home at, but she figured it was late as she had only gone to bed a little after 2am. She went into the kitchen and put the kettle on. Coffee was badly needed.

She knew that she drank too much of it, but it was a habit that she found impossible to break. She sat down at the kitchen table and looked out her window. It was beautiful out there, a gentle light mist hovering over the hills and trees. She had the most amazing view from her kitchen; she still got pleasure from it even though she'd looked at the same view every day for over eight years.

Memories of loud family breakfasts popped into her mind.

Paul and her laughing together at something funny Tommy or Katie had said. Stealing a kiss in between the demands of 'pour me a juice!' from the children. And laughter, always laughter. She tried to pinpoint when it was that Paul had stopped having breakfast with them. Last year? Two years ago? He now favoured grabbing a latte and croissant each morning in a deli close to his office. Once again she started to feel panic bubble up inside her as the realisation that her marriage had been in trouble for some time hit her smack in her face.

Sighing, she closed her mind to Paul because she had to. And try as she might, she just couldn't stop her mind drifting back to Joey. She shuddered as she remembered how he'd looked as he kicked the chair from under his feet and allowed himself to drop. He was a man who had just given up and looked so lost. She tried to think of the right word to describe what she had witnessed.

'Sorrowful.' She said out loud. Yes, that was the word alright. Joey was sorrowful.

How awful to think that the only option you felt you had was to end your life? Sarah wrapped her dressing gown around herself even more tightly, feeling cold again.

Taking a sip from her coffee, she suddenly felt a presence beside her. Sitting opposite her was Edward. 'You're up early, Sarah.'

'I couldn't sleep.' Sarah answered. 'Bad dream. I've been getting a few of them lately.'

He nodded not looking in the slightest bit surprised to hear that. 'Tell me about it.' He replied.

'Why?' Sarah said belligerently. She really wasn't in the mood for an evasive and unsatisfactory conversation with Edward. It was early, she was cold, and she couldn't justify putting the heating on just yet. She had just paid €500 for a full tank of oil and she really needed that to last till Christmas. Pulling her dressing gown tight around her once more, she felt an urge to stick her tongue out at Edward, like she used to do as a child.

Instead she answered him. 'Ok, Ok, you want to know about my dream? Well, it was about my postman. He committed suicide, hung himself. Now you know, does that make you happy?' She shivered again, though this time not with the cold.

'No, that makes me feel sad, Sarah. What do you think it means?' Edward said.

'It means that maybe I need to stop eating cheese before I go to bed.' Sarah answered glibly. Edward smiled again. 'Funny. Sarah, why do you think you dreamt that Joey committed suicide?'

Sarah shrugged. She really didn't want to think about it. But try as she could, Joey's face as he finally realised he was about to die was imprinted in her brain and wouldn't leave.

'You obviously know what it means.' Sarah said to him. 'So can't you just tell me?'

Edward smiled that same smile again; it was beginning to drive Sarah mad. She recognised it, as it was the one she used herself on the children when they were desperately trying to learn something new, but failing miserably, it was the indulgent smile of a smug parent. Right now it irritated the shit out of her.

She hated mornings, more importantly she hated early mornings, disturbed by psychic dreams and early cups of coffees with angels. She felt justified in her bad mood.

'Totally justified.' Edward said smiling that annoying smile again.

'How do you do that?' Sarah demanded crossly. He had always been able to read her mind. When she was a child she'd play a game with him and get him to say out loud the thing she was thinking about. She'd loved that game and played it for hours, much to James's annoyance, when he wanted her to go outside and play. She realised she was now smiling, at the memory.

'It wasn't all bad when I was around?' Edward asked, this time an earnest look on his face.

'No Edward. It wasn't all bad at all. In fact I had some great times with you. It was the stuff that came after I told Mam and Daddy about you that wasn't fun.'

'They just didn't understand, Sarah. And when people don't understand something they get scared. And when people are scared they can act irrationally.'

'Maybe.' Sarah said noncommittally. She had children herself now and often asked herself how she would handle something similar. And she knew that no matter what she would be on their side. She had made that vow the day she found out that she was expecting Tommy. She had promised her unborn child that she would do better than her parents had done for her.

'I get that they were scared. I get that they didn't understand. But they didn't try very hard. They didn't talk to me or more importantly, they didn't listen to me.' Sarah said with regret.

Edward nodded.

'I've thought a lot about this, Edward, in particular since I've had children of my own. All a child wants is to be loved, to feel loved and safe. When Tommy was a small baby, Paul and I used to sit for hours watching him sleep. And we would worry about his future. We'd talk about everything we could do to protect him from the bad stuff life can throw at you! I always said to Paul, that it was our duty to not only love our children, but to also make sure that they know they have a safe place to fall if they need to. Paul had that with his parents, he was lucky, but I didn't. I still don't. They couldn't handle the fact that their daughter was different. So they tried to force me to change who I was. I mean what kind of parent has their child committed for fecks sake?'

Sarah shuddered as she remembered that bleak time in her life.

'I'll never forget that day. I was terrified. I begged them to take me home. Poor James was in tears too. He was devastated that I was taken from him. We'd never been apart until that day.'

Sarah closed her eyes, hoping that by doing so she could close her mind to the bad memory.

'They found it easier to believe you were crazy, than to believe that you could talk to angels Sarah. They made a mistake, but for what it's worth, they have never forgiven themselves for doing that to you.' Edward replied.

Sarah shook her head. 'I don't know. I'm not sure I buy that. They've always been so cold towards me. They treat me very differently to how they treat James. Him, he's the golden boy. Me, I'm the mad daughter that they are so ashamed of.'

'It's complicated Sarah. For some people, when they have guilt, they put a barrier up around themselves rather than to confront the guilt and accept responsibility for their own mistakes. Have you ever considered that maybe your parents find it hard to look

43

at you sometimes because it reminds them of a time they are ashamed of?' Edward asked gently.

Sarah knew that what Edward said had an element of truth to it. She felt their guilt sometimes when she was with them. They could hardly look her in the eye when they visited, the annual, once a year visit that is. You'd swear they lived a million miles away, not less than ten miles. But she didn't have time to analyse her parents right now. The dream, try as she may to forget it, meant something.

'Ok, so is my gift to dream about things that have already happened or are about to happen? Sarah asked him.

'You know the answer to that already.' Edward replied.

'No, I don't.' Sarah said stubbornly.

'Think, Sarah; remember the details of your dream. You have all the answers you need yourself.'

She closed her eyes and allowed herself to relive her dream.

Joey sits at a table. In a kitchen by the looks of it. Oak kitchen cabinets are behind him. He walks to the fridge, opens the door and takes out some milk. There's something on the fridge door. It's a flyer advertising a table quiz at Freddie's Bar. The date is the 15th October. Joey pours himself a glass of milk. He sits down again at the table, his head in his arms. A copy of the local newspaper - The Wexford Echo, dated 16th October.

So that confirms it; her dream had not happened yet.

'It hasn't happened yet. I saw next week's paper on the table.' Sarah said triumphantly.

Edward smiled in return. 'Well done Sarah. So part of your gift is that of precognition and prophecy.'

Sarah rolled the words over her tongue. 'Precognition. Prophecy.' She stated in wonder.

'I'm struggling with this a bit.' Sarah said. 'I'm not sure I can handle it all. Is this it for me? I can look forward to bad dreams every night, about things that are going to happen that I can do nothing about?'

'You might be surprised to know that people have been having prophetic dreams for centuries. Of course many ignore them like Abraham Lincoln did, who had a psychic dream about a funeral at the White House. In the dream, he asked someone who was in the casket and they replied, "The President of the United States". He told his wife about the dream later that day but neither of them took it to heart – on the night of his assassination he gave his only bodyguard the night off. Would he have lived a long life had he taken his dream more seriously?'

'I didn't know that!' Sarah exclaimed.

'You know after the Titanic sunk, hundreds of people came forward with reports of premonitions, many of them validated, including one date-stamped letter.' Edward paused before continuing, 'Why do you assume that you can do nothing about your dreams? You have been given a unique window into the future. You now have a decision to make. You can ignore the prophecies you dream, sit back and do nothing and wait for the future to unfold, hoping for the best. Or you can apply positive action and do all in your power to change or even create a new future.'

Sarah held her head in her hands. She was scared and felt very alone. How was she going to stop Joey from committing suicide? She needed to talk to someone, someone who understood. She considered calling James, but she felt guilty about how much she had offloaded on him lately.

'I'm going to call Mary Donegan.' She suddenly decided. He nodded his approval.

It was 7am now. Was that too early to call? She'd told her to call anytime.

She picked up her phone and dialled the number. Mary answered within a couple of rings assuring her that she was an early riser and happy to chat. Sarah quickly brought Mary up to speed on Rachel Finch's murder and the dream.

'Quite a night and morning pet.' Mary answered. 'You've been busy!'

'Yes, you could say that.' Sarah replied with a smile. 'Help me, Mary. What am I supposed to do?'

'Ah, that's the million dollar question. I know how overwhelming this must feel for you, pet. I think the first thing you need to do is start understanding all that is going on right now. Something that helps me is keeping a journal. I write all the information I get from either my dreams or from talking to angels down in my journal. It's always easier seeing something in black and white, gives you a better chance to interpret.' Mary stated.

Sarah liked that. 'That's a good idea. A dream journal if you like?'

'That's it, pet.' Mary answered. 'You need to start being a detective in your dreams. You need to analyse what you are dreaming and look for clues to help you work out what they are telling you. Like what you did earlier. You looked for clues in your dream to decipher that the event had yet to happen. So at least there is some chance that a new future can happen for Joey, not the one you dreamt.'

'Well, Joey is going to commit suicide in a week's time. That doesn't give me much time. How do I stop him?'

'Well that's a tricky one. You might scare the life out of the man if you confront him about it. Maybe he hasn't even decided he's going to do it yet. You've got to tread very carefully. And remember, despite all your best efforts, you still may not be able to stop him doing this. If he has chosen this path, well then maybe nobody, not even you, can stop it.' Mary said.

Sarah refused to believe that. 'Why am I dreaming this if I'm not meant to stop him? This gift that Edward keeps referring to, well it has to be a gift so that I can help people. Nothing else makes sense.'

'I understand your frustration, pet, but you only have the power to control your own life. You can't control what Joey does. But you can influence it. Remember that. Maybe you can help him if you understand why it is he wants to die.'

'All I know is that I felt an overwhelming surge of sadness and loneliness when I was dreaming.' Sarah replied. 'Maybe I should try to talk to Joey? Try to understand why it is he is feeling suicidal?'

'Yes, that has to be your next step. But please be very careful. As I said before don't scare him by blurting out what you've seen.' Mary implored.

'I understand.' Sarah replied. 'I'll just make an excuse to speak to him when he calls with the post and I'll play it by ear. Try to get him talking.'

'Ok that sounds like a good plan. Let me know how it goes and now that your psychic self is 'switched on'; well you have to be prepared to have more dreams. They may not always be precognitive; they may be dreams of the past. They may be symbolic dreams. Get your journal ready and when you wake up, take note.'

'Do you think that my dreams will start to be about Rachel's murder?' Sarah said with alarm.

'You have to be prepared for that.' Mary replied. 'Be as prepared as you can for what may come. When is Rachel's wake?'

'I believe that she is being brought home to her parent's house tomorrow evening. James and I are going together.'

'I think you have a tough few days ahead, Sarah. Look after yourself and keep in touch. I'm here anytime you need me.' Mary said warmly.

Sarah thanked her and glancing at the clock ran upstairs to get the kids up and ready for school. She had a shift at the boutique later and needed to get Ella to Paul's mother. Rita was an amazing help to her, as she took Ella when Sarah was at work. Sarah was sitting at her window watching out for Joey by 8.15am. As soon as she saw the green An Post van pull into her drive she jumped up. She was determined to speak to him.

She opened the door just as Joey got to it.

'Hi.' Sarah said brightly. He looked a bit startled by the tone in her voice. Ok, she'd sounded like a freak then. He was used to a half-asleep-Sarah not this overly cheerful, on-a-crusade-to- save-a-life version!

'Morning.' Joey replied with a smile. He looked tired, like he hadn't slept well in a long time.

'How are you? You look tired. Is everything ok?' Sarah blurted out. 'Yeah subtle!' she thought. Way to go Sarah.

'Grand. All's well.' He replied looking a bit wary. He was clearly wondering what was with the sudden interest was in him.

Sarah knew that he was lying when he said all was ok. Not because of her dream, but because it was written all over his face. He looked sorrowful again.

He seemed to pull himself together then and asked, 'How are your lovely children?'

'They are all a bit shook up at the minute what with Rachel's murder and all.' Sarah responded.

Joey nodded in understanding. 'Awful shock for them.' He said. 'The whole village is talking about it, nobody can believe it.'

'Does anyone know anymore yet? Who would have done this to her?' Sarah asked him.

'Not that I've heard. Rachel's poor family are in an awful way. I was up at the Finch's house earlier with their post. Didn't see anyone but the drive was full of cars. Can't imagine what it must be like for them all.'

'No parent should bury a child.' Sarah said softly. 'I'm not sure I'd cope myself.'

'Funeral has been set apparently. On Sunday night she'll be going to the church. Then the Funeral mass will be on Monday. They are waking her at the house on Sunday all day. God, it's an awful business.' He shook his head as if trying to shake the sad news out of it.

'That it is Joey. Thanks for the news on the funeral. I hadn't heard yet. I know that Art said that the school would be shut on the day of the funeral and the kids would do a guard of honour. Her parents asked for that. Not sure how I'm going to get Katie and Tommy through it all to be honest. They're scared witless and not sure how to deal with it all. They've never lost anyone close before you see. They were too young when their Granddaddy Thomas died.'

'You'll get them through it. You're a great Mam. I've seen you with them.' Joey said. Then he blushed, shy suddenly at this admission.

'Thanks, that's kind of you to say. What about you, Joey?' Sarah asked him. 'Have you any children yourself?'

Sarah asked this question partly to keep the conversation going, and partly to try and understand a bit more about his home life. Although Joey had been delivering post for years to Sarah she knew so little about him. She felt slightly ashamed about that.

Joey sighed before answering, 'No children, not a one. I never married. Sure who'd have me? Just me and my auld dog, Benji.'

Sarah immediately felt a wave of intense loneliness overcome her. This was followed by sadness, vulnerability and fear. All of a sudden she felt Joey's memories flood her mind.

Joey is with his dog Benji – his best friend; there is an incredible bond between them. She sees Joey talking to Benji, playing with him, walking him. Every day Benji sits looking out his window, waiting for his beloved master to return home from work. They are devoted to each other. Suddenly Benji runs out onto the road chasing a ball. Thud! A car smashes into him. Joey is now at the vet's and the vet tells him that Benji should be put down; there are just too many injuries to save him. Joey is saying no. He begs the vet to do anything to save him. But Benji is in such pain he knows he has no choice. He makes the heart wrenching decision to have him put down, tears running down his face as he holds him close. 'Goodbye old pal,' he whispers as he strokes his coat.

Oh my God, she couldn't bear it. It was just too sad. She had no idea if Benji was dead already.

'Sarah, are you ok?' Joey said with concern. 'You're crying.'

Sarah was mortified. 'I'm so sorry.' Sarah wanted to put her arms around Joey. She had to step backwards away from him before her impulse took over and she gave the poor postman the fright of his life. 'It must be the funeral and all that. It's making me cry at the drop of a hat.'

'I'm not embarrassed to say I felt a lump in my throat too.' Joey said awkwardly. 'Go on in and have a cup of tea. I know it's hard for you, here on your own.' He moved forward as if to pat her arm, but thought better of it and stepped back awkwardly.

'I'm grand, honestly. Just being silly that's all. It is hard on my own sometimes, especially after what happened to Rachel. Plus Paul isn't at home at the moment, so I'm a little bit on edge.' She admitted and then made a conscious decision to pull herself together. She had a job to do.

'Do you have any other family, nieces or nephews?' Sarah continued.

'I was an only child, so I was. And Mam and Daddy are both dead now, may they Rest in Peace. Sure it's just me now.'

'That must be hard for you.'

He looked at Sarah, wondering what her motive was for all of a sudden asking him questions. But he only saw kindness in her face.

'Ah, I get by. Some weekends are hard but I have Benji. I know a lot of people think I'm soft, but that dog is family to me. I don't know how he works out the time, but every day when I come home he's sitting at the window, waiting for me. He's there every day watching for me to pull into the drive. And you know something, seeing him there each day, well that just makes my day, so it does.'

'That's not soft at all. Benji is a lucky dog to have you. ' Sarah said touching Joey's hand gently. Tears flooded her eyes again, the relief that Benji was still alive overcoming her.

'Maybe we're both lucky. And this job has kept me going all these years too. Meeting lovely people like you every day, well, sure that's all the company anyone could ask for.'

Sarah gulped. He was such a lovely man, why had she never taken the time to speak to him before today? He was going to be devastated when Benji died. That's what would cause it. The loneliness would just put him over the edge.

'Well we'd all be lost without you.' Sarah said fervently. 'You're a great postman.'

'Thanks.' Joey said chuffed with himself, with the praise. 'Better keep going or the rest of my route won't think the same thing! Have a good day, Sarah. Don't be worrying about those kids of yours. They'll be fine. You will too.' He nodded, almost tipping his forehead as he did and smiled as he walked away.

It was soon time for Sarah to head to work, after dropping the kids to school and Ella to Rita's. She was finding it really difficult to think about anything except Joey though. There had to be something she could do to help him get through the difficult time he was facing.

Her shift at the boutique she worked in went very quickly, thankfully. Sometimes it dragged but it had been busy all day, with lots of people in looking at the end of season sale rails. Before she knew it she was clocking off, her feet were killing her and it was time to pick up the kids from Rita's.

'Time for a cuppa?' Rita asked, alarmed when she saw how tired Sarah looked. She figured that Sarah would say no, because lately she always did, always rushing. But to her complete surprise, Sarah agreed to come in.

'How's that handsome brother of yours?' Rita asked with a smile as she poured the tea.

'Big and bold. You know what he's like.' Sarah replied smiling.

'Any sign of him settling down?'

Sarah laughed as she answered, 'Not James. He's still playing the field. There's nobody special at all'.

Taking a sip of her tea, Sarah asked Rita in a whisper, 'Have you heard from Paul recently?'

Rita started to wipe the counter furiously. She looked agitated by the question.

'You'll wear a hole in the counter if you don't stop.' Sarah said to her mother-in-law. Rita dropped the cloth and turned to her.

'He rang yesterday as it happens.' Rita answered finally. 'He was asking after the kids and you.'

'Where is he?' Sarah answered. 'It's been over a month now. I've given him as much space as I'm prepared to do. His children need him, now more than ever, what with Rachel Finch and everything. And I need some help financially. I'm struggling.'

Rita was pale. 'I know. It must be difficult.' Rita was so embarrassed by her son's actions. She couldn't make head or tail of it.

'No, you don't know. It's not just difficult. I'm broke. I've used up all our savings, what little we had left in the account that is! I don't earn enough at the boutique to support us. Christmas won't be long coming round – with three kids, I just don't know how I'm going to do it. I had to say no to Tommy last week when he asked me for new boots for his soccer. He was in tears about it. And Ella is outgrowing all her clothes. I need to buy winter bits for her now.' Sarah blurted out angrily. She knew it wasn't Rita's fault, but she couldn't help herself feeling angry with her.

Rita picked up her purse and rummaged out a fifty euro note, pushing it into Sarah's hand. Sarah pushed it back to her immediately and felt bad that she had snapped at her.

'Rita, I don't want your money. You're on a pension and I'll not take it. But I do want something from you, I need Paul's number. I don't believe you when you say you have no idea where he is. It is beyond ridiculous that the only way I have to contact my own husband, the father of my three children, is by email!'

Rita started to cry. 'I'm not sure where he is. I swear it. He always rings me with his number blocked so I can't call him back. He won't tell me where he is or what he's doing. I begged him yesterday to come home. Honestly Sarah, I begged and begged him.'

Sarah could see how upset Rita was and that she was telling the truth. She had no reason to doubt her. 'What did he say?' Sarah asked, almost afraid to hear the answer.

'He hung up.' Rita answered quietly. 'I don't know where he is but I don't think he's coming back anytime soon.'

Sarah fell back into her chair at this last statement. 'How did he sound?' she asked desperately. She needed some kind of an explanation as to how or why her husband could just abandon her and the children like this. 'It's not good enough. He has responsibilities. I don't have the luxury of being depressed. I don't have the bloody time!' She finished angrily.

Rita reddened a little bit. 'It's awful for you. I'm ashamed of him, I really am. I don't know how he could go off like that, leaving you and the kids behind. You're a great mother and a great wife. He doesn't deserve you, he really doesn't.'

Sarah held her mother-in-law's hand. She knew that this was hard for her too. She must miss her son, as much as she missed her husband.

Do you miss him though? a tiny thought popped into her head. And she wasn't even sure if she did truth be told. Paul was rarely at home in the past couple of years. He worked long hours most days. He was rubbish with the practical side of looking after the kids; she wasn't sure he'd ever given them a bath; he rarely fed or even dressed them. She had often moaned that she felt like she was a single mother long before he'd actually left her.

So what did she actually miss - the idea of having a husband or the physical presence of Paul? Did she even love him anymore? She closed her eyes and pictured his face and realised despite all of his flaws, he was her husband and she loved him and more importantly, the children adored him. She'd just gotten used to doing things on her own she supposed. However Paul working long hours and not being very hands-on at home and Paul disappearing completely into thin air were two different things altogether. Once she found him, she vowed to work harder at being a couple, not just being parents.

She looked at her mother-in-law and asked, 'Did he say anything about his job? He told me that he was out on sick leave. But surely even when he's out sick, he should still be getting paid? I've sent him several emails and got no response. His mobile says that it's no longer in use. I'm running out of patience, not to mention money.'

'Sarah, I don't know how to tell you this, but last night when we spoke, he didn't sound depressed. He sounded happy. I'm so sorry. Maybe I shouldn't have said that.'

'Happy? What is going on with him? Has he left us for good? Does he think that he can just break up a ten year marriage with just a couple of emails?' Sarah finished in a small voice.

'I don't know. I really don't.' Rita replied.

'Listen, if he calls again; tell him I'm not going to row with him. Tell him to call me for the children's sake, if nothing else.'

Rita nodded. 'I will; he promised he'd be in touch next week. I'm going to try harder to get a contact number or address. I'll tell him I've been sick and I'm worried if something happens to me, nobody could contact him.'

Sarah got up and gave her mother in law a hug. 'Thank you for that and for all your help with the children. I'd be lost without you.' She felt sorry for her all of a sudden. She could tell she was deeply embarrassed by her son, but he was still her son and she missed him too.

'It's my pleasure. I look forward to the days that you need me to mind them. I'm lonely here on my own, especially since Thomas died.' Rita's husband had been dead for five years now.

Sarah felt her guilt double at that admission. She rarely invited Rita over to her house anymore.

'You'll have to come over some weekend for dinner.' Sarah said kindly.

'That would be great, love.' Rita replied with a big smile. 'I can come anytime.'

'That's a plan so. Right, better get these kids home to bed.' Sarah called out for them and gathered up Ella from her playpen.

'By the way Sarah, I nearly forgot to tell you, I bumped into Mae Shiggins yesterday, Ruby's mother – she's back home!'

'Goodness, I've not spoken to her in years. Since Katie was a toddler I'd say.' Sarah smiled as she thought of her old friend. There was a time when they had done everything together. She often thought of her and regretted how much they'd drifted apart.

'You should give her a call.' Rita urged.

'Maybe.' Sarah replied, without any conviction. They'd nothing in common now; she doubted Ruby would even remember her.

Chapter Seven

Sarah picked up the phone to call her brother. 'Are you working on Saturday afternoon?' she asked when he answered the phone.

'Nope, why?' he answered, curiosity piqued.

'You're invited to lunch, so. I've asked Rita over and Mary Donegan. Oh, and Joey our postman is coming too.'

'Whoa there! Rita, I understand. Mary, at a push. But Joey, the postman? What on earth are you doing inviting him for?' James asked incredulously.

'It's a long story. But long story short he's lonely. So I've asked him over for lunch. And Mary is looking to date someone. She told me so on the phone. They're both roughly the same age. Sure you never know they might even get on.' Sarah blurted out.

James started to laugh. 'You're match-making a woman you barely know with the local postman! Incredible. Only you could come up with a hare-brained scheme like that! Does either of them know what you're up to?'

'Erm, yes and no. Mary knows that Joey has been lonely. She knows I'm trying to help him, and she said she'd love to meet him.' Sarah said. What she didn't know was that Sarah had hoped they would fall into each other's arms over the dessert course, declaring undying love. It could happen. Maybe.

'So why is Rita coming then?' James added. 'Is she bringing her son with her by any chance?' He finished sarcastically.

'Watch out you could cut yourself, you are so sharp!' Sarah snapped back. 'If you must know, Rita has been very supportive. And she's mortified about Paul. She's trying her best to help me track him down. She was just delighted to be asked for lunch. She loves spending time with the kids.'

'So what about this Joey dude. Does he know you're doing your own version of *Take Me Out*?'

'No of course he doesn't. We've been chatting a bit lately and I've been telling him how upset the kids are about Rachel Finch. He has a dog called Benji. So I asked him to bring the dog over for the kids to play with as they have been going on and on for ages about getting a dog. It'll cheer them up and I've asked him to talk to them about the responsibilities of owning a puppy. If I do ever get them a dog for Christmas, and that's a big if, I want to make sure they are on board with every aspect. I clean enough poop every day with Ella's nappies without adding a puppy into the mix thank you very much!'

'And he fell for that?' James said. Sarah could almost see the smirk he'd have on his face.

'I can be very persuasive, when I want to be. And anyhow, even though I may have an ulterior motive, he's a nice man. I like him. The kids always have a laugh with him. And you never know. Stranger things have happened; he might just hit it off with Mary!'

What she didn't add was that she'd had another dream last night and she saw that Benji was going to be knocked down on Saturday. She figured that if Joey was at her house, then his dog would be ok. And if Benji is ok, then Joey couldn't hurt himself. It was simple really. She instinctively felt that he needed to meet some people; she had deeply felt his isolation in her dream. He needed to get some confidence to get out and have some fun. Mary said she'd be happy to talk to him, try to build his confidence up a bit. It was worth a shot anyhow. She couldn't just do nothing and wait for him to die.

And maybe, if she was really honest, she was glad of this distraction, as it allowed her to dull the thoughts that were never far away, about Paul. If he loved her, how could he stay away? She didn't have an answer for that, so turned her attention back to James.

'Ok, sis, I'll be there. It should be a laugh anyhow watching you in action! Should I bring my iPod, download the *Greatest Love Songs* ever from *ITunes?*' He teased.

'Ha Ha, very funny. I'm sure you already have them downloaded, part of your seduction technique when you lure unsuspecting bimbos back to your house!'

'Ah, you're only jealous of my Jagger moves!' James responded with a laugh, then broke into song, "I got moves like Jagger, I got the moves like Jagger!"'

Sarah giggling said, 'Stop. My ears!'

'And another thing Cilla, if you're trying to set me up with Rita, forget it! Grannies are just not my thing!'

'If it's got a pulse and it moves it's your thing!' Sarah quickly replied laughing. 'But no, you're safe enough. Don't think Rita would ever look at another man after Thomas. She loved him too much.'

'Thank God for small mercies!' James answered with a grin. 'I'll bring some booze with me. I've decided I'm going to stay with you guys for a few nights. I want to go to the funeral anyhow. I'd rather be there just in case anything weird happens.'

Sarah was so relieved to hear that. She could do with his support with the children. 'That would be great. I'm not looking forward to it. I'm not even sure what exactly I'm to expect and Edward is no help whatsoever. He just says to be prepared. But listen, I'm changing the subject for a minute. I've been trying to get hold of Paul and he's dodging me. Not answering emails or his phone. Can you help me track him down?'

'At fecking last, sis. I don't know how you've waited this long to be honest, but never mind that now. I'll track him down, leave it with me.'

'What are you going to do?' Sarah asked, intrigued.

'I'll start by ringing his boss. They might have a contact number for him. I'm sorry, sis, but I just don't buy this whole depression story, and it doesn't sound like the Paul I know. And before you ask, I'll be discreet. This is the kind of stuff I do in the agency all the time. Don't worry.'

'Thanks bro. I owe you.'

It was one of those rare October days where the sun was shining and it was also quite warm. Summer days had often been colder and darker than today was. The kids were out the back playing on their trampoline, Ella was in her Tigger bouncer jumping and down, squealing with delight at how clever she was. Lunch was almost prepared.

Sarah was doing an antipasto for starters, served in a large dish in the centre of the table. She loved serving this kind of food that everyone can just dig into and share. This way they could take as much or as little as they liked. On the platter was Bruschetta Fegatini which consisted of toast – made with Italian style bread – covered with chicken liver pieces sautéed with just a hint of chilli. Carpaccio, wafer thin slices of prime beef, served raw with a dressing of vinaigrette and shavings of fresh Parmesan and Prosciutto, an uncooked, dry-cured ham which was exquisite and would satisfy even the biggest carnivore. Her kids adored this type of food. She also had Cannellini beans and Tuna served with olive oil, lemon juice, and a little sliced onion, with a touch of garlic, salt and pepper. And of course, the old faithful served at every dinner party in their house, garlic bread. Katie was addicted to the stuff and thought it was the height of sophistication to have a starter of garlic bread before any main course. Following the antipasto she was going to serve a Seafood and Chorizo Risotto. She could make risotto with her eyes closed and this recipe was a firm favourite. James adored it and she wanted to give him a little treat. And the added bonus was that Risotto was really inexpensive, but didn't look it.

She'd prepared most of it, but would actually finish it when everyone had finished their starter. For dessert she had made Banoffi cupcakes. This was often a dessert she made for friends the odd time she entertained. She made her usual cupcakes but added some mashed banana to the mixture instead of fruit or nuts. Then when they were cooked she took the top off the cupcakes making a little hole in the centre of them with her heart shaped cookie cutter. She then poured the Banoffi caramel into the hole, topped this with chopped bananas and some whipped cream. It really was very good and as Mary had said that cupcakes were her favourite, she wanted to surprise her with these.

James was bringing the alcohol, although she did have a bottle of red and white ready to go too. The kids had made place names for the table; they were excited at the thought of a dinner party. They even made a place name for Benji and put it on the floor beside a bowl of water they put down. She was just going to make some lunch for Ella soon and have her fed before everyone arrived. That way she would hopefully sit happily in her high chair when they all ate. It was all about timings with a little baby!

Putting Ella into said highchair she spied James out in the garden with the kids. He was a big child himself, he had his shoes off already and was jumping up and down on the trampoline like a lunatic. The kids were squealing with delight jumping on top of him every time he fell down.

Ella was in high spirits and had picked up that something important was happening. She was a really sociable baby, loved having people all around her, so she was literally bouncing up and down in her highchair, too excited to eat her food.

James walked in the back door gasping for breath. 'That trampoline is a killer. That's better than any workout at the gym!' he declared with a clink of bottles banging together as he placed the wine on the floor.

Sarah laughed; he was puffing from the exertion. 'Grab a beer and sit down. You'll survive!'

60

'Something smells gorgeous. Banoffi cupcakes?' James asked hopefully.

'The one and only.' Sarah answered.

'Before the others get here, I have to talk to you about Paul.'

'Did you find anything out?' Sarah asked quietly. Looking at her brother's face she figured he had and she wasn't sure she'd be pleased at what he was about to disclose.

'Yeah, I know where he is. You'll not like it, sis.' He said slowly.

'Go on, tell me. I've been imagining all sorts. Nothing could be worse than my imagination.' She braced herself for James's words.

James wasn't so sure. 'Saz, he's in London.'

Sarah grappled for the kitchen counter to steady herself. She had imagined many scenarios as to where Paul could be, but none of them involved him being in a different country. She'd just assumed he was in Ireland somewhere, maybe in a cottage in Cork or Kerry like one of the holiday lets they'd had in previous summers with the kids. They didn't know anyone in London, so she was at a loss as to why he was there.

'Ok, here's the deal. I rang his company and asked to speak to him. And the receptionist told me that he didn't work in Ireland any more. I asked her why, and she informed me that he'd been promoted and taken a transfer to their London Headquarters. He moved over there over five weeks ago and has been working there since. I asked her for his new number and she gave it to me. I rang them and they said he was with a client at the minute but I didn't leave a message, sis. I did ask them if he was now better as I'd heard he'd been unwell. The receptionist in London seemed puzzled and said that he'd not been absent from work at all. So I said to her that I must have him muddled up with someone else and I just hung up.' James finished, never taking his eyes off his sister. He wished he could do something to take away the look of pure horror Sarah had on her face.

Sarah felt completely bewildered. 'If he got a promotion why didn't he just tell me? Why didn't he talk to me about moving to

61

London? Did he think I'd not want to go? Why lie and tell me he's depressed and out sick. What's he playing at for goodness sake?'

'I don't know but this is far more serious than him just needing to sort his head out. He's been lying to you about work and the country he's in! What else is he lying about? I'm sorry but it doesn't look good.' James replied.

Sarah suddenly felt her body go rigid with anger. She started to pace her kitchen and felt the urge to scream. Here she was coping with the children on her own, scraping to make ends meet whilst at the same time worrying about Paul, thinking he was suffering and depressed. She thought she was doing the right thing giving him space to sort himself out as he requested, but all along he was in London working away, not a bother on him. She'd bloody well kill him.

He'd always been a bit flaky, she'd often felt let down by him over the years, but this was in a different league. She'd excused him missing birthdays or anniversaries, because in fairness he would always make it up to her. He'd come home and surprise her with a night away in 'their' hotel and they would have a blissful childfree twenty-four hours, where she'd remember what it was like to be a wife, a lover. She felt scared again and looked at her back door, wondering if she could simply run away herself. She wasn't sure she had the strength to take anymore. But then she looked at the children jumping up and down on their trampoline, pure joy on their faces and she knew that she would have to face this, for their sake.

'Do you have the address and number of where he is?'

'I do.' He handed a piece of paper over to her.

'I'm going to ask Rita to take the kids for a few days next week after the funeral. I'm going to London. I've got to see him face to face and find out what the hell is going on.' Sarah said, making the decision as she spoke.

'You can't go on your own. I'm in the middle of two cases at the minute in work, so leave it a week or so till I sort out some time off.'

Sarah shook her head. 'You're a star, as always. But no, this one I've got to do on my own. If I need you, I'll tell you. But this is my marriage or what's left of it anyhow. I've got to sort this one out on my own.'

'You're taking this better than I thought you would.' James said, a little surprised at how unemotional she seemed. He had expected tears at the very least.

'I'm too angry right now. I'm furious with him, putting me and the kids through this. It's all so unnecessary. I've wasted too many tears on him already; I'm not wasting any on him today.' She finished defiantly.

'Good for you!' James responded, squeezing his sister's shoulder. 'You hold onto that anger. He deserves it, every bit of it. Sock it to him when you see him.'

He jumped up and pulled out a bottle of red. 'Pinot Noir for the young lady?' Glancing at Sarah as she shook her head, he ignored her, deftly opening the bottle and pouring a glass for her. 'You need this, you have to be in the right frame of mind for luuurrrvvve, Cilla!!!'

Laughing half-heartedly, Sarah accepted the glass, taking a sip. 'Cheers, bro. What I'd do without you I just don't know.'

'You'd be lost, alone and miserable, that's what you'd be. A lucky girl you are that I'm your twin!' He said with a big grin. 'Now, wipe your daughter's face, she's covered in that orange mush she calls food!'

Ella looked like she'd just pressed her face into the bowl; she had butternut squash and sweet potato puree all over her. 'You little monkey!' Sarah said laughing at her baby. Ella delighted that she was making her Mama laugh, started to bang her hand on the highchair table repeatedly, squealing loudly. She was such a joy to Sarah; she really couldn't understand how Paul could just walk away from them all. She felt sorry for him for a minute. Had he any concept of what he was missing out on?

Then the doorbell rang. Sarah indicated to James to take over with Ella and ran to the door. Joey was standing there with Benji in his arms. She didn't know why, but she expected Benji to be a big dog. Joey was a big man, well over 6 foot and carried a bit of weight. He was as her mother would have said, round. So she'd expected a big old Labrador or something of that size. But Benji was a tiny Westie, a little white ball of fluff sitting comfortably in Joey's arms.

Sarah welcomed them both in and warned Joey that the kids would probably drive him mad, they were so excited.

On cue Katie and Tommy ran into the house shouting in unison, 'Can I hold him first?'

Joey laughed at their enthusiasm. 'I tell you what, Tommy. Let Katie have the first hold. Ladies first I always say. We men have to be gentlemen sometimes.' He finished with a wink.

Tommy stood up even straighter and agreed immediately. 'You can hold her first, Katie.' He said loudly. Then turning to Joey he whispered loudly. 'She's younger than me, so I have to let her have most things first you know.'

Joey ruffled his hair saying, 'Good boy. Now, Katie, sit down over there on that couch and I'll put Benji in your lap. He loves been tickled under his chin. Yes, just like that!'

Katie was giggling as she stroked Benji. 'He's lovely, Mammy! He's so cute.'

'I have a joke about a dog you know.' Tommy said to Joey. 'Do you want to hear it?'

'I most certainly do!' Joey answered. 'I could always do with a good laugh!'

Tommy took a deep breath and said, 'What did the cowboy say when a bear ate Lassie?'

Katie started to giggle and Joey declared he didn't know.

'Well doggone!' Tommy shouted in his best cowboy voice, beaming as everyone started to laugh.

'Tommy's our resident comic.' Sarah said to Joey.

Within a few minutes both Rita and Mary had arrived and Sarah and James were introducing them to each other. Benji was a great icebreaker, as was Ella. It gave them all something to ooh and aah about as they got used to each other.

James made sure that they all had a drink and they all sat down at the dining room table. Sarah placed the platter down in front of them all and watched happily as they all tucked in.

'I've never had anything like this before.' Joey said to Sarah in between mouthfuls, his eyes wide with awe as he took in all the colours and smells on the big platter.

'What's these fellas called again?'

'Bruschetta.' Katie and Tommy said at the same time.

'Bruschetta.' Joey said, rolling the word over his tongue. 'Never heard tell of them before. But they're lovely. Very tasty, Sarah.'

Tommy and Katie kept repeating the word Bruschetta over and over, laughing away at their own jokes. It was good to see them so happy, there had been far too much sadness in this house lately. Ever since Paul disappeared it was as if his departure also took a lot of the joy out of their house too. Sarah vowed to find ways to make her children laugh again, every day. 'You've gone to so much trouble.' Rita said to her daughter in law.

'Ah, it's nothing. It's worth it, just seeing those two so happy.' Sarah said, nodding at the children. 'We eat like this every day don't we kids?'

Tommy picked up his napkin and dramatically dabbed the side of his mouth before saying, 'Yes, Mama, we dine every night with three courses and the good silverware!'

Everyone burst out laughing at his mimicking of somebody 'posh'!

Tommy was delighted with himself for making the grownups laugh. Katie started to dab her mouth too, wanting to join in the fun. Sarah smiled as she looked around the table. It was going well.

When the starters were finished, Sarah got going on the risotto while the others all chatted away easily with each other. James joined Sarah in the kitchen.

'Well I left Mary quizzing Joey about his hobbies. She's got her sights on him alright!' James said with a laugh.

Sarah threw a tea towel at him saying, 'Behave, you. Everyone seems to be getting on ok though don't they? What do you think of Joey?'

'You were right. Sound as a pound that guy. I like him a lot as it happens. And he's very good with the kids. Very patient when they asked him hundreds of questions about dogs! Katie just asked him what dogs dream of every night. Poor man was trying his best to come up with an answer for her.'

'I'm glad you like him. I do too. I think we might see a bit more of him in the future. I'm going to ask him over again. He needs some friends, he's lonely.'

The risotto was a great success too. Joey declaring that it was the nicest rice he'd ever had. It was creamy; packed with lots of flavour from the chorizo and prawns.

Everyone declared themselves stuffed after they finished. Sarah jumped up and took the plate of Banoffi cupcakes from the fridge saying to everyone as she placed them on the table, 'Nobody will have room for these then I suppose?'

'Oh you're a wicked girl!' Mary said with a glint in her eye as she took in the sight before her. 'Cupcakes are my absolute favourite. They look divine!'

'Wait till you taste these, Joey,' Rita said. 'They are incredible. I've always said that Sarah could sell her cupcakes.'

Joey agreed as he took a bite of his. The sweetness of the caramel combined with the soft, light vanilla sponge was just heaven.

'That's the best meal I've ever had.' Joey said to his host. 'Thank you for having me.' He looked so grateful, Sarah was chuffed.

'You're so welcome. Thank you all for coming. Now dig in. Plenty more if you can manage it.'

Once everyone had finished Joey suggested bringing Benji and the kids for a walk.

'Can I get the present, Mammy?' Katie asked excitedly. 'Is it time?'

'Yes, it's time.' Sarah said with a smile and watched her daughter run to the utility room and pick up a little gift bag.

Joey looked gobsmacked when Katie handed the little bag to him. 'It's for Benji!' Katie shouted. 'Mammy bought it for him.'

Joey was completely stunned that these lovely people had bought his little dog a present.

'Thank you so much. Oh my, would you look at that lead, it's very fancy.' Joey said admiring the red lead with the little studs around the collar.

'I picked it, all by myself!' Katie said beaming.

'I've never bothered with a lead before.' Joey said to Sarah. 'We don't even own one so this is his first one ever!' he declared affectionately patting his dog on the head.

Sarah smiled at him and said, 'He doesn't know this area so I thought a lead would be good especially the way cars drive so fast these days!'

'You best just do as Mammy says. She will just keep nagging you till you do.' Tommy said with dramatic seriousness to him.

'Hey, watch the cheek!' Sarah said, half-laughing.

'Benji will wear this lead every day with pride.' Joey declared firmly. 'The nicest day I've ever had to be honest. Can hardly believe it.' He muttered.

With the new lead now adorning Benji, Joey, James, Rita and the kids went off for their walk.

Mary insisted that she would stay behind to help Sarah with the tidying up.

'He's a lovely man, Sarah and such easy company.' Mary said as she stacked the dishes in the dishwasher.

'He is, isn't he? I'm glad you like him. Think he enjoyed your company too.' Sarah teased.

'Would you stop, pet.' Mary said with a laugh. 'I don't think that there's any sparks flying between us, but he's good company and I think I've found a new friend. That's always a good thing.'

'No sparks at all?' Sarah asked hopefully.

'None at all, pet.' Mary replied laughing.

'Do you think that I've done enough?' Sarah asked her.

'Well, that I cannot answer, we just don't know that yet. You've taken him away from where Benji could have been killed today. But his fate was to be killed and we can't always change our fate. At least you have befriended Joey now. You've given him something else in his life other than friendship with his dog. You've opened your home and your heart to him. That's something worth living for in my book anyhow. Hopefully it will be enough for Joey too.'

Mary pulled Sarah in for a hug. 'You're a good woman.'

Sarah wiped a tear from her eyes. 'Oh, stop being nice to me. I'm trying hard not to cry at the moment.' She filled in Mary on the latest news from her wayward husband.

Mary was horrified.

'Can you help me understand something about my gift? I'm struggling with one thing. I can see things. I get that. But why couldn't I see this coming? Why couldn't I see that Paul was lying to me? Surely that's the one thing I should have been dreaming about?'

'Ah one of life's great mysteries. Why can't I pick the winning numbers for Saturday night's lottery? For me, I dream about all sorts, but never anything that directly affects or benefits me. Maybe you'll be different and be able to see things to do with yourself. But in my experience it doesn't work like that.'

'Not sure I think that's fair.' Sarah moaned. 'There has to be at least one perk!'

'I agree!' Mary laughed. 'And I hate to break it to you, but the pay is rubbish and the holiday's non-existent!' Mary quipped.

Sarah pulled a face and picked up her wine for a sip. She'd only had one glass all day, hated to drink while the kids were with her.

Mary continued. 'But back to Paul. For what it's worth I think you're right to go to London. Confront Paul and demand answers. And, pet, demand money too. If he's left you, he owes you maintenance for those kiddies of yours. He's such a silly man; does he not know what he's left behind?'

Later on, when everyone was back, the kids talked Sarah into putting the *Wii* games console on. Dividing them into two teams, with Katie and Tommy as captains, they started playing *Wii Sports Resort*. It was hilarious watching Mary and Rita try to get to grips with the *Wii* remote. Joey on the other hand was a natural, taking to the virtual world of games like a pro.

It was a great afternoon and it went by very quickly. Before long it was 7 o'clock and time to get Ella down for the night. Rita, Mary and Joey all took their cue from this and said their goodbyes, all thanking Sarah for her hospitality. It had been a good day and the kids had enjoyed themselves so much. They had relaxed for the first time in days and forgotten about Rachel Finch and their missing Daddy for a few hours.

Sarah knew she had to start thinking about the funeral and she was dreading it. She knew that it was going to be very a really tough couple of days for the children.

Chapter Eight

'What's up with you today?' James asked Sarah as they drove to the Finch's house. They were on their way to the wake, prior to the removal to the church. Rita was at home with the kids. Sarah felt that bringing them to the actual funeral service in the morning was going to be enough for them to cope with. They didn't need the added trauma of going to the wake. She'd not heard if it was an open casket or not and the chance that it might be was enough for her to keep them at home. That was too much for most adults, never mind a seven and eight year old.

'You've been in a bad mood all day. Don't deny it. Is it Paul?'

'Yeah, Paul is part of it of course. Part of me cannot wait to see him, to get some answers. But the other part of me, the bigger part, is scared. I don't think I'm going to like what I hear. But I've booked my ticket, I'm going on Tuesday. Rita is going to stay in my house for the night and take care of the kids. If we didn't have this funeral to go to, I'd be on a flight already. But there's something else that's making me worried. I had another dream last night. I dreamt of Rachel. It's freaking me out.'

'Now why on earth would dreaming of a dead woman freak you out? I just don't get it.' James responded sarcastically. 'Of course it is! You should have told me sooner. Was she dead in your dream, talking to you from the grave? Or I suppose she'd

70

be talking to you from the coffin in this case, as she's not in a grave yet, technically.'

Sarah threw her brother a withering look. 'No, she wasn't dead. There were no spooky ghosts talking to me from coffins or graves, so sorry to disappoint you!'

'Ah, that's too bad.' James replied with a wink. 'Come on, we have to keep a sense of humour here or we'll not get through this, sis. Ok?' Waiting for Sarah to nod in agreement, he then continued. 'Well then, spill. What did you dream?'

Sarah took a deep breath. 'Rachel was very much alive. She was on a date, out for dinner with someone and she was flirting with him. She was just a young beautiful girl having a date with a guy, laughing, joking, telling stories, falling in love.'

'Who was the guy?' James asked. 'Did you recognise him?'

'Don't know. She didn't say his name at all in my dream. I've been going over and over it all in my head trying to piece together some clues. Mary said that I have to be a dream detective, try to collate as much information as I can so that I can decipher them.'

'Ok, what did you come up with?' James asked with interest.

'Well, that's the frustrating bit. When I dreamt about Joey, I was able to retrace each part and I managed to work out whether it was in the past or the future.'

'Backtrack! When you dreamt about Joey your postman? What dream?'

Sarah felt guilty. She should have told James about Joey sooner. 'I'm sorry, it's just so much was going on about Paul and this murder. Well I thought that I'd off loaded on you enough and I wasn't sure how much more you'd want to take.'

She quickly filled him in on her dream.

'As of this morning, when I texted him to say hello, all was fine with him and Benji. I don't know if it's going to stay that way, Mary said that we can't always change our fates. But he didn't get run over yesterday.'

'Fecks' sake. To think that poor old Joey wanted to commit suicide. He's a nice guy, he seemed so normal, didn't seem the type when I met him yesterday.'

'But what is the type? That's the whole point with suicide; no one usually sees it coming till it's too late. He isn't suicidal right now, I'm pretty sure, but I could be wrong of course.' Sarah finished. She sighed and felt guilty again.

'I understand now why you were so adamant that Benji wore a lead for that walk we went on. I thought it was strange you buying a present for the dog; meant to ask you about that.'

'I couldn't think what else to do. It was the best I could come up with and I didn't want to take any chances.' Sarah admitted.

'You are full of surprises, sis. I might give old Joey a call myself next week and ask him does he want a pint some night. Do you think he might like that?'

'I think he'd like that very much.' Sarah smiled her gratitude.

'I keep telling you, I'm a pretty good guy you know! Now back to dream no. 2. You said that with Joey's dream you could work out the timing of it based on the newspaper. Were there any clues like that in your dream last night?'

'No, there were none at all. I mean obviously the dream is in the past, because Rachel is dead. But it was at night in the restaurant, so no clues about the weather. There was nothing in the décor of the restaurant that shows me either where it is or when it was. It was a bistro, I think. But not one I recognise. I mean it could have been anywhere. I do remember that there were some really pretty lights in the room, big chandeliers.' Sarah was getting annoyed again. She wished she could remember more about it all.

'Ok try to relax. No point getting all agitated. What did this guy look like?' James said to her.

'He was in his thirties, our age I suppose. Don't know what height because he was sitting, but he looked tall enough, seemed to have long legs. He had dark hair and brown eyes. He looked almost foreign, but I'm pretty sure he was Irish. He did have an accent, local I think. Oh, and I noticed too that his hands were calloused. They looked like he worked at hard labour kind of thing. I don't think he works in an office.' Sarah looked a bit sheepish. 'Not a lot to go on is there?'

'I'd say that's a lot to start with. But we have to remember that we don't even know if it's relevant or not, Sarah. You might have dreamed about some random date that Rachel was on. She was 24 and, as you said a good looking girl, one would imagine she probably had loads of dates.'

'That's true. I know I haven't got much detail, but there is one thing I am certain about. This guy killed her. I just know it. When I was with Joey last week I could feel his loneliness coming out of him in waves. It was the same thing last night in my dream. I got a huge feeling of foreboding when this guy stroked Rachel's hand on the table. I was terrified and woke up sobbing. He murdered her, I'm sure of it, and I think he might be going to do it again. I had a dream last week and I'm sure it was him in it. He was looking at a woman, I couldn't see her face, but there was such hatred, I'm sure of it.' Sarah sounded very tearful.

'It's ok, sis, if you say it was him, then it was him. We'll go to the house. We'll pay our respects and see if you pick up anything else. I was chatting to my mate in the Gardaí last night. She didn't have a long-term boyfriend or not that they've uncovered so far. They've interviewed all her family and any friends and colleagues that were in her life and they all say the same thing, she wasn't dating. Reading between the lines with what he didn't say rather than what he did say, they have no real leads at the minute and no real forensics either. It sounds like they are struggling big time. Whoever did this to Rachel covered their tracks pretty well. But at least we now know it was a male and someone that Rachel knew. That's a good start.'

'There was only one other thing in my dream that didn't make sense. Rachel's hair was brown. She had blonde hair though, always had whenever I met her at the school gates. That was a bit strange. Oh I don't know, maybe it was just my over-active imagination.'

73

James thought that the whole thing was a bit strange but decided to keep his mouth shut. They had arrived at the Finch's house. Taking a deep breath they both walked up to the front door. The place was heaving with people. There was about thirty or so men in the front garden chatting and smoking.

'Joe and Maureen, Rachel's parents are in the wake room right now. That's the good sitting room at the end of the hall on the right. Go down and pay your respects then come into the dining room. Tea and sandwiches will be waiting for you.' They were ushered in by a woman with sergeant like precision. Sarah felt the urge to salute in response, but instead walked quickly up the hall behind James who had scuttled off quickly, almost genuflecting as he left.

He gave her hand a tight squeeze before they walked in. Sarah steeled herself for the worst; she'd had nightmares that Rachel might jump up from the coffin to have a chat. She'd only just about gotten used to Edward turning up; talking to the dead might just be a bridge too far.

'Don't worry, I'm right beside you.' Sarah heard a whisper and there was Edward standing right behind her.

Taking a deep breath, grateful for both James and Edward by her side, Sarah walked in.

The coffin was in the centre of the room. It was a beautiful oak casket with heavy ornate handles. No open coffin. She looked around the room. There were chairs lining either side of the coffin and there were about twenty people in the room. She recognised over half of them, a couple of the mams from the school gates among them. She walked up to Joe and Maureen and knelt in front of them.

'I'm so terribly sorry for your loss,' she murmured. How trite those words sounded. Her mind flew to her own children, but she couldn't stay there for a second to even contemplate losing one of them.

Rachel's mother was quietly weeping, holding her hands over her mouth as if to stifle the sobs. Her husband nodded his thanks.

Somebody stood up from a seat and offered it to Sarah saying they were leaving. This was the way it always was with Irish wakes, a tradition that was heavily ingrained in Irish culture. It was simply the way mourners sent off their dead and said their goodbyes. They watched over their loved one, from the time of death to their burial, never leaving the dead on their own. This tradition was beginning to wane in cities as more and more people used funeral parlours, but in the country it was still active. Through the night during the wake there must always be someone who sits with the deceased. More often than not, the mourners will have a drink or two and tell stories of their loved one and this tradition played a huge part in the grieving process for those left behind.

Sarah looked around the room at the faces of the people there. All looking shocked and stricken at the heart-wrenching sight of Rachel' parents who were broken in their loss. They knew the unwritten rules to waking too. Neighbours would arrive before-hand laden down with food. There would be home cooked hams for the sandwiches and salads. Several would make steaming hot Apple and Rhubarb Tarts and pies for the tea. Sarah herself had dropped up cupcakes to the house earlier that morning for her contribution to the proceedings. Chairs would appear as if from thin air if needed, to accommodate the large numbers of mourners who were to turn up. A rota would be set up between the neigh-bours to ensure that somebody would be there always to take care of the teas and coffees and washing up. At no point would the family of the deceased have to worry about the particular burden of coping with the large groups of mourners who would trickle in and out of the house during the wake. Sarah knew that living in a small village like this was very special. Neighbours and friends were so good and all just wanted to help in any way they could.

Before Sarah took her seat, she stepped over to the top of the casket and laid her hand on the top. A picture of Rachel had been placed there. She looked beautiful and carefree in that picture; her blonde hair blowing gently as the picture had been snapped. She turned to her parents and said, 'Rachel was such a beautiful girl.'

'We had to have a closed coffin.' Rachel's mother sobbed. 'Her poor face you see. It was, it was so….' She finished on a sob, unable to complete the sentence.

Sarah felt tears running down her cheeks, she quickly brushed them away.

'It's unbearable for you both. I'm so terribly sorry.' She finished and took her seat to say her prayers.

'She was pretty wasn't she?' Rachel's mother looked wistfully at the picture on the casket.

Murmurs of agreement came from everyone in the room.

'She took after you, love.' Joe said to his wife. 'Just like you were the day we got married in that picture.' He started to sob, but Sarah could see him visibly pull himself together and stop the tears.

'She'll never get married now though, will she?'

It truly was heart-breaking watching Rachel's parents go through this. Sarah looked at James and knew immediately that they were both thinking the exact same thing – they were going to get the guy who did this to Rachel and her family, no matter what it took.

'Didn't like that bloody brown hair though!' Joe said gruffly all of a sudden.

Sarah looked up quickly catching James's eye as she did.

'Brown hair?' Sarah asked him.

'She came home two weeks ago with a new hairdo! She took a fancy out of the blue. It made her feel more sophisticated she told us. I didn't like it at all. She had lovely hair, no need to change it.' Joe answered

'That's girls for you.' Someone murmured.

Another neighbour walked in, standing awkwardly at the door of the room. Sarah took the opportunity to leave the room, offering her seat. She excused herself, signalling James to follow her. Rachel had dyed her hair brown only two weeks ago!

'Well, we know that your dream was at some time in the past two weeks then.' James said quickly, looking at his sister with a slight look of wonder on his face. The details kept proving to be correct; he wondered did Sarah have any idea at all how powerful her gift truly could be? He felt in awe of his sister all of a sudden. They had both been slightly blasé about the whole psychic issue, but this was sobering stuff.

'So she was dating, after all. Come on, let's grab a cuppa and see if anyone knows if she had a new fella or not.'

They walked into the dining room and were ushered to sit at the end of a large folding table. A plate of sandwiches and apple tart was put in front of them each and a large silver catering pot of tea was produced, and poured into two mugs. They both murmured their thanks.

'It's going to kill those two you know. Their only child being ripped from them like that is just plain wrong.' a voice from the end of the table said.

Sarah and James agreed.

'I don't know how you get over something like this.' Sarah replied. She shuddered again at the mere thought that something should happen to her children.

Sarah closed her eyes and prayed quickly to God that she would never outlive any of her children.

'Rachel was such a good looking girl; it seems hard to believe that she didn't have a boyfriend.' James said to the woman who was sitting beside him at the table.

'Yes, that's true for you. She was a lovely looking girl. But she wasn't seeing anyone at all. I can't for the life of me understand why not. Don't think she's ever really brought a boyfriend home to meet Maureen and Joe. She probably thought she had all the time in the world to settle down, poor girl.' She made the sign of the cross quickly on herself.

Sarah and James ate their food and then made room for the next group to walk in. They went out to the family room and

77

waited with more neighbours and family until it was time to stand outside and wait for the coffin to be brought out, for the short drive to the church. They stood side by side, all the neighbours and friends, as Rachel's body was carried out of the house and carefully placed in the hearse, Maureen and Joe walking behind sobbing quietly. It was a scene that Sarah would never forget, one holding the other up, following the coffin like two lost souls.

Chapter Nine

It was the day of the funeral and Katie and her classmates were outside the church. Art was organising them into two groups, lining them up on either side of the church door. The funeral service had just finished and in a moment or two the coffin would be carried out of the church. The children had played a large part in the service with several of them reading the Prayers of the Faithful. Katie had brought up one of the Offertory gifts. Her gift was one of her paintings that she had done in art class with Ms Finch. She had looked so small and vulnerable walking up the church aisle. Her bottom lip had been trembling and she gulped down her tears. Sarah's heart swelled with sadness that her children had to be subjected to death at such a young age.

When she had reached the top of church, she had faltered as she came close to the coffin. She looked around, panicked and then Tommy, who was one of the altar servers, edged forward and whispered quietly, 'Katie, over here.'

He gave her a little smile of encouragement and she walked slowly, gingerly, towards Tommy and Fr. Mulcahy. Sarah was once again grateful for Tommy and how he always looked out for his sister. Katie had quickly handed over her painting and bowed her head to the priest, before turning and walking very quickly to the back of the church to her classmates. Sarah had wanted to grab her and hug her close and had to physically sit on her hands to stop herself. She would hug her shortly.

The bells rang and interrupted Sarah's thoughts and she caught the smell of incense wafting towards the door as the priest swung his censer backwards and forwards. A bell tolled as the four altar servers followed Fr. Mulcahy, one of them Tommy. He looked very sombre and all of a sudden very grown up for his young age. Every day he looked more like Paul, but today, the resemblance seemed uncanny.

She looked around her quickly, hoping fervently that he had turned up and was making his way to them right now. She'd emailed him the details of the funeral and although he'd not answered her, maybe he would surprise them. The thought of having his strong arms around her right now made her ache with need. She knew it was a long shot, but even so, the disappointment that he had not shown up was crushing.

The pallbearers walked slowly, arms around each other as they carried the coffin carefully towards the graveyard. As the coffin passed by the children, they sang the very poignant *Over the Rainbow*. This song had special meaning, as the children had started working on their school play, and it was to be *The Wizard of Oz*. As family, friends, neighbours walked through the guard of honour; there was hardly a person there who wasn't wiping away a tear. Sarah herself was quietly crying. James was beside her, his face all scrunched up as he desperately tried to hold back the tears.

'It's ok to cry, James.' She whispered quietly.

'Not what Dad would say.' James replied. 'Real men don't cry, sis. Isn't that what we learnt?'

Sarah smiled at her brother. She knew that they were both sharing a memory of the time that their grandfather had died when they were only eight years old. When they were in the funeral car, following the hearse, Sarah and James had been both crying. Their father had admonished James strongly calling him a cry baby, telling him crying was for the girls. Sarah could still remember James wiping his face with his sleeve and scrunching his face up in an attempt to stop the tears coming. She caught his hand and gave it a squeeze. James squeezed back, grateful that Sarah understood.

Following the burial they all assembled back at the local hotel, The Ballyaislinn Tavern, where the Finch's had provided soup and sandwiches for the funeral party. Sarah hated these occasions but she knew that they were a necessary part of the grieving process. Another tradition steeped in Irish culture, the same as the wake. Funerals were a two to three day affair. First the wake for at least twenty-four hours at home, then the funeral removal to the church, followed by the funeral mass and burial, finished with a gathering of the funeral party for a meal and drink. It must be exhausting for Rachel's parents, Sarah thought. Looking at them both she surmised that they would much rather have been at home on their own. But maybe they needed this; maybe it was this very tradition that was keeping them going.

Sarah was sitting with some of the other parents; the kids were playing with their friends in the corner. It was getting late and she wanted to start making tracks home, where Rita was babysitting Ella. She gathered her things together and said her goodbyes, calling to the children that they were leaving. Now, where was that brother of hers? He had said he was going to work the room talking to as many people as possible about Rachel, hopefully picking up some glean of information. He'd also told her that in a large percentage of murder cases, the murderer would actually go to the funeral. It sounded so macabre and very sick to Sarah, but she supposed she really didn't want to ever get inside the head of a murderer. She said her goodbyes to Rachel's parents and made her way into the lounge next door and James was holding fort at the bar with five other men. She walked over to them and nodded in greeting to each of the men with James. Most of them were the husbands of the ladies Sarah had just been sitting with. They had children Tommy and Katie's age too and over the years their children had been in each other's houses for birthday parties.

Her eyes moved to the last of the group, she didn't recognise him at first. But as she got closer she stopped in shock and with her heart pounding she took in his face. Although she had never met this man before, there was no doubt that she did recognise him. He was the man from her dream, the man that was on a date with Rachel Finch. She started to shake.

'Sarah, what's up?' James said as he took in his sisters white face. 'You're as white as a ghost!'

Sarah couldn't answer him.

'Come on over and have a brandy. You look like you need it!' said one of the men in the group. 'It's an awful day for everyone.'

Before Sarah could protest a brandy was produced and placed in front of her. She picked it up and took a large gulp. The warmth of the brandy immediately hit the back of her throat, burning it, and the sharpness gave her the jolt she needed to finally be able to speak.

'Thanks.' She nodded at her neighbour.

James went around the group introducing each of them to Sarah. He finally came to the mystery man.

'And this guy is Mal Wickham. Mal, meet my twin sister Sarah.'

Mal smiled at Sarah. 'See she got the looks, James!' he joked as he shook Sarah's hand.

His hands were rough, and scratched Sarah. She shuddered as she remembered noticing the hands in her dream two nights ago. 'I've farmer's hands,' he said, holding the culprits up. He flashed a look of annoyance at Sarah and she realised that he had noticed her shudder and he didn't like it. They were big hands and as he waved them in front of Sarah, she had a flash of something. She flinched, almost feeling the pain as she saw images of a blunt piece of driftwood making contact with Rachel's body.

A dog is barking as he tries to defend his mistress. But neither the dog nor the young woman are a match for the man standing in front of them. Rachel screams in horror as she tries to protect her body from the assault. She tries to run but he is too quick for her and she falls to the ground all the time begging him to stop.

Sarah knew she had to get out of there. She felt like vomiting and was shaking like a leaf.

'James, I have to go. Can you come to the car with me, please?'

'Back in a minute, guys.' James said to the men.

Sarah put Tommy and Katie into the car, checking that they were buckled in ok. She then closed the door so that she could talk to James without being overheard.

'Your new friend in there, Mal, he's the guy from my dream, I'm sure of it.'

'What the— ? ' James replied in shock. 'Mal Wickham? No way! Are you 100% sure?'

'I'm 110% sure. I've never met that guy before in my life till just now. But I'd have recognised him a mile away; he's the guy that was with Rachel.'

'Could it just be someone who looks like the guy you dreamt about? He's tall and dark, half of the male population in Ireland look like Mal!'

'Credit me with some sense. I'm not making this up. I dreamt about this guy two nights ago. A guy I'd never seen before in my life. He was with Rachel. They were dating, they were intimate. I could tell.'

'I don't know, Sarah. This guy is married. I met his wife earlier. She's lovely, a real stunner.' He replied doubtfully.

'For the third and final time it's him. I don't care who he's married to or what she looks like, he was seeing Rachel. And I'm pretty certain he killed her.' Sarah said firmly.

'And what makes you think he killed her?' James asked.

'I just know!' Sarah said feeling a bit defensive. 'Don't go looking at me like that. I know how crazy this all sounds. But I need you to believe me. I saw images – flashes of pain and hurt and anger. Her dog attacked him, trying to save Rachel and I saw him bludgeon the dog too. And standing beside him right now, I can't put my finger on it, but he just exudes evilness. I can't shake it. It's him, I'm sure of it. I'm trying my best to make sense of it all James, but this is freaking me out!'

'Relax, Sarah.' James said, putting his hand lightly on her shoulder. 'If you say it was this guy in your dream, I believe you. But unfortunately it's not enough to go to the guards with. If we can prove they were having a relationship that would be great. And a murder weapon would be handy.'

It was Sarah's turn to pull a face at her brother, 'You don't want much, do you?'

'Hey don't shoot the messenger, but I need something more before I can go to Roger and get him to take me seriously.'

'I know that. But I don't know what to suggest. All I can tell you is what I see or feel. I need your help. What should I do now?'

'What you should do right now is go home. I'm going to go back in and have another drink with the lads and see what I can find out about Mal. I'll see how much I can find out from him and how well he knew Rachel. It will be interesting to see what he's willing to admit to.'

'Thank you.' Sarah said. 'Be careful though, he's dangerous. I know that much, even if I can't prove that he murdered Rachel yet.'

'Go home.' James repeated with what he hoped was a reassuring smile. 'I can take care of myself. I'll follow you home soon.'

As Sarah drove the two miles back home to her house she tried to digest this latest revelation. Edward was sitting beside her in the front seat. She couldn't talk to him as the children were behind her, but she was glad he was there. He had a habit of popping up beside her when she needed him. More often than not he'd sit there quietly, as he knew that Sarah couldn't chat to him, while she was busy being a Mammy. But it was a huge comfort to feel his presence. And right now, she needed that comfort.

'Trust your instincts, Sarah. They are not letting you down.' He said firmly.

She nodded in return. Arriving at home she was surprised to see another car in the drive, beside Rita's. The children realised whose car it was before she did.

'Joey's here!' Tommy and Katie shouted with glee. They had really fallen for him and his little dog, Benji. Since he had been with them for lunch, they had talked about him constantly and were disappointed if he didn't get to them with post before they went to school.

She went in and Joey stood up from the couch.

'I hope you don't mind me calling in, Sarah. I just wanted to see if you and the children were ok after the funeral. And I wanted to give the kids this.' Joey mumbled.

He handed them a large jigsaw puzzle of a Westie dog.

'That's the best present EVER!' Katie squealed and ran over to give Joey a hug of thanks.

'Thanks, Joey.' Tommy agreed. 'Mammy, can we make it now?'

''Course you can guys. Do it at the kitchen table.' Turning to Joey she added, 'Thank you so much. It's very thoughtful of you to do this for the children. And of course I don't mind you calling in. The kids and I love seeing you.'

'Ella has been as good as gold. She's still trying her best to crawl. Thought she was going to do it a few minutes ago, but she just flopped down instead!' Rita told her.

Sarah laughed. The whole family were waiting with bated breath for Ella to start. At the minute she moved around the room by rolling and could get from one side of the room to the other quite effectively like this. But she was very close to crawling; it was coming very soon.

'I'll make you a coffee. Joey, fancy another one? White, two sugars isn't it?' Rita said.

'Oh, you've a great memory! That's the way I like it. Thanks Rita.' Joey said a big smile breaking out.

'You've a great smile, Joey.' Sarah said to him. 'You look really handsome when you smile.'

'Ah, go away out of that!' He answered with delight.

Rita came back in with coffees for them all. 'So, how was it?' She asked Sarah.

'Tough, sad, senseless.' She answered quietly. 'The kids were amazing. They were obviously upset and scared at times, but they got through it all very bravely. Art, was fantastic. You couldn't have faulted him. He has a quiet strength that seems to calm everyone around him.'

Changing the subject, Rita asked, 'You all set for tomorrow, Sarah?'

Sarah sighed. 'I'm dreading it to be honest.'

'What's tomorrow?' Joey said with concern.

It was strange. She'd only just become friends with Joey, but she knew instinctively she could trust him. He was a good man.

'I'm going to London tomorrow to find Paul. James found out that he's working over there. He took a transfer with his job, just didn't bother to tell me or the children he was doing it.'

'Or me either.' Rita said with a sigh of her own.

Joey patted Rita on the hand and said, 'What kind of an eejit is he? Does he know you're going?'

'Nope, even if I wanted to tell him, I've no number for him. And I'm not having this conversation on the phone anyhow. Tomorrow, I'll be playing the mad wife surprising the runaway husband. I'm on the early flight in the morning. I'm going to go to my hotel, check in, freshen up, and then head to his office early afternoon.'

'I just don't understand it. I didn't raise my son to run away from things.' Rita said, distressed.

'Not a word to the kids. They don't know that I'm going to see Paul. They are finding it extremely hard to believe that Daddy's still away on business this long. I'm going to have to give them some answers soon enough. I just hope I get the answers that they will want to hear tomorrow.' She ended softly.

She had tried her best not to think about what might happen when she saw her husband, but whenever it came into her mind, which was every five minutes it seemed, her stomach started to heave. No matter which way she looked at this, it couldn't be good news.

Chapter Ten

Why on earth had she booked a flight at 7.15am Sarah asked herself again. She could blame nobody else; she'd decided it would be good to get going early. But that was before she knew that she would have spent the night before tossing and turning with bad dreams. It was getting to be a horrible habit and one she was not thankful for right now.

'Coffee, Tea?' the air hostess asked with indifference. Sarah normally would pass on inflight coffees, but she needed this one. She handed over her €3.00 and took the small cardboard cup from the girl who was looking slightly irritated at the handful of change she had just received. Sarah had emptied her purse and counted out all her small cent coins. Seeing the girls irritation appealed to Sarah's mischievous nature and she held back a giggle. It's the small things that get you through a bad morning, she thought to herself.

Sarah picked up her journal from her handbag. She had taken Mary's advice and was now keeping a record of everything she either sensed or dreamed. She looked at the notes she had made yesterday after James had called in on his way home from the Ballyaislinn Tavern. Joey had gone home and Rita was playing Monopoly with the children. She had walked into the living room and closed the door firmly behind her.

'Well, did you find anything out?' Sarah asked him.

'I managed to learn quite a bit actually. Marie and him have been married for two years with no kids. He's a farmer, cattle, I'm pretty sure he said, out Rosslare direction.'

'I knew most of that already.' Sarah said irritably. 'Did he say anything about Rachel?'

'Well, I could hardly ask him outright if he was having an affair with her and then killed her. Could I?' he said exasperatedly to Sarah.

'Ok, sorry. You're right, it's just so frustrating knowing this but not being able to prove anything!' Sarah replied.

'Listen, it's early days. I'm going to do some digging into this guy. Have a chat with Roger about the case. I've got to tread carefully though, I've got to come up with a reason as to why I'm focussing on Mal Wickham all of a sudden. I can't say for definite but I think he's not even on the Gardaí's radar right now. And I certainly can't tell them that my twin sister is having psychic dreams about the murderer. Not until you dream something that I could use as actual evidence.'

'I hate this. I wish I knew something else. Sorry, go on.' Sarah said earnestly.

James felt sorry for his sister, but there wasn't much he could do to help right now.

'He didn't say much else to be honest. Bit of a closed book when I started to question him a bit more deeply. His wife came over though and she was far chattier. They met only two and half years ago and they got married within six months. It was a whirlwind romance by all accounts. She's from Dublin, a real city girl, and he's the farmer from Wexford so polar opposites. She's like a fish out of water, from what I can gather, out in the sticks on the farm.'

'Did they seem happy?' Sarah asked.

'Well, at first glance I would say yes, she was all over him, calling him baby. But when you look a little closer, there are a few cracks.'

'How so?' Sarah said. This was getting more interesting now.

'He seemed a little less amorous than her,' James replied. 'like she was trying very hard to please her husband, but he wasn't as bothered about pleasing her if you know what I mean. He was quite short with her as if she irritated him. I did find out though that she went to college with Rachel and they were pretty good friends back then. So that's the connection. At least we know how they all know each other. Marie did say though that they had drifted apart since she got married.'

'That's a bit strange isn't it? Marie marries a Wexford man and moves here but her best friend and she don't reconnect?' Sarah commented. 'I'd have thought that living in the same county again would mean that they would be even closer than ever.'

'Exactly what I thought. Marie said to me that Rachel was at their wedding and that after their honeymoon the three of them went for a drink one night. But they didn't really stay in touch much after that. She whispered to me that Mal hadn't really liked Rachel and wasn't keen on them spending much time with her.'

'Well, that much we know to be untrue. I wonder if Marie has any idea that her husband and friend were having an affair?' Sarah wondered out loud.

'I don't know, but it wouldn't surprise me if she had a slight inkling of something. Everyone had a good few drinks yesterday but I wasn't drinking, just sipping the same pint, so I was in a good position to keep my eyes and ears open. When I realised that Mal wasn't going to say much about him or Rachel, I focussed on Marie. I liked her as it happens. She's a nice girl, a little bit dim, but nice.'

'Imagine being married to him.' Sarah said and then stopped suddenly as a thought struck her and made the hairs on the back of her neck stand. 'Maybe it was her that I saw in my first dream. Maybe Marie was the woman in danger!'

'Oh man, this is getting serious.' James answered, feeling more and more alarmed every second.

'Did she say anything else?' Sarah asked.

'I asked her if Rachel had a serious boyfriend or not and she made a face. I asked her what the face was for and she just said, 'Let's just say that Rachel liked a lot of boys. She was a real flirt. The night we went for a drink she was practically all over my Mal.'

He laughed at Sarah's face, her jaw had dropped open.

'Now, that's when I started to get real interested in what she had to say.' James continued.

'So do you think she knows that they were having an affair?' Sarah asked excitedly.

'Not sure about that. But she definitely had the hump about Rachel flirting with her husband. I reckon that's the real reason why she lost touch with her. She was afraid of what might happen between the two of them.'

'James, surely you can tell Roger to bring him in for questioning about the affair from that information?'

'What affair? I need more than a dream and a snide comment about flirting before I can go to the guards with this one.' James said.

'We're no further along.' Sarah said with a sigh, feeling deflated again.

'I wouldn't say that, sis.' James answered. 'In less than twenty-four hours we now know the name of the guy in your dream. We also know where he lives and a little bit more about him. If he's the guy who murdered Rachel, we'll get him. We just need to do a bit more digging first.'

Sarah tried for hours to go to sleep after James left, but just couldn't stop thinking about Paul, the children, Rachel Finch and now Mal too. Her head was just ready to burst with everything as her mind flitted from one thing to the next. She finally drifted off to sleep about 2am, knowing that she only had a few hours before she had to be up again.

However, once again her sleep had been disturbed, when she dreamt about Mal and Marie.

Marie looks out her bedroom window, watching the lights of her husband's jeep pull into their yard. She sees him take something out of the boot and head into the barn. Marie runs downstairs and throws on one of Mal's work jackets and a pair of old wellies, then she walks to the barn. As she opens the door she sees him put a piece of wood onto the log pile.

'What are you doing?' *she shouts causing him to jump at the sound of her voice.*

'Sorting out kindling to keep you warm for the winter, you stupid woman!'

'But it's three in the morning for goodness sake!' *she exclaims.* 'Where have you been till now?'

'I've been out. That's all you need to know.'

'Why are you being like this, there's no need to be so rude? You said you were going to see someone about selling some cattle and you'd be home in an hour or two. That was at seven o'clock this evening! You wouldn't answer your phone; I didn't know what to think.'

Her husband is never at home these days, out all night at least four or five times a week.

'I told you where I was going. Stop your bloody nagging. Have you ever thought that maybe I'm tired? I've been working all the hours that God made just to keep this farm going. Have you thought about that, woman? Nag, nag, nag. You'd drive a man to drink.' *He bellows at her. With that he storms out of the barn and walks towards the house leaving Marie to trail behind him, close to tears.*

When they get to the house Marie notices something on their carpet. What was it that Mal was dragging into their house? It looks like sand from the soles of his shoes. That just didn't make any sense. But she is afraid to ask him about it. She is still reeling from the accusations of nagging. Maybe she is on at him too much. She'd just hoover the mess up in the morning and say no more about it. She'd also make a huge effort not to nag any more. It wasn't fair on Mal. She'd try harder to be a better wife.

Sarah had woken up hearing her alarm going off and the first thing she thought of was the beach. Then it started to come back to her. He had sand on the soles of his shoes! So she grabbed her journal and scribbled down every detail she could remember. She'd ring James later. She remembered the feeling of desperation that radiated from Marie. She was a woman who knew she was losing her husband and she was desperately trying to hold onto him. Sarah felt so sorry for her and then her mind went to her own marriage. What was she going to have to do to save her own marriage later today? Maybe Marie and she had more in common than she first thought.

The sound of the PA system stated fifteen minutes to landing and snapped Sarah back to reality. She finished her coffee quickly, handing the empty cup to the hostess. She was going to put Mal, Rachel and Marie out of her mind. She had to focus on her own marriage. In a few hours she'd be confronting the man who'd run away from her and their children. This was the man that a couple of months ago she would have sworn she loved with all her heart. They had been married for ten years, together since Sarah was eighteen. Paul was her first and only love and she couldn't imagine a life without him in it. It was just so confusing, because right now she wasn't sure if she even liked him, never mind loved him.

Before long she felt the thud of the aircraft as it bounced onto the tarmac runway at Heathrow. She watched in amusement as the hostess tried unsuccessfully to get everyone to stay buckled in their seats, until the plane actually stopped. One guy stood up as the aircraft was still taxiing down the runway, opening the overhead bin, trying to pull down his bag. Where did he think he was going, she wondered? The hostess was walking towards him with major irritation on her face as she demanded he sit down immediately. As soon as the plane stopped everyone was up and out of their seats and standing in the aisles waiting impatiently for the doors to open. Sarah stayed seated. There was nothing she hated more than to be squeezed up close between strangers in the aisle of an aeroplane, just to save a few meagre seconds on her arrival time.

Successfully getting through arrivals and customs, Sarah followed the signs for the underground. Reading the map was tricky, as it resembled a science project at first glance! But before long she had worked out that each line on the tube was colour coded. She needed to change at Earl's Court and then get out at Victoria. Her hotel was a few minutes' walk from the station, according to Google maps and Paul's office about a five minutes' walk from there. She was soon sitting in a carriage, the whole process relatively pain-free. She found it fascinating people-watching. Everyone kept their heads down, avoiding eye contact with their fellow travellers, many reading the free paper or a book. Practically everyone had an *iPod* on and was clasping their luggage between their legs as the train trundled along.

She realised she had arrived at Victoria Station and Sarah could not believe the sheer size of it. It was the biggest station she'd ever been in. Oscar Wilde popped into her head as she navigated her way around, looking for the correct exit. She had always loved English in school and had studied *The Importance of Being Earnest*. The title character had been found as an infant in a handbag in Victoria station.

As the station was so big, that meant that there were hundreds of nameless people walking in different directions, all either arriving or leaving, heads down, intent on their destination only. Sarah thought of her sleepy village Ballyaislinn at home in Wexford and the small train station there. *We're not in Kansas anymore, Toto*, she thought with a smile. After a couple of wrong turns she was on her way and soon had arrived at her hotel. It wasn't a very expensive hotel, and looked a bit shabby, but with her budget it was all she could afford. She walked up to reception to check in.

Understandably, as it was only 10am they didn't have a room ready for Sarah yet. The receptionist was very pleasant and promised to do her best to get a room ready early for her once Sarah explained how tired she was from her early start. So with at least an hour to kill Sarah decided to go for a walk and check out the neighbourhood. She really hadn't come prepared to do any sightseeing or shopping, so without any plan formed, decided to just see where she might end up. Wandering up and down streets she enjoyed the colour and bustle of London street life. There were buskers on what seemed like every street corner, the sounds of both folk and pop songs blending into each other beautifully. She had just seen a guy with the pinkest head of hair playing Tom Jones's *Delilah*. She found a little souvenir shop on the corner of the road she was on and picked up a couple of pencil cases in the shape of Big Ben for Tommy and Katie. She found a cute little teddy bear wearing a Union Jack t-shirt for Ella. She'd like that. It would be stuffed in her mouth as new teething material as soon as she got her little hands on it. Thinking of the kids made Sarah's heart ache suddenly. She's only been gone a few hours and they would be at school now anyhow, so she knew she was being silly. But she'd missed giving them their breakfast and it seemed like a long time ago that she held her baby Ella in her arms and felt her nestle into her neck.

How on earth could Paul stay away from his children this long? Ok, if he didn't want to be with Sarah anymore, that was one thing. This was followed quickly by a sharp pain in her chest as it tightened with just the mere thought. Surely there would be another explanation. They had been together so long; everyone always said they were the perfect couple.

There wasn't a reason on this earth that Sarah could think of that would keep her away from her children, so she found it impossible to forgive him for abandoning them. Leaving her behind, she could come to terms with, but she wasn't sure she could forgive him the children's pain. She wondered again if perhaps he was ill and suffering from some sort of brain tumour. Then she felt guilty for even thinking that he would be seriously ill. Imagine that thought being actually preferable to him not wanting them all?

Feeling a bit tearful again, Sarah walked purposefully forward. This was not going to get her anywhere; she had to be strong today. No tears! And then all of a sudden she looked up. In front of her, in all its palatial glory, was Buckingham Palace. It was beautiful and majestic. She quickly took out her phone and snapped a few pictures. She thought of Princess Diana as she walked in front of the Palace gates. She remembered so clearly the day she died and the days that followed, the pictures on the news of people pouring their grief out in this very area. She could remember the flowers, a sea of pinks, and purples, greens and reds, lining the street pavements. She had watched Diana's funeral service all day and cried tears at the sad loss, with her friend Ruby by her side. Funny, she hadn't thought about Ruby in years and now she kept popping into her head all the time. Maybe she should give her a call as Rita suggested.

Her reminiscing was interrupted suddenly by the shrill sound of her phone ringing. It was the receptionist at her hotel, Sharon.

'Mrs Lawler?'

'Yes, speaking.'

'I've moved a few things around and I'm delighted to let you know that we have a room ready for you.'

'Oh, thank you so much. That's so kind of you.'

Chapter Eleven

Sarah was sitting in the bright reception of her husband's firm. The receptionist, a pretty young girl called Tracey, had asked her to take a seat and said she would call to see if he was available.

'Mr Lawler, sorry to bother you, but your wife is in reception and says that she needs to see you urgently.' Sarah heard Tracey say into her headpiece efficiently.

Sarah couldn't hear the response but it was obviously not one that included delight that his wife had tracked him down and he'd be right out to scoop her into his arms and tell her all was ok.

'Certainly, I'll let her know that.' Tracey replied again into the headpiece.

She walked over to Sarah and said, 'I'm terribly sorry Mrs Lawler, he is in meetings all afternoon, but assures me that he will give you a call as soon as possible.' This was all relayed in a voice that receptionists all seem to share. Sarah wondered if there was a school for receptionists, where one of the modules they needed to pass was how to speak in an irritating singsong voice. If that were the case this one was a natural and must have passed with flying colours.

How had it come to this? Ten years of marriage, with three children and they were resorted to communicating via 'Tracey'! She felt overwhelming sadness. She fought the urge to run away from this situation, because whatever was going on here, she knew that it was going to hurt her.

'You're stronger than you think you are.' Edward whispered. 'You can do this.'

Sarah drew strength from Edward's confidence in her and turned to Tracy, who was eying her up inquisitively. She refused to be ignored and ushered away by a twenty something receptionist in a pencil skirt that showed a bum that clearly defied gravity while her husband skulked and hid in his office. She was married to 'Mr Lawler' and hadn't come all this way to be palmed off in such an offhand way.

Sarah squared her shoulders back and said firmly, 'Tracey, please give Mr Lawler the following message. Tell him that his wife will not be leaving this reception until he comes out to see her, even if his wife has to wait here all day and night.'

It was impossible to miss the look of pity that crossed Tracey's face. But in fairness to her, she quickly recovered and with a smile responded, 'Certainly.'

A moment later, after she had finished whispering on the phone, Tracey said politely, 'Can you follow me, please?' She indicated a room to the right with a flourish of her manicured hands. 'Mr Lawler will see you in our Tara Suite meeting room.' 'Thank you, you've been most helpful.' Sarah gave the receptionist the benefit of her most winning smile.

She stood up and smoothed down her Diane Von Furstenberg wrap dress. It was nearly ten years old, something she'd bought in America in one of the outlet malls on her honeymoon. It hadn't fitted her for years, so it had hung in her wardrobe unworn. She had been pleasantly surprised when she tried it on last week and it had fitted perfectly. She wouldn't recommend the stress diet to anyone, but in fairness it was effective!

She felt nauseous as she contemplated seeing Paul. Why had he been lying to her for nearly two months now? What else has he been hiding? She took a seat. It was ultra-modern with a white boardroom table, surrounded by lime green chairs, with pink walls. After what felt like hours, but in fact was only moments, Paul walked in. Sarah watched the man she barely recognised in slow motion. His glasses were gone. His normally flat mousey brown hair was cut short, spikey with hair gel. He was wearing a sharp three-piece suit, in grey pinstripe, with a blue shirt underneath, no tie. He looked tanned, rested, younger and very well.

Every core of her being was insulted by the cut of him.

'For a man with depression, you look awfully fit on it.' Sarah said stung by his appearance. Her stomach was flipping, she felt her heart beat start to quicken. She had promised herself that the first thing she said wouldn't be an attack, but seeing Paul looking so obviously well was such a shock for her. She didn't need her sixth sense to let her know that something was very wrong. This did not look like a man on the brink of suicide as she had been terrified of.

Paul at least had the decency to redden. He stood at the door, unsure as to what to do or say. But then he shifted into 'salesman' mode. She'd seen him like this before, when she had played the dutiful wife at big sales dinners with customers. He'd become another version of himself, one that she had never really cared for. Now it seemed he was going to try to charm his way out of trouble.

'You look good too, Sarah.' He said with a smile. 'You've lost weight.'

'I lost my appetite at the same time I lost my husband funnily enough.' Sarah retorted with irritation.

The fantasy she had clung to that upon seeing her husband again, of the two of them falling towards each other, all right in the world again as they came together, splintered into a million pieces.

She knew that the two sentences she had spoken since her missing husband had walked into the room were both loaded with sarcasm, but her whole body was throbbing from fear, hurt and humiliation. There she was sitting at home, defending her husband to James and friends, saying that he was depressed and now to come face to face with him, to see him looking so well, it cut her beyond anything she could have imagined.

'It suits you, Sarah.' Paul went on, ignoring her last comment with another smooth smile. 'You should keep the weight off, makes you look younger. Is that dress new?'

Sarah had a moment where she saw herself climb up onto the boardroom table, pick up one of the horrendously bright green chairs and hit him over the head with it. But she didn't move. She needed to keep her cool. Sometimes it's easier to pretend you don't care than to show that you are dying inside.

'No, the dress is not new Paul. It's over ten years old as it happens. Enough about how I look, I couldn't care less about that. I want to know what's going on. I'd like to know why it is that I had to find out from someone else that my husband had taken a new job and moved to another country.' Sarah demanded.

'That's understandable.' Paul said nodding. 'You've just thrown me a bit. I wasn't expecting to see you here today. You won't believe this probably, but I was going to come to Ireland next month and talk to you. Honestly, I was.'

'Sure you were.' Sarah said, trying to bite back the sarcasm. 'Well, I've saved you the trouble. Now talk, I need an explanation. You told me that you were having a breakdown and needed to get away to sort your head out. In the few measly emails I've had, you said that your doctor advised that you have some "solitude"', that you were feeling suicidal. And at no time in the past six weeks have you thought fit to tell me that you've changed jobs and emigrated!' Sarah ended her voice raised several octaves.

'I know I've been a coward. It's unforgiveable. How did you find me?' He said lamely.

'It didn't take Sherlock Holmes to find out. James rang your office and they told him you'd transferred over here. Up until right now, I still didn't quite believe it. Why on earth would you take a transfer to London headquarters without telling me?'

'Should of known good old "knight in shining armour" James would be involved somewhere, Sarah!' he replied accusingly.

'Don't try and deflect away from this horror by turning it into a rant about James. You should be grateful that my brother has been around. He's been amazing with YOUR children, helping them deal with an absent without leave father.'

Paul put his head in his heads. He looked up eventually and said quietly. 'I was too scared to talk to you Sarah. You love Ballyaislinn, always have done. I knew you wouldn't want to leave that village. But I hated it there. I hated living in Ireland. This is such a great opportunity for me. It's a promotion, much bigger client base. I've been stifled back in Ireland. I needed a change and this job; well it's given me a new lease of life. London is where it's all happening right now.' His voice had gotten more and more excited with every word he said.

'Oh that explains everything!' Sarah snapped. She sighed, composed herself and tried to remain calm.

'How can you glibly tell me that you needed a change and just went for it? Do I need to remind you that by making that huge life change you have left behind a wife and three children? By the way just when were you going to ask how they were?' Sarah asked angry once more despite her best intentions.

She needed to smack him hard. It was taking every inch of her resolve not to.

'I was just about to.' He answered defensively. 'Give me a bloody chance. I feel terrible about leaving the kids behind. I miss them so much. It's been horrible for me, bet you haven't even thought about that once.' He finished on a whine.

'It's been horrible for you!' Sarah exploded. 'How unbelievably self-absorbed you are! Do you know something, I've secretly thought that about you for years and years, but tried my best to ignore it. But this takes the biscuit. You want me to think about how hard this is for you? I've done nothing else but do that for weeks now. Worried sick you were going to do something stupid. So please, whatever else you say, don't say that.'

'I'm sorry. You're right, I'm being selfish.' Paul replied.

100

'How could you have made me think you were ill?' Sarah tearfully asked and Paul moved closer towards her, regret all over his face.

'I was a coward. It seemed like the kinder thing to say at the time, but the lie just grew and before I knew it, I felt I couldn't admit that I wasn't unwell.'

'Who are you?' Sarah said. 'I don't recognise you anymore.'

She held her head in her hands.

'You know what hurts the most?' She asked him. 'You knew exactly what you were doing. You might as well have stuck a knife in my heart.'

They sat in silence, then Paul spoke, 'Tell me, how are Katie, Tommy and Ella?'

'They are well physically.' Sarah replied, softening a little. 'But emotionally, this has been difficult for them. Tommy and Katie cried for you on and off for about two weeks. Where's my Daddy? When's my Daddy coming home? Then after about two weeks, they stopped asking. But every now and then I hear crying coming from their rooms and Tommy is in tears and your seven year old daughter is trying to comfort him. Or vice versa. They don't understand why you disappeared like that and my excuse about work just doesn't cut it with them. As for Ella, she probably has forgotten all about you by now.'

'Don't say that! That's nasty, and you were never nasty.' Paul said, wounded.

Sarah sighed. She wasn't getting anywhere by shouting at him. She changed the tone of her voice; did her best to remain calm and reasonable.

'You know when I found out that you'd moved to London and that you were working away here; I tried to make sense of it. How could you leave me and the children, with no money coming in, and no contact? It just didn't add up. So I persuaded myself that you really were having a breakdown and that somehow or another you'd gotten amnesia. You'd banged your head or something. There had to be an explanation as to why you would do something like this. Is there, Paul? Help me understand, please.'

101

Paul remained quiet, not responding. He wouldn't look Sarah in the eye; he kept shifting in his chair like he was sitting on nails.

'This isn't just hard on me and the kids. What about your mother? Rita is heartbroken too by the way, in case you're bothered.' Sarah continued. This sparked a response at least.

'Of course I'm bothered.' Paul answered angrily. 'I love my mother!'

'Well she doesn't feel very loved right now Paul. She's been amazing, helping out with the kids. She even tried to give me some of her pension last week, which of course I refused.'

Sarah got up from her chair and faced her husband. 'Ok, let's pretend that I'll go along with this great promotion you got, and that you were too scared to tell me about it, because I wouldn't want to go. That's bullshit by the way; we both know that, just for the record. I've always been supportive of your career.' She paused for a moment then reached out to touch Paul's hand. 'Yes, I love Ballyaislinn, but I love you more.'

Paul looked embarrassed again. She waited for him to tell her that he loved her too, but he remained chillingly quiet and her stomach started to flip, anxiety growing with every second. She took a deep breath.

'Let's just move on from that for now. What I can't get my head around is the fact that you've left me without any financial support. You lied to me and said you had no money coming in, that you were trying to sort out sick pay, when all the time you were working here in London. That's something that I am really struggling with. How could you do that to us? I assume with this big promotion came a big pay rise, you needn't deny it!'

'It's expensive moving to a new country. I had to find a place to live, deposit, rent in advance. I needed to get some new clothes; it's different over here. People expect you to look the part. I'm not in bally-go-backwards Ballyaislinn now!' Paul said indignantly, the whine back in his voice again.

Sarah was incredulous at his sheer neck. She could hardly believe her ears. She wished she had brought James with her now, because right this second she knew he would have decked Paul right out on the pristine white carpet. And maybe that might have made it easier to listen to his words.

'So while I've been scraping together money, digging into our meagre savings, working extra shifts at the boutique, you've been splashing out on new clothes to keep up with the bloody Joneses!!' Sarah exploded angrily.

'You make it sound so terrible.' Paul moaned. 'I'm just trying to make something of myself. Don't I have the right to live the life that I want?'

Sarah was speechless. Is this what a mid-life crisis looked like? She had tried to envisage what he might say, what excuse he might give. She'd heard a lot of rubbish lines come out of Paul's mouth over the years to make up for broken promises, but this really won the prize. There was only one more thing she had to ask Paul. She already knew the answer, deep down, but she needed him to say it. Sarah took a deep breath.

'I have one more question for you and I'd appreciate an honest answer from you.' Sarah closed her eyes for a second. She was terrified to ask the question, but she knew that it could not be avoided.

'Does this new life of yours, this new apartment, have any place for your wife and children?'

Paul reddened, sighed dramatically before he sheepishly replied. 'It's complicated, Sarah. You wouldn't like it here. And the kids, getting them into new schools, well, they'd hate it. It's a bad time to be shifting them to a new country. It's not me I'm worried about at all, I'm thinking of all of you really, honestly I am.'

Sarah fell back into a chair. Even though she'd half-expected him to say something like that, in that moment of betrayal by her husband, her soul shook.

'Even though I saw it coming, it hurts so much.' Sarah whispered to herself.

Paul moved towards her, then thought better of it and stepped back again.

'I'm ashamed of you, Paul. You've done some terrible things during our marriage together, but this time I'm truly ashamed.' Sarah said wiping away tears furiously.

Paul had tears in his eyes too. 'I'm so sorry. I didn't mean to hurt you. I'm so sorry.' He repeated.

Sarah felt claustrophobic. Every breath she took hurt, like her ribs had been broken and were pushing into her lungs. She needed to leave and fast. Then she heard Edwards voice whispering in her ear.

'Sarah, ask him for support. Don't leave without it. It's what the children and you are entitled to.'

She paused as she got to the door, turned around and said to him.

'Sorry is just a word, Paul. And sorry doesn't pay the mortgage or pay for the groceries. Get your cheque book out, I need some money before I go.'

Paul looked shocked at the request, offended almost with her bringing up the subject of money.

'Don't look so surprised. Surely you knew that you couldn't just walk out on us all and not pay maintenance? You have obligations, Paul. Now be a man for once in your life. Don't have me ask you twice. We can do this amicably ourselves or I will get a solicitor who will make sure you pay, you mark my words.'

'I don't have any cash on me or a cheque book. Nobody carries a cheque book anymore.' He said with a last ditch attempt to avoid paying up.

'What has happened to you?' Sarah said with contempt. 'You have changed beyond all recognition. The man I married would never try to shirk his responsibilities. Ok, you obviously don't love me anymore. But you have three children and I cannot believe that you don't love them anymore. You have a duty of care to them.'

Sarah placed a card with the name of the hotel she was staying in on the table between them.

'This is where I'm staying. I'm checking out tomorrow at noon, for an afternoon flight. You have my mobile number. Text me and let me know when you'll be calling by with some money. Don't have me come back here in the morning to make a scene. Because I will if I have to, I'll make such a scene that your new London colleagues will be gossiping for months!'

Paul stuttered, 'There's no need for any scenes.' Sarah could see the panic in his eyes. Having a hysterical ex-wife really didn't go with this new image he'd cultivated for himself. He continued. 'It's no problem at all on the money. I wasn't going to walk away from my duties as a father. I was going to send some on soon, honestly. I'll call into the hotel after work at around seven.'

Sarah held her head as high as she could, squared back her shoulders and looked at her husband,

'I'm sorry we were not enough for you.' Then walked out of the building with each step she took a symbolic step of walking away from her marriage. She couldn't stop the tears; they were like a fountain and as quickly as she wiped them away, more would flow.

The walk back to her hotel happened in a blur. 'Are you ok, Mrs Lawler?' the receptionist asked with concern.

Sarah was about to say that she was fine; the standard response one makes when asked if they were ok, even when clearly anything but. She smiled in an effort to put a halt to the tears that simply would not stop.

So she quietly said to the kind girl who looked so worried about her, 'No, I'm not ok, not ok one little bit. My husband has just informed me that he's left me and our three children. As of today, my marriage of ten years is over. So truth be told, I'm having a shit day.'

She walked to the lift without giving the poor girl a chance to even respond. She knew she shouldn't have off-loaded on her, it wasn't fair. But she'd needed to say it out loud she supposed. She really couldn't get her head around how selfish her husband was. Ex-husband she corrected herself. That would be difficult to get used to – but she might as well start trying.

Chapter Twelve

Feeling desperately alone, Sarah heard Edward whisper to her, 'You need a friend right now. Give Ruby a call.'

'Sure we've not spoken to each other in years!'

'Trust me, you need to call her.' Edward repeated. 'You have her number. Go on, do it.'

Sarah picked up her mobile and scrolled through the contacts till she found Ruby's mobile number. She looked at Edward again who nodded and then dialled.

Ruby answered almost immediately.

'Well, as I live and breathe, Sarah Lawler!' Ruby's voice said with excitement.

Hearing her voice brought the tears rushing back again and Sarah could hardly speak, 'Ruby...'

'Oh feck, what's wrong?' Ruby immediately asked with concern.

'It's Paul, he's left me.' Sarah answered, crying harder with every word.

'Ah no Sarah, I'm so sorry!' Ruby replied, listening in horror to her friend sob down the phone, unable to string a sentence together.

'Who's with you? You can't be on your own right now. Is James there?'

'I'm in London, I've got nobody!' Sarah wailed.

This evoked a squeal from Ruby in response. 'No fecking way! Ok, you will not believe this, but so am I! I'm here for an overnight with work, for training!'

Sarah stopped crying at that and looked at Edward who was looking pretty pleased with himself.

'Listen I'll get out of dinner early tonight with the work gang and I'll head to your hotel as soon as I can, ok? Hold it together for a little bit longer, I'll be there soon.'

'That looks good.' Paul said to Sarah, pointing to her Amaretto. He had walked up behind her as she was sitting at the bar, her back to the door. He smiled at her and despite herself she felt herself smiling back.

For a moment Sarah daydreamed and allowed herself to believe that the afternoon had never happened. Paul had come to his senses and they'd go home hand in hand. She could just see Tommy and Katie's face as they saw Daddy arrive home with her. Not to mention how happy Rita would be. They would probably laugh about it all, in years to come. OK, it would take time for her to forgive him, but for the sake of the children she'd try.

Paul indicated to the barman two more of Sarah's drink.

'I'm really sorry about earlier.' Paul said quietly. 'I was an asshole.'

Sarah looked at her husband intently. He did look genuinely sorry. Was he going to beg her for forgiveness? Could she forgive him? She would of course have to make it difficult for him, make him sweat it a bit. But maybe, just maybe, it was going to be ok.

She smiled. 'Yeah, you were an asshole. But in fairness, I did catch you off guard.'

They moved from the bar to a booth at the back of the dimly lit room.

They both took a sip of the Italian liqueur that they had become enamoured with years ago on a trip to the Amalfi coast before the kids came along. The sweetness of the almonds caressed Sarah's tongue, before the hit of the alcohol stung the back of her throat.

'How many of these would you say we've drank over the years?' Paul asked.

'Enough that we should have bought shares!' Sarah quipped back.

The familiarity of drinking 'their drink' was not lost on either of them. She felt more relaxed and sank back into the back of the soft seat, letting the tension in her shoulders go for the first time that day.

'Do you remember the night in that tiny restaurant we loved? What was it called again?'

'Santa Carina's!' They both shouted at the same time.

'We drank so many Amarettos he ran out of it!' Paul said.

'I was mortified! Imagine drinking a place dry!' Sarah laughed.

'Ah but fair play to him, he got more in for us the next night!' Paul replied. 'His best customers! You've got to love the Italians.' Paul said raising his glass slightly.

'Cin Cin.' Sarah replied in Italian, almost shyly. Would he remember?

'Cin Cin.' Paul answered laughing. 'We haven't said 'cheers' in Italian for years. We used to say it all the time after that holiday. When did we stop that?'

Turning to look at Paul, she shrugged and then asked him. 'I keep asking myself questions just like that. How did we end up here? Was our marriage that bad?'

'No, of course it wasn't. We've had some great times together. Some of my happiest memories are with you and you're an unbelievable mother. The kids are so lucky to have you.'

'Then how can you leave this life behind?'

'We've been drifting apart for a long time now; you have to agree with that.'

Sarah realised with a start that he was right and she acknowledged his words with a slight nod. 'I'll admit that things have been a bit flat lately. But I truly didn't see this coming, Paul. I mean, all marriages go through rocky patches.'

'They do.' Paul replied then looked at Sarah and continued. 'But I felt completely trapped and I've been so unhappy for months now. I dreaded coming home every night. It was just the same thing every day. So when I found out about this opportunity in London it just seemed like the answer to my problems.'

The answer to 'my problems', Paul had said. Not 'our problems' but 'my'. Sarah could feel herself getting irritated again. Why was it always all about Paul? But then again she'd let him dictate how things went in their marriage for years now. She had wanted a small wedding, him a huge extravagant affair. Paul got his way. Two hundred guests were invited, most of whom Sarah didn't know and they ended up with a huge debt to start their married life off with. She'd wanted to have children immediately. Paul hadn't, so they waited and waited until eventually Sarah had to practically bully him into it. Maybe that was the problem she thought suddenly. She'd bullied him into having kids when he wasn't ready. Ok, they had been married for three years before she'd pushed the point with him. But maybe he'd resented her for this?

A voice in the back of head whispered. 'Don't be so hard on yourself, Sarah.' It was Edward again. She knew he was right to an extent, but she had to accept some responsibility here.

'I'm so sorry you felt like that. I wish you had been able to come and talk to me. Maybe we could have worked something out.'

'Maybe we could have.' Paul said, smiling gently at Sarah. 'You just seemed so busy with the kids all the time, especially since Ella came along. I just felt like you didn't need me anymore.'

'Of course I needed you. I still do.' She finished on a whisper. She wasn't going to beg him, but she wanted to let him know that they had a chance to get back their life.

Paul looked at his wife quizzically and replied softly, 'I need you too.'

'Now, isn't this cosy?' A woman's voice with a London twang said, interrupting them.

Sarah looked up startled, wondering who the voice belonged to. A woman in her mid-thirties Sarah guessed, who was extremely glamorous, from her long, wavy and glossy brunette hair to the perfect red pout she was now prettily pointing in her husband's direction.

'Can I help you?' she said to the woman, who had sat down beside Paul, and then placed a manicured hand on the top of Paul's thigh in a way that clearly showed she was intimate with him.

'Aren't you going to introduce me, sweetheart?' she purred.

Sarah thought she was going to faint. She could feel her heart quickening again and tears springing to her eyes. She knew that an axe was about to fall and cut the life she had into millions of pieces.

Paul looked like he wanted to be anywhere but there, and had lost his voice suddenly.

In what felt like slow motion, the woman leaned over Paul and held her hand out to Sarah.

'Hello, you must be Sarah. I'm Michelle McGuirk, Paul's partner.' She purred again.

Sarah inched back as far as she could from the both of them. She had just been contemplating packing up everything and moving to London with the children, just to make Paul happy. And all along he had a girlfriend. She could feel her face redden with embarrassment. Earlier she had been deeply ashamed of her husband but now she felt her whole body shudder with her own embarrassment.

Fool me once, shame on you; fool me twice, shame on me. The phrase popped into her mind and kept going around and around on a loop.

She looked at Paul and finally found her voice, 'She's with you? Paul, please tell me she's lying.'

'Take a drink.' Michelle said, her voice dripping with fake concern. 'You've had a shock.'

She then leaned in again over Paul and said, 'You know what Paul's like. He hates to hurt people, so I thought it best to come here myself and meet you. Just so we are all on the same page. It's less messy that way, wouldn't you agree?'

110

Sarah could not believe the gall of the woman. She was both cruel and ruthless. It was obvious she wanted Paul and was not going to risk the inconvenience of a wife getting in her way.

Paul still had said nothing and kept his eyes firmly on his glass.

'Now, I hope that you're not going to make a scene.' She said with a smile to Sarah. 'I'm just not up to the stress right now, not in my condition.' She finished triumphantly.

'Michelle.' Paul finally found his voice and warned her, 'You promised.'

'Don't be silly.' She said to him. 'Sarah is a grown up. She would want to know everything. Wouldn't you?'

Sarah felt every fibre of her body fighting to run away from this situation. But she had to stay and hear exactly what her husband had done to them.

'What condition, Paul?' Sarah said turning her body away from Michelle's. She refused to even speak to the woman draped across him.

'I'm – I'm so sorry. I never meant to hurt you.' He stammered pathetically. 'Michelle and I fell in love. We didn't mean it to happen.'

'What condition?' Sarah said again, her words like ice.

'We're having a baby.' He whispered back.

Sarah couldn't help herself. She glanced down at the non-existent stomach of the woman sitting next to her husband so possessively.

Michelle caught the glance and tapped her stomach gently. 'Three months pregnant, the time is just flying by.'

'Three months.' Sarah spluttered. 'Three months. You left home a little over six weeks ago, Paul. And it's not even five hours since I found out that you'd left me. You bastard.' Sarah stood up and grabbing her Amaretto, threw the contents into his face.

'What's on earth is going on?' A voice interrupted and Sarah turned around to see Ruby standing behind her, her face horrified by the scene unfolding.

'Ruby, you remember Paul? I've just been introduced to his pregnant mistress.'

And despite the years of drifting apart and no contact, Ruby quickly moved over to her friend and pulled her hand into hers.

'You'd better lawyer up, Paul, because that's exactly what I'm going to do as soon as I get home. I want a divorce. Sweetheart.' She finished, imitating the drawl of the woman who clearly enjoyed her world being torn asunder.

The sad thing was that he seemed relieved when she mentioned the word divorce. He didn't even try to talk her out of it. He had his new life now and it seemed he had replaced one family with another younger, smaller one.

Ruby walked over to Paul and Michelle, holding Sarah's hand tightly and looked them both up and down with disdain. 'You know what, Paul? When Sarah married you I always thought she was way too good for you. And I'm so fecking disappointed that you proved me right. Shame on you Paul Lawler, shame on you! As for you,' she said, turning to Michelle, 'remember this, once a cheater always a cheater. Good luck with that.'

She walked away quickly, pulling Sarah with her. Paul began to run after them into the lobby.

'Sarah, wait up. Please, wait.' He begged.

Sarah turned to look at the man she had loved for over a decade. She thought that she knew everything about him; she thought that she understood him, all of his intricacies, his good points and his bad. But the man standing in front of her was unrecognisable now.

'For what it's worth, I'm deeply sorry. Michelle was way out of order coming here. I told her not to.'

He waited for a response, but seeing none was forthcoming he continued.

'I know I have done things all wrong and I know I'm a coward. But I do want to do right by you and the children.' He handed Sarah an envelope.

'It's €1000. We'll agree a regular monthly payment immediately. But until then it will tide you over.'

€1000 would just about cover their next month's mortgage and bills. But she couldn't get into that now. She just needed to get away from Paul. She could feel her pulse quickening again, her heart hammering in her chest, her breath getting shallow.

'She's a nice girl when you get to know her.' Paul added pathetically, as she pushed the button on the lift. 'You'll like her, honestly you will.'

'Un-fecking-believable!' Ruby exclaimed.

Sarah turned around and looked at her husband in disbelief. 'Did you just tell me that I'd like THAT in there? What she did tonight was malicious and intentional. But these past few months you have shown a side to yourself that is cruel beyond my wildest imagination. You know what? I think that you both are well matched. Guaranteed to make each other miserable for years to come!'

For once, timing was on her side. The lift door opened and as Ruby and she walked in, at least, if nothing else, she had the last word.

Chapter Thirteen

Ruby quickly took control as soon as they walked into the room. She pulled from her handbag a bottle of Prosecco and rinsed out two glasses.

'I'm glad I stopped in M&S now!' She declared. From her large tote handbag, she pulled out several bars of chocolate and laid them down beside the glasses. 'Right, while I get this open, fill me in. I take it this was your first time meeting her ladyship downstairs?'

Sarah nodded then quickly brought Ruby up to speed with the previous few months' events, leaving out Edward of course.

'I'm just gobsmacked. I mean he did all of this with forethought. That's a whole new level of cruelty.'

'Did you always think he was a weasel?' Sarah asked her suddenly.

'I kinda did. He was always just so full of himself.'

Sarah flinched at the words. 'Go on.'

'Look I won't lie, Paul is a charmer, I'll give him that. We always had a laugh didn't we, when we'd all hang out together, back in the day?'

Sarah smiled at the memory.

'But he was always flaky, he'd take up a new hobby and then five minutes later it seemed, he'd run out of the enthusiasm for the same thing he'd only just been waxing lyrical about.'

Flashes of Paul in tennis gear, with golf clubs, in hiking boots, badminton racket in hand all skimmed across Sarah's brain. All fads he started and got bored of.

Ruby continued, 'It's just that commitment comes from staying loyal to something you said you are going to do, even when the mood you said it in has left you. I worried about that aspect of Paul's personality.'

'How did I not see any of that?' Sarah asked with self-reproach. 'He obviously had started the affair with her before he left home. She said she's three months pregnant.'

'You never suspected a thing?' Ruby looked sceptical at that.

'You think I'm stupid.' Sarah stated. 'I am stupid.'

'Not in the least! Only one gobshite in this equation is and it isn't you!' Ruby assured her. 'Listen, one thing I've learnt over the years with men, is that it's easy to believe someone when they're telling you exactly what you want to hear!'

Sarah smiled at her friend, 'When did you get to be so wise? I'm so glad you are here. I can't believe you are, to be honest. Thank you.'

'You've popped into my head a few times over the past month! Isn't that weird?' Ruby said.

'Not weird at all. I kept thinking of you too Rubes!' Sarah reached over and squeezed her hand tightly.

'You know today when you called? Well I never have my personal mobile phone on during the day in work. Never! But I had overwhelming urge to turn switch it on, just before you called.'

Sarah smiled and knew that somehow or other it wasn't a coincidence that had caused that.

She looked at her old friend. It had been years since they'd spoken, yet it didn't feel awkward or strained in the least.

That was the way it was with good friends. There was a time when they were inseparable, but life moved them in different directions and years had passed without any real contact. But nothing had changed at all. Sarah realised she had so much to catch up on.

'What about you Ruby? I heard you were back in Ireland. Are you? Last I heard you were working on cruise ships?'

'Yeah, I ran the fitness lounge for the past few years for one of the big liners. But when I heard that the Ferrycarrig Hotel was looking for a new gym manager I decided to apply for the job and sure would you believe it, I got it! Mam is having her hip replaced shortly; I wanted to be around to help her recuperate.'

'And is there anybody special in your life?'

'Depends what your definition of special is, Sarah. I mean the sommelier from the hotel I'm staying in, he felt pretty special last night. Just saying!'

Sarah started to snort with laughter. 'You didn't!'

'I did. Three times!'

The two friends burst into peals of laughter until tears streamed down their faces.

'Good to see you laugh.' Ruby told her.

'It's been a while.' Sarah admitted.

'Well it's a good job I'm back so.' Ruby declared. 'Now I think I'd better call room service. We're going to need another bottle!'

Chapter Fourteen

'This is so not like Tommy.' Sarah said worriedly. She was sitting in Art O'Leary's office.

'I agree. Tommy has never been in a fight before in school. But I was in the school yard when it happened so I saw it myself. Young Joseph O'Dowd passed the basketball to Tommy and it hit him on the head, but purely by accident. The next thing I knew he was running at Joseph and had him on the ground, punching him.'

She glanced outside the window of Art's office and saw Tommy sitting on a bench, head down, sullenly kicking a stone with his foot. Katie was playing hopscotch in front of him.

Ella was asleep in her pram beside her.

'Is everything ok at home?' he asked gently. He'd heard rumours that Paul had left her, but didn't know how true they were. 'You look a little pale?'

Sarah looked up at him to assess if he was being nosy, but no, he seemed genuinely concerned.

'The gossips have been having a field day over my life.' Sarah said quietly.

'I'm not interested in rumours and gossip.' Art answered gently. 'How you and the children are doing, well, that's a different matter.'

'Paul and I split up. He's moved to London and has a new girl-friend. I had to tell the children that Daddy has moved out. They are not taking it too well. I still have the joy of telling them about Michelle, Daddy's new girlfriend, who incidentally is a piece of work.'

Art drew in a breath and replied, 'That's rough. It explains a lot. I can't imagine how much of an adjustment it must be for you all.'

They sat in silence for a bit then Art said, 'You don't have to allow Michelle to see the kids surely? Can't Paul see that it would be better for the children to do things in stages and see if this relationship with Michelle is going to last before he introduces her to them?'

'Bit late for that Art, they are having a baby. So the kids are going to have a new brother or sister soon. I think Michelle is here to stay.'

'Sarah, that's bloody awful.' Art said shocked. 'When I split up with my girlfriend I found it really hard to deal with but there was nobody else involved or any children either. This must be really messing with your head.'

'You could say that alright.' Sarah replied. 'I've just explained that their Daddy has changed jobs and has met a new friend in England. You'll understand if I ask you to keep that to yourself?'

'Absolutely. Nobody will hear any of this from me I can assure you. How did they take it?' Art said, glancing to the door of the office. 'Stupid question, sorry. Doesn't take a genius to work out that the fight Tommy was in was all connected to his Daddy going.'

'I could kill Paul.' Sarah said fiercely. 'This is such a mess.'

'Have Tommy and Katie got anyone that they can talk to?' Art asked.

'I think that Tommy thinks he's got to be the big man now. Katie cried when I told them, Ella is just too young to understand and Tommy clammed up and just said that he'd look after all of us. He's a kid, I want him to have a childhood, not feel that he has to grow up overnight.' Sarah felt so sad and so very tired all of a sudden.

'And who do you have, Sarah?' Art asked her gently. 'Do you have someone to be strong for you?'

Sarah looked up at him quickly. He was staring at her so intently that she felt herself blush under his gaze. When he said her name again, she realised that she had been staring at him and she could feel herself getting even redder. Flustered, she quickly answered, 'Yes, I'm lucky in that regard, Art. I have James, my brother, and also some good friends. Paul's mother, Rita, is a rock too.'

Sarah glanced out the window at her son. 'What should I do about this situation with Tommy and Joseph O'Dowd? Should I ring the O'Dowd's and apologise?'

'Don't you be worrying. Joseph is one of five brothers and as tough as old boots. Tommy didn't connect any of his punches to Joseph's face thankfully, so no harm done. I've spoken to Joseph's Mam and she's fine about it all.'

'That's something to be grateful for.' Sarah said ruefully. 'I'll talk to him tonight. Try to work out what's going on in his little head. I'm so sorry for all of this. Thank you for your help.'

'All part of my job. I'll keep an eye on the two kids in school. I'll talk to each of their teachers too. On top of Rachel's death, well, it's been a hard year for them both.' Art summed up.

Sarah felt her eyes drift to Art's arms. His white shirt sleeves were rolled up and she wondered how she'd never noticed before how muscular and tanned he actually was. She quickly looked up, flustered again and stood up quickly. What on earth was wrong with her?

'It's taken its toll.' Sarah agreed quickly. 'But Katie's new teacher seems to be a big hit. She was full of praise for Mr Brennan yesterday.'

'He's a good guy. He's very musical too, so he'll throw himself into the *Wizard of Oz* play. I know the kids loved that with Rachel.'

'Apparently he looks just like the teacher Will from *Glee*!' Sarah said with a smile. 'I think my little girl has got her first crush.'

Art started to laugh. 'She'll have to join the queue! All I heard in the lunchroom yesterday from the other teachers was just how gorgeous young Mr Brennan is! I'll have to check this *Glee* out and see what the fuss is all about.'

Sarah laughed and thanked Art as it was time to go get the kids. Suddenly she felt tired and so sad and she wasn't sure she had the energy to deal with any more problems. She felt like crying – again. She was going to have to toughen up. But the past couple of weeks had taken their toll. As it seemed they had on her son too.

'Sarah?' Art enquired quietly. 'You ok?' Seeing that she was far from ok, he walked over to her and pulled her into his arms. Sarah's first instinct was to pull away from him, but it felt good to be held, to have someone comfort her.

She relaxed and allowed herself to move closer into Art's arms and closed her eyes, lost in the moment, and then the tears that had been prickling her eyes, came thick and fast.

'Sshh.' Art said to her as he stroked her hair. 'It will be all ok, you'll see.'

Sarah pulled away from Art quickly, feeling embarrassed that she had gotten so upset.

'I'm so sorry.' Sarah was mortified as she noticed mascara smudged onto Art's white shirt. 'I seem to have made quite a mess.'

'Come's with the territory.' Art joked. 'Comforting damsels in distress, that is!'

Sarah smiled and as she didn't trust herself to speak, she left quickly.

She walked outside to get the kids, pushing Ella in her pram in front of her.

'Come on you two.' She said with a big smile, hoping that they wouldn't notice she'd been crying. 'Who's hungry?'

'Me!' replied Katie. 'Is Tommy in trouble?' She added with just a hint of joy at the thought of her big brother getting into trouble.

'Never you mind, little monkey.' Sarah said to Katie. She squeezed Tommy's hand tightly in hers.

When they got home she did what she swore she'd never do, but more and more she had to rely on, she turned on the TV and used it as a babysitter for Katie and Ella, so that she could talk to Tommy.

'Tommy, would you mind helping me chop some veggies?' Sarah said to her son.

He looked at her suspiciously. He was waiting for her to start giving out to him, but so far she was acting all normal.

'OK, Mammy.' He said without any enthusiasm.

She handed him the peeler and some carrots. 'You can start with these.' she said gently to him.

Soon they had gotten into an easy rhythm. Tommy was scraping the skins off the carrots then he would hand them to Sarah who topped and tailed them, before chopping them into small batons. The children would only eat them in that shape, they didn't taste the same if they were round apparently.

After a few minutes, Sarah asked Tommy. 'How are you doing, kiddo?'

He shrugged making a non-committal sound.

'That good, huh?' Sarah replied.

'Things are a bit weird right now, aren't they?' She continued chopping her carrots, so that Tommy would not feel pressurised into answering her.

'I'm sorry for hitting Joseph.' Tommy said quietly, staring at his peeler intently.

'What made you do that?' Sarah asked him.

'Don't know.' He answered.

She continued chopping, placing batons into the saucepan on her right. She didn't want to push him too much. She knew her son; he'd open up to her in his own time. If she pushed him, he'd clam up like a shell and she'd never find out what was going on in his head.

'I heard some kids talking. They said that you and Daddy were getting a divorce.' Tommy said in a whisper.

'Hmm, I can imagine that must have been horrible for you. Hearing somebody talking about your life is never nice.' Sarah responded mildly, even though her heart broke into a thousand pieces.

'Are you getting a divorce, Mammy?' Tommy asked her, his eyes full of tears.

Sarah put down her knife and turned to her little boy. She sighed quietly, wondering how they ever got to this point; she just wanted to make it all ok.

'I think we might be, Tommy.' Sarah replied. 'I'm so sorry. I wish it wasn't like this.'

'Why did Daddy go? Was it something that I did?' Tommy said, a big fat tear falling down his cheek. 'I didn't do well in my spelling test the night before he left. He was cross with me for only getting five out of ten. Is that why he went?'

Sarah pulled her little boy into her arms. 'No, Daddy is not cross with you or with Katie or Ella. Daddy loves you all very, very much. And both your Daddy and I are always proud of you as long as you try your best.'

'If he loves us so much, then why did he go?' Tommy said with the logic that only children have.

Sarah wished she had a magic answer for her son. She also wished that Paul could see all of this first hand. He had no idea of the devastation he was leaving behind, as he had run away to start his new life. She could have cheerfully strangled him.

'Sometimes people do things that we don't understand.' Sarah said to Tommy. 'And even though they hurt us, they never stop loving us.'

'How do you know?' Tommy said, wiping away his tears with the back of his sleeve.

'Because he has told me so, silly.' Sarah said with a smile. 'The day you were born, your Daddy looked at me, as he held you in his arms and he said that it was the proudest day of his life.'

'Really?' Tommy asked his eyes wide.

'Yes really.' Sarah replied. 'It was my proudest day too, Tommy. I was so happy to finally meet you. And you've grown into such a funny, loving, happy little boy. Every day has been a joy for me. Truly.'

Tommy snuggled into his mother's arms. 'I love you, Mama.' He said in a whisper. She hadn't heard him use the word mama in nearly two years. It was always Mammy now. She had to fight back the tears yet again.

She held him close for a few more minutes, then pulled away to look him in the eye.

'Now, I know that today you were upset and angry that some children were talking about you. But you know better than to get into a fight.'

'I know, Mammy.' Tommy said. 'I'm sorry. I won't do it again.'

'Promise me?' She asked her son.

'Promise.' He said.

'OK, we'll say no more about it then. But you remember that I'm here for you. I know that this is tough, but you can talk to me about anything anytime. I'm always on your side, buddy.'

'I know. Can I go watch some cartoons now?'

Sarah shooed him out of the kitchen with a smile. She peeped in at the children; they were all happily playing together. While they were quiet she picked up the phone to talk to Paul. He needed to know what was going on. Despite any battles they may have regarding maintenance in their divorce, they were always going to have to be parents together and do what was best for the children. She had to make him see that.

Chapter Fifteen

James knew that he was treading on ice right now. He was parked outside the office where Marie Wickham worked. Ever since Sarah had filled him in on her dream regarding the night Mal came home late with sand on his boots, he couldn't get it out of his head.

This was way out of his league, he knew that. He had done stakeouts many times before but normally on behalf of an insurance company checking up on a suspicious individual who claimed they had whiplash, or following a man whose wife suspected he was having an affair. And while he took his job seriously, it wasn't life or death stuff he was dealing with. This was different. Mal Wickham had brutally murdered a young girl. And who knew what he was capable of? If Sarah's intuition was right, someone else was in mortal danger right now too.

He'd spoken to his friend Roger in the Gardaí about his conversation with Marie Wickham and told him that he'd gotten a feeling at the funeral that Rachel might have been involved with Mal. That of course was a slight stretch of the truth. But Roger had understandably told him to back off unless he had something concrete to base his hunch on. And he couldn't very well tell him that he was basing his conjuncture on his twin sister's psychic dreams. Try as much as he could, the image of Mal's smug face wouldn't leave him. Sarah truly believed that he murdered Rachel and she also believed he was dangerous. He couldn't just sit back and do nothing, plus he had promised Sarah he would do everything he could to help her make sense of her dreams about this guy. Marie Wickham was a good place to start.

He looked at his watch, five o'clock. He had been waiting for over an hour now; he figured that Marie would have to be out soon. Within five minutes he saw her coming out the door. He jumped out of his car and walked over to her. She got a fright when she saw him walking towards her, not recognising him at first.

'Marie? Not sure you remember me? We met at Rachel Finch's funeral. James Codd.' He said quickly.

'Oh yes, I remember.' She replied in a worried voice. 'What are you doing here?'

'I wondered if you had five minutes for a quick chat.'

'About what?' She asked quickly. 'I'm married, James, in case you've forgotten and I'm not sure that Mal would appreciate me talking to you.'

'We can do this quietly here or down at the station if you like?' James said recklessly. Now he was really crossing the line. He pulled his ID card out of his jacket pocket and flashed it quickly at Marie. 'I'm a detective and I have a few questions I need to ask you. Nothing for you to be frightened of.'

If Marie looked at his ID badge she would see quickly he wasn't a detective in the Gardaí's but a private investigator and had absolutely no jurisdiction over her.

'Have I done anything wrong?' Marie said in a frightened voice, barely glancing at his badge.

'Not that I'm aware of.' James replied quickly. 'I just want to have a chat with you regarding Rachel. Five minutes I promise you, and then you're free to go home.'

'OK.' Marie replied. 'But can we get in your car? I feel like the whole office is looking at me.'

'Sure, if that makes you feel more comfortable.' James replied.

They walked to his car and James opened the passenger door, allowing Marie to get in. He sat in the driving seat and turned to face her. She was as white as a ghost and she seemed to be really agitated, looking all around her, as if she was afraid to be seen talking to him.

'Marie, please don't be scared. I just need to ask you some questions, that's all.' James said to her, in a voice that he hoped would calm her down. He was afraid she'd burst into tears and he was beginning to wonder if this was a good idea or not.

'We have reason to believe that Rachel was seeing someone just before she died.'

Marie looked surprised. 'I thought she was single?' She replied. 'At least that's what her mother told me at the funeral.' He studied her face; she did seem genuinely surprised that Rachel had a boyfriend.

'Well, I can't go into the details, the seriousness of the crime prevents me, you'll understand.' He said cryptically.

Marie nodded energetically in return. 'I understand.'

'I know that this is a delicate question, but I need to ask you something. I got the feeling when we chatted at the funeral that you didn't much care for Rachel. Was I right?'

He watched Marie's face as she ran through scenarios as to what to reply. He could see she was worried that she might get herself into trouble.

'No law against not liking someone.' He said in a friendly voice to Marie. 'If there was I'd be in jail myself, as there are one or two individuals I can honestly say I don't care for much!'

'Oh.' Marie said, laughing nervously. 'Well, in that case, you're right. I didn't much like Rachel. Or rather I didn't much like her anymore. There was a time when we were great friends.'

'Tell me about your relationship with her.' James urged her. 'This would be most helpful in my investigation.'

'Well, I don't like to speak ill of the dead…' Marie said.

'Of course, I understand.' James said smiling encouragingly. 'But…'

'Well, in college she was different. We just had fun together, going out, clubbing, drinking, boys; you know what it's like. We did everything together; I thought that we'd always be in each other's lives.' She sounded wistful.

'Sounds like it was a lot of fun back then.' James said.

Marie nodded.

'So what changed?' James asked her.

'Well back then, Rachel was always popular. She was big flirt, she had a way with men, and she had a way of making them want to do everything for her. I don't think she ever completed any of her own essays herself. There was always a guy who was willing to write 3,000 words on whatever subject was needed. It was hilarious watching her and the way she played them. She always had lots of them all vying for her attention. She could have had her pick of them really. But she never wanted to settle down; she said that she didn't want to be stuck with one man forever, marriage was for losers. As soon as someone got close, she would back off.'

James was picking up on an edge in Marie's voice.

'That seemed to bother you a lot?' He asked her.

'It did bother me a bit if I'm honest but not too much, at least not then anyhow. We were both single and having fun. Besides we had one rule, no flirting with each other's boyfriends.'

'Sounds like a good rule to make.' James agreed. 'So what happened between college and you getting married?'

'Well we lost touch for a while after college. She had an affair with one of our lecturers in college and I didn't approve.'

'Did you tell her that?

'Yeah, we fell out over it. She actively went after this guy. It was a game for her, the more he tried to push her away protesting he was happily married, the more attractive he became. It was cruel. He eventually gave into her charms. Men always did. Before long they were headlong into a passionate relationship. But as soon as he left his wife, declaring himself in love with her, she dumped him. She completely ruined that man's life, and for what? A game.' Marie said bitterly.

'She sounds like a piece of work alright.' James agreed. This was a side to Rachel's character he'd not heard of when chatting to her family and friends in Ballyaislinn.

'So that's why you lost touch?' He asked.

'I suppose it was. She knew that I didn't approve of her relationship with this guy. It was fine when it was just single guys she was messing with, but I couldn't just say nothing to her when marriages were being torn apart. I saw something in her character that I didn't like and she sensed my disapproval. We didn't really have a big fight, we just kind of mutually moved away from each other. Rachel came back to her home town and got a job teaching in a local school. I was working in Dublin by then. But then by a twist of fate, I met Mal and we got married. And as Mal was from Wexford, it made me think of Rachel. I was lonely for my friends and family in Dublin, so I called her and we met up. But she was different to the Rachel I had known back in college. She'd changed, was harder.'

'How so?' James pushed.

'Well, for one the old rules didn't apply anymore apparently, about leaving each other's men alone. She flirted openly with Mal; she seemed to enjoy how upset it was making me.'

'That must have been hard for you to see that.' James said with genuine sympathy now.

'Yes, it was. It hurt me a lot.' She answered truthfully.

'And Mal, how was he with Rachel?'

'He's a man, James. He reacted like most men would, he was flattered.'

'I don't want to upset you, Marie, but do you suspect that your husband and Rachel might have had an affair?' James asked the girl bluntly.

She looked up at him sharply. 'No, I didn't. Or at least I didn't until now.' She replied tearfully. 'Or maybe I did suspect, I just don't know anymore!' She ran her hands through her hair and as she did so, James caught sight of a large bruise on the side of her temple. Her long fringe had been covering it.

James took a proper look at the woman sitting beside him. She had her makeup on pretty thick. At first he had thought it was just her way of applying make-up, but looking closely now, it was definitely a way of covering up some bruising to her face.

She noticed him looking at her bruise and quickly pulled her hair down over her face.

'What happened to you?' James said to her very gently.

'It's nothing.' She replied quickly. 'I'm just so clumsy, it's ridiculous.' She looked at his face and continued. 'It's not what you think!' She could feel her face redden with embarrassment. She knew that she sounded like a cliché, trying to make out that she'd walked into a door. But she couldn't say the words out loud to anyone, because if she did that, well it would make them real.

'What do you think I'm thinking?' James asked her gently.

'That my husband hit me! All because I'm a stupid woman who nags him, that if I only thought before I spoke, then my marriage wouldn't be in pieces. That's what you're thinking.' She said tears forming in her eyes.

'I'm so sorry, Marie.' James said, reaching over and touching her hand. 'You're right I do think that your husband hit you. But that's all. I don't believe for one minute that any of this is your fault. No man has the right to do this to a woman, even if that woman nagged him from morning till night. You can file a complaint. You have to do something, because in my experience, it's not going to go away, it will only get worse.'

Marie looked over at James. 'You don't understand. I love my husband. It's not his fault, I'm very annoying. I can't help myself sometimes; I can hear myself always nagging him over and over. And I know it drives him mad. I hate myself for it. I promise myself every day when I get home that today I won't say anything to annoy Mal. And everything is fine at first. I make our dinner; he comes in from the farm. He eats his dinner. Then he disappears upstairs and comes down all dressed up and tells me he's going out. Every night he goes out and won't take me with him, so I'm at home thinking

129

all sorts. And sometimes it's the middle of the night before he gets in. Last Sunday night I accused him of having an affair. He hit me. Said I couldn't love him if I could imagine such an evil thing. That I must be thinking of having an affair myself. And I'm not thinking any such thing, honestly.' She finished sobbing.

James felt sorry for the woman. This was no way to live a life. No wonder she was scared to be seen in his company. She was worried her husband would find out and accuse her of having an affair. He wanted to drive to the farm right now and show Mal how a man hits a man. Let him pick on someone his own size for a change. But he knew that although that would give him some short-term satisfaction, it wouldn't help in getting the guy locked up. And he wanted to make sure that Mal Wickham was locked up for a very long time and couldn't hurt anyone else ever again.

'Listen to me, Marie. You have to leave him. That's no way to live your life, living in fear constantly.'

'But I don't want to be on my own.' Marie answered flatly.

'Sounds to me like you're living on your own already. You have been for some time now.'

Marie didn't disagree with him. 'I'm not brave enough to leave him. I love him.'

James wouldn't believe that what Marie felt was love. But he wasn't in the situation she was in and he knew he shouldn't judge. He'd learnt in his job that relationships were very complicated and very often when in the hands of an abuser it was very hard for the victim to walk away. They lived their lives in such fear, they were afraid to just make the break.

Marie took out a tissue and wiped her eyes. She turned to James again saying, 'You think that Mal was having an affair with Rachel don't you?'

'Yes, I do.' James replied.

Marie sighed. She was lost in her thoughts.

'I think that Mal has been cheating on me. It's been on my mind for months now, like an itch that just won't go away. I didn't know it was Rachel though, honestly. He told me that he didn't like her, that she was too vulgar for him, too obvious. And I believed him. But if I'm honest, well, I've been suspecting that my husband isn't truthful to me. As I said earlier, he's out till the wee hours several nights a week. He stayed in for a few weeks after Rachel died. But in the past few days he's out again, at all hours.'

'It must be awful for you.' James replied, aghast at the life this poor woman was living.

'It's not the marriage I envisaged.' Marie replied bitterly. 'Now unless you have anything else you want me to answer, I'd better get home. He'll be looking for his dinner at six.'

'Listen, Marie. I'd rather you didn't repeat any of this conversation to your husband right now. It's a confidential matter as you can appreciate I'm sure.'

'Don't worry, James, I'm not going to mention this to him. I don't want more of this.' She finished, pointing to her head.

'Let me get you help.' James begged her. 'There are places that can help you, take you in. I'll go with you to get your things. I'll bring you to a safe house.'

She shook her head. 'No I can't do that. I married him and I'm going to try and work this out.'

James handed Marie his card. 'Here's my number. Keep it. If you need anything, ever, just call me. And if you think of anything that might help us with our investigation, give me a call too. No matter how small it might seem to you, it might be of help to us. Maybe you might remember something about Mal's movements around the time of Rachel's murder. Like if there was anything unusual to report about him coming home late at night, acting strangely.'

Marie shoved the card into her handbag. 'I've got to go.' She jumped out of the car and ran to her own.

James sat watching until she drove away. He felt like he had gotten nowhere and everywhere both at the same time. He picked up the phone to call Sarah and fill her in.

Chapter Sixteen

'Mammy, why do I have to wear Tommy's stinky old costume from last year?' Katie whined. 'It's not fair. Jessie got a new costume and I'm going to look stupid wearing Tommy's. Everyone will know.'

'No they won't.' Sarah replied calmly. 'I'm sorry we didn't get any new costumes. I told you I'd make you a cat costume but you said no to that. Wearing Tommy's vampire costume from last year is your only other option. Come on, look in the mirror, you look fantastic. And by the time I do your face paint, you are going to look so scary!'

'Ella's wearing your old costume from when you were a baby, Katie.' Tommy said to his little sister. 'And you know there are lots of kids in school not getting new costumes.'

'It's ok for you; you look cool in Uncle James's costume.' Katie said to her brother.

'Well you couldn't be Sherlock Holmes, you're a girl!' Tommy shot back straight away. He was delighted with his gear. Uncle James had given him a Sherlock Holmes costume he had from years back. It was very cool actually and even had a pipe and hat.

'Enough already about the costumes, please, I beg you!' Sarah said to them both. 'New costumes cost money and money doesn't grow on trees, you know.' Sarah cringed inwardly. She sounded just like her mother then. 'We all have to make sacrifices for a little while until I get the money situation sorted.'

'I know, Mammy. We're in a session.' Katie said solemnly. 'Mr Brennan told us.'

'A session?' Sarah said looking a bit worried.

'A recession, dumbo.' Tommy said.

'That's what I said. A session.' Katie replied throwing her eyes to heaven.

Sarah smiled, listening to their banter, Ella watching her brother and sister intently, laughing away at them.

'I have a recession joke.' Tommy said to Katie. 'Do you want to hear it?'

'Yes, Tommy, tell me!' Katie squealed.

Tommy took a deep breath. 'Money is so tight, 50 cent had to change his name to 10 cent!' he said triumphantly.

Sarah started to laugh. 'That's very funny, Tommy. You're a funny guy!'

'I don't get it.' Katie said crossly. 'Who's 50 cent?'

'A singer. A rapper.' Tommy explained.

'Like wrapping paper?' Katie said. 'Wrapping paper with 50 cent on it? That's silly, Tommy.'

'I give up!' Tommy said walking out of the room, shaking his head as Katie ran after him, all moans about their costumes forgotten for a minute.

Soon they were all set and they left the house ready to go trick or treating. Sarah had been dreading this. Every year the tradition had been that Paul would bring the children out and she would stay at home getting food ready for their return – burgers and hotdogs. And of course she would be at home too to give sweets to other trick or treaters. Disaster was averted only when Nana Rita arrived to see the children dressed up and said she'd stay and answer the door to anyone who came. Katie was most upset at the thought of some of her friends calling and not getting their rightful sweets.

She'd asked James to come with them but he was working, unfortunately. He'd felt really bad but she was going to have to start relying on herself a lot more. She couldn't keep calling James to keep her company.

In the end they had a great time going from house to house. Halloween had become such a huge occasion in Ireland now, most of the adults dressed up as well as the kids. Sarah herself had gotten into the spirit and gone as a witch. She'd just put on one of her black dresses, used liberal amounts of dark make-up and stuck an old witches hat of Katie's on her head. A yard brush as her witches broom, with a small stuffed kitten of Ella's glued to the end of the handle, completed the look. Not bad for a homemade costume, she'd thought as she'd gotten ready.

They had a wobbly moment when they'd met a large group of kids, about ten of them in total. And they were accompanied by their Daddies – four of them together all dressed up. Sarah watched Tommy and Katie looking longingly at the children's fathers and she cursed Paul in her head. Damn him and damn bloody Michelle. She'd called him earlier in the week and asked him to come and do Halloween with them. It was hard to make that call, but she was determined that they do right by their children wherever possible. He'd put her on hold and said he'd call Michelle to check with her. But apparently Michelle felt it was a very bad idea as it would give the children false hope that their Daddy was coming home. So for the children's sake he wouldn't come. She was so angry with him. I mean how long had he'd known this Michelle woman and she was already making decisions that affected their children? But what could she do? She thought it was ironic really. James had told Sarah about a colleague of his who was fighting his ex-girlfriend for access to see his daughter. He had to take her to court to try and ensure he got to see his daughter on a regular basis. And here was her husband, who couldn't care less. She'd be taking him to court to make him see their children more often at this rate.

After an hour of trick or treating the children were getting tired and were happy to go home to check their loot.

'Let's go see if Nana has eaten all of Ella's chocolate buttons!' Sarah said to them jokingly.

They all laughed and made their way home.

Soon they were all sitting around the kitchen table pouring the contents of their pumpkin cauldron bags out. There were jellies, chocolate, marshmallows, and bars of every description tumbling out.

'Whoa now, kids. Just one thing each until we have our tea. Then you can knock yourselves out!' Sarah said.

Sarah walked into the kitchen where Rita was busy cooking the burgers and sausages.

'Thanks, Rita. You're a star.' She said gratefully.

'We're almost done.' Rita replied brushing off the thanks. 'Chips are in the oven, five more minutes and they'll be finished. Ella went down about fifteen minutes ago. She was all done in, poor pet.'

'The excitement wears her out.' Sarah said smiling. 'She loves watching the kids playing and tonight was great fun for her, watching everyone get dressed up. She looked adorable in her pumpkin outfit, didn't she?'

'She did, the angel.' Rita replied. 'She's the image of Tommy.'

Sarah nodded. And the image of Paul too, they were both thinking.

'He should be here, Sarah.' Rita said. 'I'm disgusted with him. I called him and said as much.'

Sarah walked over to her mother-in-law. 'Don't be getting yourself worked up. I appreciate you sticking up for us like that, I truly do. But he's your son; it must be difficult for you. I don't want you to feel stuck in the middle of all this.'

'He might be my son, but you're my daughter as well, as far as I'm concerned.' Rita replied.

Sarah walked over and gave the old woman a kiss on her cheek.

'And you've been more of a mother to me than my own.' She replied quietly. They gave each other a quick hug until a funny smell made them look around.

135

'Oh feck, my onions are burning!' Rita said laughing.

Within minutes they were all happily munching their burgers, onions caramelised beautifully! Ketchup was dribbling down Katie's chin.

'I can't see what's fake blood and what's ketchup anymore!' Sarah said to her daughter, laughing.

'I know a vampire joke.' Tommy said to his family. 'Want to hear it?'

'As long as it's better than the session joke.' Katie said seriously.

'Session?' Rita enquired.

'I'll explain later!' Sarah answered. They weren't going down that road again.

'Ok, Tommy. Go for it, funny boy. What's your vampire joke?'

'What did the ghost say to the vampire when he said goodbye?' Tommy said with a big grin.

He waited for everyone to answer, 'I don't know. What did the ghost say?'

Pausing dramatically for effect, Tommy shouted 'So long, suckers!'

They all laughed together. 'That's a good one, Tommy.' Katie gave her vote of approval.

Sarah glanced at the empty seat beside her. Paul's spot. Funny how families end up always sitting in the same position at the table for every meal. Or was that just her family? So far, in what was an unspoken agreement amongst them all, everyone avoided his seat. She wondered where he was right this minute. He wasn't trick or treating that's for sure. She figured he would be in a swanky wine bar somewhere in London, eating Tapas, laughing, not a care in the world.

'Penny for them?' Rita asked gently.

'Oh you can guess. I'm thinking that right now his view is a hell of a lot different than ours is here.' Sarah nodded to their kitchen window, where all you could see was hills and trees.

'I daresay you are right.' Rita acknowledged. 'But I know one thing for sure. He's missing out on one of the most spectacular views there is – that of his children.' Rita stood up to gather the plates up, but walked over to her daughter-in-law first and kissed her forehead tenderly.

'You are doing a great job pet. And from where I'm standing, you're the lucky one. He doesn't know what he's missing, but he will do one day. He'll realise, I promise you and he'll be so sorry.'

Sarah reached up and hugged Rita tightly, whispering her thanks.

Chapter Seventeen

James was expecting the bank and phone records of Mal Wickham emailed to him any minute. And yes, here they were. He already had Rachel Finch's. Sometimes it paid to have contacts.

Opening the first attachment he saw Mal's bank statement.

'Let's see what you've been up to, Mr Wickham.' He said to himself. It was amazing the amount you could find out about somebody by looking through their records. Where was he spending his money? Would the bank statement give any clue as to where Mal had been on the day Rachel was murdered? As if he didn't know. He just needed the proof.

He scanned through the transactions and stopped suddenly when he saw an entry for an online dating company. Wickham had a monthly subscription it seemed. Ok, that's not a bookable offence, but interesting all the same. It was another insight into his character. The word Sleaze with a capital 'S' sprung to mind. Poor Marie, she'd no idea who she was married to at all. Looking through the statement line by line, he saw a trend developing. Every couple of nights he was taking out cash, but, the interesting thing was, the cash machines were all in Dublin. And fair enough, he lived quite rural in Rosslare, but James was pretty sure that there were bank links nearer to him than 120 kms up the N11. Dublin was a fair old trek just to get some cash. So that's where he was disappearing to every night. And to back this up, he could see several payments to various petrol stations along the N11. Expensive thing, dating, when you have to commute to Dublin from Wexford every day, James thought. Wonder who the lucky lady is? Or plural, ladies. Goodness knew how many he had on the go.

'Ok, now let's go back further,' he thought, hitting the 'older entries' button on the statement. He wanted to see what Wickham was up to on the day of Rachel's murder. Sarah said she saw them in a restaurant in her dream. Would it be too much to hope for that he paid for that restaurant by one of his credit or debit cards? Come on, Wickham; do me a favour, James thought. No such luck. But hang on one minute, bingo, here we go; a lead worth following. Things were looking up suddenly. Mal had withdrawn money from a bank machine in Gorey town at 3pm on the day Rachel was murdered. Now as he lived in Rosslare, Gorey was just a tad out of his way. Just what was he doing there he wondered? Was that where he met Rachel?

If he could find a way to link Rachel and Mal together he could give that to Roger and let the Gardaí take over.

He then looked through the phone records and there was nothing in the statement that jumped out at him. One thing for sure was the fact that he wasn't using this phone to call Rachel. But logically, being a married man, he'd not want to use this phone to call his mistress. Marie might get suspicious and check his phone for texts. He had to have another phone, he was sure of it. The only problem was if he had a phone that was pay as you go, he could have taken it out under any name and it would be harder to trace. Not impossible but it would take a little bit of time.

Think, James. Think. There was always another angle. He needed that missing phone number and quickly. He looked at the bank statements again and then it hit him. If he was doing speed dating and online dating, he'd have to give a contact number to the companies involved. He googled the speed dating company listed in his direct debit and soon was speaking to its owner. It didn't take long for James to persuade him that it was in his interest to pass on the phone details of Malcolm Wickham, in order to avoid having a search warrant produced and the messy newspaper coverage that would surely follow. As soon as you mentioned the word Detective James Codd, he found most people assumed he was in the Gardaí and started to own up to all sorts of stuff. And sure enough he had confirmation that the number listed for Mal Wickham was a different number. Ok, it was time to get the phone records for this new number. He rang his contact and asked for them to be emailed to him as soon as possible.

A few hours later they arrived. To his delight he discovered two numbers that popped up on a regular basis. He pulled open the details he had on file on Rachel, and cross referenced her home number and her mobile. Bingo, again – James practically punched the air, he felt on fire. One of them was Rachel Finch's. Mal was calling her on a regular basis right up to the day she died. In fact he called her the morning of her death on his mobile. The call lasted three minutes. The second number was one he didn't recognise. He checked the phone records and the mobile belonged to a Denise Young. He was calling her daily for the past week. So she was the new girl on the scene by the looks of things.

He now had something to go to Roger with. This should be enough to bring him in for questioning, at the very least. They finally had proof that showed Rachel and Mal had a relationship. And who was to say that the new girl Denise wasn't next on his list? He murdered once, he could do it again. Never mind his poor wife Marie, who already was a victim of physical and mental abuse.

He thought about ringing Roger straight away but then reconsidered. He didn't want to leave anything to chance; when they brought him in he wanted them armed with enough evidence to charge him. So he decided it was worth checking out that bank machine. See if the bank had any cameras over the machine. And also if he could work out where they both were that night and how Rachel ended up on Ballyaislinn beach. So many questions still.

James felt he was getting close to a breakthrough. He drove to Gorey and parked the car on the main street. Within a few minutes he had found the bank machine that Mal had used. And yes, there was a camera looking down onto the machine. He walked into the bank and requested to see the manager flashing his ID again. He was soon ushered into the bank manager's office. He explained he was involved in a homicide investigation and judging by how wide the bank manager's eyes had gotten, he was impressed. 'So you see, I'd really like to see your video footage for October 3rd please?'

'You're out of luck, Detective Codd.' The bank manager said. 'We only keep our video footage for one month, unless there's an exception. I'll check for you, but unless something happened on that day, we'll have reused the tape by now.'

'It's only November 3rd for goodness sake!'

'I know that.' He replied. 'We started reusing the tapes yesterday on the 1st. Do the same every month. We use the first on the first of the next month, the second on the second, so on and so forth. Unless there's an exception, then we put in a new one today.'

'Yes, yes, so you said.' James answered irritated. This was just his bloody luck. Had he come yesterday he'd have been fine. 'Can you go check?'

'Right away.' The bank manager said picking up the phone to call his assistant in.

'What tape did you put in the video yesterday morning?'

She looked worried. 'Last month's one. Why, is something wrong? There was no note of anything wrong for October 3rd.'

'No you've done nothing wrong. Don't worry.' Turning to James, he said, 'Sorry, you're out of luck.'

James walked out of the bank cursing their efficiency. He looked up and down the street. He could see several pubs and restaurants. He figured that chances were if he was in Gorey and took money out of a bank machine here, he was meeting Rachel around here too. It was time to go knocking on some doors. He had a photograph of Rachel with him but he didn't have any of Mal, but it was worth a shot. She was a pretty girl. Someone might have remembered her.

He walked into a Chinese restaurant two doors up and asked to see the manager; he showed the picture to the staff.

'Do any of you remember serving this girl a month ago in this restaurant?'

They all looked at the picture closely and a chorus of no's murmured from them all. He had the same response in every bar and restaurant he called into. James was getting weary. He'd been into every possible location he could think of in Gorey town and nobody recognised Rachel. Although there was one woman who recognised her from her picture in the papers following the murder, which was no use whatsoever.

Feeling deflated he decided to call it a day and started to drive out of town. He was on his way towards Sarah's house when he spotted a sign in the middle of the roundabout that caused him to do drive around the roundabout a second time to re-read it. 'Margaret and Francis's Wedding. This way!' It was a trend he'd seen develop a lot of over the years, couples putting directional signs up for guests on how to find their church or hotel for their wedding.

Of course, he thought, The Seafield Hotel was just a few miles out of Gorey town. He'd been focussing entirely on the town centre of Gorey. But who was to say that he'd not met Rachel outside the main town? A discreet spot for a romantic meet up, slightly off the beaten path, not many locals called in there, mainly out-of-towners for spa breaks or weddings. He quickly turned the car around.

He spoke to the Duty Manager there – Bryan, who didn't recognise Rachel at all. He did however check his records to see who was working in the restaurant and bar that night.

'The team that were working on 3rd October are not on shift now.' Bryan said to him. 'But if you leave the photograph with me, I'll check it out for you.'

'That would be great. Thank you.' James said to him giving him his card.

He jumped in his car and continued on his way to Sarah's. They had lots to catch up on and Mary Donegan was also going to be there. Sarah had invited her over for the evening along with Ruby. He checked his watch; he was running late. The kids wouldn't be impressed.

He got there in twenty minutes and his heart melted as he saw Katie and Tommy peeping out the living room window, waiting for his car to pull into the drive. Times like these made him feel a little bit lonely and he wished he could find the right woman to settle down with and maybe have children of his own. He'd be so proud to have kids like those three in there. They were absolute starbars.

He ran in and was soon engulfed in big hugs.

'Uncle James, Uncle James.' Katie squealed. Tommy put his little hand in his and gazed up adoringly at his uncle.

'Catch any bad guys today, Uncle James?' Tommy asked.

'I caught ten of them. Bad to the bone, they were!' James answered. 'I locked them all up personally. Streets are safe now for pretty ladies like you, Katie.' He said to his niece, much to her delight, tipping an imaginary sheriff's hat at her.

'Come in here "Wyatt Earp" and sit down.' Sarah shouted out to him laughing.

'Howdy ma'am.' He said in his best western drawl. 'Mighty fine day.'

Tommy and Katie were in hysterics laughing at him and he heard a few giggles coming from the others too.

'Hi Mary. Good to see you again.' James said to her.

'You've quite a fan club there I see.' She remarked.

'Mutual appreciation society between my children and brother.' Sarah said laughing to her friend. 'I don't get a look in once James comes over!'

'Proper order!' James said in reply to his sister.

'What's for dinner? This sheriff is mighty hungry!'

'I have a Sheriff joke.' Tommy said to his uncle.

'He wants to be a stand-up comedian when he's bigger.' Katie explained.

'Knock, knock.' Tommy said.

'Who's there?' James replied

'Gopher.'

'Gopher who?

'Gopher your gun, Sheriff!'

James started to laugh. He praised his nephew. 'A mighty fine joke!' he said in his western drawl again.

'It's stupid.' Katie said sticking her tongue out at him.

'We don't use the stupid word in this house.' Sarah reminded her daughter.

'Sorry, Tommy.' Katie said to her brother. 'The joke wasn't stupid. It just wasn't very funny, that's all.' she said very seriously.

Tommy raised his eyes up and said dramatically, 'The world's a critic!'

'Funny guy.' Sarah said laughing. 'Right time for dinner, everyone. Wash up, on the table in five!'

'I hear there's a new sheriff in town.' A voice said from behind James, causing the hairs on the back of his neck to stand on end. He turned in surprise, wondering who it was who owned the voice that sounded like chocolate. The most beautiful woman that James had ever seen in his life walked into the living room. She looked familiar, but he couldn't quite place her. Tall with killer curves, long chestnut coloured wavy hair that bounced onto her shoulders and he knew he was staring at her, but he simply couldn't look away. Big brown eyes were intently watching him back, with amusement. His heart started to thump furiously in his chest and he felt a line of perspiration appear on his forehead. He'd never ever experienced a reaction like this to any other woman he'd ever met.

'You ok there?' Ruby asked him, amusement written all over her face.

'Ruby?' He replied incredulously, then made a supreme effort to pull himself together and stop looking like an imbecile.

'All grown up now, James.' She said to him with a grin, giving a little curtsey.

'I can see that!' He answered with a smile. She was a woman who knew how to dress her curves and make every single one of them count. 'Sorry, I didn't recognise you Ruby! You've changed since the last time we met. Come here, gorgeous!' He walked over and pulled her in for a hug.

She smelt good and suddenly James felt out of his depth. He pulled away quickly and noted that Ruby was still looking at him with amusement

'You're looking good. Still the charmer I see?' Ruby teased.

'Never worked on you!' James answered. 'We could have been so good together!' He finished dramatically.

'In your dreams!' Ruby answered laughing.

'Ouch, that hurt!'

James looked at Ruby, trying to equate the ponytailed young friend of his sister's with this glamorous young woman in front of him. He started to run through all the witty one liners he'd ever used in the past, he needed just the right one for Ruby. She was incredibly beautiful; why hadn't he noticed that before? He wondered how quickly he could bring up the subject of orphans dying. But then she spoke again and he realised that there wasn't a single line that he could use on someone like her.

'It's good to see you again, James.' Ruby said to him and he marvelled at how the sound of her voice as she said his name could stop him in his tracks. She made it sound very intimate, like it was just the two of them in the room. A woman's voice had never had that effect on him before. But then she touched his hand and he jumped back as he felt an electric shock run through him.

'Ow!' He yelped in surprise at the jolt. Ruby just smiled serenely at him like she was enjoying a private joke.

He couldn't speak; he couldn't find a single word to say.

What is up with you?' Sarah interrupted, looking puzzled. James had a strange look on his face.

James couldn't answer. He wasn't usually lost for words but then again, he'd never met someone who had this instant effect on him. He tried his best to smile at Ruby, but it came out like a grimace. She simply smiled at him again, obviously used to having this effect on men.

'Come on everyone, let's eat.' Sarah said again, glancing at Mary as she walked out the door who was taking in the scene intently.

Mary responded by raising her eyebrows in the direction of James and Ruby, a knowing smile on her face, and started to hum quietly as she stood up, *'There could be trouble ahead, but while there's music and laughter and love and romance, let's face the music and dance!'*

Chapter Eighteen

James wiped his hands on his jeans. He was sweating and he could feel a line of perspiration forming on his brow. Ever since he spent time with Ruby yesterday he couldn't get her out of his mind. He knew he'd made zero impact last night at dinner. He'd sat there all evening in virtual silence, feeling like a teenager; all tongue-tied because the pretty girl next door was visiting. Sarah kept throwing him worried looks; he knew she couldn't understand why he was so quiet. In his twenty-five odd years of dealing with the opposite sex he could safely say that no woman had ever had this effect on him. God knows what Ruby thought, he'd hardly uttered a word to her. She was the most perfect woman he'd ever seen. Her skin was flawless, it was almost translucent. And her voice, whenever she spoke he literally melted. Katie and Tommy had also both been charmed with her. Tommy had his first crush, James thought. And who could blame him?

Both Katie and Tommy had fought over who sat beside Ruby for dinner. Normally they fought over sitting beside him! In the end Ruby had to sit in the middle between them both. Tommy went into overdrive telling jokes to her, beaming with pride each time she laughed. Katie had stared at Ruby's jewellery, every now and then stroking her bracelet or touching her necklace, in awe at the glamour of this new guest.

And she was glamorous, in an understated way and although she had been wearing jeans and a top, she managed to make them look like she was straight off the catwalk.

When they left, Sarah had asked him, 'I've never seen you so quiet. What's with you tonight?'

'Nothing.' He'd said sulkily.

'Goodness knows what everyone thought of you.' Sarah had moaned. 'You were quiet to the point of almost being rude!'

He really hoped Ruby didn't think he was rude. He just couldn't find any words to say to her. Every time he thought of something, he'd stop and second guess what he'd been about to say, thinking Ruby would think it silly. So he'd end up saying nothing. She even tried asking him about his job, but he'd just stammered that he was very busy right now. Normally he'd have talked up how dangerous his job was defending the weak and defenceless. Women usually loved it when he did that. But he just couldn't find the words with Ruby. It seemed like a cheap trick and not worthy of a woman such as her.

He had woken up this morning and after a bad night's sleep, dreaming of Ruby, he'd decided he was going to ask her out. He knew where she worked at least. She was the new manager at the gym in the Ferrycarrig Hotel in Wexford. So after breakfast, he'd headed there to meet her, before he headed to work.

Checking his appearance quickly in the mirror of the entrance hallway he decided he'd do. 'I'm here to see Ruby Shiggins.' He'd said to the receptionist at the entrance to the gym.

'You her nine o'clock appointment?' she said, and before he had a chance to say no, she pushed the intercom button. 'Ruby, your client is here.' He figured if it meant getting to see Ruby, he'd go along with it. Sure, what harm could it do?

Hands sweating again, James tried to look nonchalant as he stood by the door. The door opened and Ruby walked out and James swore his heart actually stopped beating as he watched her. She was wearing a tight Lycra top over a pair of yoga pants, with her long brunette hair tied back into a ponytail. She wasn't wearing any make-up and he didn't think he'd ever seen a more breath-taking vision in his life. She just radiated beauty. And James knew right then, without a shadow of a doubt, that for the first time in his life he was in love.

She seemed taken aback when she saw James standing there.

'James, what are you doing here?'

'Hi, Ruby.' He answered shyly.

'You're here for an assessment?' she said with a smile. He nodded quickly still unable to find his voice. He'd have to work on that if he wanted to ask her out later.

'What a coincidence, you never mentioned you were booked for one last night.' Ruby said to him.

James didn't know what to say, so decided not to break this new habit of his, and said nothing.

'Do you want to get changed and we'll get started?' she continued.

'Changed?' James said dumbly.

'You need to get into some gym gear.' Ruby continued gently. 'You'll be more comfortable than in your jeans.'

She was smiling at him again and somehow he got the feeling she was laughing at him, but her face was expressionless.

'Erm, I didn't bring any gear with me.' He replied, feeling a flush of embarrassment forming. This wasn't the time to admit he wasn't her client. In fact he was half-expecting someone to come in any second and shout 'Imposter!' at the top of his lungs. James could feel himself sweating again at the thought of being caught out.

'Don't worry. You're wearing trainers and we always have some spare kit if needed.' Ruby said to him. She walked behind the receptionist desk into a small office and returned a moment later with a pair of black Lycra cycling shorts and the brightest pink polo shirt he'd ever seen.

'Problem?' She said when she saw the look of horror on his face. 'I think they're your size.'

'No problem.' He responded, looking sharply at her. This time there was no doubt, Ruby was definitely enjoying this! She could hardly suppress the giggles as she handed over the pink top.

'Changing rooms are to your right. I'll be in the gym when you're ready.'

And with that she walked back into the gym, her ponytail bouncing along behind her.

James walked into the men's changing room hoping it would be empty. Yep, he was in luck. Most of the early morning gym bunnies were already on their way to the office by now. He quickly took off his jeans and striped Ben Sherman shirt. He'd spent ages that morning deciding what he should wear to meet her. He'd changed his shirt four times till he found just the right one. The irony was he'd actually taken off a turquoise shirt because he thought it was too bright, and here he was standing in a bright hot pink polo shirt, about to try and impress a girl.

Maybe it doesn't look too bad, he hoped, as he walked to the mirrors to take a look, turning around trying to see how his bum looked in the skimpy Lycra shorts.

'Ah, Jaysus no.' He thought when he looked in the mirror. He'd always thought his legs were in pretty good nick but he reckoned Brad Pitt would have a job pulling this look off.

The bloody top was so small it barely covered his bum; he desperately tried to stretch it a bit. He could feel himself sweating again. This wasn't good.

'Feck this.' He thought. 'No girl is worth this, I'm outta here.'

He went back to his locker and pulled out his jeans, determined to get dressed and run out the door, he never wanted to see Lycra again never mind wear it. Then he heard Ruby's voice.

'You ok, James?' The way she said the word James, he actually thought his legs buckle slightly. He found new resolution.

'Feck it.' He thought. 'Let's get physical!'

'I'm on my way.' He said, and standing up tall, he puffed out his chest. If he was going to pull this look off, he'd need to adopt some attitude.

He strutted as best he could to the gym, difficult, he thought, for anyone to pull off in hot pink.

He passed a big guy by as he left the changing room, on his way back in. He looked James up and down and started to laugh as he passed him by. As James walked out the door he could hear him laughing.

Ruby had her head in a clipboard when he walked out, but when she looked up she slowly looked him up and down and with a quick smile she said, 'Good, they fit. Snug.'

She was making fun of him again, he knew it. Why he hadn't just told her at reception that he wasn't there for a fitness review, he'd never work out. God, the messes he got himself into sometimes were unreal.

'So, what is your goal for today's assessment?' Ruby said in a very efficient voice.

To secure a date with you, James thought to himself. But decided he'd not share that right at that minute.

'Erm, to just get fitter, I think.' He replied. He hadn't prepared for any questions!

'So, would you say your goal is to get healthy?' Ruby said looking up from her clipboard.

'Yes. Exactly, get healthy.' James repeated. He was a moron, if he didn't up his game; she'd never go out with him.

'And lose some weight?' Ruby then added.

Was she looking at his stomach? James thought in panic. He was sure her eyes lingered on his love handles for a second.

James quickly sucked in his stomach. She thought he was fat. Was he fat? He had always thought he was fairly trim. There were mirrors everywhere in this bloody gym, he thought. No matter which way he looked there were images of him glaring back. And he couldn't help notice that he looked a little bit pudgy right now. But he supposed he had been eating a lot of pasta lately. Damn Sarah and her lasagnes. He was addicted to them.

'I guess I could drop a few.' He mumbled to Ruby.

'Don't worry; I'll soon work off those pesky pounds you're carrying.' Ruby said smiling.

She was killing him.

'And would you like to work on your muscle tone?' she then went on.

'What's wrong with my muscle tone?' He answered feeling aggrieved. He could feel himself flexing his arms. He might not be *Thor*, but he had muscles.

'Oh, nothing at all. But we can work on building them up. You'd be surprised at what we can achieve in just a few quick sessions.'

'Was he actually going to have to do some sessions? He was perfectly happy with his current muscle tone. She better be worth all this, he thought. Then she touched him lightly on his arm and he was in no doubt that she was worth every humiliation he was currently enduring.

'Ow.' He felt an electric shock. 'Did you feel that?' he asked her curiously. She hadn't flinched like him.

'Feel what?' she asked him. 'Now, let's get you weighed and measured.'

She wrote something else down on her clipboard. What the hell was she writing on that damn thing? He tried to peep over her shoulder as he followed her to the scales, but couldn't see anything.

'Right, pop on the scales for me.'

He jumped on and pulled his stomach in automatically. He was regretting that breakfast roll he'd eaten an hour ago now.

'Hmmm.' Ruby said enigmatically, scribbling away on her clip board again. That clipboard was really beginning to irritate him now. Just what could she be writing?

'Now, I'm going to do some measurements. Let's start with your height.' Ruby continued.

She guided him to a wall and quickly confirmed what he could have told her, he was 6′ 2.

She then took out a measuring tape from her pocket.

'I need to measure your calves, thighs, chest and upper arms now. Wait there, please.'

James panicked. The thought of her touching him while measuring him was more than he probably could cope with without grabbing her and kissing her. And that would really scare the life out of the girl! But then again, maybe if she's up close doing the measurements, maybe she'll feel what I'm feeling, we'll have a moment, and I'll ask her out. It'll be magic. He felt a goofy smile appear on his face as he daydreamed about what was about to happen.

'Hey, man.' A nasally voice said interrupting his daydream.

'This is Seamus, my colleague. He'll take your measurements.'

James looked up and saw a geeky looking teenager standing in front of him, who couldn't have been more than eighteen and was covered in acne.

'That's ok, Seamus.' James said to him. 'Sure, Ruby will just do them.'

'Afraid not.' Ruby said to him. 'Club policies. Guys measure guys, girls measure girls.'

'Oh.' James replied crestfallen. He quickly looked to see if Ruby was enjoying this turn of events, but she had her head in that damn clipboard again, scribbling away.

'Right, work away.' He said to the teenager. Ruby was furiously writing down the numbers as Seamus called them out in a flat voice.

'Ok, that's the measurements done. Let's see how your fitness levels are.' Ruby then said. 'Follow me.'

She then proceeded to the treadmill and James hopped on.

'Let's just start with a gentle run for five minutes and we'll see what your heartbeat is like then.'

'No problem.' James replied. He'd easily do five minutes he reckoned. He used to run a lot. Ok, that was a few years ago, but he was still pretty fit, he thought. He started to run. This is a gentle pace? He wouldn't want to be assessed on a tough run if this was a gentle one. He could feel his heart pounding already. He glanced at the time on the machine. He'd only be running for sixty seconds and he thought his chest was about to explode.

The next twenty minutes were the most humiliating James had ever had. He didn't realise how unfit he was until now. He practically fell off the treadmill when the five minutes were up. But that wasn't the end of the torture. She had him doing stretches to check his flexibility and he couldn't even get close to touching his toes. He was mortified with his performance and all along she was scribbling away on that clipboard saying nothing, except for the odd 'Erm' or 'Ok'. Finally his ordeal was over.

'Well done. You've done really well for a guy in your condition and I'm sure that we can work a programme out for you that will have you reaching all your goals in time for Christmas. Why don't you go get showered and changed and I'll meet you in reception with your fitness plan.'

James didn't have the breath in him to speak. He simply nodded and limped back to the changing room. He was exhausted.

He showered and dressed quickly. He just wanted to grab his fitness plan and get out of there quickly. He was running late for next appointment, with a potential new client. After all of that and he wasn't even going to get a date! When he thought of all the girls he'd dated over the years and how little he'd had to do to impress them, he was gobsmacked that he'd allowed himself to be manipulated to do that assessment. It wasn't like he was short of female attention. He had two girls he was dating on and off right now, they were both mad about him. He didn't need Ruby. Ok, he felt some sort of weird chemistry every time she spoke, but he'd get over that. He'd chalk it up to experience he reckoned. He'd laugh about it all in a few years. She obviously didn't feel any connection with him at all; she'd not once given him any indication that she thought of him in any other way than that of a client. She just assumed he was there for an assessment, the thought of him asking her out didn't even cross her mind. The more he thought about it, the more mortified he felt. He wondered if there was a back door to get out of the gym without having further humiliation.

No such luck on that front, there was only one way out and Ruby was standing right in front of it in reception waiting for him. She handed him a bottle of water when he walked towards her.

'You look like you need that.' She said kindly.

'Thanks.' James said. 'I've a bit of a cold on me, that's why I wasn't at my best in there.' He nodded in the direction of the gym.

'Oh, is that what it was?' Ruby said with a smile.

She could see straight through that lie, he could tell. 'I'd normally do that type of workout in my sleep.' He added for good measure. He wanted to shut up, he knew he was talking bull, but he just couldn't stop himself.

'You're actually in quite good condition.' Ruby then said. 'I was very impressed.'

She was letting him off the hook but James could feel himself start to feel better immediately.

'Oh, well I do try to keep in shape.' He said trying to sound cool.

'I can tell.' Ruby answered him.

She looked down at her clipboard again and scribbled something else. He wanted to get that clipboard and throw it out the bloody door.

'Why don't you give the receptionist here a call and schedule in some sessions at a time that works for you?'

'Yeah, I'll do that.' James said.

'Well, it was nice seeing you again, James.' Ruby said.

'It was lovely seeing you too.' He replied. He didn't move, he just stood there looking at her, a big goofy smile stuck on his face.

'My next appointment is here, I've got to keep going.' Ruby then said indicating a guy who was sitting down a few feet from them.

'I've been here for over 30 minutes.' the guy moaned.

'I'll be with you in a sec.' Ruby said to him. 'I'm so sorry you've been delayed. There was a bit of a mix up with my first appointment.'

James reddened as she said that.

She then pulled a piece of paper off that stupid clipboard. She folded it in half and handed the paper to him.

'Oh, and by the way, the answer is yes.'

'Sorry?' He said looking confused.

'Yes, the answer is yes.'

'I haven't asked you a question.' James replied. 'Yes to what?'

'Yes, I'd love to go out with you.' Ruby replied smiling at him. 'That's my phone number. Give me a call.' And with that she turned around and walked back into the gym, her ponytail bouncing again.

'Oh.' James managed to lamely say as she walked away. Then realising what had just happened he did a little jump and whooped, 'Yes!' as he walked to the door, and put the number in his jacket pocket.

Chapter Nineteen

The past couple of weeks had just flown by and Sarah could hardly believe that it was now almost December. She had found a divorce lawyer, a guy called Conor Burke. He came highly recommended apparently. Ruby had a friend at work that had used him in his divorce the previous year. It was one of the most unnerving and scary things Sarah had ever done going in to meet him for the first time. When you fall in love, get married and start a family, you never ever see a future where a divorce lawyer plays a part in it. She really didn't know what to expect. But she'd need not have worried, as Conor was extremely understanding and helpful. She supposed he saw people like Sarah all the time, looking for help to do something that ultimately they never really wanted to do, but circumstance had driven them to his door. She had vowed to herself that she would do everything possible to keep things as amicable as possible for the children's sake, although there were times over the past couple of weeks that her resolve in that vow had very nearly weakened. It would be very easy to play the bitter and twisted ex-wife. And truth be told she felt she had earned that right to a certain degree. Had they no children she might have played that role with glee, but, for her children's sake, she decided to stay on her moral high ground and do the right thing. She just hoped that Paul would do the same.

They all wanted to get an agreement fostered without the need for a court case. With this in mind Conor had written to Paul over a week ago and hoped that between Paul's lawyer and him they could start negotiating on access and maintenance fairly quickly. Sarah hoped that Paul felt the same way about avoiding court, because every time Sarah thought of it her stomach just flipped. She'd never even been in court before, her only reference for what went on there was from watching soap operas. And she wasn't sure that was a good source of information!

Another issue she had to deal with was financing it all. Money seemed to be always an issue these days. She just couldn't get over how much it all cost. She had received an invoice from Conor already for €242 for just the letter he'd sent Paul. District Court could cost up to €5000, so she was really hoping that Paul would work with her, not against her. She had called him several times and begged him to come and visit the kids. Tommy was still struggling with his Daddy not being around and he was quick to lose his temper lately, which was very unlike his usual self. The sins of the father, a true phrase in this case. He'd not been in any more fights in school, he'd promised Sarah he wouldn't, and was true to his word. But it was hard to miss the effect that Paul's absence was having on the children. With Christmas fast approaching both Tommy and Katie had admitted to Sarah that they were scared that their Daddy wouldn't be home before then. Finally, Paul agreed that he would visit this coming weekend and he was due to arrive any minute.

Sarah was so nervous about seeing him again; her stomach started doing flips at the mere thought of him. Despite the brave face she tried to put on during the day, once it was the cold dark of night, all her resolve would weaken. She had cried a river in the previous few weeks every night when the children were asleep. She was careful to cry into her pillow to muffle her sobs though; she didn't want Tommy or Katie to see her in such a state.

She knew she was being morbid and it was like picking at a scab when you knew it was the wrong thing to do, but every night she would put on their wedding DVD and look at her face and Paul's face over and over again as they said their vows. She was desperately trying to see something in his face back then, that she had obviously missed. Were there any signs there that one day in the future he would show that he didn't really love her at all? But no matter how many times she looked at their video, each time she saw the same thing. Two young, happy people in love. She no longer recognised herself in that video, as long gone was naïve carefree Sarah. So much had happened since then.

Realising that her marriage was over, she realised was like coming to terms with a death. She was in mourning, as if Paul had died. And in many ways it seemed exactly like that because one day he was here and then suddenly he was just gone. The grief blindsided her so much that some mornings she struggled to get out of bed. If she didn't have the children to see to, she thought she would have happily stayed there with the duvet over her head.

She'd spoken to Ruby about it quite a bit. It was funny how someone could come back into your life at exactly the right time and now it was as if she'd never been away.

She wasn't trying to rewrite history and pretend that Paul and she were deliriously happy or anything before he left, she just thought that they had been muddling through and that they were content enough. She had gotten it all so wrong. While she was busy doing sleepless nights with the night feeds for Ella, Paul was off falling in love with Michelle. And to top it all off she had to get her head around the fact that Tommy, Katie and Ella would have a new brother or sister soon, and that little baby would be nothing to her but everything to them. Today was a good day though she supposed, she'd not cried yet. After all the crying of the previous few weeks, she'd no more tears left. And that was a good thing, because she really didn't want to break down in front of Paul. She was desperately trying to hold onto what was left of her dignity.

One positive thing was that she was finally coming to terms with her psychic gift and she found that she was even getting used to the dreams she had every few nights. So far she'd not had any more in relation to Rachel's murder, but she was dreaming nevertheless on a semi-regular basis. Some of her dreams were just too cryptic to understand and some were quite boring. She dutifully wrote all of them down in her journal which was getting really full already. Mary said that maybe one day the ones that seemed boring might make some sense.

Right now, her mind was on a pensioner who lived in her village, about a mile out. Her name was Bridie Moran and she lived on her own. Sarah tried to work out how old she would be now and figured it would be at least eighty. She'd often see her at mass and she was quite sprightly for her age. She did have a family, both a son and a daughter, but they were married and living in Dublin. It was one of those dreams that had awoken Sarah in a panic, as last night Bridie had died in a snow blizzard. Sarah closed her eyes and recalled the dream once again.

The weather is horrendous and everyone is housebound, as a white blanket of snow covers the ground Bridie gets more and more anxious as she is running low on groceries and fuel for her fire. She decides to walk to the local shop not realising how treacherous the roads are. But as she reaches the end of her lane, she slips on the snow. No matter how hard she tries she doesn't have the strength to get herself back up. She dies on an icy bed, alone and scared.

Sarah had been dreadfully upset when she awoke with a start. She ran to the window as soon as she got up, half expecting to see that it had been snowing all night. But there wasn't the slightest sign of any white in her garden. She'd checked the weather forecast first thing, but so far it wasn't predicting bad weather. She had made a promise to herself to keep an eye on the weather channel. She shuddered again just thinking about poor Bridie shivering in the cold in her house and she was going to do everything in her power to ensure that Bridie didn't die like that alone, even if she had to move her into her own home to make her safe.

No time for morbid thoughts now, as she glanced at the clock. Paul would be here soon. She stood up and went to check her appearance one more time. She had spent an age on her make-up this morning. She had no desire to win Paul back or anything like that, but she had her pride. She was determined not to look like the shabby ex-wife now that Paul had his shiny new accessory, Michelle.

Thank God for concealer, she thought. It had effectively covered the fact that she'd not had much sleep lately. Satisfied that she was looking good, Sarah peeped in the living room at the kids.

'Mammy, there's nothing on worth watching.' Katie moaned. 'I want to watch *I Carly* and none of the stupid channels have it on!'

Sarah sighed. She'd really thought long and hard about cancelling her satellite subscription, but in the end the maths just didn't add up. She was only working part-time and she just didn't have the money for the luxuries that her family had become accustomed to.

'I know it's hard to adjust to only nine channels when you've been used to hundreds, but we've talked about this several times. You are old enough to understand that money is tight right now. *I Carly* might not be on but I don't believe that there is simply nothing else on worth watching on all those channels we do have! And last time I counted you guys had over twenty different DVD's in your collection!' Sarah said. She really did not need her daughter making a big deal out of this; she'd enough on her plate. She felt bad enough that she had to cancel it. But until maintenance was sorted and Sarah knew how much cash she had, she had to be sensible and make cutbacks. Tommy, in fairness to him, had been great and took it on board pretty quickly, but Katie was evidently still adjusting to the loss. As for Ella, bless her, as long as there was a TV remote control to chew, she didn't mind what channels it switched on.

Sure enough, Ella was sitting at Tommy's feet, chewing something. Sarah smiled at her, her heart bursting with pride. She was just doing so well. She was crawling now and chattering away to anyone who looked in her direction. It had been great last Sunday when she crawled her first few inches. And luckily they were all there to watch her. And in addition to that every now and then there was even a word thrown in that they all understood. Tommy and Katie were besotted with her and loved playing with her, singing to her, dancing with her, anything that made her laugh, made them happy.

Sarah counted her blessings once more, three healthy children, a house, good family and friends, she wasn't doing too badly. And then she heard a car pull up into the drive – Paul.

'Kids, your Daddy is here,' she called to them.

They stood up and walked to the window. Sarah had expected them to run out the door to meet him, but instead they stayed close to each other in the living room, shy all of a sudden of the man who answered to the name Daddy. Sarah could feel her temper rising again, she was just so angry with Paul for putting them through this. Taking a deep breath Sarah opened the front door to the beaming smile of her soon-to-be ex-husband.

'Hello.' She said quietly.

Unbelievably Paul leaned in to give her a kiss on her cheek, his arms open wide to pull her in for an embrace. She pulled away to one side quickly leaving him kissing air. It was an incredibly awkward moment, but what on earth was the idiot thinking? He felt like a stranger to her, he wasn't the man she'd loved and married.

He looked hurt that she'd rebuked his embrace. Had he really thought that they could just pretend he'd not had an affair? He obviously thought he would be getting a hero's welcome when she opened the door. They had promised each other on the phone to be civil in front of the children and Sarah fully intended to keep up her end of the promise. But kissing him was a level she wasn't prepared to go to. She didn't think that they would ever be back on kissing terms again.

'Where are the kids?' Paul eventually said, cutting the silence.

'Inside.' Sarah said pointing to the living room. Paul dropped his bags and walked in, expecting to be knocked down by Tommy and Katie as they rushed to hug him. Instead they stayed by the window, both of them unsure of themselves. Katie looked like she was about to start to cry and had started to suck her hair, something she hadn't done in years. Tommy looked really angry again, like he wanted to punch Paul rather than kiss him.

'Say hello to your Daddy.' Sarah said gently to them.

'Hello,' they both chorused quietly.

'Hey you guys.' Paul said loudly. 'Come here and let your Daddy give you a hug.'

They walked over slowly to him. Katie was in the lead, Tommy bringing up the rear, constantly looking at Sarah for reassurance.

'I missed you, Daddy.' Katie said tearfully as she gave him a big hug.

'I missed you too princess,' he answered her.

'You were gone an awfully long time.' She said to him.

'I know.' Paul replied with tears in his eyes. 'Too long, Daddy's so sorry.'

Sarah watched as Tommy offered him a half-hearted hug. He kept his two arms firmly by his side and looked down the whole time Paul tried to hug him. He was going to be a harder nut to crack. She could see how hard this was for Paul, seeing the consequences of his absence first-hand in his children's reactions.

Ella then decided it was time to make herself heard and started to bang the remote control on the wooden floors, letting a few shouts out.

'She's gotten so big.' Paul said in awe as he looked down at her. 'She's beautiful.' He walked over to her and picked her up, kissing her chubby cheek. She looked at him with her big eyes and then turned to Sarah with her arms out, crying.

'Don't be like that,' he sounded very disappointed.

'She doesn't know who you are!' Tommy said with vengeance, before kicking one of Ella's teddy bears that was on the floor. 'She's forgotten who you are!'

163

Paul looked stricken at his son's words.

Sarah walked over and took Ella from his arms soothing her quickly.

'Three months is a long time to be gone, Paul.' Sarah said to him. 'You can't expect to walk back into the life you left and expect nothing to have changed. It's going to take a bit of time for you to reconnect with each of the children. '

Paul nodded miserably.

'Should I go after him?' Paul said, nodding in the direction of the door.

'He's upset. Let me talk to him for a few minutes. Katie, why don't you take Daddy into the kitchen and show him the cupcakes we all made for today.'

'They're pink, Daddy!' Katie said excitedly, grabbing his hand and leading him into the kitchen. Leaving Ella in her playpen, Sarah went looking for Tommy.

He was in his bedroom lying on his bed face down. His little body was heaving as he cried into his pillow.

'You ok, buddy?' Sarah asked her son gently. Stupid question she knew, he was obviously far from alright.

'I hate him, Mam.' Tommy said defiantly. 'I wish he wasn't my Daddy!'

'No you don't. You love your Daddy. You just don't like him very much right now.' Sarah said to him gently. She let her words just sit there, then continued. 'Isn't that right?'

Tommy looked up at her shrugging his shoulders. 'Don't know.' He mumbled.

'And it's ok to not like him right now. Your Daddy hurt you when he left and you're angry with him, right? I was pretty angry with him too so I understand.'

'Were you Mammy?' Tommy asked her, his eyes filled with unshed tears.

'Yes I was.'

'Are you still angry with him?' Tommy asked her.

164

'Yes, I am, a little bit. But it's very hard for me to stay angry with your Daddy, because he gave me the most precious gifts in the whole wide world.' Sarah replied.

'What?' Tommy asked.

'He gave me you, Katie and Ella. How could I stay angry with him when I have you three precious children?'

Tommy smiled and wiped his tears with the sleeve of his sweatshirt.

'Come here.' She said to him, opening her arms for him to fall into.

He snuggled in close to his Mammy, the warmth of her embrace soothing his tears. She held him close until his body stopped shaking.

'Your Daddy loves you very much Tommy, don't ever forget that.' She said to him gently.

'If he loved me he'd have never left me.'

Sarah sighed. It was so unfair. Part of her wanted to kick Paul out of the house right then and there and tell him never to come back. But she knew that wasn't in the children's best interest. She had to put them first.

'Tommy, have you ever done something that you wish you hadn't?' Sarah asked her son.

'Suppose.' He mumbled back. 'I wish I hadn't broken Katie's Littlest Pet Shop house. She moaned about that for weeks and weeks,' he ended dramatically.

There had been murder over that one!

'Well sometimes grownups do things too that they wish they hadn't also. Grownups make mistakes just like little boys do.'

Tommy nodded solemnly.

'And well, your Daddy is really sorry he has been away for so long. He had to go and work and he got so caught up in his new job, he just forgot all about the time, and didn't realise it had been so long since he saw all of you. That was his mistake.'

'When I'm excited over things I sometimes forget the time.' Tommy said to Sarah. 'Like when I went to Joey's house to play last week, I forgot to come home at five like I promised.'

'That's exactly it, just like that.' Sarah said. 'Daddy just forgot the time, but he's here now. Do you think that maybe you can forgive him?'

Tommy scrunched his nose up as he thought about this. 'When I was late home from Joey's I had to say sorry. Is Daddy going to say he's sorry too?'

Before Sarah could answer him, Paul walked in. He had tears in his eyes; he'd been listening at the door the whole time.

'I'm really sorry. I did a bad thing forgetting the time.' Paul said to his son. He sat down on the bed beside Tommy. 'I promise never to do that again.'

Tommy looked at his father and decided that he really meant what he said. He did look very sorry.

'Ok.' Tommy said. 'I forgive you.' He leaned in and gave Paul a hug, his face breaking into a huge smile.

Paul looked up to Sarah over Tommy's shoulder and mouthed quietly, 'Thank you.' He knew that Sarah could have used the situation to her advantage, making the kids hate him, but she had been fantastic, sticking up for him. For the first time since he had walked out of their marriage he thought that maybe he'd made a mistake. He had forgotten how amazing Sarah was. Michelle quickly popped into his head; she was forever complaining and nagging. He was exhausted at the minute, waiting on her hand and foot as she was so tired with the pregnancy. He didn't remember Sarah ever being like that. She was brilliant when she was pregnant. His daydream stopped when he saw Sarah walk out of the room to give him a moment with Tommy alone.

Sarah went back to the kitchen to find Katie feeding Ella pink icing from a cupcake.

'She loves them Mammy!' Katie said giggling, her face sticky from the frosting too.

'It appears she's not the only one, you little monkeys!' Sarah said with a laugh. 'Leave one for the rest of us!'

166

The day flew by very quickly with Paul reacquainting himself with all three children. Very quickly Ella was charmed with him and happily bouncing on his knee, listening to him singing *Incy Wincy Spider* out of tune and shrieking with delight with it all. Paul helped Sarah put the children to bed, promising them he'd be over early in the morning. They were going to spend the day at Rita's house all together. Sarah had agreed that while Paul was in Ireland he should spend as much time as possible with the children.

'Thanks for today.' Paul said, looking at Sarah. They were in the kitchen drinking a cup of coffee, all the children finally asleep.

'You're welcome. The kids loved seeing you. They've missed you.'

'I know. I didn't realise how much I missed them too till today. I'm so sorry, Sarah. For everything I've done.'

She sighed. His apologies didn't really mean much to her. It was how he behaved in the future that mattered. 'I hope you meant what you said earlier.'

'About what?' Paul asked.

'When you promised Tommy you wouldn't forget the time again. You can't just disappear for months on end again. It's too cruel on the children. I know it seems like they've gotten over it now, but you going away like that left a mark. I won't have them hurt again.'

Paul put down his cup and leaned in close to Sarah. 'I meant every word I said. I'm ashamed of myself. Honestly, I am. I saw myself through the children's eyes today and I didn't like what I saw. I've been a selfish fool.'

'I won't argue with that.' Sarah replied tartly.

They drank their coffees in silence for a few more minutes.

'I've been thinking. What if I came home once a fortnight for the weekend? I could get the flight home after work on Friday and spend all day Saturday and Sunday with the children, head back on the red-eye flight on the Monday morning. Would that be ok with you?'

'That's fine with me. But don't promise anything that you can't follow up on. What about Michelle? How will she feel about you coming to Ireland every other weekend?'

'What about her?' Paul replied sharply. 'She's not my boss. I can come and go as I please.'

Sarah raised her eyebrows. There was trouble in paradise already by the sounds of it. But no matter what Paul said she reckoned that Michelle was very much wearing the trousers in their relationship. It certainly seemed that way when they met a few weeks previously.

'You have to tell the children about Michelle and the baby at some point too, Paul. I'm not doing that for you. But I think you should leave it a few more weeks. Let them see you a few more times and then get into a routine before you add this to their plates.'

Paul looked miserable. 'How do you think they'll take it?'

'It's going to be a really hard thing for them to deal with.' She said. 'I should know, it's pretty horrific for me to get used to and I'm an adult.'

'I've been such an asshole.' They were both silent for a few moments, the words left hanging in the air.

Sarah looked at Paul and tried to work out if he really meant it and he really did seem to. 'My solicitor is going to call yours next week. I've told him to be fair.' Paul said to her.

Sarah nodded without saying a word. She wasn't going to thank Paul for doing the right thing. He had responsibilities and she was grateful he'd finally owned up to them, but that was as far as it went.'

'How are you fixed with money? Tommy mentioned you had to get rid of the satellite TV.'

'We've had to do some serious cutbacks here. I'm only working the odd shift in the boutique and the money from that barely pays for the groceries. I've had to dig into the savings to cover mortgage payments and they are nearly gone now. Why on earth we didn't save more over the years I'll never know.'

Paul nodded. 'We were too busy living the good life I suppose.'

Paul reached into his pocket and pulled out his wallet. He counted out €200.

'That's not going to go very far.' Sarah said bitterly. She hated how she sounded these days. She didn't want to become the bitter ex-wife always begging for money.

'I know it's not much. But it's all the cash I have on me right now. I'll not leave you short I promise you. I'll pay half of all the children's expenses. But maybe it's time you got a full-time job too.' He finished, slyly looking up at Sarah waiting to see her reaction. Michelle had insisted he suggest that.

'Just like that?' Sarah shook her head in exasperation. 'I've not been working full-time in almost nine years since we had the children. There's a recession on, jobs are not that easy to come by. And who will take care of the kids while I'm at work?'

'I haven't all the answers.' Paul snapped at her. 'I was only suggesting something. You don't need to be so tetchy!'

'Tetchy! Are you insane?' Sarah said her voice rising despite all her good intentions to remain calm and unflappable. 'I'm worried sick. I'm trying to make money stretch and stretch and you know what, it can only stretch so far before it's going to snap. Christmas is almost here.' She stood up and walked to the counter top, picking up the *Smyth's* catalogue and throwing it on the table. 'Take a look through that Paul. Go on.'

Paul picked up the catalogue and flicked through. The children had marked pages with big black markers, circling the items that they wanted from Santa. It was something that they had done ever since they were old enough to hold a crayon in their hand.

'Right now, I'm frantic about how I can explain to the children that Santa has a smaller budget this year, without ruining Christmas for them! Its Ella's first Christmas and it should be so special for her. But I'm too busy being stressed out over the fact that she's growing so fast I need to buy more clothes for her, how can I even think about presents? And you think I'm being tetchy! I'm SO sorry.'

Paul looked shocked, Sarah rarely raised her voice. 'I'm under pressure too, Sarah.' Paul threw back at her. 'Michelle's pregnant and she's got this fancy consultant she's going to. He's costing a bloody fortune. And our apartment in London is huge rent. It's not easy for me.'

Sarah could not believe her ears. He was actually looking for sympathy from her. 'Oh boo hoo to you!' Sarah said sarcastically. 'My heart goes out to you. Maybe you should have thought about all of that before you left this life and decided to start another!'

Paul stood up. 'Maybe it's time I left.'

'Leave? You left a long time ago.' She felt like picking up her coffee cup and smashing it against the side of his head. No court in Ireland would charge her, she was sure of it. Goodness knows she had provocation.

'He's not worth it.' Edward whispered. Sarah looked around; Edward was standing just behind her. She felt instantly more relaxed, his presence always had that effect on her.

She took a deep breath. 'Look this is getting us nowhere. We need to remain civil for the children's sake. Let's do our best for them and try to keep our own feelings to one side.'

Paul nodded, grateful for the olive branch being extended.

'I'll pick the kids up at ten tomorrow. Ok?'

'Fine. We'll see you then.'

'And Sarah, whatever is needed for Christmas, just let me know the total and I'll go halves.'

Sarah's stomach flipped again. It was all very well Paul saying he'd come up with half of the Christmas expenses, but just how was she supposed to come up with the other half?

Chapter Twenty

'You and James are quite the schemers, I kinda like it!' Sarah said as she sipped a gin & tonic in her local pub Freddie's.

'Listen, as shitty days go, seeing your lying, cheating, good for nothing ex-husband rock up your drive, is right up there with the best of them. I figured you might need a drink by the end of it, so I called James and he happily said he'd babysit. No biggie.' Ruby explained.

'No, it is a biggie. I'm so grateful I have you in my corner now, Rubes.' Sarah said sincerely.

'We were both to blame for losing touch, but listen, best friends are hard to find and when you do get a good one, they are even harder to lose, so I guess we're always going to be here for each other, ok?'

Raising their glasses, they clinked them together in a silent toast.

'Did you see Paul's face when James walked in?' Ruby said suddenly laughing again. 'Fecking weasel nearly passed out!'

'I'm just relieved James behaved himself. I thought they were going to come to blows!' Sarah admitted.

'I think if Paul had said one word to him, he would have given James the excuse he needed to let fly! He was wise to leg it when he did!'

'They've always had a tetchy relationship.' Sarah admitted. 'Paul has always been jealous of how close I am to James.'

'Imagine being jealous of a twin brother! Honestly Sarah, the more you tell me, the more I feel like giving him a slap myself!'

Seeing Sarah giggling again was good. Ruby had been very worried about her. She just looked so sad and dejected lately.

'Right, truthfully now, how are you doing? I've been thinking I need to stage an intervention.' Ruby said, half seriously, half joking.

'Dr Phil style?' Sarah giggled. They had both spent many a happy Saturday morning, lying on the couch watching Dr Phil dole out his wisdom to unhappy Americans, mimicking his southern drawl.

'And so how's that workin' for you?' Ruby said in her best Dr Phil drawl to which they both started giggling again.

'What you put up with you end up with!' Sarah threw in another Dr Phil saying.

Sarah and Ruby dissolved into peals of laughter. The laughter became funnier than their silly Dr Phil impression and they had to hold their aching bellies such were the snorts coming from them.

'Ssstop, honestly stop, I'm going to pee!' Sarah begged holding her hand up towards Ruby.

Eventually when they stopped laughing, Ruby asked Sarah, 'Seriously, what's going on with you?'

'I'm struggling. Most days it's an effort to get dressed, never mind do anything else. But I've got to keep going for the kids.'

'Please tell me you're not still watching your wedding DVD over and over?' Ruby said, thinking about the last time she'd called over to see Sarah and found her watching it, not for the first time she suspected.

Sarah looked sheepish. 'I can't help it, it's like car crash TV! I keep looking at myself walking down the aisle, thinking you poor cow. I wish I could warn me.'

'What would you say? And would your younger self believe you? I think not. And whatever else the weasel has done, he does good kids. Tommy, Katie and Ella are adorable.'

Sarah nodded at this truth. All the heartache and pain at Paul's betrayal were worth the privilege of being their Mammy.

'Desperate times, desperate measures and all that, so I am doing a DVD intervention and confiscating it. It's not healthy, Sarah.'

Sarah knew her friend was right, but felt so tired again just thinking about Paul. She could feel depression sneaking up threatening to undo the joy of the laughter she'd just experienced. It was time to change the subject.

'What about you, Ruby? I've missed so much about your life these past few years. Have you ever come close to getting married?'

'Not since Eric.'

'Jeepers, there's a blast from the past!' Sarah confessed. 'Where is he now?'

'I've no idea. Sure, it's ten years since we split up. He's probably married with kids. But he was the only one I ever considered settling down with.'

'I liked Eric.' Sarah said.

'I loved him.' Ruby answered quietly.

They sipped their drinks again in quiet reflection.

'What did happen with you two?' Sarah asked.

A look of such pain passed over Ruby's face; Sarah grabbed her hand and said, 'Oh Rubes.'

'Sometime, not now, I'll tell you about it. Promise.' She picked up her glass and took a large gulp.

'I know most people think I'm running around desperate for a man to 'save' me, but I'm doing very well on my own! I date, I have fun and if the right guy comes along, great. If not? Well, there's always a cute sommelier somewhere looking to hook up!' Ruby joked.

'Ready to pop your cork?' Sarah teased to which they both started laughing again.

'Exactly! Eric is my past, no point dwelling on that now. And you never know what the future will bring? Who knows, maybe my Mr Right is close by.' Ruby smiled. 'And speaking of which, don't look now but there's a seriously cute guy over by the bar checking you out!'

Of course Sarah couldn't resist and immediately swung around to look, with Ruby exclaiming, 'I told you not to look!'

'Oh my god!' Sarah exclaimed as she waved back to the man who was now heading their way.

'Hi Sarah.'

'Oh hi, Art.' Sarah could feel herself blushing. What was it with this guy that he had such an effect on her!

Ruby looked on in amazement as she saw them both shyly smiling at each other. Sarah had been holding out on her!

'Hello there, I'm Ruby.'

'Oh sorry, Rubes!' Sarah apologised, flustered again. 'Art is the children's principal.'

'Well now, the scenery has certainly improved from when I was a pupil in Ballyaislinn National School!' Ruby exclaimed taking in the toned, tanned man before her. 'Ow!' Sarah gave Ruby a dig in her ribs to make her shut up.

'Can I get you ladies a drink?' Art asked.

'Yes.' Ruby answered.

'No.' Sarah replied at the exact same time. 'It's just we are on a girls night out.'

'Don't mind her.' Ruby gave Art one of her dazzling smiles. 'Two gin & tonics and then I insist you join us to tell me all about your job!'

'Well maybe just for one.' Art said looking at Sarah to make sure that was ok.

Once he walked over to the bar and was out of earshot, Ruby turned to Sarah and joked, 'Jeepers, get a room you two!'

'I don't know what you are talking about!' Sarah huffed in reply.

'I'm talking about 6'2 hot teacher over at the bar that can't take his eyes off you and you blushing like a schoolgirl, that's what I'm talking about!'

'He's been very kind since Paul left.'

'Evidently!' Ruby said with a laugh.

'Not like that. I've only ever been with Paul, as well you know!' Sarah said. 'I'm not interested in dating anyone; my head is literally melted from all this Paul and Michelle stuff.'

'I know. I get that, I honestly do. But you mark my words; Teach over there likes you. And he's hot. Seriously hot.'

Sarah looked over at Art's back as he happily chatted with some people at the bar.

'You are allowed to have a life after Paul you know. If you move on, it doesn't mean you didn't love him or aren't grieving for your marriage still. But it might make it a bit easier to deal with.'

Ruby just didn't understand what it was like for her, Sarah realised. The very thought of being with another man sent her into a panic. It was as if a heavy anchor of fear held her down and she was drowning. She could not breathe.

'I need to get some air.' Sarah gasped and ran to the door, much to the astonishment of Ruby and Art who had returned with drinks in hand.

'Shit! Sorry. Back in a minute.' Ruby apologised then ran after her friend.

She found Sarah outside holding onto a bench, her whole body shaking. Ruby pulled her friend into her arms and held her close. Intuitively she recognised that this was a time for no words, just strong arms to calm the storm that was raging within her friend.

After a few minutes Sarah could breathe once more.

'I'm sorry.'

'Don't you dare apologise.' Ruby declared. 'My fault for teasing you about Art. It's too soon.'

'It is too soon. Problem is though, my mind says that, but my body seems to say something else!' Sarah admitted.

'I knew it!' Ruby shouted. 'You do fancy him!'

'But that doesn't change the fact that I'm not ready to do anything about it.' Sarah said firmly. 'It's just every time I see him, I can't seem to stop looking at his forearms. And then my imagination moves on from that to his chest. What is wrong with me, Rubes?!'

'How long since you and Paul had sex?' Ruby asked gently.

'I'm embarrassed to tell you.' Sarah said.

'Spill!'

'I'd say at least five months.'

'Well that right there is what's wrong with you! Of course you can't stop looking at Mr Sexy Teach in there! You need to get laid & quick!'

Sarah started to giggle. 'I keep telling you, I'm not ready.'

'And I keep telling you that the best way to get over one man is to get under another. That's all I'm saying!' Ruby replied with a wink, gratified to see Sarah begin to giggle.

'Seriously Sarah, you have all the time in the world. If he's meant for you, he won't pass you by, so how about we go in and have that drink with him, just have a laugh? Nothing else and I'll try to behave, honestly.'

Smiling in response, Sarah agreed and the two girls went back in to Art.

'All ok?' He asked when he saw the girls returning. 'I thought you'd legged it on me!'

'Just needed some girl talk.' Ruby replied with a smile. 'And don't know about you Sarah, but it's made me thirsty! Cheers!'

Chapter Twenty One

The kids were at Rita's house with Paul for the day, which maybe wasn't a bad thing, as she was rocking a serious hangover from the night before. Together with Art and Ruby, she had been the last to be chucked out of the pub. It was a fantastic night and one that they had all promised they would make a more regular occurrence.

She thought about the horrendous moment earlier when Paul drove off with the children in his hire car. Not a Kodak memory for the family album that was for sure. It was such a surreal feeling getting the children ready for a family day out, but one without her, their mother. It was the 'new normal' Sarah supposed and one she needed to get used to. She smiled brightly as she waved them off, with the sound of Ella crying in protest at leaving her Mama behind and it just broke Sarah's heart. She knew that the children were in safe hands and in fairness Paul had always been a good daddy. Rita would be there too and that gave Sarah an extra layer of comfort as the children loved her.

While they were out, Sarah decided she would use the time to get working on her paperwork for the solicitor. She had been given the job of outlining all her living expenses for the children and the house, so that a maintenance schedule could be drawn up. Paul had intimated that he wouldn't want them to sell the house, but he wasn't prepared to pay the full mortgage every month, only a percentage of it. It was down to the solicitors to start horse-trading now. Whatever magic Conor managed to do, Sarah knew that she was still going to have to come up with more money herself.

She'd already spoken to the boutique and they had no more shifts to offer her. In fact Martina the owner was almost in tears herself. Her sales were down by 50% on the previous year and she was struggling to remain open. Sarah sympathised with her, it was an awful situation to be in. She thought about all the money Paul and she had squandered during the better days – the so called 'Celtic Tiger'. They'd had two holidays every year, the kids had been given every toy and gadget they'd ever expressed an interest in. She had a wardrobe full of handbags and shoes that she'd never in a million years ever wear. What had she been thinking? If only she could go back in time she'd have never bought all those things. Then inspiration hit her.

'I'll sell some of my handbags on eBay!' Sarah had used eBay before to buy decorations for the kid's birthday parties. This time she was going to be a seller rather than a buyer.

Paul had bought Sarah several expensive handbags over the years for various occasions. When he got a big bonus in work, he'd normally buy her something then too. She went upstairs and decided to have a sort out on items she could easily get rid of.

There were two *Marc Jacobs* bags, both of which could go. She also had a *Louis Vuitton*, *Prada* and two *Orla Kiely* bags. Her *Guess* bag and her *Fendi* spy bag were both well used, she didn't think she could give them away never mind sell them, so she put those back on the shelf in her wardrobe. But the others could all go as they were as good as new really. She picked up her *Chanel* handbag. Looking at it tugged at her heartstrings. This was her pride and joy, it was the first designer bag she'd ever owned, and she took it out for all special occasions. One day she dreamt she'd pass it on to Katie. No, she was going to keep this one. She placed it back reverently on the shelf. If things got worse she'd sell everything in her wardrobe if she had to, but she hadn't gotten to that point yet.

She was on a mission now, and continued routing through her wardrobe. She found a Hermes scarf. Paul had won that in a sales competition. He had been so proud handing it to Sarah when he came home. Tommy and Katie were only toddlers at the time. She smiled at the memory. Paul and her dancing around their kitchen with the scarf wrapped around both their necks, pulling them in close.

'I love you.' He'd whispered and she replied as she had always done, 'I love you more.'

She closed her eyes to erase the memory and, like a bubble popping, it disappeared. If someone had suggested that in a few years she and Paul would be on the brink of divorce she would have laughed out loud at the ludicrously of it. They were rock solid in those days, the two of them against the world.

Sarah shook her head. She knew that memories didn't buy Santa gifts so put the scarf on the pile of handbags.

She also found two pairs of Jimmy Choos. She had only worn each of them once, so again they were in perfect condition. They could go too. She piled everything into a wicker laundry basket and headed downstairs to the computer to start listing everything on eBay.

She looked at her clock, surprised to see that it was midday already. Setting up the sales had passed the morning quickly for her. She felt invigorated right now. The feeling of taking control of her finances was wonderful. Now to take control over the rest of her life.

So much about her future was unsure, but the time for wallowing was gone, it was now time for action. She knew now that Edward's arrival had come at a time when she was at her most vulnerable. Before she even recognised that she needed him, he was by her side. And she was going to need him to help sort out her next problem. She flicked onto her Google homepage and checked the weather. Snow was forecast for the following day and rest of the week on the east coast of Ireland. She jumped up and grabbed her car keys. Time to sort out Bridie.

Sarah had formulated a plan on how to help the pensioner earlier that morning. An hour later, Sarah was driving down the lane to her house. It was a narrow lane and in bad need of some work on the potholes. She could see Bridie peeping out of her front window, obviously wondering who was calling. Sarah jumped out and opened the back door of her car, pulling out a large box.

Bridie looked in surprise at Sarah and the box she was carrying.

'How are you Bridie?' Sarah asked her neighbour.

'I'm in fine form. What have you got there?' She asked curiously.

'Can I come in?' Sarah enquired.

'Of course, I'm delighted for the company!' Bridie said, opening her door wide.

Sarah walked into the front room where a big fire was crackling away.

'It's cosy here.'

'I love an open fire.' Bridie said with a smile, giving the fire another poke. 'Nothing like it.'

'Do you have any central heating?' Sarah asked her.

'I never bothered with it. I got a back burner on the fire, which heats the radiators lovely. I'm only in here or the kitchen or bedroom anyhow.' Bridie replied.

Sarah nodded, feeling worried. If that fire went, so did her heating for the whole house.

'Did you hear that snow is on its way?' Sarah continued.

'Yes, I saw that on the news earlier. The kids will all love that I'm sure. What age are yours?'

Sarah told her, smiling as she always did whenever she thought of the children.

'I remember my two when they were that age. Full of mischief the pair of them.' Bridie answered.

'Do you see much of them?'

'They're both very busy with their own families now. But even so, they both come and visit me at least once a month. And they're always begging me to go visit them too.'

'Would you not think of going up to stay with one of them for a few days? It's to be awfully cold this week.' Sarah asked her.

'Oh no, I'll not leave my house. I'm as cosy as anything here. Anyhow, speaking of visiting, I'm sure you haven't called here to listen to me talking about my children. What can I do for you?'

'Well I was concerned about you when I heard about the snow. So I pulled together a box full of groceries that I thought you might need in case you get snowed in.'

Bridie stood up to look in the brown box Sarah had placed on the sofa, close to tears. 'Sarah that's so thoughtful of you. Well I never.' She finished, at a loss for words. 'It's like Christmas has come early!'

'It's not much.' Sarah protested. 'But some tins of various things that are non-perishable in case you can't get out for a few days with the weather. I've also put in some basics like tea and coffee and bread and milk with a few cupcakes that were made fresh this morning.'

'That's the nicest thing anyone has ever done for me. Let me get my purse. How much do I owe you?'

'Oh I don't want money.' Sarah said immediately. 'It's only a few bits from Centra, it didn't cost very much. I've some coal for you in the boot too and some logs. To help you keep that fire going for you.'

'It's too much.' Bridie said protesting. 'I can't accept it all.'

'Not at all, it's my pleasure. And listen, I want you to promise me one thing.' Sarah said seriously to her neighbour. 'Just promise me that you won't go out into the snow for any reason. It's going to be treacherous and if you fall it could be very bad for you.'

'Sure I won't need to go out now; you've got everything in for me!' Bridie exclaimed happily. 'But I insist on giving you some money.'

'I won't hear of it. But here's my number, ring me if you need anything else. And also, I've spoken to Colm in Centra, I've asked him would they do deliveries if it snows badly and he's agreed they would. Here's their number. Call them for more fuel if you need some and a list of any groceries you need. They're happy to come up here with them; Colm has a big jeep that he said would get around most weather conditions.'

'I just can't believe you've done all that for me.' Bridie said and this time she couldn't help herself and started to cry.

'Sure, you'd do the same for me.' Sarah replied. 'Neighbours have to help each other out.'

'I'll not forget this.' Bridie said grabbing Sarah's hand and holding it tightly between both of hers. 'I'll never be able to repay you. But if you ever need anything you need only ask.'

'Well there is something you can do for me.'

'Anything!' Bridie exclaimed.

'Put that kettle on, I'm parched!' Sarah said. laugh.

While Bridie prepared the tea, Sarah looked around the cosy living room. A pile of books on the coffee table and beside that the TV Guide, where Bridie had circled her favourite programmes to watch that day. Was she happy? Sarah wondered. Was this the life that she could look forward to one day? Children living miles away immersed in their own busy lives and she, on her own, reliant on a friendly neighbour to help her out? She remembered a night that seemed a lifetime ago now, lying in bed, her head resting in the crook of Paul's shoulder. He whispered to her, 'I hope that I die first, because I don't want to live a day without you.' And they had both fervently agreed that neither could be without the other.

Yet here she was. Living without him.

Chapter Twenty Two

The next day Paul once again collected the children. They were all having Sunday lunch with Rita who had in fairness invited Sarah to come too. She'd begged her in fact to join them, saying it was unthinkable that she'd be on her own. Rita was still struggling to get her head around all the changes. But Sarah was happy to decline. Even Rita's wonderful roast potatoes couldn't entice her to join them. She needed to get used to the fact that they were no longer the family they used to be and that every second weekend the children would be with their father. The children had been having a great time thankfully. Each day they had gotten more and more excited and animated about having their Daddy back. And this morning, they were both sitting at the window waiting for his car to arrive. They practically knocked Sarah down as they ran to meet him at the door.

Paul was chuffed with the reaction and even got a big smile from Ella when he walked in. Traitor! Sarah thought quickly, but, in all honesty, she was happy that the children were excited. Plus to make things even better, it had snowed heavily during the night and they had already been out building snowmen. They couldn't wait to show off their handiwork to their Daddy. Paul had always been the snowman expert for previous snowfalls, so they were very beside themselves at the thought of building more at Rita's house with his help.

The conditions were driveable, but it was to get worse, so Sarah asked Paul to have the children home by four o'clock. She didn't want to take any chances.

She made a cup of coffee and decided to have one of her cupcakes. She was thinner than she'd ever been in her whole life, so she could afford the calories for once. The phone rang and Sarah jumped to answer it.

'Hi, sis. Thought I'd call in for a coffee later on if that's ok.'

'Course it is. Since when did you ring in advance to let me know you're on your way?' Sarah asked him curiously. Normally he'd just arrive at the door; they'd never stood on ceremony ever.

'Em, well I just thought I'd let you know because I'm going to bring someone with me.' he declared.

'What kind of somebody?' Sarah asked.

'A date kind of somebody.' Sarah could hear the smile in his voice.

'Oh lordy, must be serious,' she replied. 'Who's the lucky lady?'

'You'll see when we call around.' He said mysteriously. 'Three suit you?'

'I can't wait!' It was about time her brother settled down and maybe this mystery woman was the one to do it with him. She picked up her cupcake again but the phone rang for a second time. She was never going to eat that cake the way things were going!

But it wasn't James this time, it was Bridie.

'You'll never believe it, but I've just had a delivery from Centra! I rang them like you said and they took my order no problem and arrived out here a few minutes ago. Colm even brought the coal into the house for me and put the groceries into the kitchen. I can't believe it. And they didn't even charge me for delivery. Can you believe that?'

Sarah laughed at how incredulous Bridie sounded. 'That's great. 'Course I can believe it. You're a good customer to them, why wouldn't they look after you?! You warm enough over there?'

'Oh it's lovely here. The snow looks so pretty. But I've not been outside at all. I was watching the news last night and there was a woman on who died from the cold. Awful shock it was when I saw it. Made me think of you and how you made me promise not to go out. I'll not forget it.'

'It was nothing. I'm just happy that you're ok. Stay inside and don't even attempt to go out until this all thaws.'

'I won't.' Bridie promised. 'Oh by the way where did you buy those cupcakes from? I asked Colm and they didn't know which ones I was talking about. I was going to order another box.'

'I didn't buy them. I made them myself.'

'Well they are the nicest cakes I've ever had. You should sell them. I'd buy them.'

'Are you serious? I hadn't thought anyone else would buy them!' Rita too had always said she should sell them but she always thought her mother-in-law was simply biased.

'Of course they would.' Bridie responded. 'Why don't you give Centra a call and see if they'll sell some for you. They've a customer already with me for sure!'

'I might just do that!' Sarah said laughing. She put down the phone and thought to herself maybe it's not such a bad idea. Everyone said that they loved her cupcakes. And she loved making them. She needed to find a way to earn some extra revenue without incurring huge childcare costs. This could be the answer. She could work from home with the children here.

Feeling bold, she decided to strike while the iron was hot! She picked up the phone. A bit of market research wouldn't hurt at all.

With luck on her side it was the manager Colm who answered the phone.

'Hi Colm, its Sarah Lawler here.'

'Hi Sarah. You looking for a delivery of groceries?'

'I'm grand, thanks.' Sarah replied. 'I hear you've been out and about though to Bridie's. She's delighted.'

'It was a great idea of yours. We put a message up on Facebook saying we'd do deliveries for the cold spell and we've been inundated with requests. My sales are up actually on last year despite the bad weather!'

'I'm delighted for you.' Sarah said smiling. 'It's nice to hear of a good news story these days.'

'I should get you to come work for me!' Colm said laughing. 'Best marketing campaign I've ever done, doing free deliveries.'

'Well funny you should say that, I am calling with a proposition for you. I make cupcakes as a hobby and I'm thinking about starting a small business selling them. I wondered if I could put up an advert in your shop? Or maybe you'd sell them for me in the shop?'

'Are they the ones Bridie had me driven demented about? I brought her some tea cakes we stock and she sent them back to me, saying that they weren't the ones she'd gotten from you!' Colm declared.

'Yes, they're the one and the same.' Sarah replied, chuffed that Bridie had really loved them that much.

'Well, one good turn deserves another, so I'd be happy to give them a go for you. Why don't you drop down about two dozen of them tomorrow morning and I'll see how many we can shift? Can you email me your pricing later?'

Sarah was gobsmacked. She thought she'd have had to talk Colm into it. But he seemed happy to give her a try. 'I'll get working on my pricing straight away, Colm, and I'll email it on to you. Thanks a million.' Sarah replied before hanging up.

She jumped up and danced around her kitchen! Yes! At last something that might just bring in some money. She ran to the computer to do some market research on how much cupcakes were selling for these days. Very quickly she found out that they sold individually for anything from €1.50 to €2.00 each. She decided that in the current climate she needed them to go on the market for €1.50 each. She quickly opened up a spread sheet and started working out how much each item would cost to make. She listed out all the ingredients she'd need to make a dozen cakes and then worked out a single unit cost price. Even factoring in electricity, she figured she could make them and sell them to Colm giving them both a healthy margin.

She quickly started looking through her recipes she had collated over the years. What flavours should she try? Tommy and Katie's faces popped into her mind immediately and she knew that her Rocky Road cupcakes were definitely a must for Centra. Her kids just loved them and she hoped that children would see them in the shop and beg their parents to buy them. And in fairness they had always been a hit with the adults too as James loved them too. Now for the second flavour; Sarah wondered what she should do. She had so many ideas of different flavours she could try to sell, but in the end she figured her Pistachio, vanilla and raspberry cupcakes would be an ideal contrast to the Rocky Road ones. Maybe she'd start with twelve of each initially and see how they sold and then she could start introducing some of her other flavours. Her head was bursting with ideas.

She opened up her cupboard and started pulling ingredients out. Flour, sugar, icing sugar, colourings, pale pink paper roses, tiny marshmallows, chocolate chips and vanilla essence. She also pulled out some of the pretty cupcake paper cases that she had in the store cupboard. She'd a habit of picking them up whenever she was out and about and had managed to amass hundreds of different styles. She found just the ones for her inaugural batch as they had a vintage feel to them, with a chintzy flower print on them in duck egg blues and pinks. She walked to the fridge and pulled out eggs, milk and some butter. Now to get baking she thought. These had to be just perfect!

Soon the kitchen was filled with the wonderful aroma of vanilla and chocolate as the cakes were baking in the oven. Her tummy started to rumble loudly and she realised that she had never actually drank that coffee earlier, or finished her cupcake. She was ravenous all of a sudden, when had she last eaten? The stress of everything going on had meant her appetite had all but disappeared. She made herself some beans on toast quickly and sat down to eat. Not quite a Sunday roast, but it was the best tasting meal she'd had in weeks. She licked her lips and ate every morsel on the plate. She felt alive again and for the first time in a long time the feeling of helplessness that had plagued her seemed to have vanished.

She put the cupcakes on a wire rack to cool while she went about making the icing for them.

She started with the Pistachio, vanilla and raspberry cupcakes. She wanted a pale green icing for these. She added a few drops of her green colouring to the icing and mixed until it was exactly the right colour. Soon it was the perfect Pistachio colour. She iced each of the cakes very carefully and then gently placed the pale pink paper rose on each. They looked beautiful, she thought proudly.

She then moved onto the Rocky road cakes. She broke her chocolate up into small pieces and placed it in a bowl. It was 70% cocoa solids and absolutely delicious in icing. She then heated her cream and when it was almost boiling she poured it over the chocolate, allowing it to melt and let them blend into each other. She left it to cool for about thirty minutes until it was smooth and glossy. She then spread the chocolate mixture over the cakes and sprinkled her marshmallows, and chocolate chips on top of that in a little pile. They looked fantastic, the best she'd ever made in fact and she knew exactly how she wanted to display them in the shop. A few months ago she'd bought a large white cupcake stand, and it had several layers to it, that you could use or not use, depending on how many cakes you wanted to display. She had used it for Ella's christening, having sixty cupcakes sitting proudly on the five layers of the stand, with a large cupcake on the top. It was a wonderful christening cake and a big hit with all of the kids. She was going to ask Colm if she could display her cakes on the stand. She knew it would make them stand out so much more than if they were just placed beside each other on the shelf.

Sarah had never run her own business before but she did know how to sell. Having worked in the boutique for years she knew how to make the merchandise stand out. Thinking about the christening cake she'd done, gave her a further idea. Maybe she should think about advertising her cupcake business, start looking for birthdays or christenings to supply. She wondered if Colm would mind her putting an advert up in his store.

She sat down and started listing all her ideas as they came thick and fast into her head. Dinner parties, children's parties, Christmas cupcakes, she was on a roll with all her ideas. Her heart was racing with excitement.

'I haven't seen you looking so happy in a long time.' A voice interrupted her thoughts. It was Edward, now sitting opposite her smiling.

'You here long?' Sarah asked him with a smile.

'I'm always here.' He pointed to the cakes standing proudly in a row on the counter top. 'Those look good. Makes me wish I could eat one,' he finished with regret in his voice.

'Why can't you?' Sarah asked. 'You look like a human, you sound like one, seems unfair you can't have a few treats the odd time too!'

Edward smiled at Sarah. 'That would be nice wouldn't it? But it doesn't work quite like that. God created us so that we don't grow or age like you do. We take on human form because that's easier for you. If I stood here ten foot tall, floating, with wings, it might send you running!'

'Are you ten feet tall?' Sarah asked in awe.

'I'm actually closer to eleven feet.' Edward replied with a grin. 'Despite our human form, angels don't have internal organs and cavities like you. So that's why we don't eat or drink – we never feel thirst or hunger, so it's ok. I've watched you making cupcakes for years mind you and the pleasure they give the people who eat them too. It made me want to try one.'

Sarah laughed at him. He sounded like one of her children just then. 'I wish you could try one too. Do you think that they'll sell?'

What if nobody bought one? She started to panic, thinking that maybe she'd be left with the embarrassing task of having to take them all back unsold.

'Have faith.' Edward said to Sarah. 'Good things happen to good people. Look at how you unselfishly helped Bridie and that act has now brought you to this!' He indicated the sumptuous cakes lined up.

The doorbell rang and Sarah realised that it was after 3pm, it had to be James and his new girlfriend she realised. And she must look a right mess, she thought. Not to mention that the kitchen was in disarray. She'd completely forgotten the time. Oh well, she hoped James' girlfriend was the type to just take them as she found them.

She quickly smoothed her hair down and wiped the icing sugar from her cheek. It would have to do. She opened the door and, to her utter surprise, standing beside her twin brother, was Ruby. They were both looking at her with big beaming smiles, holding each other's hand.

'Ruby!' Sarah exclaimed.

'Can we come in?' James said with a laugh. 'I have to tell you, your face is a picture!'

'You've taken me by surprise that's all. Come in, come in.' Sarah said beaming.

They all sat down in the living room.

'How you doing with the kids with Paul gone?' Ruby asked with concern.

'Enough about me and my marriage Rubes, that's enough to put anyone in a bad mood and I'm determined to hold onto my good one today! I'd much rather talk about this new romance. When did you two get together?'

James had Sarah in stitches as he regaled her with the story of his fitness assessment.

'And all along, she knew I was only after a date, but she still put me through all of that!' James said with a laugh, playfully pushing Ruby's shoulder with his hand.

'I couldn't help myself.' Ruby said bubbling with laughter. 'I kept expecting him to fess up that he wasn't there for an assessment, especially when I brought him out the cycling shorts!'

'I'm so happy for you both.' Sarah said to them. 'I never saw this coming! But now I see you sitting beside each other, it makes total sense! You make a gorgeous couple.'

'Thanks, sis.'

'Why didn't you tell me earlier?' Sarah asked him puzzled. They'd been dating for a few weeks now and James had been over a few times during that period.

'Ah you were having a rough time, sis.' He said. 'It wasn't the right time to be talking about romance when you were going through so much over here, what with Paul and everything.'

Sarah felt terrible that her unhappiness had stopped her brother and best friend feeling free to celebrate the fact that they'd fallen in love. And she reckoned by their faces that's exactly what had happened. James was smitten she was sure of it. She'd never seen him like this before. And Ruby too.

'Well I'm glad you've told me now. I couldn't think of anyone more perfect for you James, than Ruby. And you needn't worry about me anymore; I've had a very good day!'

She quickly filled them in on her activities, her sales on eBay and her new enterprise. They were both extremely enthusiastic about it all.

'You've been busy.' James said laughing. 'Alan Sugar better watch out, there's a new apprentice in town!' He finished jokingly.

They all laughed at this.

'You need a name.' Ruby said to her. 'Have you thought of one yet?'

'No I hadn't thought about that. But you're right, I suppose I do.'

'Right, brainstorming session needed pronto.' James declared. 'Go make us a cuppa and we'll try some of the cupcakes out, it will help get the brain cells flowing for inspiration! Wait till you try the Rocky Road ones, Ruby. They're the business!'

'Coming right up!' Sarah said with a mock salute to her brother.

A few minutes later they were all munching away.

'They look amazing and taste even better.' Ruby declared. 'Remember Mary described your cupcakes as little pieces of heaven. Nail.On.The.Head!'

'There's a name so.' James declared. 'Sarah's little pieces of heaven cupcakes.'

'It's a bit of a mouthful.' Sarah said looking a bit worried.

'Ok. Let's think again.' James replied. 'How about just Heavenly Cupcakes.'

'Better.' Ruby said. 'You need to add your name to them though. Heavenly Cupcakes by Sarah Lawler.'

'Doesn't sound right yet for me.' Sarah said. 'It's nearly there but not quite.' She glanced up and saw Edward standing in the corner.

'I know what I'll call them.' Sarah declared. James and Ruby looked up.

'Go on.' James said impatiently.

'Angel Cupcakes by Sarah Codd.' Sarah said formally.

'Angel Cupcakes by Sarah Codd.' James repeated with his eyebrows slightly raised. Sarah was using her maiden name again. 'I like it! And it's very apt on the angel front anyhow.'

'Why so?' Ruby said.

'Oh just that it ties in with the whole heavenly comment.' Sarah replied quickly, giving James a look. He understood immediately that she didn't want Ruby to know about Edward.

'Right, I'll go grab some more coffee!' Sarah said and James jumped up, offering to help too.

'Are you ok with this?' James asked.

'I'm more than ok with it.' Sarah reassured him. 'But don't mess it up, James. She's my best friend and I've only just got her back. I don't want to lose her again because she's a broken heart courtesy of you!'

'If anyone is likely to get a broken heart this time, it's me. I've fallen for her. Hard.' James confessed.

192

'You can't tell her about Edward.'

'I know.' James replied. 'But one day you will have to. You can't keep hiding who you are from everyone who loves you.'

'I can't risk losing everyone I love either!' Sarah replied. 'I'm not strong enough to deal with the looks of horror on their faces when they find out. What if they don't believe me?'

'Don't tar everyone with Mam and Dad's brush,' James told her. 'And for what it's worth, you are stronger than you think you are.'

'So Angel Cupcakes is a good idea?' Sarah asked.

James nodded in agreement. 'When you think about it, angels brought Ruby and I together too. Good old Eddy!' he ended jubilantly! 'I'd kiss him if I could see him right now!'

'Funny that just as you said that, Edward disappeared!' Sarah said laughing.

They both started to laugh then and once they started it seemed hard to stop. It was so good to see James looking so happy.

Ruby walked into the kitchen and walked over to James and into his embrace, smiling as she saw them both laughing.

Despite feeling genuinely happy for them, Sarah felt a slight stab of what she recognised as jealousy as she watched them together; their bodies seemed to mould into each other's perfectly. They were obviously very much in love already and all of a sudden Sarah felt lonely. She hadn't felt that intimate touch of a man in a long time and realised she may never again. She quickly shook the feeling off. This wasn't the time to get all maudlin. She didn't want to ruin a happy moment by being selfish.

'Are you sure about going back to your maiden name?' James asked with concern through mouthfuls of chocolate icing. 'It's a big step.'

'I know.' Sarah replied, 'But this is a new beginning for me. It feels right that I go back to being Codd again. I stopped being a Lawler when Paul left me I suppose. That name belongs with my marriage, in the past. My solicitor said I needed to decide if I was going to keep the name or not. Well, the decision has just been made.'

James walked over to his sister and gave her a hug. 'I'm proud of you, sis. You're doing brilliantly through this whole mess. I don't think I'd be able to cope as well as you have.'

Sarah smiled at her brother, grateful for his kind words. It meant a lot to her, gave her the strength to carry on.

Just then his mobile beeped and he broke away from Sarah. He walked outside to take the call, returning a few minutes later.

'Got to go. Sorry about eating and running, but that was the Seafield Hotel. Finally one of the staff who is working tonight remembers Rachel and Wickham. I'm going to go interview them quickly before they disappear again.'

Ruby quickly jumped up. 'Oh is this the case you are helping the Gardaí with? We better go quickly, that's a big breakthrough! Sarah seriously, those cupcakes are amazing. They'll be a huge success, I just know it.'

Sarah hugged them both warmly as they left, 'I'm just so happy for you both!'

Chapter Twenty Three

James was having a pint with Roger. He needed to find a way to persuade him that Mal was a suspect, without giving Sarah away.

'So let me get this straight.' Roger said a little sharply. 'You have been playing Sherlock Holmes based on a hunch?'

'Something like that, mate. I've done some digging around that guy I told you about, Wickham, and I have some suspicions I think you need to hear.' James said.

'I thought I told you to back off this whole hunch thing?' Roger said with more than a little annoyance.

'Rachel Finch was my niece's school teacher. And my sister's kids were devastated when Rachel died. It was upsetting; I just wanted to help make it right.' James said truthfully.

'That I get.' Roger said. 'And I'd say every parent of every child from Rachel's class felt the same. But I don't have any of them sitting in a pub with me telling me they've been having a go at solving a murder!'

'Fair point.' James acknowledged. 'Hey, I'm a frustrated private investigator! Shoot me!' He tried to add some humour to the situation. Roger was a mate; he couldn't stay mad at him for long.

'Right, start at the beginning.'

'It started at the funeral. I was in the bar at the Ballyaislinn Hotel and was chatting to some friends and we were joined by a guy there. It's hard to explain, but there was just something off about him.' James replied.

'How do you mean off?' Roger replied.

'I just didn't trust him, I suppose.' James replied. 'I can't put my finger on it, but there was something about him that made me feel uncomfortable.'

'Ok, so what brought you from not liking a guy to making him a murder suspect?' Roger continued.

'I know that this sounds crazy.' James replied. 'His wife Marie joined us at the bar and it was her that actually made me suspicious. She was good friends with Rachel apparently but they had a falling out and there was something about the way she spoke about Rachel and her husband, that made me think that there was more to their story.'

'Why not ring and tell me that straight away?' Roger replied.

'Would you have listened?'

There wasn't a reply to that so James continued. 'I decided to follow up on it. I went to see Marie and spoke to her. And she admitted that she thought they had been having an affair. And listen to this, Roger, this guy Mal is really messed up. She had bruises on her face and head, which she'd tried to cover up with make-up; she's terrified of him.'

Roger was deep in thought listening to this, picking up a beer mat and twirling it in his hand over and over.

'The fact that he knocks about his missus makes him a dickhead, but it doesn't make him a murderer.' Roger replied. 'I need more.'

James picked up his pint, took one mouthful and put it down again. He wanted a drink, yet he didn't; he needed a clear head. 'I know for definite that Mal and Rachel were having an affair now. I've found his second phone, a pay-as-you-go. I bet there's a number you have been trying to trace from Rachel Finch's phone records?' James received a nod of acknowledgement from Roger on that one.

'It's Mal's second phone. Marie told me that he's never at home. She hardly sees him he's out so late every night. And when I asked her about the night Rachel was murdered she admitted that he came home very late and that he had gone to the barn and she followed him there and saw him at the log pile. Doesn't that sound strange?'

James knew he was treading on thin ice here. It was actually Sarah's dream that told them about the late night visit to the log pile not Marie, but he couldn't say that to him.

'Would she be willing to make a statement?' Roger asked sitting up, finally throwing the beer mat down.

'I don't know.' James answered truthfully. 'She's terrified of him. But listen, this guy is a predator. He's up and down to Dublin all the time going to speed-dating events. His poor wife is at home worried sick as he's out till all hours. He's dangerous. He needs to be stopped. What if he does something to Marie next?' James said passionately.

'Hold on a second.' Roger said putting his hand on his friends shoulder. 'We don't know that he has any intention of hurting Marie any further; let's not get ahead of ourselves.'

He took out a pen and started writing down some facts in his diary.

'OK, so far you know that Rachel and Mal were having an affair. And that he is a creep who is sleeping around and is also fond of his fists. That's convinced me to go to Sarge.'

'I've more for you.' James said with a small smile of pride.

'I'm nearly afraid to ask. Please don't tell me you've gone and arrested him on my behalf? Should I just go and put my feet up?' he added a little sarcastically.

'Well I have a positive ID that Mal was with Rachel on the afternoon she was murdered. I found out that Mal withdrew money from a cash machine in Gorey that afternoon at 3pm. He then met up with Rachel in the Seafield Hotel . They had something to eat there. I've got the name of the barman and he is willing to come and make a formal statement. He's only just back from a visit to his mother in Poland, hence only getting this statement last night. As it happens he'd served them quite a few times over the past few months so remembered them both clearly. And apparently Mal Wickham never left a tip; it pissed this guy off. What he didn't know was that Rachel had been murdered.'

'So we can thank Mr Wickham for being a tight arse for the barman remembering him.' Roger said.

'Have you enough to bring him in?' James asked hopefully.

'Assuming the phone and bank records check out as you say they do and we get a statement from the barman, then yes, I would say we can certainly bring him in for questioning. You never know he may just feel the need to get something off his chest and confess all his sins.'

'I wouldn't bet on it.' James replied. 'He's one cool customer, this guy.'

'I reckon we'll be talking to Mal Wickham. You did well.' Roger said shaking his hand. He couldn't wait to get back to the station to tell his colleagues. They had all been waiting for a break in the case.

A few hours later, having briefed the rest of his team, Roger and his partner Johnny arrived at the farm. Parking their car up, they walked to the farmhouse and rang the bell. No answer. They saw a tractor in the distance coming towards them.

'Reckon that's him?' Johnny asked.

'Reckon so. Let's wait for him to come to us.'

A few minutes later the tractor entered the farm yard. Sure enough it was Mal Wickham. He jumped down from the cabin and walked over to them.

'Can I help you?' he asked with suspicion. He did a double take when he saw the uniforms.

'You can.' Roger replied. 'We'd like a chat with you about Rachel Finch.'

Mal hesitated so Roger added a bit more pressure, 'You've gone a bit pale there. Something wrong?'

'Of course not.' Mal replied, recovering himself quickly. 'It's just shocking to think about poor Rachel. I'm not sure how I can help you in your investigation, but I'm happy to try.'

'That's very good to hear Mr Wickham; your co-operation is much appreciated. We've a few questions to ask you.' Roger said to him. 'We'll need to bring you in to the station for some questioning.'

'Are you arresting me?' he asked, his voice steely.

'No, we are not arresting you at this point.' Roger replied. 'We just need to ask you some questions.'

'Is it necessary for me to come to the station?' Mal asked. 'I'm sure I've nothing I can tell you that would help in any way with your investigation, I barely knew the poor girl.'

'All the same, we'd still like you to come in.' Roger continued firmly.

Johnny walked over to him and grabbed his arm. 'This way Mr Wickham.'

'If you don't come voluntarily, we'll have no choice but to arrest you.' Roger told him. 'If that helps you make up your mind.'

'Can I at least get changed?' he demanded, indicating his over-alls and wellies.

'Sure. We can wait five minutes for you to change. Lead the way.'

They followed him into the house and waited as he got ready.

Soon they were back in the car and heading to the station, all the time Mal asking them why they wanted to question him, declaring he had absolutely nothing he could share with them that would be of any help.

Roger and Johnny stayed quiet and ignored his pleas of innocence.

'My wife will come home from work and be worried as to where I am. How long will this take?' He asked with more than a hint of annoyance in his voice.

'Not long, Mr Wickham.' Johnny said firmly. 'As long as you co-operate with us, you can be finished up very quickly.'

199

'I'll do anything to help.' He said, flashing a smile their way.

Roger kept driving, keeping his eye on the road. It was still really bad weather out there; it had started to snow again.

Roger sat down beside Johnny, opposite Mal.

'You comfortable, need anything? Some more water?' Roger said convivially to Mal.

'I'm fine thanks.' Mal responded. 'Look I've been here over an hour already. Are you going to let me know exactly what it is you've brought me in for?' he demanded.

'We just have some questions to ask you. We're going to record the interview; it's standard practise.' Roger said to him.

'Do I need a lawyer?' Mal said, a line of perspiration forming on his upper lip.

'You tell me Mal, do you need one?' Roger retorted quickly. 'By all means if you want a lawyer go ahead. You're not under arrest; we're simply here to ask you some questions. But I'm happy to suspend the interview for an hour if you want to get a lawyer organised.'

He watched him run through his options in his head. If he looked for a lawyer it might make him look like he had something to hide. On the other hand if he flew solo here it would show them he was as innocent as the day he was born.

Mal leaned back in his chair and crossed his legs. 'No, that's fine. I don't need one. Let's get this over and done with.'

'Glad we have that sorted. We'll get going, so.' Roger said to him giving him his brightest smile.

He hit the record button on the recorder and looking directly at Mal said, 'This is Detective Roger McElvoy and Detective Johnny Murphy in the homicide case of Rachel Finch. It is 12.45 pm on December 4th 2012. The subject of the interview is Mr Malcolm Wickham who has just declined a lawyer.'

Roger looked at Mal and asked him. 'For the purpose of the tape please state your name.'

'Malcolm Wickham.'

'Thank you. Now, tell me about your relationship with Rachel Finch.'

'You've got that wrong to start with.' Mal said smoothly. 'She's my wife Marie's friend, not mine. They went to university together.'

'When did you first meet Rachel?' Roger asked.

'Let me think.' Mal replied. 'The first time was actually at our wedding I'm pretty certain.'

'Nice wedding, was it?' Johnny asked.

'Yes, as it happens it was.' Mal responded. He wasn't sure if Johnny was being sarcastic or genuine in his question, but he was smiling at him intently.

'Ok, you met Rachel initially at your wedding. When did you see her again?' Roger continued.

'About a month or so after our honeymoon, Marie arranged to meet up with Rachel. We went for dinner and then a few drinks.'

'And how did that go? Did you like Rachel?' Roger continued.

'Not particularly. She was Marie's friend. I only went along because she asked me to.' He shrugged his shoulders and smiled his most charming smile to them both. 'You know what it's like; sometimes you have to just do what your wife says!' He actually winked at them at this point. Roger looked at Johnny and they both smiled back at Mal. Let him think they were all buddies.

'True.' Johnny answered him. 'My wife certainly wears the trousers in our house.'

Roger watched Mal visibly relax. His shoulders dropped slightly and he sat back further in his chair. It was time to shake things up.

'So is it Malcolm or Mal, which do you prefer?' Roger asked him.

'Most people call me Mal, or at least my friends do. You can call me Mal.' He replied smiling again.

'Good, that's agreed then. So Mal, tell me something. At what point after that night out did you and Rachel Finch start sleeping together?' Roger threw in quietly.

Mal sat up quickly, a look of shock all over his face. 'How dare you! Rachel was Marie's friend. I never slept with her. We were just friends. I'm a married man!'

'That you are.' Roger agreed. 'But I have it on very good authority that you were more than just friends with Rachel.'

'Friends with benefits, maybe?' Johnny said with a wink of his own.

'As I said, I'm a married man!' Mal once again protested.

'Ok. So as friends did you see much of Rachel?' Roger asked.

'On occasion we might bump into each other.' Mal replied. He was sitting up now with his arms folded across his chest.

'And did Marie know that you occasionally bumped into Rachel, as you so delicately put it?' Johnny interjected.

Mal didn't answer.

'Answer the question, Mal. Was your wife aware that you saw Rachel occasionally?' Roger said a little more loudly this time.

He hesitated, and then finally admitted. 'No, she wasn't. And that was only because she'd have taken it the wrong way. You know how women can be. She was very jealous of Rachel and would have gotten the wrong end of the stick.' Mal explained.

'Of course.' Roger said. 'Let's leave your relationship with Rachel Finch to one side.'

'I had no relationship with her!' Mal protested. 'I love my wife dearly.'

'You're sounding a bit like Bill Clinton there.' Johnny said jokingly. 'I did not have relations with that woman,' he drawled in his best American accent.

Mal gave him a dirty look, clearly not enjoying the comedy routine.

'Mal, how many mobile phones do you own?' Roger asked.

'One.' Mal replied quickly. 'Why?'

'It's important that you realise that I know how many phones you really do have Mal. So for your own sake, take a sec and rethink and then answer my question again.' Roger said firmly.

Mal thought about this for a moment, then stated nonchalantly, 'Well now that I come to think of it, I have a second phone for emergencies. I don't use it very often, so that's why it slipped my mind.'

'That wasn't hard, was it?' Johnny said sarcastically to him.

'Now you're going to have to help me out here.' Roger said to him. 'Why would a guy like you need a second phone?'

'I have it for personal use. I don't like to mix up my work with pleasure. That's all. It's not a crime is it?' Mal said to them.

'No, of course not.' Roger replied calmly. 'Don't worry; we'll not arrest you for owning more than one phone, of that I can assure you!'

Mal smiled in relief. He could get out of this yet. They'd nothing on him; they'd have arrested him immediately if they had.

'Out of interest, does Marie know about the second phone?' Johnny asked.

'I can't remember.' Mal replied tetchily. 'Probably, I'm sure I've mentioned it.'

'Oh that's good. Not great to have secrets in a marriage, I think.' Johnny said.

'Out of interest, which phone is your business one and which one is your personal one?' Roger asked him. He showed him both numbers written down on a piece of paper. 'It's just that the second phone doesn't have a record of you ever calling Marie on it or receiving a call from her either. And as she's your wife, that seems a bit strange. So, I'd say that must be your business phone, so.'

Mal nodded.

'Maybe I'm a bit slow here.' Roger continued. 'We've established that the second phone is your business phone, that's why Marie never calls it. But why would Rachel text and call you on it for months? Were you in business together?'

Mal didn't know how to answer. He felt his hands start to get clammy and sweat begin to form in a pool on the small of his back.

'No answer to that?' Roger said to him. 'OK, let's get back to Rachel Finch again. When did you start your affair with her?' Roger asked again.

'I told you, we weren't having an affair!' Mal almost shouted back.

'Oh I beg to differ.' Roger responded. 'Mobile phones are great things aren't they? What would we do without texting? I must send about a dozen texts every day to my girlfriend. Big problem with mobiles though is that all the data is recorded. All the numbers you called, all the numbers that called you, all held together in your history, waiting for someone like me to come along and have a nose through. What do you suppose we found when we looked through your phone records Mal?'

Mal reddened, as the realisation hit him that the texts sent were incriminating. 'Ok, I'll put my hands up guys. I was having a fling with Rachel. She was a good-looking woman and damn near threw herself at me. What man could refuse?' He held his hands up in the air, feigning a look of innocence.

'Now, that wasn't so hard was it? So now that we've finally all agreed that you were having an affair with Rachel, maybe you can clear a few things up for me.' Roger said amiably.

'Sure. I'm happy to.' Mal replied in a tone that left no doubt that right now he was far from happy.

'When was the last time you saw Rachel before she died?' Roger asked.

'Let me think.' Mal said, looking up to the ceiling. 'About a week before she died I should think.'

'Really?' Roger replied opening a manila folder in front of him. He started to leaf through the papers that were in the folder.

'Yes I think that's about right.' Mal said again smiling broadly.

'It's just I have a witness who says that you were with Rachel on the day she died.'

Roger enjoyed watching the colour drain from Mal's face.

'Who is this witness?' Mal demanded.

'You're a fan of the club sandwich in the Seafield Hotel aren't you?' Roger said still looking down into his file. He glanced up and enjoyed the startled look that had appeared on Mal's face. He was clearly beginning to get rattled.

'What day was Rachel murdered on again?' he asked Roger. 'Maybe I've gotten my days muddled up.'

'That seems very likely Mal. You see we know that you were in Gorey on the 3rd October, that you withdrew €30 from the AIB bank link machine on the main street. We also know that you then went to the Seafield Hotel and met Rachel in the bar there, and ate your usual club sandwich and fries. So again I'll suggest that you rethink your answer. Were you with Rachel Finch on the day she was murdered?'

'So what if I was!' He shouted back. 'There's no crime with two people having a bite to eat is there?'

'Absolutely not.' Roger replied. 'Calm down, Mal. If you've done nothing wrong, then there's nothing to be afraid of. What time did you and Rachel leave there?'

Mal knew that there was little point in making anything up. The staff there obviously remembered him and had landed him right in it.

'We left there at about 5pm.'

'And where did you go from there?'

'I went home.' He said defiantly. 'I said goodbye to Rachel in the car park and that was the last time I saw her.'

'So you're having an affair with a hot woman and you just have something to eat, then say your goodbyes and that's it?' Johnny asked incredulously.

'Yes. That sounds about right.'

'I find that hard to believe, Mal.' Johnny said with a wink. 'If I was going to risk my marriage by having an affair, I'd at least like to see a bit of action. Don't think a sandwich and a chat would be worth the risk for me!'

'I'm not an animal.' Mal said indignantly. 'We had a sandwich together then we said our goodbyes.'

Roger looked at Johnny and shook his head indicating that they should stop the interview.

'Interview suspended at 1.51 p.m.' Roger said.

'Suspended?' Mal said with irritation in his voice. 'What do you mean suspended? Does that mean I can leave?'

'I'm afraid not, Mal. Let's all just take a break for a short while. Someone will bring you in a coffee. You need to have a good think about what happened the night of the 3rd October. We all know that the last time you saw Rachel wasn't in the Seafield Hotel car park. Don't have me embarrass you again as quite frankly it's getting boring catching you out every five minutes in lies.'

Roger enjoyed seeing the look of panic fleet across Mal's face. He quickly covered this with another broad smile.

'You don't have anything on me!' He said quickly. 'This is actually pathetic watching you guys trying to act all *CSI* Wexford.'

'He's a funny guy.' Johnny said to Roger, shaking his head in mock disbelief. '*CSI* Wexford. I must tell the missus that tonight. She'll enjoy that!'

'And Mal.' Roger said, pausing for a second as he was leaving the room. 'You'd be surprised what jokers like us two have up our sleeves!'

Chapter Twenty Four

Sarah was standing in her local Centra supermarket, admiring her handiwork.

'It looks great.' Colm said walking up behind her.

Sarah turned around to the supermarket manager. 'Do you really think it's ok?'

'Absolutely. I'm tempted to go grab one of those chocolate lads myself!'

'Go ahead.' Sarah said with a broad smile. 'They're delicious, I can promise you!'

'I don't doubt it! And by the way you have your first order already!'

'You're kidding me? Oh that's wonderful.' Sarah said delightedly.

'Yes, Bridie rang earlier to place an order for more logs and I told her we were now stocking the cupcakes, so she has ordered three to be delivered with her fuel!' He laughed as he told her.

Sarah started to giggle. Thank God for Bridie.

'That stand is a great yoke altogether.' Colm said. 'Reminds me of one my granny used to have when I was a little fella. She'd take it out every Sunday when we called to visit.'

'All things retro are very in now.' Sarah replied. 'I wanted to show you something if you have a minute to spare.'

'Fire away.' She opened up her handbag and pulled out some snapshots she'd taken of the christening cupcake she had done for Ella. Colm looked impressed as he looked through them.

'They look great.'

'Cupcakes have been popular for weddings for a good while now. I decided to give them a go for Ella's christening and they went down a treat. All the children at the christening spent ages standing in front of the cake stand, choosing their favourite cupcake. It was hilarious watching them. And I think the adults all enjoyed eating them too!'

'I'm sure they did.'

'So, I was thinking that I'd like to advertise that I can do Angel Cupcakes for special occasions. I've put together some pricing. I thought that for every order you secured I'd pay you commission. I've typed up the details for you to look at.'

'It's not a bad idea at all. Tell you what, let's see how the cakes go over the next few days. If we sell them all in the next forty-eight hours we can then think about this idea of yours.'

Sarah beamed at him. 'Thanks a million. Here's hoping that everyone is hungry for cake!'

She walked back to the car practically floating on air. She just had to hope and pray that the cupcakes sold for her. If they did well at least she had a chance at making a go of her new enterprise. Who needed Paul now?

'Right, time to get home to Ella now'.

Tommy and Katie were in school, although it had been touch and go as to whether it would open or not. The snow was continuing to fall every few hours. Art had sent a text earlier saying that it was possible that school would be closed if it got worse. Paul was with Ella at home. He was leaving for the airport in an hour and called in unexpectedly just as Sarah was about to head to Centra, so she left Ella with him while she made her delivery.

She wondered why he had called in. He'd already said his goodbyes last night to the children when he dropped them home. She'd soon find out she supposed.

Just as she was getting into the car, she stepped on a really bad slippery patch of ice and before she could right herself her legs went from beneath her. She went crashing down to the ground quite hard, winding herself in the process.

As she hit the cold ground and felt the wet, icy snow on the back of her head she saw the strangest thing. Lying beside her in the snow was Paul. She looked at him puzzled. When had he gotten there? What a coincidence that he fell at the same spot as her. Then she quickly thought about Ella. If he was there, where was Ella? She tried to get up and started shouting her name.

'Ella, Ella.' She felt panic rise through her body.

'Are you ok, Sarah?' A voice interrupted her shouts. 'Let me help you up.'

Sarah looked up and saw Colm standing there. He grabbed her hand and pulled her to her feet.

'Ella.' Sarah said again, looking around for her. 'Where's Ella?' She looked down to the ground to ask Paul. But he wasn't there anymore.

'Where's Paul gone?'

'I haven't seen him in months.' Colm replied looking around him, half expecting to see someone standing there.

She looked around and there was no sign of him.

'But he was lying here beside me just now.' Sarah said panicking. 'You must have seen him too. And he has Ella. Where's Ella?' She was getting hysterical now.

'Paul wasn't here I promise you. I saw you fall and came straight out. Honestly. You must have bumped your head harder than I thought. Come in and I'll make you a cup of tea.'

'I have to ring him.'

'Come on in and we'll ring him inside. You're wet through. This bloody snow, I'll be glad when the thaw comes in.'

Once inside the store she picked up her mobile phone and quickly dialled Paul's number.

'What's up?' He said cheerily.

'Where are you? Where's Ella?' she demanded.

'She's at home waiting for you!' he answered, sounding exasperated. 'Where else would we be!'

'Oh, ok. That's great Paul. I'll be home soon.'

'Are you ok?' he asked.

'I fell on the ice, that's all.' Sarah explained. 'I'm fine. I'll be home in a few minutes.'

She sighed with relief and turned back to Colm. 'He's at home.'

'That's good. Now come on, have a cup of coffee.' He'd made one for her while she made the phone call. 'Get warmed up and then I'll drive you home.'

'No, I'm fine, honestly.' Sarah assured him. 'I'll drink the coffee but I'm fine to drive. I just got a scare that was all.'

'Did you bang your head?' He enquired. 'You must have done if you were seeing things. Should I call the doctor?'

'Don't call the doctor, Colm. I'm so sorry for causing all this fuss. I'm fine, I promise you.'

She drank her coffee and after a few more minutes of reassuring him that she was fine, she made her way home.

'Were you checking up on me?' Paul asked her when she got home. 'Did you not think I could cope with Ella on my own for even one hour?'

'No I didn't think that for one moment.' She replied quickly.

He saw how wet her clothes were. 'You're soaked through.'

'I told you, I fell in the snow outside Centra.'

'You ok?'

'Yep, nothing wrong except for feeling like a complete fool!' She answered. 'I'm just going to get changed. I'll be down in a sec.'

What was that all about? She thought to herself. It was so strange. She'd have sworn that Paul had been lying beside her in the snow. Maybe she had banged her head? But it had seemed so real.

She changed quickly and ran downstairs to Paul and Ella.

'So have you two had fun?' She asked them, giving Ella a big kiss on her lips.

'She's just the most amazing little baby.' He said with pride. 'I can't believe how much she's grown in such a short time.'

'I know. A few months is a long time in a baby's world, they change so much so quickly.'

'When she waves at me and says Daddy, it just melts my heart. You're doing a wonderful job with her. With them all.'

'They're good kids.'

'I made some tea.' Paul said, indicating the pot on the kitchen table.

'Thanks.' Sarah replied.

'I want to talk to you about the children. I've just had the best time these past few days. Thank you for making it so easy for me to spend time with them.'

'You're their father. No matter what happens between us, I'll never use them as a weapon. It's very important to me that you are in their lives.'

Paul was silent for a few minutes. 'I've told Michelle last night that I'll be coming home once a fortnight to see them.'

'Good.' Sarah replied.

'She wasn't very happy about it.' He said.

Why didn't that surprise her? Sarah thought.

'She thinks that every two weeks is too often. She wants it to be once a month.'

'I don't believe this.' Sarah said; the annoyance in her voice unavoidable to miss.

He put his hands up in the air. 'Hold your horses. I've told her that no matter what she says, I'll be coming home to the children every fortnight.'

'When the new baby comes it might be a bit tricky for a few weeks to get away.' He added.

'That's fine. I'm reasonable and I'll make sure the children understand that you need to be at home then.'

'I don't want to miss out on any more.' Paul said pointing to Ella, who was happily playing in her playpen.

'There's no reason why you should. I'll not stop you seeing them.' She said truthfully. 'They need you.'

'I've been thinking too that I'll look into transferring back to Ireland again in a year or so. Michelle and the new baby will come with me; that way I'll be closer to the children.' Paul continued.

Sarah was surprised and thought that it was unlikely that he'd actually do that. 'Sounds like a good plan.'

'And as I said the other day, I'll make sure that the maintenance is sorted quickly.'

'Well, I've sent my schedule of expenses to my solicitor. They should be talking today about them I think.'

'I'll ring my solicitor tomorrow morning, Sarah. I promise to not drag it out. You'll have your first maintenance payment in your account by the end of the week.'

'That would be great. I've included how much Christmas presents will cost too. Speaking of which, will you be home for Christmas?'

'I'm not sure yet.' Paul said going red slightly. 'I have to talk to Michelle about it.'

'Well, if you are home for Christmas, you are welcome to come and spend it here with the children and me. But I'm not asking Michelle too. The kids aren't ready for that complication yet. And nor am I.'

'That's decent of you. And if I'm honest, I'm not sure I'm ready for the complication of spending Christmas Day with my ex-wife and pregnant girlfriend either!' He started to chuckle and looked at Sarah, expecting her to be doing the same.

'I'm not ready to joke about this, Paul.' She said quietly. 'If I seem okay about it all, it's because I am doing everything I can to make this transition as easy as possible on the children. But this is very hard for me. I've not yet accepted the fact that you've gotten a new family.' She couldn't believe that Paul thought that she could just snap her fingers and forget about what he'd done to her during the past year.

'I'm sorry.' Paul said. 'Don't think I don't realise how hard this is for you.'

'Well knowing that you'll get the money sorted and come visit the children regularly is making it easier. My biggest concern is that they are okay. I'm an adult, I'll get through this, but they need some kind of normalcy again.'

'I know.' He acknowledged.

'By the way, did you know about this big romance of my Mam's?' He asked. 'Fecking ridiculous!'

Sarah looked up with surprise.

'Rita and a romance? Well she kept that one well hidden! Who with?'

'Some old geezer called Joey apparently. I'm not supposed to know, but I heard her on the phone with him a few times.'

'Joey!' Sarah exclaimed, starting to laugh.

'Do you know him?' Paul asked, his eyes widening.

'Yes I do and so do you! Joey is our postman.' Sarah said with a laugh.

'That bloody old codger.' He said. 'How on earth did she meet our postman?'

'Aw I think it's cute, Paul. And he's a lovely guy as it happens. The children and I have gotten to know him quite well over the past few months. And as for how she met him, I introduced them!'

'I turn my back for five minutes.' Paul grumbled.

'And are they definitely dating?' Sarah asked.

'I asked her last night after I heard her call him "love" on the phone. Love! She says that they are "friends", but every time he rings she jumps up and gets all flushed-looking. It's making me feel sick.'

'Don't be so selfish.' Sarah admonished. 'You're in London and your Mam has been lonely for a long time now. If she can find some happiness with somebody at her age, well good luck to her. And Joey is a really great guy. I think they'll be really good for each other.'

'I suppose.' He responded, sounding very unsure.

'Hadn't you better get moving?' Sarah asked him looking at the clock. She had loads she wanted to do. Apart from doing a couple of loads of laundry, ironing two baskets of clothes, sorting out dinner, she needed to do some work on Angel Cupcakes. She was itching with ideas on how to market her new enterprise. She was planning on checking out Facebook. Ruby had texted her this morning and suggested she do that. Apparently lots of companies had Facebook pages.

She got up to walk Paul to the door. He leaned in again to give her a kiss goodbye and this time she let him kiss her cheek. The familiarity of his touch, his smell, took her to a place where Michelle and London didn't exist. But quickly the pain of knowing that he was no longer hers blindsided her. She pulled away. Then before she had time to gather herself she remembered the flash of him lying in the snow.

Frantically she said, 'Listen to me, Paul. You're to be very careful in this weather. It's treacherous out there. In fact, maybe you should just stay here and travel back to the UK another day?'

'Relax, Sarah. Just because you fell doesn't mean that I will.' He said with a laugh. 'Nice to know you still care though!'

'No you don't understand, and I don't have time to get into it, but Paul, you have to listen to me. I've – I've been having dreams recently. Dreams about things that are going to happen. Dreams that come true.'

'Yeah right!' Paul replied laughing.

'I'm serious. And I'm scared you are going to get hurt.'

'Oh I've heard it all now! Never mind Mystic Meg, more like Septic Peg!' Paul said, bursting out laughing. 'Psychic dreams! Of all the silly things you've ever come out with, Sarah, that takes the biscuit. Is this some kind of attempt to get me to stay here with you? Because if it is, I'm sorry it won't work, I've to get back to London and Michelle. She did say you'd probably try to make me feel guilty and stay with you.' He looked with pity at Sarah.

'Don't be ridiculous!' Sarah replied stung by the look on his face. 'I'm not that desperate I'd make up a story. I'm telling you the truth, believe me or not. You have to be careful. I'm worried for you. I might not like you very much, but I don't want you to get hurt!'

He looked at her face and saw genuine concern. 'Ok, ok, calm down. Are you sure you didn't bump your head earlier?'

'No, I didn't bump my head, but I think you're going to, that's my point!' She said.

'Ok, I promise you. I'll be careful. But you needn't worry, I've got grips on my boots – see?'

Sarah nodded and in fairness he was dressed ready for the snow. She could see that he didn't really believe her but maybe her word of warning would just make him be a little bit more careful. As she had no idea when he was going to fall she had no timeline to guide her when it might happen, it could be years away for all she knew.

She walked to the door and watched him make his way carefully to the car.

Then all of a sudden, 'Help me, Sarah!' He shouted at her. 'I'm slipping!' He had a mischievous twinkle in his eye, one Sarah knew so well, and laughed the whole way to the car as he pretended to fall.

Sarah felt like picking up a lump of snow and throwing it at him. Right then she was glad he was her ex-husband. He was really annoying.

Closing the door behind her though she couldn't get rid of the nagging feeling that something bad was about to happen.

Chapter Twenty Five

Roger was on his way to Wickham Farm. They had Mal in custody and were letting him sweat it out in a cell for a few hours.

He was glad of the break from the interrogation room as he wanted to personally supervise the search warrant. There was a team out on the farm already. Apparently Marie was there too, she had come home from the office and was hysterical. Roger hoped that in her hysteria she might just say something that would help them with their case.

The roads were treacherous. He'd passed a couple of cars already who'd been in a fender bender. Nobody was hurt thankfully, but if the snow kept up like this he was sure that there would be some fatalities from it. Ireland just wasn't geared up for cold spells.

He arrived at the farm and pulled up behind the Gardaí squad cars that were already there. Another car pulled up beside him and he realised it was James.

'What are you doing here?' Roger asked his friend. 'I told you to stay away.' He had called him on the drive over to Rosslare.

'I thought Marie might open up more if I was here.' James said in response. 'I'll not get in the way I promise, it's just I've met Marie before. I might be able to help?'

Roger nodded. Maybe he would come in handy. Standing in the drive, looking half–perished, was Marie. But sure enough she seemed relieved when she saw that James had arrived.

'James. What's going on?' She asked him tearfully. 'Nobody will tell me anything.'

He felt sorry for the woman. She really didn't have a clue who she had married.

'Let's go inside, Marie.' He said to her gently, leading her towards the farmhouse. 'This is Detective Roger McElvoy. He's a good guy honestly. He'll explain everything.'

They walked inside and he brought her over to the Aga stove that was in the kitchen.

'Warm yourself there. I'll make a cup of tea for you.' James said kindly.

He found the kettle and put it on, finding the teapot and cups quickly enough. When the tea was made he poured a large mug for Marie.

'Here, drink this.' He said, as he heaped a couple of spoons of sugar into it.

'All I've been told is that you've got a search warrant. What are you looking for? I don't understand any of this.' She sounded hysterical again.

'Marie, I need you to calm down. Take a sip of the tea.' James said reassuringly.

She did as he asked like an obedient child. 'Where's Mal?'

'Mal is in the station helping us with our murder enquiry.' Roger replied.

'Rachel's murder.' Marie stated flatly.

'Yes, that's right.' Roger replied. 'You don't seem surprised.'

'You think he did it, don't you?' she asked in a small whisper. Roger nodded.

'Have you arrested him?'

'Not yet. At this point we're still questioning him.' He wasn't looking forward to breaking Marie's heart, but she needed to know what was going on. 'I take no pleasure in telling you this, but you have the right to know, Mal has admitted to an affair with Rachel.'

He watched her reaction carefully. She looked shocked at first, and then resignation crept into her face, as if she had been expecting to hear something like this for a long time.

She started to cry quietly. 'I don't know why I'm crying. I knew that he was having an affair already. Or at least I suspected as much.' She picked up a tea towel and used it to wipe away the tears.

James looked closely at the woman in front of him. She barely resembled the glamorous blonde he'd met the first time at Rachel's funeral. Her blonde hair was now streaked with dark roots. She had bags under her eyes and without any make-up on he could see the remnants of a large bruise. She'd also put on quite a bit of weight. He could hardly fathom how a woman could age so much in such a short space of time. It made him so angry to see the physical repercussions of a living with a cruel man.

'Are you okay?' James asked her gently.

'Not really.' She replied. 'I can't get my head around all of this. Ok, I believe he was having an affair. As I said I've suspected it for months. But why do you think he's murdered Rachel?' she finished in a whisper.

'Do you not think he's capable of murder?' James asked her. 'Is he not capable of acts of extreme cruelty? If anyone knows what he's capable of, it will be you Marie. You've lived with him now for a year or so.'

'Oh he's cruel alright.' Marie said, bitterness creeping into her voice.

Roger and James sat there quietly, waiting for her to continue.

'You know he hits me almost on a daily basis now.' She continued in a whisper. 'Anything seems to trigger him off. I used to get really upset that he would be out all evening. I knew he was with another woman. But lately, I've been praying that he'll go out and stay out all night. That way I'll not be on the end of his fist.'

'I'm so sorry.' James said to her.

'Why are you sorry? It's not your fault.' She replied tartly. 'It's my bad. Marry in haste, repent in leisure, isn't that what they

218

say? I just thought he was the perfect man. He was so charming when we met and I fell in love with him so deeply,' She smiled at the memory. 'I thought we'd have children together and grow old together. That's not going to happen now is it?'

'It can still happen.' James replied, grabbing her two hands between his own. 'But just not with him. You hold onto that same dream and one day in the future you'll meet the right guy and he'll treat you with the love and respect you deserve and I've no doubt you'll have those children you crave.'

She smiled at James, 'You're a kind man. I'm not so sure I believe you though.'

She picked up her tea again. 'What are you looking for outside?'

'The murder weapon.' Roger replied. 'Can you think back to October 3rd, the night of Rachel's death? Can you remember what time Mal came home that night? We know he was with her that evening. Anything at all that might help us.'

Marie closed her eyes and rested her head on her hands. She felt so tired and she just wanted to pack a bag and drive home to her parent's house in Dublin. She needed to feel the warmth of their love; she needed her Dad to tell her that everything was going to be ok and her Mam to fuss about her and tuck a blanket around her legs.

'I don't know. I can't think. My head is about to burst!' she shouted, tears falling again.

'Marie, I believe that Mal murdered Rachel Finch brutally. She may not have been a good friend to you; in fact it's fair to say that she treated your friendship appallingly. So I can understand you feeling angry with her for having the affair. But you're a decent woman, I can see that. No matter what she did to you, you answer me this, did she deserve to die in such a brutal and callous way?' Roger pressed on.

Marie shook her head. 'No, she didn't deserve that.' She replied quietly. 'Nobody deserves that. But what can I do about it now?' She started to cry again.

Roger needed her to toughen up if he was going to get any answers from her. She was falling apart in front of his eyes.

'Marie, you listen to me. Your husband is a vicious man. Look what he's done to you. You've admitted that he hits you on a daily basis. What else is he capable of? You can walk away now and pretend that none of this is happening. But could you sleep at night knowing that you may have helped a murderer go free? You can help us ensure that Mal never gets out of jail and hurts you or any other woman again.'

Marie stood up from the table and walked to the kitchen window, wiping her face once again with the tea towel. Mascara was running down her cheeks, a black river, her nose was running. She sniffed and turned around to face Roger.

'I do remember that night.' She said quietly. 'To the day I die, I'll never forget it.'

Roger looked at her, feeling his pulse quicken. This was it. 'Tell me about it.'

'Mal didn't come home until almost 3am. I know that for definite because I was awake waiting for him and when he pulled into the drive I looked at the clock.'

'That's good. You're doing brilliantly.'

'I was so angry with him. It had been weeks and weeks of him not coming home till all hours and he never had a reasonable explanation. He was so offhand with me whenever I asked what he was doing. I didn't need to be Einstein to know that something was going on. That night I'd had enough and I was determined to confront him once and for all.'

'Were you not scared?' James asked her.

'I was , but I was more angry, I suppose, so I ran outside to ask him where he'd been and was surprised to see that he wasn't on his way inside at all. I remember thinking that was very odd. I went looking for him and found him in the barn.'

'And would he normally go to the barn when he got home?' Roger asked.

'No, that's why I remember it so clearly. It didn't make sense to me that he would go out there at three in the morning. When I got to the barn he was over at the wood pile.'

'What was he doing?' Roger asked.

'He had his back to me, so I couldn't really see. But he was definitely putting something on top of it.'

'Could you guess what it was that he put on there?' Roger asked.

'No, as I said, he had his back to me and I couldn't see properly. I asked him what he was doing and he said that he'd been sorting out firewood.'

'Did you not think that was strange?' Roger asked her.

'Yes of course I did. But it was his face that I remember the most. He looked guilty when he turned around and saw me. It was like I had interrupted him doing something wrong. But then he seemed relieved that it was only me there.'

'If you had to guess as to what he was doing, could you?' Roger asked.

'I suppose he looked like he was hiding something.' Marie replied.

'Did you question him about it at all?'

'I was scared to. He got very angry with me. And there was something else too. When he walked into the house, he trailed sand into the hall carpet.'

Bingo, James thought.

'Surely that must have made you curious as to why he had sand on his feet?' Roger asked again.

'It did and I was going to say something to him about the sand, but he was in a temper and I was afraid to upset him further. So I decided not to say anything more on the subject. Didn't matter though, despite me saying nothing he still lost his temper with me.'

'What happened?' Roger asked gently.

'When he went to bed, I got back up and went out to the barn. I couldn't shake the memory of how guilty he'd looked when I interrupted him. I wanted to see what he'd put on the woodpile.'

Roger was holding his breath. 'What did you see?' He asked her quickly.

'Nothing really unusual or so I thought at the time. It was just the usual load of chopped wood piled there. But underneath a couple of logs, sticking out slightly, was a lump of driftwood, it was really worn and aged. It looked odd lying there among the freshly cut logs. It stood out I suppose.'

'Did you see anything else?' Roger asked with hope.

'I don't know. Because the next thing I knew somebody was grabbing my hair from behind. Mal had woken up and followed me to the barn. He was furious with me for going out there.'

If it was possible for her face to go even paler, it had just happened. She was deeply distressed remembering that night, it was evident to see.

'He slammed me hard onto the floor of the barn. I felt winded, it had happened so quickly. I thought my head was about to explode into two. He was standing over me, shouting at me for being a nosy bitch. With every shout he kicked me, over and over again.'

Roger felt the bile rise in his mouth. He had dealt with domestic violence several times in his career and it was one of the parts of his job that he hated. He felt guilty just for being a man, listening to what some women had to go through.

'I begged him to stop. Please Mal, I'm sorry. I won't do it again. Please stop. It hurt so much, but he didn't stop.'

'I had to take a week off work after that. I was black and blue from head to toe.'

James wanted to kill Mal himself. He didn't care what happened; he was going to get that bastard even if the Gardaí didn't.

'Do you know what I remember the most about that night, James?' James shook his head.

'His face as he kicked me and hit me. He was smiling. He enjoyed it.'

They were both silent for a few moments. James felt that anything he could say right then would only be trite.

'So you can see that the reason I remember that day so well, is because that night was the first night that Mal hit me. One minute I was out at the log pile, the next minute I was barely conscious on the barn floor.'

She was crying again, the memories flooding back. She was a victim in this too and Roger made a silent vow that he wouldn't rest until Mal Wickham was behind bars.

'Marie, I'll need you to come into the station and make a formal statement about everything that happened that night.'

She looked scared again. 'He'll kill me.' She said. 'He told me that night if I ever spoke of what happened he'd kill me. I believed him.'

'If you make that statement it's going to help make sure that Mal Wickham never kills anyone ever again, I promise you. I'll make sure you are protected, I just need your help first of all.'

'I'll do it.' She said, a hint of strength coming back into her voice. 'I want to go home to Dublin to my parents though; can I leave?'

'Of course you can. Why don't you pack a bag now and then come back to the station with me. I'll make sure someone drops you to the train station afterwards personally. You can't drive in these conditions and frankly I don't think you're in any fit state to.'

'I'll go with you, Marie.' James said kindly. 'I'll drive you to the train afterwards myself.'

She stood up and headed towards the stairs, stopping suddenly to say, 'You'll not find anything on that log pile now you know. He put that piece of driftwood on the fire the next day, I watched him do it. And we ran out of logs last week. The stuff that's out there is a new load that Mal brought home a few days ago.'

'Damn.' Roger said under his breath. He'd not really believed that Wickham was stupid enough to leave the murder weapon just lying around, but it would have been nice. Still at least he had Marie's statement now. It was only circumstantial evidence again, but it was all beginning to add up. Surely it would be enough to get a conviction?

Chapter Twenty Six

The phone rang suddenly, Sarah ran to answer it.

'Hi Sarah, it's Colm here from Centra.'

'Oh hello is everything ok?' Sarah asked. All of a sudden the thought that she might have poisoned half of the village crossed her mind. She wondered if she could be arrested for that, a crime of cupcakes!

'Not a bother. I'm just ringing to let you know that those cupcakes have gone down a treat. I've sold every single one of them already!'

Sarah wanted to whoop out loud, she was so happy. But she took a deep breath instead, thinking it was best not to frighten Colm with shrieks!

'Are you still there?' Colm asked.

'Sorry, yes I'm here.' Sarah replied, her voice full of emotion. 'I'm just so relieved that they sold so quickly. I was half afraid you were ringing to ask me to take them back!'

'Not at all, in fact if you can get me another two dozen tomorrow I'll take them again.'

'I could try some more flavours if you like.' Sarah offered.

'What do you have in mind?'

'Well, I was thinking about doing some Christmas cupcakes, with cranberry and pear in them?'

'Sure we'll have some of those, so.'

'I have the most beautiful cupcake cases for them. They're white and look like lace. I think they look very Christmassy.'

'It all sounds good to me.' Colm said. 'I'll tell you what; I'll trust your judgement on what flavours you want to sell. But I have to tell you, the chocolate ones grabbed the kid's attention. They're a winner.'

'Yes, I'll definitely include the chocolate Rocky Road again. How about I make a dozen of those and a dozen Christmas cupcakes?'

'Do you know what? I'm feeling reckless. Throw in another dozen of a different flavour too. If they go as quickly as the ones today I'll need more anyhow.'

'That's great. I appreciate you giving me this chance.' Sarah said gratefully.

'Oh, it's my pleasure. And I've already told the girls at the check-outs to start spreading the word about taking orders for special occasions too. And while we're on the subject of special occasions, I'll give you your first order. It's our wedding anniversary next week. Think I might surprise the wife by cooking a meal. Did you mention you could do cupcakes for desserts?'

'I most certainly can. I've quite a few that would be beautiful for a special meal. I could do a lovely Banoffi cupcake or perhaps a Black Forest cupcake if you prefer. Both are with fresh cream and make a lovely dessert. I've another idea I've been thinking of too. How does a vanilla and white chocolate cheesecake cupcake sound to you?'

'Oh I'm licking my lips listening to all of those! Tell you what; the wife loves cheesecake, so I'll have six of those for next Monday.'

'I'm writing it down now. I'll hand deliver them to you person-ally and make sure that they are just perfect to help make your meal special.'

She opened her laptop up and set up a template for orders. She would print out a dozen or so of the order forms and drop them in with the cakes tomorrow. She wanted to be prepared just in case anyone else wanted to order special occasion cakes. She listed the flavours she was going to sell indicating that the minimum order of these would be six. She then went onto eBay and found a stockist who sold little boxes that she could put her cakes in. She also found some ribbon in different colours that she could use to tie around the boxes. Sarah knew that packaging was extremely important. She wanted the cupcakes to be a whole experience for the buyer, not just a special treat. eBay was fast becoming her best friend these days, she thought. She even had cash in her PayPal account from the sale of the handbags and shoes to pay for the supplies. It was all coming together nicely.

All of a sudden she could feel excitement bubbling up inside of her and she was energised! She hadn't felt so young and carefree in such a long time and she simply couldn't sit still. She jumped up and started pacing the floor, her mind exploding with possibilities. The business would work and it would help her current financial situation, she just knew it.

Suddenly Katie appeared before her, she had just been dropped home from school by a neighbour and she was also beside herself with excitement for a different reason!

'There's no school tomorrow, Mammy!' Katie screamed with delight as she ran into her arms.

Ella couldn't stop squealing with excitement as she watched her Mama and her big sister run around the house whooping.

'I'm sorry I didn't quite catch that. What did you say about school again?' Sarah teased tickling her daughter.

'No school, no school, no school!' Katie continued screaming, running around in circles in their kitchen.

'Alright monkey, go get changed out of your uniform.' Sarah said to her daughter. 'Where's Tommy, did he go straight to his room?' With all the excitement she must have missed him.

'I don't know, Mammy.' Katie replied. 'He came home at lunch.'

'What do you mean he came home at lunch?' Sarah said as her stomach flipped.

'He told me at lunch that he was going to come home to see Daddy. I told him that he would be in trouble.' Katie said looking worried. 'Is he in trouble?'

Sarah's heart sped up and prickles of sweat began to form on her forehead, as she began shouting for her son, running around each room, one by one. But there was no sign of him anywhere. She could feel the blood draining from her face.

She picked up her phone and called Art. He answered pretty quickly.

'Is Tommy at school still?'

'No. Not as far as I'm aware. All the kids are gone home. What's up?'

Sarah told him what Katie had said. 'I'm going to go talk to Tommy's teacher. I'll ring you back in a minute.' Art replied.

Sarah texted James quickly and asked him to come over.

The phone rang and it was Art who confirmed that Tommy had gone home at lunchtime and had given his teacher a note from Sarah, saying he had permission to leave early to say goodbye to his father.

'I didn't sign any note.' Sarah said to Art, panic making her voice rise several notes.

'I tell you what; I'm going to look around the school and double check that he's not still here. And then I'll walk to your house. Retrace his footsteps.' Art replied calmly.

'Where is he?' Sarah said, panic now really taking over.

'We'll find him.' He promised. 'Keep your phone with you and we'll stay in touch.'

Katie was standing watching her mother anxiously.

'What exactly did Tommy say to you, Katie?' Sarah asked her. 'Don't worry, no one is in trouble.'

'He said that he was going to talk to Daddy man to man and tell him that he had to come home. He said he was going to make him stay with us Mammy.' Katie said tearfully. 'Did he make Daddy stay?'

227

Sarah cursed Paul once again.

'Don't worry.' Sarah told her. 'Mammy needs to make a phone call. You watch your little sister for me.'

She ran around each of the rooms in the house once more and checked and double checked in case Tommy was actually at home and hiding somewhere. It wouldn't be the first time that he had played hide and seek with her. But despite a thorough search, there was no sign of him.

Art called and said that he'd checked the school and hadn't found Tommy either so was going to walk up to their house.

She had a terrible feeling of foreboding. She called Paul, but just got his voicemail. He should be at home in London by now she assumed. She left him a message and decided to call Rita. She might need Rita to come mind the children, so she could go look for Tommy. Where was he? She felt tears prick her eyes again but shook them off. She didn't have the time or the luxury to fall apart right now.

She sat down and closed her eyes in an effort to compose herself before she rang Rita. And then suddenly Tommy's face flashed into her mind. She recognised that she was having another vision.

She is with the children in their hall, she can see snow falling outside, a white carpet on their driveway. Tommy is laughing and asks her, 'You want to hear a good joke about the snow, Mammy?'

'I can hardly wait!' Sarah replies smiling back at him.

'What two letters of the alphabet do snowmen prefer?' He asks with a grin. 'Bet you can't guess!'

'Oh that's a tricky one. Go on tell me.'

'I.C.' He declares loudly, bursting into giggles. 'Do you get it Mammy? I.C. is like Icy!' He explains.

'Oh I got it alright, it was very good! I like that one.' Sarah ruffles his hair affectionately and pushes him towards the hall. 'Now get changed!'

'Nope, first of all, it's conga time, Mammy!' he squeals.

Katie starts whooping with delight at this and they both quickly form a conga line behind their Mammy.

'Here's to Angel Cupcakes, here's to Angel Cupcakes, lalalala, lala-lala!' They all chorus before falling to the ground in a heap giggling.

'Does this mean we're rich now that you have the big order from Colm?' Katie asks, her eyes are alight thinking up things she can buy.

'No, not rich yet honey, but let's just say that Christmas is no longer cancelled!' Sarah replies laughing. 'I tell you what; I need a logo for my Angel Cupcakes business. I've found a place online that will do stickers for me and if I send them a photograph of my logo they'll put it on the labels for me. Could you both work on some drawings for me?'

'What will we draw?' Tommy asks.

'Angels and cupcakes silly!' Katie replies throwing her eyes up to heaven. 'Don't worry, Mammy, I'll make sure he does something nice.'

'I know he's in safe hands with you Katie.' Sarah answers her mock-seriously.

Sarah felt her heart contract with love as she the scene unfolded in her vision. She knew that it was what *should* have happened today had Tommy come home.

She sets the dining room table with paper and colouring pencils and soon they are busy working away on their designs. Tommy is drawing a cupcake and Katie is working on an angel. She laughs again at Katie who has her tongue stuck out, as she always does when she is concentrating hard.

'Mammy. Mammy. Mammy.' Katie's frightened voice brought Sarah crashing back from her vision. She had tears falling down her face. Where was Tommy? Why hadn't he come home? She thought she might vomit, her stomach was actually heaving in fear at the possibilities that were racing around her mind.

'I'm scared.' Katie said to her.

'I know, sweetheart.' Sarah said scooping her daughter into her arms. She needed to get Rita over quickly to look after the girls. She had phone calls to make. Maybe Tommy had gone to one of his friends' houses. But in the meantime, Sarah knew she had to find something to distract Katie. Then she had an idea, using the vision for inspiration, she said to her daughter, 'Katie, could you do a drawing for me, a picture that I could use on my leaflets to sell my cupcakes? That would be such a help.'

Katie was extremely excited to do this and quickly ran to her bedroom saying she would get her art supplies.

Sarah picked up the phone again and rang Paul, still no answer.

She then called Rita. 'Tommy hasn't come home from school and I'm getting worried. I've been trying to get hold of Paul but his phone is going straight to voicemail. Have you heard from either of them?'

'Oh good lord!' Rita exclaimed. 'I haven't heard a thing. But I wasn't expecting Paul to call. I'll try to get him for you.'

'Can you come over here? I need you to watch the girls, I think I'd better go look for him.' Sarah said sobbing.

'I'm on my way.' Just then the doorbell rang. Sarah ran to open it, praying it would be Tommy. But it was Art.

Taking one look at Sarah's face he concluded correctly that Tommy wasn't home.

'There's no sign of him at school or between there and here. I checked the playground and the football pitch. They were deserted in this weather.' Art told her. 'Have you tried any of his friends?'

'I've been trying to get hold of my husband but haven't got an answer and I've called my mother-in-law, she's on her way over. I was just about to start calling his friends. Katie has confessed that he was coming home at lunchtime because he wanted to see Paul before he left for London. But he must have missed him. I just don't understand where he is. He'd never not come home, he knows I'd be worried sick.'

'I'll start ringing his classmates.' Art said. 'I have the entire class and their parents' numbers on this.' He pointed to his Blackberry. 'You keep trying to get Paul.'

'But why would he be at friend's house if he left school at lunchtime?' Sarah asked. 'Did one of Tommy's friends take the afternoon off too?'

'No, I'm afraid not.' Art replied. He'd checked the very same thing earlier. 'I know it doesn't make sense, but maybe one of his friends knows where he is. He might have confided in one of them what he was up to. I'll try Alan first of all; those two are thick as thieves.' He looked at Sarah intently for a moment, then continued, 'Is there any chance he's run away?'

Sarah was despondent at the thought that she and Paul had screwed up their son's life so badly that he would choose to run away rather than come home. She thought they had a better relationship than that. They were close. Or at least she believed they were.

'I don't believe he would run away.' Sarah said. 'But who knows? He seems happier these past few weeks, since his Daddy came back to visit.'

She heard Edward's voice whisper to her. 'Trust your instincts, Sarah. Listen.'

Sarah closed her eyes and pictured her son's face. She was certain of one thing. 'Tommy hasn't run away.' She stated. Then continued, more firmly, 'don't ask me how I know that for certain, but I do. If he's not here, he's in trouble of some sort. So we have to find him. Please ring his friends, but if there is no sign of him within the hour, I'm calling the Gardaí.'

Chapter Twenty Seven

James walked back to his car from the train station and as he walked he picked up his phone and rang Ruby.

'Hello, James. Are you ok?' Her beautiful voice felt like a caress. She sounded concerned about him. He liked it.

'Hi, beautiful.' He replied. All the years he'd spent making up cheesy lines for different girls, what had he been thinking of? He'd wasted so much time on those other women.

'How's the case going?' She asked him earnestly, she knew all about the murder case now, just not Sarah's involvement.

'It's been a long day, I won't lie. I've just dropped Marie Wickham to the train; she's on her way home to her parents. Mal is still in custody and Roger and the lads are questioning him. Roger said that he's a tough nut to crack, he's not sure he'll admit to anything.'

'They have to find a way!' Ruby said to him. 'I dread to think of someone like him loose on the streets. They will find the evidence they need to arrest him, they have to. You made this happen James. I'm so proud of you.'

He felt he was ten feet tall when she complimented him.

'It can't have been easy for you today, though.' Ruby continued, frowning with worry.

'To be honest, today was horrific. Listening to Marie Wickham talking about the awful time she's had with that bastard, so much abuse. I still feel sick when I think of what he's done to her.' James admitted.

Ruby shivered. 'You have to be careful. He's obviously a dangerous man. What if he finds out you helped the Gardaí?' She sounded worried.

'Don't worry about me, beautiful.' He replied. 'I'm going to be just fine. I just wish I could see you right this minute. I wouldn't say no to a hug right now.'

'Come on over. I'm home. Maybe I can find a way to de-stress you?' She teased and James could hear the smile in her voice.

'You're trying to get me to crash the car!' James groaned. There was nothing he would have loved more right this minute. 'But I can't right now. I've had a text and couple of missed calls from Sarah. She wants me to call over. Don't know what's up, but she sounded stressed, so I'm going to head there now.'

'Oh, I hope all is ok.' Ruby replied. 'Tell you what; I'll meet you over there too.'

James marvelled at how he felt better at just hearing her voice. It helped balance out the negative energy he got from talking about scumbags like Mal Wickham.

He should have told her he loved her, he thought when he hung up the phone. Because he knew without a shadow of a doubt that he was in love. But saying it on the end of a phone wasn't really romantic, maybe it was better that he kept it to himself for a bit longer. He thought she felt the same way, but maybe he was wrong. He felt slightly panicked just thinking that she didn't feel the same way about him.

He shook the feeling away quickly. He dialled Sarah's number quickly to check up on her.

'Paul?' Sarah asked when she answered the phone.

'Nope, it's James.' He replied. 'All ok?'

'Where the hell are you?' Sarah answered sobbing. 'Tommy is missing.'

James nearly dropped the phone he got such a fright from her words. 'I'm on my way. Have you rung the Gardaí?'

'Yes.' Sarah replied. 'Please hurry,' she ended in almost a whisper.

He buckled up and drove as quickly as he could to her house.

Chapter Twenty Eight

'How long more is this going to go on for?' Mal demanded. 'I have rights you know. I'm entitled to make a phone call!'

'I have absolutely no problem whatsoever with that.' Roger replied. 'Once we've finished this interview you are free to make that call.'

'My wife will be concerned.' Mal responded. 'She worries about me.'

Roger once again marvelled at the gall of this guy. 'Don't worry about Marie, she's perfectly fine.' Roger said.

'You've been speaking to her? Is she here?' Mal demanded.

'She was here earlier, yes.'

'Why wasn't I told? She must be beside herself.' Mal said.

'She was upset, but that's to be expected when you find out that your husband has been having an affair with one of your friends.' Roger replied dryly.

'You had no right to tell her that!' Mal exploded. 'It's not what you think!'

'Tell us what we think? Enlighten me.' Roger said.

'You think I murdered Rachel Finch, go on, and just say it!' He said. 'But I didn't and you've no proof. If you had, you'd have arrested me by now!' He looked triumphantly at both Roger and Johnny.

'Patience, Mr Wickham.' Johnny said quietly. 'All good things and all that.'

'What did you tell my Marie?' Mal said. 'If you've upset her I'll be talking to your superiors!'

'I'm shaking in my boots!' Johnny said to him.

'I mean it, if you've done anything to damage my marriage, I'll…'

'You'll what? Bludgeon us to death with a piece of driftwood?' Roger shouted at him.

'No, of course not!' He exclaimed. He looked from one of them to the other, then fell silent, obviously pondering his next move.

'Marie has been most helpful in our investigation. I'm sure that will please you.' Roger said to Mal.

'What do mean by that?' Mal asked. Roger watched him closely. He could practically hear his brain ticking over as he went through possible scenarios.

'Let's cut the bullshit and talk about what really happened the night of 3rd October. We have finally all agreed that you had something to eat in the Seafield Hotel with Rachel Finch. Tell me what happened next.'

'I went home and watched TV, then went to bed.'

'Really? That's very strange because we have a signed statement from your wife stating that you didn't come home until almost 3 am that night.'

'You're looking a bit peaky there, Mal.' Johnny decided it was time to start poking the bear again.

Mal picked up his water and took a sip. 'She must have gotten it wrong; she probably muddled up her days.'

'I'm not surprised considering the amount of times you've hit her!' Roger shouted at him.

Mal recoiled back from him. 'I've never laid a hand on her, if she said anything different she's lying!'

'I don't think so somehow or other. Do you want to know why she is so certain about the time you got home at on that night? It's quite simple really – you see that date is imprinted on her brain. Do you have any idea why that date is so unforgettable for her?'

Mal shook his head.

'Well it seems that you were a busy boy on the 3rd October. After you murdered Rachel, you went home and beat the crap out of your wife, on the barn floor.'

'Nice guy.' Johnny said raising his glass of water to Mal.

'No! I most certainly did not!' Mal exploded.

'What are you saying no to? Just out of curiosity which of the two things are you denying? Is it the murder of your mistress or the beating up of your wife?' Roger asked him.

'I deny both! I never laid a hand on either of them.' He protested. 'She's making it all up just to get back at me because I had an affair!'

'Well somebody sure as hell laid more than a hand on Rachel Finch.' Johnny remarked. 'Who do you suppose that was?'

'I never touched her! She was fine when I left her.'

'Unfortunately Rachel is not here to back up that story.' Roger said to him mildly. 'Your wife Marie however is very much here and she had some interesting things to say to us about that night.'

'It's all lies. She's always been venomous!' he spat at them.

'Make you mind up, dude.' Johnny said to him. 'One minute you say that she'll be beside herself with concern for you, the next she's a right evil cow. I'm getting confused here!'

Johnny turned to Roger then and said, 'If looks could kill…'

Roger smiled at Johnny; he was playing a blinder. 'Well, you'll have to let me know exactly where you were between 5pm and 3am that night, Mal. Because right now from where I'm sitting, it's not looking too good for you! So far you're the last person to see Rachel alive. And despite saying you went home after you said goodbye to her, your wife states that this is absolutely not true.'

'I can't remember where I was.' Mal said lamely. 'I think maybe I went for a drive. The more I think about it that's what I did do. I was just feeling so guilty about my indiscretion with Rachel, I needed time to think, to sort my head out.'

'I suppose there's nothing quite like a long drive for hours and hours to help clear a conscience.' Johnny remarked. He was happy to see that his little needles were really irritating Mal. He intended to continue poking the bear until he got a reaction.

'So while you were having this long drive, where did Rachel go?' Roger asked.

'She said she was going to get her dog and then go for a walk.'

'That makes sense.' Roger said to him. 'And you didn't feel like a walk yourself?'

'No, I told you I said goodbye to her at the hotel.'

'So you said. But I'm finding that hard to believe somehow.'

'It's true; you'll have to take my word for it.' Mal said defiantly.

'I'm afraid I won't be doing anything of the kind.' Roger replied. 'You see you've lied to me at least three times that I can recall so far today.'

'More like four times.' Johnny piped in.

'So you can see where I have a dilemma. If you've lied to me so much already, why should I believe you now? So on this long drive of yours, you say you drove continuously for hours and hours?'

'Yes, right up to nearly 3am.' Mal answered quickly.

'Did you stop anywhere for coffee or something to eat maybe? There could be somebody who could come forward and confirm your whereabouts then?'

'No, I didn't stop anywhere. I just drove and then I went home.' Mal replied.

'So you drove from roughly 5pm till roughly 3am. That's a lot of driving.' Roger said to him.

'I had a lot of thinking to do.' Mal responded, sarcasm beginning to edge its way into his voice again.

'So it appears.' James replied. 'But in this long drive of yours, surely with all those miles you must have clocked up, you'd need to get petrol.'

Mal looked up startled at this.

'You hadn't thought of that had you?' Johnny said with a smile. 'If you're going to go making things up, you're going to have to get a little bit cleverer with your lies mate!'

'I did get petrol, I've just remembered.' Mal answered.

'Where and what time did you get this petrol?' Roger shouted back at him.

'I can't remember.' Mal said to him, lifting his chin defiantly. 'Do you remember every petrol station you ever go into?'

'That's a valid point.' Roger replied. 'However, the great thing about modern technology is that it's not necessary to remember every detail such as that. We have things like bank statements and mobile phones and they can paint quite a picture when we start to look into the secrets they hold. I have your bank statements, Mal. And the thing that really puzzles me is that on the 3rd October there isn't a mention of you buying petrol anywhere.'

'I must have paid cash.' Mal responded.

'Oh that would clear that one up. That's very plausible.' Roger said amicably.

Mal looked relieved to hear the detective say that.

'I have a slight problem with that though. Do you know what the definition of a pattern is Mal?'

Mal looked confused and shook his head.

'For the benefit of the recording, Mr Wickham said no. Well, let me illuminate you. A pattern is a type of theme of recurring events or objects, sometimes referred to as elements of a set of objects. And these elements always repeat in a predictable manner.'

'Very interesting.' Johnny said to Roger.

'It is because I have Mal Wickham's bank statements here in front of me and I can see quite a pattern in the entries here.'

'I'm on the edge of my seat.' Johnny responded.

Mal looked more and more worried as the exchange continued.

'He always pays for his petrol with his laser card. Isn't that correct, Mr Wickham?' he shouted to him, throwing the statements down in front of him.

'So I'm surprised that you broke your usual routine and paid for your petrol on this occasion with cash. The very time that you need some proof of your whereabouts.'

'Sounds a bit dubious to me.' Johnny remarked to Roger.

'I thought so too.' Roger replied. 'What do you think Mal?'

'What can I say?' Mal said sarcastically. 'I fancied a change!'

'OK so where did you buy this petrol? We'll send someone off immediately to check their CCTV and we'll clear this whole misunderstanding up. We can have you home in a few hours. I'll even drive you myself.'

Mal didn't answer.

'You take a sec there; we have all the time in the world.' Roger responded.

'I can't remember the name of the garage.' Mal whispered back.

'What was that?' Johnny said. 'You'll have to speak up.'

'I said I didn't remember the name of the garage.' He shouted back. 'I've had enough of this, it's harassment!' He pounded on the desk with his fist, his face purple with rage.

'That's some temper you have on you.' Johnny said to him. 'It'll get you into trouble one day.'

'Is that what happened with Rachel?' Roger said to him. 'She made you lose your temper? Something snapped and you just went for it. Maybe it all got out of control?'

Mal took a deep breath and smiled sweetly at them both. 'I don't remember the name of the garage; I've nothing else to say on the matter. It's the truth,' he said, smiling at Johnny. 'what would you have me do, make up the name of a garage just to appease you?'

'Well let's try to narrow it down a bit. What time did you stop for petrol at? What town were you in? Help me help you.' Roger said.

'I can't remember, how many times do I have to tell you?'

'Maybe you don't remember where you stopped for petrol because it's another lie.' Roger said raising his voice again. 'Let's just cut the crap. We all know that you went to Ballyaislinn beach with Rachel Finch and you murdered her there. Just be a man and admit it and then we can all leave this bloody interview room!'

'I told you, I didn't go to Ballyaislinn beach and I didn't murder Rachel Finch.'

Roger stood up and leaned over the table. 'I've another question for you Mal. When you stopped at this unknown garage to buy this imaginary petrol, at a time that you can't remember, in a place you don't remember driving to, did they sell you firewood too?'

Mal looked startled at this line of enquiry. 'No. I didn't buy any firewood. What kind of question is that?'

'The regular kind.' Roger answered tersely. 'I just wondered where you bought the firewood.'

'I told you I never bought any firewood.'

'Well that's very strange, because in the statement we obtained from your wife, she stated that when you returned home at 3am, instead of going inside straight away, you went to the barn and put something on the wood pile.'

Mal slumped back in his chair.

'Lost for words for once, I see.' Johnny said.

'Would you ever just shut the fuck up?' Mal shouted at Johnny jumping to his feet. 'I've had enough of this harassment!'

'There's that temper again.' Johnny said, smirking back at him. 'I did warn you it would get you into trouble.'

Mal sat down again and said, 'I've had enough of this. I'll not say another word until I get my lawyer here.'

Chapter Twenty Nine

Rita and Joey arrived at Sarah's house. 'Any sign of them?' Rita asked immediately.

Sarah shook her head. 'I'm expecting James any minute. This is Art, Tommy's principal.'

'Has Paul arrived back in London yet? Sarah asked.

'No. I'm starting to get worried now. I rang Michelle earlier after I spoke to you. I couldn't get any answer on Paul's phone. She said he wasn't home yet and to be honest she gave me short thrift. She didn't seem too worried about the fact that he'd not arrived home.'

'She was bloody rude to you!' Joey interjected, annoyed on Rita's behalf.

He threw his eyes up to the ceiling.

'I didn't think too much about it at first, thought the flight he was on must have been delayed. As Michelle didn't seem worried, I thought no point in me fretting. But then Michelle rang me back.' Rita went on. 'She was extremely irate, shouting that she wanted to speak to Paul. I told her that he'd left here hours before, but she kept screaming abuse down the phone. It was as if she thought I was hiding him in the house or something.'

'She seems a bit unstable if you ask me.' Joey said.

'I'm going to give her the benefit of the doubt, maybe she was just upset.' Rita replied.

'You always think the best of people, love.' Joey said with a note of pride in his voice.

Rita smiled at the intimate use of the word love. Sarah noticed it too but right at this minute didn't have the inclination to acknowledge their happiness. When her little boy was safe at home with her, then she would.

The doorbell rang and this time it was James, followed closely by Ruby. 'What's going on, Sarah?'

'Tommy is missing and I think that Paul is missing too.'

'Paul's missing again?' James said incredulously. 'Sure, we've only just found him!'

'I think Paul could be hurt.' Sarah whispered to him, pulling him away from Ruby and the others. 'I had one of my visions today.'

Sarah filled him in on what she'd felt when she fell on the ice. 'But right now I'm more worried about Tommy.'

'Is there any chance that Tommy is actually with Paul?' James asked.

'I don't know.' Sarah responded. 'But if he was, surely he'd have called me to tell me? Why would he keep that from me, he would know I'd be frantic?'

'It doesn't make sense for it to be anything else though. Tommy leaves school at lunchtime to talk to Paul and now Paul and Tommy are both missing. Was Paul acting weird? Would he snatch Tommy?' James asked.

'Never!' Rita exclaimed, walking over to them. 'I know my son and I know he's got a lot of faults, but he'd never take Tommy from Sarah or his sisters.'

Sarah agreed with Rita. Something didn't feel right.

'Trust your instinct. Listen.' She heard Edward whisper.

She glanced over at Art who was playing Guess Who with Katie. He glanced up at her and held her gaze. It was good of him to stay.

She walked towards Tommy's bedroom. Sitting on his bed she closed her eyes and concentrated, thinking of her son. And then she saw him. And she knew where he was.

Paul is smiling as he drives out of her driveway. He is oblivious to the fact that Tommy is crouching down on the floor of the back seat, out of sight.

'Tommy is with Paul. He's with Paul.' She shouted as she ran back into the living room. 'He hid in the back of Paul's car. Paul didn't know he was there when he left here to go to the airport.' She started to shake.

'How do you know that?' Rita asked.

Sarah ignored her question.

'That's good.' James said. 'Now we know where he is. He's safe with Paul.'

Sarah screamed. 'You don't understand. He's not safe. Paul is in danger. I told you that. And that means so is Tommy. Edward where are they, god damn it, just tell me where they are?'

'Who's Edward?' Joey asked looking around.

Rita shrugged in response, tears in her own eyes. 'What do you mean Paul is in danger and Tommy too, Sarah? I don't understand what she's saying.' Joey put his arm around her.

Sarah ignored her mother in law and screamed again, 'Edward don't you dare give me one more line of bullshit telling me to trust my instincts. Just tell me where they are!'

Rita and Joey looked at the wall where Sarah was screaming, puzzled. Art and Katie had stopped their game of Guess Who and were staring at Sarah too.

'Has she been drinking?' Ruby asked James and walked closer to Sarah. 'What's going on Sarah? Who are you talking to?'

'I can't tell you where they are.' Edward replied gently. 'But you can work this out Sarah. You know you can. Tommy is alive. Both of them are. You can feel that too.'

Sarah closed her eyes and thought about her gorgeous son and she could sense him. Edward was right; she could sense he was alive. But she also knew that he needed her and was in grave danger.

She turned to her brother. 'They're in trouble, James. It's dark out there. We have to find them. Before it's too late'

James paled, listening to his sister. 'Do you know what time his flight was? Maybe he's still on the way to the airport. Maybe whatever you have seen hasn't happened yet? It's plausible isn't it? Think about what nearly happened to Joey. You stopped that.'

'What about Joey?' Rita demanded. Sarah looked around the room and saw only confusion and fear in the faces of all there. She recognised the look, it was the same one her parents had when she told them about Edward all those years ago.

'It's happening again.' She whispered. Memories of her childhood came flooding back. The fear. The anger. The realisation that nobody believed her.

But she didn't have time to worry about what they all thought about her right now. Her son needed her. The man she'd shared so many important moments with over the last ten years needed her and she wouldn't let either of them down.

'Art, can you do me a favour, could you bring Katie and Ella to Katie's room and read her a story?' Sarah asked.

He looked completely bewildered with the conversation he'd just overheard but to his credit he got up and asked no questions, coaxing Katie to come with him, scooping up Ella at the same time.

'I know you are all wondering what's going on, but right now I can't go into it. Can you just trust me and leave it at that.' Sarah asked.

Ruby walked over to her and said, 'I've always felt that you were hiding something from me, all these years. And whoever this Edward is, he's part of it, isn't he?'

Sarah squeezed her hand in response and turned to her mother-in-law.

'Please don't ask me any questions right now, I promise I will explain, but not now!'

Rita looked unsure, then Joey spoke, 'She'll tell us in her own good time what's going on.'

So Rita nodded at Sarah.

'Right, by any chance do you know what flight was he booked on?' Sarah asked. 'I want to work out what time he would have gone to the airport at.'

'I know it was with Aer Lingus, but that's about it.' Rita said apologetically.

'That's a start.' Sarah said. 'I'll go grab the laptop and I'll see if I can find out if the flight left or not. Maybe he's found Tommy and they are on their way back here. His phone is always out of battery.'

Rita smiled and started to relax, 'Oh yes, that makes sense.'

'Absolutely.' Joey said, patting her on her hand. 'I never think to charge my phone. If I had a euro for the amount of times I get caught out with my battery dead, well I'd be able to retire early!'

Sarah felt a shiver run down her spine; the feeling of dread once more creeping up on her. She hoped that she was wrong, but somehow she felt that there was bad news coming.

'Joey, why don't you go put the kettle on.' Rita said to him. 'Make us all a cuppa.'

Sarah sat down with the laptop and switched it on.

'Ok, let's see what I can find out.' She logged onto the Aer Lingus website and quickly found the area that showed all the daily departure and arrival details. 'His flight was supposed to be at around four, I think.' Rita said.

'Right, here we go, I've got the flight. There was only one flight at that time, so it has to be this one.'

'Well was it delayed?' Rita asked.

'Nope, doesn't appear to be.' Sarah responded. 'No word on any flights being delayed. Tell you what; I'll go ring them, just in case the information is not correct online.'

She picked up the phone and called the helpline. After a few minutes of frustrating conversation with a couple of different people she returned to the living room where Joey was pouring the tea.

'They can't release passenger lists, no matter how much I begged and pleaded with them.' Sarah said. 'But I'm sure he wouldn't get on a plane with Tommy, nor would he leave him behind on his own. So wherever they are, it's not in London.'

'Try ringing him again.' Sarah said to Rita.

She picked up her mobile and hit redial. 'I can still get no answer from him.' Rita said. 'I'll ring Michelle again and see if she's seen him yet or heard from him.'

It was evident from the shouting on the other end of the phone that he'd not turned up yet.

'No joy?' Joey said to Rita when she put the phone down.

'She's livid.' Rita said.

'Maybe he's hiding from her.' Joey said dryly. 'If he has any sense he would.'

Sarah thought to herself that on another day she would be cheering that Michelle was not showing herself in the best light to Rita and Joey. She felt threatened enough about Michelle being in Paul's life and, eventually, the kids' as well. But right now all that nonsense seemed so trivial.

'It's just typical of Paul disappearing like this.' Rita said, her eyes beginning to tear up. 'He swore he'd never put me through this again. Not after the last time.'

'I hate to be the one to say this, but somebody has to. He does have form, doesn't he?' Joey said. 'Maybe he's done a runner again?'

'I've been thinking the same.' Rita admitted quietly. 'I know that you said he seemed completely fine earlier today, but, Sarah, in all honesty, can you say that you had any inkling he was going to run away the last time? Because I certainly didn't!'

Sarah had to admit that she hadn't. 'But Tommy hadn't stowed away in his car the last time.'

She kept thinking about the image she'd seen of Paul earlier. What if he was already hurt? She closed her eyes and thought about the image she'd had earlier when she slipped on the ice – Paul lying motionless and the bright red blood staining the white snow.

She didn't want to worry Rita any further, she looked scared enough, but she couldn't just pretend that everything was fine either. Rita and Joey had no idea about Sarah's psychic abilities yet, but she was afraid to share them. What if they thought she was stark raving mad? Actually scratch that, after witnessing her screaming at the wall at someone called Edward earlier they all most definitely thought she was off her head. She thought about Art and felt sad all of sudden. Whatever they might have had in the future was gone before it had a chance to start, she was sure of that.

The more people that knew, the more on edge she felt. Rita was the same generation as her mother and father, likely to react the same way. And she'd only just reconnected with Ruby; she couldn't bear to lose her either. Her instincts told her only to tell people if she absolutely had to.

Sarah desperately tried to think of something she could do to help track Tommy down. Anything that meant she didn't have to tell them about her visions.

'James, what should we do now?' she pleaded with her brother.

'Let's ring his car hire company.' he said. 'We can see if he returned the car or not before his flight. Okay, million dollar question, anyone know what car hire company he used?' James asked them.

Rita shook her head. Sarah too.

That would have been too easy, he thought. He picked up Sarah's laptop and googled car hire in Dublin airport.

'Twenty companies operate from Dublin Airport.' James said to them. 'Could be worse I suppose! Right, might as well start with all the As!'

James rang the first company on the list.

'Oh hello, I wonder if you can help me. I'm Paul Lawler; I'm calling about the car we hired from you this weekend. I seem to have left one of my children's toys in the boot. Would you mind checking if it's there please? My baby is simply crying her eyes out and just won't settle without that toy.'

'He's good.' Joey said with admiration to Rita.

James took a mock bow to them both.

'You have no record of us hiring a car from you? Oh I'm terribly sorry I must have dialled the wrong number.' James pressed end to the call.

'Well it's not them, 1 down, 19 to go!' James said to them all.

Eight phone calls later and James struck gold. 'We're on; they're going to check the car for me!'

'So he has dropped the car to the airport.' Rita said. 'At least we know that much. So where the devil is he now?'

After about five minutes of waiting James frowned as he put down the phone thanking the clerk.

'Paul hired the car from them, but he hasn't returned it yet. It's way overdue.' This was met with silence as they all digested the news.

'Is it possible that he left the car in the wrong car park and he got that flight to England and brought Tommy with him? But he hasn't gone home to your woman Michelle?' Joey said to the two women. 'I mean, she's pretty narky that one. He might be delaying going home because he knows he'll be getting it in the neck when he does arrive home with the little boy!'

'What do you think, Sarah?' Rita asked her. 'Maybe Joey's right, he's just avoiding Michelle and that's all?'

Sarah would have loved to agree with Joey. It would be just like Paul to dodge going home until after he thought Michelle was asleep if he knew she was in a bad mood. He'd often not come home till really late with Sarah, rather than face the music for whatever he was in trouble for. And while she would be furious with him for taking Tommy without her permission, it was preferable than them both being missing. But Sarah kept coming back to the image of him lying in the snow. She knew without Edward saying so, they were in trouble.

'I think maybe we should call the hospitals.' James said quietly 'Let's be safe rather than sorry. And I'm going to call Roger, see if he can help.'

'You think he's hurt don't you, you think something has happened to them?' Rita asked him, panic creeping into her voice again.

'I don't know Rita, but I won't lie to you, I'm a bit worried myself. I just hope I'm wrong.' James admitted.

The phone rang and they all jumped.

'It might be Paul!' Rita said.

Sarah answered it quickly, 'Hello?'

'Is that Sarah?' A cultured English accent asked.

It was Michelle. She'd never forget that voice ever; it would haunt her for a long time.

'Hello Michelle.' Sarah responded.

'So I presume he's with you!' Michelle accused. 'You begged and begged him to stay with you so much you wore him down. I knew this was going to happen!'

She looked over at Rita and Joey and mouthed to them, 'Michelle.'

'You were always going to wear him down doing a big guilt trip. I knew it would only be a matter of time before you dragged him back to you and your children. What I'd like to know is how you can live with yourself, have you no self-respect? He doesn't love you any more!' She spat down the phone to Sarah.

Sarah was flabbergasted. The absolute nerve of the woman was incredible. She'd had affair with her husband and he'd left her and their three children for her, and somehow now it was Sarah that was supposedly guilty of trying to steal him back. She tried to speak but each time she opened her mouth Michelle just kept shouting and screaming down the phone. And the more she spoke and shouted the more her posh accent seemed to unravel. Sarah was getting fed up listening to the tirade of abuse and no matter how much she tried to step in and explain that Paul wasn't hiding in her attic, Michelle just continue to speak over her.

Eventually she decided she had no choice but to try to shout over her, talking just wasn't working!

'Michelle if you let me get a word in I'll be able to tell you that Paul isn't with me.'

Let's see if that got through. No, she didn't hear that. She was too busy telling Sarah that Paul wouldn't stay with her; he'd soon get bored again and come back to her again.

God, she was a vile woman. Sarah almost felt sorry for Paul. What had he gotten himself messed up with?

'I'm going to try to speak again, but if you don't shut up and let me I'm hanging up!'

The tone in Sarah's voice seemed to work and this time Michelle went quiet.

Sarah said to her gently. 'I promise you that Paul is not here. He left my house today to get his flight. And I've not heard from him since. And I've more than Paul on my mind right now as Tommy our son is missing too. We think he snuck into Paul's car before he left for the airport.'

Quiet again. 'Michelle, are you ok?'

'If he's not with you, then where is he?' Michelle started to cry. 'My poor baby, my poor little Paulie baby.'

Sarah couldn't believe her ears. Not one word of sympathy or acknowledgement that a little boy was missing. She was about to let her have it, but she thought of the baby that Michelle was carrying and no matter what she thought of that woman, she was pregnant and getting upset wouldn't do her or the baby any good.

'I don't know where he is. But we're trying to find that out. My brother James is here and we have called the Gardaí. I promise you that we'll call you as soon as we know anything. And Michelle, if he turns up with you, will you do the same and call us?'

She promised she would and they both hung up.

'She's a right madam that one.' Rita said crossly. 'I could hear her yelling down the phone all the way over here!'

'Maybe it's just her hormones?' Sarah said in an attempt at being magnanimous.

'Well I've seen you through three pregnancies Sarah, and you've never shouted like a common fishwife in any of them!'

Sarah smiled at her. 'I probably felt like it once or twice though. She's just upset and worried.' Sarah was stunned that she was even sticking up for that woman. She surprised herself a lot these days. 'I'm going to go check on the kids, make sure they're ok with Art.'

Art was standing at the door of Katie's room and beckoned Sarah to look. Katie was lying still in her bed with her teddy bear held in tight to her chest. She couldn't sleep unless she had one of her cuddly toys wrapped up tightly in her arms. Sarah went in and kissed her daughter tenderly. She wanted more than anything to shield her from any distress. She was oblivious to the fact that Daddy was missing along with Tommy. She really didn't think Katie would be able to cope if he disappeared for the second time again. As for Tommy, they were best friends. Ella was also fast asleep tucked up into the corner of her cot. She always needed to feel something up against her head to get to sleep. No matter how many times Sarah put her in the middle of the bed; she'd find her way to the top or the bottom.

'Art, I can't thank you enough.' Sarah said to him. 'I can't believe you got them into bed.'

'I'm happy to help. They are great kids.' He acknowledged. 'Any news?'

'Not yet. I'm scared though.' She whispered. She looked up at him warily. 'About before, I'm sure you must be wondering who I was talking to?'

'I'd be lying if I said I'm not curious as to what all that was about. But it's not important right now. You can explain all when Tommy is back.' He looked at her intently and seemed to make a decision. Walking over to her purposefully he pulled her into his arms and held her close. She was shocked to find that in this extreme circumstance she could still feel so relaxed in his embrace. He reached down and caressed her cheek and whispered so quietly, 'Sarah, beautiful Sarah,' that she wondered had he said it at all.

He then cupped her face in his hands and, with more tenderness than she'd ever been shown, he leaned in and kissed her gently for just a second.

She looked up at him, confused once again by the reaction this man could get from her.

'I'm sorry.' Art began to apologise. 'I shouldn't have done that.'

'There's nothing to be sorry about.' Sarah replied feeling herself blush. 'But I can't do this right now. I must get back to the others.' She scurried away to the living room again, flustered by the encounter.

She heard Roger's car pull into the drive. 'It's snowing again.' He said as he ran into the house. 'It's absolutely bitter out there. And the roads are treacherous too. There's hardly anyone out at all. Sorry it took me so long to get here.'

He walked in and stood in front of the open fire, trying to warm up.

James walked over to him and filled him in on what they knew so far.

'First thing to do is to see if I can find out if he was on that flight or not with or without Tommy. At least we'll know what country he's in then.' Roger said to them all.

'They wouldn't tell us.' Rita said. 'Sarah called them earlier.'

'They'll be happy enough to tell me, don't worry.' Roger said to her.

Roger stood up and walked into the kitchen, dialling his phone as he walked.

Sarah, Rita and Joey sat in silence waiting for Roger to come back in.

'He never made that flight.' Roger said to them all. 'So at least we now know he's in Ireland.'

'He has had an accident on the ice somewhere between here and the airport. They are hurt and need help, I'm sure of it.' Sarah said emphatically.

'What am I missing here?' Roger asked no one in particular.

'When you work it out, let me know!' Ruby answered him, then added under her breath, 'Because Sarah sure as hell is keeping something from us.'

253

'It won't do any harm to check out if he's been admitted to any of the hospitals in Dublin.' Roger said.

Twenty minutes later he had determined that Paul hadn't been admitted to any hospital that day.

'So a dead end once again.' Rita said. 'We still don't know where he is?'

'If he's any sense he's in a hotel taking shelter from this weather.' Joey said to them all.

James looked over at Sarah. She shook her head.

'They are in trouble, James.'

'Let me think.' James said.

Rita picked up her mobile and dialled Paul's number again. 'Still no answer, why won't he answer?' She said and finally the tears that had been lingering all evening finally fell. She put her head on Joey's shoulder. 'I know he's caused a lot of trouble over the past couple of months, and I know he's been a terrible father and husband, but he's still my son.'

'There, there.' Joey said stroking her hair gently, pulling her into him for a hug.

James raised his eyebrows at the tender gesture. He hadn't seen that one coming. It was fairly common knowledge that he hadn't much time for Paul, but seeing Rita that upset tugged his heartstrings. And he was going to move heaven and earth to find Tommy; he loved him like he was his own. He trusted Sarah and if she said Paul needed help, he thought he'd better do everything he could to help.

'We have to go look for them.' James said. 'They left here this afternoon heading for Dublin. They have to be somewhere on the route.'

'This is no night to be out driving.' Roger said to James. 'I'll check with the station and see if any accidents have been reported in.'

Sarah closed her eyes and tried to focus. Why couldn't she see Tommy? Why was she only seeing Paul lying in the snow?

Edward was beside her again. 'Look around the area you see Paul in. Look for a clue to where they are. You can do this. You have the power to find them. You are letting your emotions stop you focussing.'

She walked to the corner of the room and closed her eyes.

Paul's face is as white as the snow he lies on. She allows herself to let her eyes travel down his body and startles as she sees Tommy's little frame lying on top of his father's chest. Oh please God, let Tommy be alive. She looks and his little body is heaving as he cries. He is white and shivering. But there's no doubt – he's alive!

Sarah takes a moment to steady herself, then forces herself to focus on looking around her.

They are in what appears to be a field. She sees snow and ice glistening on a ditch nearby. She sees the car then, its nose buried in the ditch – they have crashed. And then her eyes stop on rows upon rows of white plastic tunnels; almost obscured, blending into the white blanket of snow.

A memory teases her, just out of her minds reach. She has seen them before, but where?

She opened her eyes and saw everyone watching her.

'Sis?' James said with concern. 'You were talking out loud.'

She realised her face was awash with tears again.

'They've been in an accident. They are in a field with white tunnels all in a row. I've been there. I know I have.' Sarah said to James.

Rita turned to Sarah looking extremely confused and angry. 'What's going on? You keep saying that you're sure that Paul is hurt, that he's fallen on the ice. That Tommy stowed away in Paul's car. But how could you know that? Just now you seemed to just pluck from the sky that there had been a car accident. Speak up now, young lady.'

James shouted, 'Wait just a minute. Let me think.'

They all watched him in silence. 'It's the fruit farm in Gorey. That's where those tunnels are.'

Sarah knew it to be true; she could feel it with every fibre in her body. 'They are there, I know it.'

'Roger, call an ambulance and get it over there immediately.'

He looked at both their faces and was about to tell them he would do no such thing unless they gave him one good reason why, when a strong feeling overcame him, one that told him that he should just do as they asked. He'd always trusted his gut before and it had done him well, so he picked up his phone and made the call.

'James, Ruby, can you stay with the children. I'm going to Gorey.' Sarah said.

'Not without me.' James added. Ruby quickly nodded her assent to stay with the children.

'And I need to be on my way too.' Rita declared.

'The roads are in an awful state.' Roger said. 'I really don't think you should travel anywhere tonight. Let's wait and see if they are found first.'

'I can't stay here and do nothing!' Rita cried back. 'He's my baby, my only child. I'll not leave him on his own.'

'And you don't have to Rita, love. I'll drive us up there.' Joey said. 'If there's one thing I've picked up on over twenty years of delivering post, it's how to drive in all kinds of weather.'

'Right, that's settled then. Let's get going.' James said.

They agreed and quickly they were at the door ready to leave.

'James, ring me as soon as you get there, no matter what time it is. I'll not sleep till I hear from you.' Ruby said.

With a quick kiss, he promised to do so.

Chapter Thirty

As they were navigating their way towards Gorey, James's phone rang. It was Roger. He put the call on speakerphone for them all to hear.

'The ambulance. They've found them. Exactly as Sarah predicted.' Roger said with just a little awe creeping into his voice.

From the back seat, Joey gasped, he just couldn't help himself. He glanced at Sarah in amazement.

'How are they?' Rita asked tearfully and summoned all her strength up to ask, 'Are they alive?'

'Yes, they are both alive. It looks like Paul is in a bad way. Tommy is cold and upset, but seems to be unharmed.'

'What's wrong with Paul?' Rita asked.

'He's cracked his head and lost a lot of blood apparently,' Roger replied. 'They're taking them both to Arklow Hospital.'

Sarah clasped James's hand in relief that they had been found and all she could think about was holding her child close to her and never letting go.

Sarah was in shock, she could barely take it all in. She was so relieved that Tommy was ok on one hand and all she wanted to do was feel his arms around her neck and hear his little voice call her Mammy. But coupled with that she was still so worried about Paul. She felt like she'd let him down, the guilt was overwhelming.

James thanked Roger, then turned to Sarah and said, 'This isn't your fault, Sarah. You couldn't have done any more than you have done.'

'Somebody ought to ring Michelle.' Joey said.

'I can't face it.' Rita sobbed. 'I can't deal with her right now.'

'I'll do it.' Sarah replied.

It was one of the most surreal moments she'd ever had. Michelle answered the phone on the first ring. 'Yes?' she whispered. Her voice sounded croaky from crying.

'It's Sarah. I'm so sorry to tell you this, but they've found Paul. He's been in an accident.'

'I know Sarah. The hospital called me a short while ago.'

Sarah was confused. 'How did they have your number?'

'I'm listed in his phone as his 'in case of emergency' person.' Michelle replied.

That shouldn't have surprised Sarah, but it still did.

'I've just booked a flight to Dublin. I'm packing, so won't stay on the phone, you understand.'

Sarah wished her a safe journey, confused at how Michelle being listed as next of kin for Paul could upset her so much.

'Michelle already knew.' Sarah said to them all. 'She's on her way.'

She felt very strange. He was still her husband in name, but they were no longer married in any true sense of the word. She longed to see Tommy with every fibre in her body, but she wanted to see Paul too, to tell him that she was here for him. But it wasn't her that he'd want to see when he came to. It was Michelle. She was his 'in case of emergency' now.

Everything was just so complicated. She was pretty sure she wasn't in love with Paul anymore, but he had played a large part of her life for so very long, it was impossible to not care about him. She wasn't sure she would ever be ready to let him go.

They arrived at the hospital within the hour and split up – Rita and Joey went to Paul, Sarah and James to Tommy.

258

As soon as Sarah walked into Accident and Emergency she saw Tommy sitting on a hospital trolley, with blankets wrapped around him and all pretence at being strong vanished. She ran towards him and he fell into his mother's arms, crying his little heart out. Through the tears Sarah had found out exactly what had happened. Tommy had decided that it was up to him to persuade his Daddy to come home. So he forged a note so he could leave school early and hopped into the back of his Daddy's car while he waited for him to come out. But he fell asleep and it was only halfway to Dublin that he woke up. Paul had turned the car to bring him home. Unfortunately on the return journey he skidded on ice and crashed.

Neither of them had been hurt in the crash miraculously, but the car was stuck in the ditch. So Paul had tried to push it but had slipped in the ice and cracked his head on a stone as he hit the ground. A silly, senseless, quirk of fate.

Tommy had tried to ring Sarah, but couldn't get a signal on his Daddy's phone so he couldn't do anything. So he just lay on top of him, trying to keep him warm and prayed that someone would come rescue them soon.

He was so distraught and already had decided he was at fault for the crash. James and Sarah had both told him all about the road conditions saying it would have happened either way, but Tommy wouldn't believe them.

Eventually he fell asleep in Sarah's arms and he was still asleep now. The hospital said that they would keep him overnight for observation, but that tomorrow he would be discharged to go home.

'James.' Sarah whispered to her brother. 'Will you stay beside Tommy in case he wakes up? I want to see Paul.'

James nodded, 'Take your time, sis. I'm going nowhere.'

Sarah walked towards Paul's room, dreading what she would find there, but knowing that she needed to see him. Rita and she had called in on each other a few times already during the night, but there was little news so far on Paul, other than he was in a bad way.

Rita and Joey were in the visitor's room, Joey dozing on a chair, but Rita stone-faced and wide awake. Walking beside Sarah was Edward. His face looked very solemn. Sarah was afraid to ask him if Paul would live or not, afraid of the answer he might give her.

'It's bad.' Rita stated trying to hold back the tears. 'He's in critical condition. He had extreme hypothermia from all those hours lying in the snow. A nurse just told me that if we hadn't found him when we did, he'd be dead by now. So that's something to be grateful for. You saved his life you know. I don't know how you did it, though.'

Sarah brushed that aside. She still felt the crushing weight of guilt, that maybe she could have done more.

'What treatment are they giving him?' Sarah asked.

'It's not just the hypothermia. He has had a bad blow to his head and he's lost a lot of blood. He's unconscious and they have put him on life support. I've been told to prepare myself for the possibility that he might have brain damage.' Rita finished on a sob.

Sarah burst into tears at this, she couldn't hold back any longer. 'Oh Rita, no.' She cried.

'I know. I can't believe it. They promised me that they are doing all they can. Michelle will be here in the morning, I'm dreading telling her this.'

Sarah understood how hard that would be for Rita, as she was reeling at the thought of telling the kids. That poor woman, pregnant and to hear news like that?

'Sarah, the nurse also said that if there was any family who needed to say goodbye, we should have them close by. In case ...' Rita finished with a cry.

'Oh, Paul.' Sarah sobbed herself. 'I don't know if Tommy and Katie are up to all this.'

'I can't stop thinking about the children too. You're they're mother so I'll let you decide if you think that they should be here or not.'

Sarah felt her head spinning. She was at a loss as to what to do.

'I'll have to think about this some more before I make my mind up.'

'Of course.' Rita said. 'You put those kiddies first. If you think that it's too much for them to handle, keep them away. Paul wouldn't want them to be any more traumatised than necessary.'

'No he wouldn't.' Sarah agreed.

Sarah closed her eyes and silently called out for help. 'Edward help me, should I bring the kids to see Paul or not? I don't know what to do!'

Edward walked over to Sarah and sat down beside her.

'Think about when you were their age.' Edward said to her. 'What would you have wanted if it were your father that was critically ill?'

'I'd want to see him.' She answered without hesitation. 'They'll want to see him won't they?'

'I think they'll need to see him.' Edward gently corrected her. 'Don't underestimate your children. They are very like their mother, they're strong.' He said gently.

'I think they'd want to see Paul, but right now, I'd like to go in and sit with him, if that's ok?' Sarah asked Rita.

'Of course it is. You don't have to ask me that!'

Sarah walked into Paul's room and walked over to the bedside of her husband. He looked like he was perfectly fine, just having a deep sleep. He was pale, that was true, but apart from that she couldn't see a mark on him. She heard the faint buzz of the machines that Paul was connected to. He had a tube down his throat and one also in his nose. He was connected to a drip.

'Oh Paul, my darling.' Sarah sobbed. She leaned in and kissed him tenderly on his lips, then sat down to hold his hand.

'This is a right mess! I bet you wish you hadn't called me Septic Peg now!' Sarah joked lamely. 'You should have listened to me, but then again you never did so I suppose why start now!

But darling, don't worry about Tommy, I know you must be thinking of nothing else. He is absolutely fine. He's fast asleep right now and I know he'll wake up starving! He's always hungry; you know what he's like.'

She looked down at her ex-husbands left hand, bare now as he no longer wore a wedding band. She glanced at her own hand where she still wore her own rings as she'd not been brave enough to take them off. Silly really, how much a piece of jewellery could become a symbol of so much more than just a marriage? Sarah knew that when she took her rings off, she was finally letting go of the life she had shared with Paul. No more Mrs Sarah Lawler, wife to Paul.

'Do you remember our wedding day?' She whispered. 'The sun was shining, despite it being October. An Indian summer, everyone said! You made me promise not to be late, but of course I was. I always am. But I couldn't wait to walk down the aisle to you. You told me that you wouldn't look till I got to the top of the church, but you couldn't stop yourself and you peeped! And then you smiled at me and I just wanted to run to you and throw myself in your arms right there that second. we were so in love, Paul.'

She brushed tears away quickly. She closed her eyes and in a moment and was back in Paul's arms, for their first dance.

'You insisted on choosing the first song, do you remember? I was so annoyed with you, I wanted to pick it! I mean, who chooses Elvis Costello's *She*?

But when the music started and I heard the words...... You got me, Paul. I still can't listen to that song without crying.' Sarah started to hum their song.

'You always said it was the end bit, that was why you chose it.' Sarah leaned in and kissed him again and began to sing softly,

'I'll take her laughter and her tears
And make them all my souvenirs
For where she goes I've got to be
The meaning of my life is
She'

She laid her head on Paul's hand and closed her eyes.

Chapter Thirty One

Tommy had been given the all clear and was discharged, so with Sarah and James, they had joined Rita and Joey in the family room. Paul was still in intensive care, no change.

Sarah rang Ruby to fill her in on the news and check on the children.

'Is there any news?' Ruby asked her.

'No change. He's having some tests done as we speak and a consultant and his team are with him now. He's been for a CT scan already. They said that they'll talk to us later on and let us know how he's doing.'

'Has Michelle arrived yet?' Ruby asked.

'Any minute. She'll be in a taxi by now I should think.' Sarah answered. 'Ruby, could you do me a favour? Can you pack some things for the children and bring them up here to me?'

'Absolutely.' Ruby replied. 'I'm way ahead of you. I've already rang work and taken a couple of days annual leave. And I have an overnight bag packed too, so I'm ready to leave. I may need some help though in what I need to bring for Ella! I don't have much hands-on experience with babies, but sure, how hard can it be?' This she said with a laugh. 'I figure I can look after Ella at least when you bring the children in to see Paul. Or just be a shoulder to cry on if you need it.'

Sarah had been concerned about how she'd manage all three children herself in a busy hospital.

'I'll not forget this.' Sarah told her.

'Too right you won't! Repayment will be accepted in copious amounts of gin & tonics in Freddie's bar!' Then looking towards the children, Ruby added. 'Plus, I've got ulterior motives! I get to spend lots of time with your beautiful children and I just know that's going to be a whole lot of fun for me!'

'I won't lie, I'll be glad to see you Rubes. This is the stuff of nightmares.' Sarah admitted.

'Yep, it's pretty hard-core. You must be in bits, but I'll be there soon. How's Tommy holding up?'

'Scared and worried. .' Sarah answered. 'But he is taking it in his stride.' Sarah was as always extremely proud of him. What he'd been through and he was coping extraordinarily well.

'By the way, Katie was asking questions at breakfast, so I had to tell her something. I told her that Daddy had banged his head and he was asleep right now, but having lots of fun dreams about his three kids.'

'That was a lovely thing to say to her.' Sarah said.

'Katie was so cute. She said to me, 'Maybe he's in Chocolate Land in his dreams? He might be climbing the Toblerone tree right this minute. The imagination she has!'

'We all visit Chocolate Land every night in in our house.' Sarah explained to Ruby.

'I figured as much! I told Katie that it sounds like a fun place to dream about, so I think that's where your Daddy is alright. I know that if I was sleeping right now, that's where I'd like to be!'

'Thanks, I'd be lost without you. Can you tell Katie that Mammy said, Daddy always loved Chocolate Land and I bet he's having a swim in the Cadbury's swimming pool now.'

'Will do. Oh and I delivered those cupcakes to Centra for you too an hour ago. So that's one less thing for you to worry about.'

'I'd totally forgotten about those! For that, you get a packet of dry roasted peanuts thrown in with the G&T's!' Sarah said smiling.

Sarah marvelled at how she had ever managed without Ruby.

She then gave Ruby details on what she needed to pack for the children before saying goodbye.

'Ruby is on her way with Katie and Ella shortly.' She told the others, noting James face lighting up as soon as her name was mentioned.

Rita was relieved to hear they were on their way too. She didn't want to frighten Sarah any more than she had to, but she was very worried. The words 'critical' were being bandied about a lot and Rita was terrified that she was going to lose her son. She could hardly bear it.

Chapter Thirty Two

Stubble was beginning to grow on Mal's chin and he looked tired. Nothing like a night in the cells to take its toll on your appearance, Roger thought to himself. Sitting beside Mal was a woman with a sharp face and short black hair.

She stood up to greet the two detectives, offering her hand to Roger. 'Elaine Rochford.' She said to them both in a clipped tone that matched her face perfectly. 'Mr Wickham is now officially my client. And I'm a very busy woman, so let's get this wrapped up quickly shall we?'

Roger nodded to her in greeting and sat down.

'So Detective McElvoy, how much longer are we going to continue this little façade of yours?'

'What façade would that be?' Roger asked her mildly.

'The façade I am referring to, Detective McElvoy, is the one that you are pretending you have even one whit of evidence to hold my client here. You've been questioning him now for over twenty-four hours and I'm seriously considering issuing an enquiry into how you've handled this.'

Roger looked and Johnny and smiled. She was going straight for the jugular, trying to frighten them both into releasing Wickham.

'So unless you're going to charge my client, we'll be leaving right now.' She stood up again and gestured to Mal to do the same. He looked like he was going to cry with the relief.

'I'm afraid that I can't allow that.' Roger replied coolly, holding his hand up to stop them both. 'We haven't charged Mr Wickham yet, but nor have we finished our questioning either. The district court has very kindly extended our period for questioning your client for up to 7 days. So you won't be leaving us anytime soon, Mr Wickham.'

'That's preposterous!' Mal shouted at them. 'They can't do this can they?' he said to his lawyer.

'I'm afraid they can Mal.' Elaine said to her client. 'But don't worry; we'll soon put an end to this ridiculous persecution.'

'Not enjoying our hospitality?' Johnny said to Mal. 'Food not up to scratch?'

'Right.' Roger said. 'Since we last spoke have you by any chance had divine inspiration as to where you were on the night Rachel Finch was murdered, between leaving her at 5pm and arriving home at 3am.'

'No, I'm afraid I can't remember where I was. I was just driving.' He answered defiantly.

'And have you remembered where you might have picked up that firewood?' Roger continued.

'I have a habit of picking up wood if I see it on the side of the road. I'm always doing it. I can only think that I saw a fallen tree somewhere and I just picked it up and put it in the boot.' He said to him.

'That the best you can come up with?' Johnny asked incredulously. 'All that time to think and that's it?'

'Detective Murphy, there's no need for that.' Elaine rebuked him. She turned then to Roger and continued. 'As I said earlier, you have obviously not got one single whit of evidence. My client has admitted to having an affair with Rachel Finch and nothing further. Unless you have a new line of questioning I once again request that we terminate this interview immediately. My client has had to deal with a conspiracy of lies thrown at him; you have nothing but circumstantial evidence. And exactly what is my client's motive to kill supposed to be?' she finished dramatically. 'No murder weapon, no evidence, no motive equals no case Detective McElvoy!'

The smug smile had appeared on Mal's face again. Roger was looking forward to wiping it right off.

Roger picked up his folder and opened it. 'Well that's where you are wrong, Ms Rochford. We have every reason to believe that your client had a very strong motive to kill Rachel Finch, we were just coming to that.'

Earlier that day, they had finally had a break in the case. Interviews with friends of Rachel's finally had paid dividends and they now had a written statement from a friend, who had been in regular email contact with Rachel. She had spoken about her relationship with Mal and the email spun quite a tale.

'Listen Mal.' Roger said, leaning in close to him. 'This is your best chance to tell us exactly what happened that night. We know that you and Rachel were having an affair and we know that you were with her the night she was murdered. It will look better for you if you just admit that you murdered her upfront. Get it off your chest, you'll feel much better for it. I'm thinking of you, mate.' He finished with a smile.

Mal looked disconcerted. He turned to look at his defence lawyer. Elaine simply shook her head. 'Do not admit to anything.' She stated.

'I didn't murder her. I cared deeply for her.' he continued. 'I was devastated when she died.'

'Yeah, right.' Johnny said sarcastically.

'Did you ever argue?' Roger said, quickly changing tactic.

'No, we never argued.' Mal replied.

'Not once in your entire relationship?' Johnny remarked. 'Extraordinary.'

'We never had reason to argue. We got on very well together in fact.' Mal replied.

'So even when Rachel begged you to leave Marie, you never argued? Roger asked.

'I don't know what you're talking about!' Mal shouted back.

'And when you said you'd never tell Marie about the affair are you telling me that Rachel just smiled? From what I've learned about Rachel's character during this investigation, I'd say she wouldn't take that too kindly!' Roger said to him.

'I don't know what you're talking about. We never discussed me leaving Marie – it was never on the agenda ever.'

'Because you don't believe in divorce, do you?' Roger shouted. 'You said as much already to us in our first interview!'

'No, I don't believe in divorce, big deal. Half the country agrees with me on that one,' he shouted back.

'What are your thoughts on children?'

Mal was taken aback by the new line of questioning.

Roger continued. 'How did you feel when Rachel told you she was pregnant with your baby?'

Before he had a chance to respond, he shouted, 'Because I reckon when Rachel told you that you were about to become a Daddy forcing your hand to leave Marie, you panicked. Did you tell her to have an abortion and she said no? Did you lose that temper of yours that we all know you have and follow her to the beach to get rid of all your problems!'

Mal looked terrified. 'No, that's preposterous!' he screamed in a high pitch voice.

'Really!' Roger shouted, throwing the emails he had in his file down on the table between them. 'Luckily for us, Rachel and her best friend were a right pair of chatterboxes. Sending each other emails on a daily basis!'

Mal went white. Elaine intervened, 'You don't need to say anything further.'

'It's all here in black and white. You and Rachel were in love. Or at least she was in love with you. I'm not sure that murdering someone constitutes love really! She demanded you leave Marie. You were furious with her for suggesting it. There was no way you were going to allow Marie divorce you and take half your precious

269

farm! But Rachel wasn't the type of girl to take no for an answer. So she told you she was pregnant. What really happened that night on the beach Mal? Did you plan to murder her or did she provoke you and you lost control? That's the piece of the puzzle I'm trying to work out!'

Mal looked like he was about to start crying.

'Stop these lies once and for all.' Roger urged him. 'We already know you have a violent temper. Your wife bears the bruises to prove that! Did you decide to shut Rachel up once and for all?'

'My client has nothing further to state.' Elaine said. 'Either charge him or let him go.'

'Interview suspended 11.14 am.' Roger said, pressing stop on the recorder. 'We'll be back.'

Chapter Thirty Three

Ruby had finally arrived at the hospital. The roads were not too bad as it happened and they made good time, despite two toilet breaks for the kids. They were all waiting to greet them in reception.

Sarah opened her arms wide and gathered all three into her for a group hug.

'How's Daddy?' Katie asked. 'Is he awake now?'

'No darling, he's still sleeping.' Sarah replied.

'Michelle is with him now.' Sarah whispered to Ruby, who was now holding hands with James. She'd not met her yet herself, she'd arrived while Sarah was with Tommy.

'Who's Michelle?' Tommy asked, not missing a trick.

Damn it, Sarah thought. She'd not even had time to think about how she would play that one.

'Michelle is Daddy's friend.' Sarah replied.

'He never told me about her before.' Katie said in wonder.

'She's a new friend. They work together in his job in England.' Sarah responded.

'Oh.' Katie replied. Having thought about it she said, 'I'm glad he has a new friend. He said that he missed us all over in London.'

'I'm glad too.' Sarah replied.

'Any further news from the consultants?' Ruby asked.

'No, we're still waiting to hear from them. Shall we get a cup of tea?' Rita asked.

Sarah smiled at this. The world would be coming to an end and the Irish would be all making pots of tea.

'The nurses have our mobile number, they said they'd call if …' Joey said.

'I could do with food.' James said. 'Let's all go to the canteen, grab something and we can make our plans then.'

'I want to see Daddy.' Katie said to her Mammy.

Tommy was conspicuously quiet.

'I tell you what; let's go get a cold drink and something to eat first. Let's give Daddy's friend Michelle some time to talk to him before we go in.' Ruby coaxed.

'Ok.' Katie said appeased by the thought of a drink and maybe even a treat.

'Come on love.' Joey said to Rita. 'Let's grab your grandchildren and buy them a few sweets.'

Sarah took Ella to the changing room to get her sorted and then followed them down to the café.

'I think I should go up on my own for a bit. I'd like to meet Michelle and have a quick chat with her, before I bring the kids up.' She told the others.

'You go on up ahead of us and we'll follow you in twenty minutes or so. But don't take any S.H.I.T. from her ladyship.' Ruby stated firmly.

Michelle looked terrible. She was very pale.

'Hello.' Sarah said, trying her best to smile.

'Oh it's you.' Michelle said ungraciously. 'I hoped it was the doctor.'

Sarah walked over to Paul. He looked much the same as he had the night before. She wanted to put her arms around him and hold him and tell him that he would be ok but she was acutely aware of Michelle's presence, eyes boring holes into her back. Instead she just held his hand for a second, hoping that Michelle didn't notice it.

The irony that she, Paul's wife was trying to hide holding his hand, in front of the mistress wasn't lost on her. But she wasn't his wife any more, nor Michelle his mistress. Damn it, she had better get used to this new upside down world quick.

'How are you?' Sarah asked.

'How do you think?' Michelle spat back. 'The man I love, the father of my unborn child is lying comatose, how do you think I feel?'

Sarah was once again astounded at the selfishness of this woman.

'I'm sure you are terribly upset as we all are. The children are here, they'll be up shortly and I'd like them to spend some time alone with Paul.' Sarah asked.

'I have every right to be here. I am his partner!' Michelle said her voice rising.

'I'm acutely aware of that.' Sarah replied mildly. 'I'm not trying to make you leave. Paul would want you here, so you should stay. But I'm just asking you to give the children some time with their Daddy. They are very scared right now.'

'I suppose I could do with a cup of tea and something to eat.' She said sniffing.

'Michelle, the children don't know that you and their Daddy were together. I've told them that you are Paul's friend, but that's it. Please don't say anything about being pregnant to them just yet. It would just be too confusing.'

'My baby is going to be their brother or sister! You can't keep this from them forever you know.'

Sarah took a deep breath. She was finding it very hard to remain civil with her. But this was neither the time nor the place.

'Can we just deal with one crisis at a time? They are too young to have to understand their Daddy being so sick, never mind the fact that he was having another child with somebody other than their mother. I'll tell them about you and the baby when the time is right, I promise you.'

'Ok.' Michelle said sulkily. 'I'll be back in 30 minutes. Have your precious alone time.'

'Out of interest, are you like this all the time?' Sarah asked her suddenly, genuinely curious.

'Like what?' Michelle said.

'Every time I've spoken to you, you've been deliberately rude and quite vile. I'm just wondering if this is your normal manner or do you save up all your nasty just for me?'

Michelle, for once looked completely gobsmacked by Sarah's question. She didn't have an answer for it so she picked up her handbag and gave Paul a lingering kiss on his lips before walking out. Sarah shook her head at how childish Michelle was.

'Hello.' She said turning back to Paul. 'What on earth did you see in that one? She's a weapon. You can do a lot better my love.' She leaned in and kissed his cheek.

She stroked his hair, moving his fringe to one side.

'I have a surprise for you. The children are having a treat with your Mam, but they'll be here any minute. They can't wait to see you. Katie thinks that she'll be able to wake you up by shaking you. So I'm warning you to be ready! For such a little girl, she's quite strong.'

Sarah half expected him to open his eyes and wink, telling her all would be fine.

But he didn't move a muscle, he simply remained motionless.

'Your mam is so worried about you. You've got to get better for her sake. She needs you. And so do I. I need you to help bring up our children. Tommy feels he is to blame for the accident. He was so happy these past couple of days having you home with him. So don't you be getting comfortable there lying in this bed. I know it's lovely to have a rest, but it's time you woke up now,' she said, tears now pouring down her face. 'You always said that it was impossible to sleep each night because I was always chattering away in your ear. Well, I'm going to keep chattering to you until you wake up and tell me to shut up!'

Then the strangest sensation overcame her. As the tears flowed she felt that washed away amongst them was all the anger and bitterness she'd carried inside for months. At some point during the night, between when she had sat with Paul and now, something shifted. All that was left now was compassion and love for this man she'd married and had three children with. She knew he didn't love her any more and that was fine. She also realised with wonder, that she wasn't in love with him anymore either. That was fine too, because she knew she would always care for him. They had a shared past and children that would link them forever. That was enough.

'So this is what acceptance feels like,' she whispered to him. 'But I'm not ready to say goodbye to you yet. Do you hear me Paul?' she said, kissing him on his forehead again.

A knock on the door made her jump. Rita and the children walked in, followed by James, Ruby and Joey.

Tommy and Katie looked worried when they saw that Sarah was crying.

'Mammy?' Katie asked.

'Don't be scared darlings,' she said to them both. 'I'm just having a little cry that's all. Come over and say hello.'

'Is he awake?' Katie whispered.

'No darling.' Sarah replied.

'I'm scared, Mammy.' Katie said, moving closer to the door.

Sarah walked over to her and held a hand out to each of her children. 'There's nothing to be scared of. That's your Daddy and that's all you need to know. Ignore all the wires that are attached to him, they are just to help him breathe. He might be asleep, but I bet anything that he can hear every word we say.'

'Really?' Tommy asked.

'Yes really.' Sarah answered. They walked slowly to his bedside.

'Hello, Daddy.' Katie said to him. 'Shall I shake him, Mammy?'

'I don't think that shaking him will work this time darling.' Sarah answered her. Seeing her face she went on, 'But if you want to try, you go ahead.'

Katie used both her hands to shake his arm and said, 'Daddy, it's morning time.'

She shook him a second time, but with no joy.

'It's not working.' Katie said starting to cry.

'Come here, pet.' Rita said pulling her granddaughter to her.

Tommy was just staring at his father.

'Do you want to say something?' Sarah asked him gently.

Tommy nodded.

'Go ahead. He's right here, listening.'

Tommy wiped the tears that were falling from his eyes on the back of his jacket sleeve. 'I'm sorry Daddy.' He whispered. 'It's all my fault.'

'It's not your fault Tommy.' Sarah quickly said.

'Yes it is Mammy. I've been so angry with Daddy because he left us. And sometimes at night I've wished he would get hurt. So I made this happen!' Tommy started to sob hysterically and Sarah felt a piece of her die inside, looking at her son suffer so much.

'Tommy you listen to me and you listen hard. This is nobody's fault. You cannot wish an accident on someone, no matter how much you try.'

Tommy looked at his Mammy doubtfully.

'Think about it, Tommy. Did you wish that your Daddy would get hurt before this weekend? I mean before you got to see him this weekend?' She asked him.

He nodded through his tears.

'And did you still want him to hurt himself yesterday when you snuck into his car after your weekend together?' Sarah asked him.

Tommy thought about this and then shook his head.

'So you see Tommy, this can't be your fault. You didn't want your Daddy to hurt himself yesterday did you?'

'No Mammy.' Tommy leaned into his mother for a hug. 'I just wanted Daddy to come home.'

James walked over to Tommy and crouched down low in front of him. 'You trust me?' he asked.

Tommy nodded.

'Well then you listen to me. This is no more your fault than it is mine. You can't wish someone to get hurt. You hear me?'

Tommy nodded again and James pulled him in for a hug.

Sarah continued, 'You made your Daddy so happy this weekend. He told me. He knows you love him.' Sarah said to her son, who moved into her arms again. 'It's ok baby, Mammy's got you. I'm right here. I'm not going anywhere.' She held him close and whispered words of reassurance.

Joey was standing in the corner and he felt like his heart was going to give in, seeing the family he'd grown to love going through so much anguish. It was too much for him.

'Back in a minute.' He said gruffly trying to cover up his sob as he left the room.

Rita took out a packet of tissues and handed one to each of them. 'I'm going through boxes of these at the moment!'

'Give me one of those.' Ruby said. She was in awe of her friend, the strength she had for her children.

Sarah said to the children, 'Didn't you say you wanted to make a get well card for Daddy?'

Katie nodded yes.

'Ok, go look in my handbag, you'll find some paper and some colouring pencils. Why don't you both get working on a design for him now?'

'Ok, Mammy.' Katie agreed, always willing to do whatever Sarah asked. 'I'll do a picture of a football for Daddy.'

'That's a good idea.' Sarah responded.

They sat down on the corner of the floor and started to make their cards. Ella was in Ruby's arms.

'The consultant is on his way, Sarah.' Rita said. 'He wants to speak to us all.'

'Me too? Sarah asked.

'Yes, you're his wife, so technically his next of kin.'

'Oh, Michelle won't like that.' Sarah whispered back.

'She'll have to get used to it!' Rita hissed back. 'I've had as much of her as I can manage right now.'

Sarah grabbed her baby into her arms and held her close.

'Daddy.' Ella said, her timing perfect.

She started to bounce up and down in Sarah's arms as she looked around the hospital room. It was full of new things for her curious little eyes to greedily soak up. She started to wave at Tommy and Katie who were still making their cards. They both smiled at their baby sister. She was funny.

'James, Ruby, when the consultant comes, can you take the children for a walk or something?'

'Of course we can.' Ruby answered. 'When they've finished doing their cards, I've a great game to play with them.'

Joey walked back into the room then. 'I'll help look after the small ones too.' He said to Sarah and Rita. 'I just needed to get some fresh air earlier. Your one is on her way back up too. I passed her by a minute ago. Thought I'd try to warn you she was nearly here.'

Sarah could hear the music from *The Wizard of Oz* playing in her mind, the score that played whenever the wicked witch of the west was flying by on her broomstick.

With that the door opened and Michelle walked in. She'd used the time to apply some make-up and she now looked more like the glamorous woman Sarah had first met.

'Quite the party going on here.' She said disdainfully to the room when she came in.

'We're his family.' Rita answered firmly. 'And we're not going anywhere!'

'I never said you had to.' She answered Rita sweetly. 'It's just I'm worried that too much noise would be too much for my Paulie.'

'Oh I have your number alright.' Rita replied. 'And as Paul's mother I know that he would want Sarah and the children here with him.'

'Is that Daddy's new friend?' Katie asked her Mammy looking the woman up and down.

'Yes. Come over you two and say hello.'

They walked over and stood in front of Michelle and they all looked each other up and down.

'I like your coat.' Katie said admiring the white woollen trench coat that Michelle had on. She leaned in to stroke it.

'Don't touch it.' Michelle snapped at her.

'Hey!' Ruby said moving in quickly towards Katie, throwing Michelle a look of contempt.

'She was only looking.' Tommy said to her. He wasn't going to let anyone snap at his sister. 'She's not very nice.' Tommy said in a loud whisper to Katie, which elicited a snort of laughter from James.

Michelle threw him a dirty look.

Sarah looked at this woman sharply. 'As Paul's friend I would say that you must be very pleased to meet his children. You must know how much he loves them, how important they are to him. He would expect any friend of his to always be nice to his children. That would be very important to him.' Sarah said pointedly.

The message in Sarah's words wasn't lost on Michelle. 'Of course I'm happy to meet them.' She said smiling one of her false beams their way. 'Come here and let me give each of you a hug.'

'Do we have to?' Tommy whispered to Sarah.

'You most certainly don't!' Sarah said to him.

Tommy and Katie both moved to the other side of the room as far away as possible from Daddy's new friend.

The door opened then and the consultant walked in.

'Hello, I'm Professor Donald Malone.' Seeing the children he immediately walked over to them. 'And who do we have here?' He asked them.

'I'm Katie.'

'I'm Tommy.'

'Well how nice to meet you both. Is Paul your Daddy?' he asked them gently. 'Not that I need ask you young man, you're the image of your father.'

279

Tommy nodded, a smile breaking out. He loved people saying he looked like him.

'Well isn't he a lucky man to have such lovely children as you two.' He patted them both on their heads affectionately. 'I know I'd be extremely proud if I was him.'

'Don't forget Ella!' Katie said pointing to her baby sister who was still in Sarah's arms.

'Well I couldn't miss you now could I?' he said to Ella, who gave him the benefit of her most winning smile.

'Well you're going to go a long way in life, little lady. You've worked out at this tender age that by smiling at us silly men, you'll get us to do anything for you!'

They all laughed at this. He was a nice man.

'Now, I need to talk to your Mammy for a minute.'

Sarah stepped forward and introduced herself.

'I wonder if one of your friends would take the children for a walk while we have a chat about Paul.' He asked nodding at the rest of the room.

James, Ruby and Joey stepped forward pulling the children in close to them. Katie who always was quick to grab an opportune moment, asked 'Uncle James, can I have ice-cream?'

'I reckon so.' James said, picking her up in his arms.

'We need to have a chat about your husband's condition. Would you like to do this somewhere more private?' Professor Malone said looking around at Rita and Michelle. Before Sarah could answer him, Michelle was on her feet.

'She's his ex-wife.' Michelle said quickly, jumping in. 'I'm his partner. It's me you should be talking to.'

The poor doctor looked embarrassed. 'I'm sorry, I didn't realise.'

'She's still his wife, Michelle. You're simply the mistress.' Rita retorted back. 'So I'd sit down if I were you.'

Sarah looked at her mother-in-law with both gratitude and embarrassment. She hadn't realised how much of a warrior she

280

really was. She was glad she had her on her side, but was slightly alarmed at having her business discussed so publicly!

The room went deathly silent and Ruby seeing the look of mortification on her friend's face stepped forward and turned to Professor Malone.

'I can assure you that this isn't a sketch from Jeremy Kyle.' She joked, to take the tension from the situation. 'It's actually really simple. Sarah is Paul's ex-wife, they are now separated. Michelle is Paul's partner. And you've met his mother Rita already. You need to speak to all three of them. The rest of us are going for ice-cream!'

'That makes perfect sense to me.' Professor Malone answered calmly. 'Make sure and have two scoops!' he told the children. Then when they had left he turned to Rita, Sarah and Michelle and said, 'Let's all take a seat.' He gestured to the row of seats at the end of the bed.

Rita leaned over and took Sarah's hand for moral support.

'There's no easy way to say this. I'm afraid the news is not good. Paul suffered a major blow to his head and he lost a lot of blood. Coupled with the extreme hypothermia he suffered, his vital organs have started to struggle. That's why he is now on life support.'

He stopped and allowed this news to sink in.

'So what can you do to help?' Sarah asked. 'Does he need surgery?'

'I'm afraid that surgery isn't an option in Paul's situation.' Professor Malone responded.

'But you can't just do nothing!' Michelle said.

'I know that this is incredibly difficult for you as his family to hear, but I'm afraid that we are out of options.'

'So we just wait and see if he improves himself?' Rita asked tearfully. 'Could that happen?

'I'm afraid that's just not going to happen. Even if we could find a way to save Paul's heart, he would never recover consciousness. We have done extensive tests and they are all conclusive. Paul is brain dead. He will never wake up from this coma.'

Michelle started to cry, 'My baby, my baby.' Sarah didn't know if she was referring to Paul or to her unborn child. Either way, it was obvious that Michelle was deeply distressed and for that Sarah felt sorry for her. She held out her other hand and grasped Michelle's in hers. Michelle didn't pull away and squeezed it back.

'I don't believe it.' Rita said quietly. 'He's my son. I'm supposed to go first, that's the natural order of things. Please Professor Malone. There must be something you can do.'

He shook his head sadly.

'Sarah, talk to him.' Rita begged. 'Make him try harder. There's always another way.'

Sarah wanted to get up and run out of the room. She couldn't bear to hear the words the doctor was saying to her. Paul, the man she had spent pretty much all of her adult life with, was never going to talk again, never would hold their children in his arms again. Time stood still. The room became deathly silent.

'I wish I had different news to tell you all, I really do. But you have some decisions to make now.' Professor Malone said. 'As Paul is brain dead, we need you to think about your next step which is when to discontinue life support.'

'But he'll die!' Michelle shouted.

'He's already dead though.' Rita shouted back. 'Isn't he? Isn't that what you're saying to us? Or as good as!'

'I'm so sorry.' He said again. 'I wish I had something else to say to you.'

'The children,' Sarah sobbed. 'How will I tell the children?'

Rita walked over to the girl who she thought of as her own daughter. 'We'll do it together, Sarah. I'll not leave you on your own doing that.' Sarah and Rita embraced and sobbed together for the man they both loved. Michelle walked over to the other side of the bed and held Paul's hand, tears falling down her face.

The three women in Paul's life united at last in their horror and grief.

'There's one other thing I need you to think about. I know how awful this is for you all but I have to ask you if you would like to donate Paul's organs, when the time comes. Paul could save so many lives, if you agree. I will answer any questions you have if you would like to discuss it further.'

All three women looked at the doctor open-mouthed, reeling from the news that had just been delivered.

'I'll leave you for now.' Professor Malone said, 'But just ask the nurse to get me back anytime.'

'Send in some tea to them.' He said to the nurse when he walked out. 'And whenever they want to talk, just buzz me. I'll come back as soon as I can. I don't envy the decision they have facing them.'

Rita, Sarah and Michelle sat in the small hospital room silent; locked in their own personal hell.

Eventually Sarah spoke. 'I wonder what Paul would make of this? The three of us, together.'

'He'd be in a cold sweat.' Michelle said. 'If he could move right now, he'd be out that door…' she finished on a sob.

'What are we going to do?' Rita said.

'I don't know.' Sarah replied. 'My head is spinning. How are we supposed to make a decision like this?'

Nobody answered her. 'Does anybody know how Paul felt about life support?' Rita asked. 'We never discussed it; it never even came up in conversation.'

'He never spoke about anything like this to me either.' Michelle said. 'We didn't have any real serious conversations at all come to think about it. We were too busy having fun – dinners, parties, and the theatre.'

Sarah looked at her sharply. Was she trying to rub her nose her nose in it? She didn't think so this time however. Michelle seemed lost in her own reminiscence.

'I don't think that Paul would want us to give up on him.' Rita said. 'We should leave him on life support, you never know, there could be a chance he'll come round!'

'We spoke about this after Thomas died.' Sarah said quietly.

'Who's Thomas?' Michelle asked.

'Paul's father.' Sarah answered her.

'I never really knew him at all, did I?' Michelle said in wonder. 'I didn't even know that.'

'Maybe you knew a side to Paul that I didn't.' Sarah replied.

'Maybe.' Michelle said quietly.

'Thomas was in terrible pain in those last few weeks of his life.' Sarah continued. 'He begged Paul to help him die, until by the end he didn't even know his own name, never mind who his family were.'

Sarah glanced at Rita; she knew her words were so painful to hear.

'The night that Thomas died, Paul and I sat up for hours talking. He said that he'd never want to end up his days like his father had. He said that he'd rather die with his dignity than end up not even knowing who he was.'

'So are you saying that he'd want us to pull the plug?' Michelle said bluntly.

Rita looked like she had been slapped across her face. 'Please don't use that term again. You make it sound like all we have to do is turn the TV off!'

Michelle just shrugged. She looked like she was back in form again. For a short spell she had seemed almost human, but the wicked witch of the west was back in the room with them.

'Sarah, do you think that Paul would want us to discontinue life support?' Rita said to her, taking one of her hands. 'Is that what you're saying?'

'Yes, I think I am.' Sarah replied.

'I don't think I have the strength to do that for him. What if in a few years they find some new science to cure people?' Rita replied.

Sarah nodded. That thought kept coming into her mind too.

'What if they don't?' Michelle said. 'Do you think Paul would want to lie here for years, only breathing because a machine did it for him? Do you want to put your children through that Sarah,

284

living in false hope for years and years for a father to come back to them that never could? I don't want that for my child.'

Sarah could not answer that.

'What about my child?' Rita demanded. 'I'll not agree to it, do you hear?'

'We don't have to make a decision straight away.' Sarah said to them both. 'I for one am not ready to yet. Let's leave it for a few hours. But whatever happens, we all must be in agreement, ok? Right, I need to go for a walk, to clear my head.' She turned to face Michelle, 'Not a word of this to the children if they come back here. Or so help me Michelle, I will kill you.'

'Not before I got there first.' Rita muttered.

'Michelle?' Sarah asked her.

'I know I'm a bitch sometimes, but I'm not completely heartless. I'll not say anything to your children. They've enough coming their way, without me adding to it.' Michelle replied.

'Thank you.' Sarah said to her.

Sarah gave Rita a kiss and left. It was at times like these that she wished she still smoked. She hadn't wanted a cigarette in over ten years, but now she'd kill for one.

She eventually ended up outside the hospital chapel. It was as good a place as any to sit quietly, so she entered.

She was unsurprised to see Edward waiting for her.

'I can't do this.'

'It's an impossible situation.' Edward replied.

'How can I tell the children that their Daddy is dead?' Sarah started to cry again. 'I need you to help me. You have to answer me truthfully.'

Edward nodded.

'Is there any chance that he could be ok? Is Paul still in there somewhere, trying to wake up and come back to us?'

Edward looked at his friend and he wished with all his heart that he could take away the pain that Sarah was facing. She was so brave trying to decide what to do, but she was in so much pain. 'I'm sorry but he's not coming back. He's waiting to move on now.'

'You mean he wants us to switch the machine off?' Sarah asked.

'Yes, he's ready. His father is waiting for him. He wants to bring him home.'

'Thomas is here?' Sarah whispered. 'That's good.'

Sarah put her head in her hands. 'I don't think I can do this.'

'Yes, you can Sarah. You will do what's best, I have faith in you.' Edward replied.

'I'm not sure that Rita will agree. I don't blame her, if it were one of mine...'

Sarah sighed and closed her eyes to pray for strength.

'Do you trust what I've told you?' Edward asked her, his eyes burning into Sarah's.

'You know I do.'

'Then let him go, Sarah. It's his time to go.'

When Sarah got back to the ward Michelle was on the phone in the corner, talking to her mother, quietly weeping again. Rita was sitting holding Paul's hand saying a decade of the rosary.

Michelle put down the phone. 'I can't handle this right now. I have to think of my baby. I'm sorry, I loved Paul, but it's too much. I'm going home.'

'You deserve a say in what happens to him.' Sarah said to her, incredulous that she was leaving.

'I don't think I do.' She replied. 'I think he loved the idea of me, but we never had what you two had. We had a few months of fun and who knows, if I hadn't gotten pregnant it would probably have fizzled out by now. I didn't even know his father's name! And you want to know why I didn't know that? Because, I didn't care. If you love someone you want to know everything about them. So you see, it's not my decision as to what happens to him. You two should make it, you both loved him. Call me when you decide. But either way, I'm going home tonight and I'm not coming back.'

'You have to be the most selfish woman I've ever had the misfortune to meet.' Sarah said.

'I'll let you away with that. I probably deserve it.' Michelle stated.

She walked over to Paul's bedside and kissed him lightly on his lips.

Rita stood up and walked over to her. 'I'm sorry that you feel you the way you do. I know we haven't hit it off, but that baby you're carrying is my grandchild. Please don't cut me out of your life.'

She nodded and looked again at the man lying on the bed. 'I'm sorry.' She turned and walked out.

Chapter Thirty Four

Sarah and Rita joined the others in the family room. All three children were curled up on a couch, fast asleep.

'They were exhausted.' James told Sarah, 'I put on the TV in here and about five minutes later they were zonked.' He looked up at his sister and walked over quickly to her, 'What is it? What's happened?'

Sarah told them the news.

James was shell-shocked. He'd hated Paul for months for what he'd done to his sister and more than once he'd wished he'd fallen over a cliff, but he'd not really meant it.

'So what happens now?' Ruby asked.

'We have a decision to make.' Sarah replied softly.

'I can't do it. I won't do it.' Rita said firmly, Joey close by her side.

'We have to think about what Paul would want.' Sarah said gently to her.

'He'd want to live!' Rita declared.

'Not like this.' Sarah continued. 'We have to let him go, Rita. Thomas is here waiting for him. Paul wants to go to his father; he's ready to move on.'

'No.' Rita shouted, looking alarmed. 'Stop it! Stop saying such things!'

'What do you mean Thomas is here?' Ruby asked.

James walked over to Sarah and asked, 'Edward?'

'Yes.'

'Ok, that's the second time you've mentioned Edward.' Ruby stated. 'What's going on? Is this to do with how you worked out where Tommy and Paul were?'

Sarah looked around her. Rita, Joey, Ruby and James all staring at her. Sarah felt sadness overcome her wondering which of these relationships would be a casualty of her confession? Who would find it too much to cope with, just like her parents had?

But she could no longer hide from the truth of who she was. Eventually she answered Ruby, 'You're right; I didn't just pluck that information from the sky.'

James walked over to stand closer to Sarah, showing his support.

She took a deep breath, then continued. 'I'm psychic.' She let that sit for a moment. 'I know that this must seem very strange to you, but it's very real I promise you.' Sarah said earnestly.

'When we were children Sarah spent a large chunk of time playing with her guardian angel.' James interjected.

Sarah continued with some steel creeping into her voice. 'Edward – my angel's name is Edward. You see, my earliest memories always included two people.' She reached over and held James' hand and said. 'Edward and James. They were both always with me; I had such happy memories with them. The two most important people in my life.'

James squeezed Sarah's hand, glad that he was here with her now. He knew by this admission, she would be dredging up some very painful memories; she needed all the support she could get.

She could see the look of scepticism flash across their faces. Joey made the sign of the cross on his chest, as if something evil had just come into the room. In that action she instantly regretted her admission. They wouldn't understand.

'Give them a chance.' Edward said to her. 'Don't give up without even trying to help them understand.'

'I haven't seen Edward since I was ten years old, but then about two months ago he came back into my life and I started to have psychic dreams and visions, mostly while I was sleeping, but sometimes they even happen when I'm awake too. And they seem to be pretty accurate.'

Rita looked like she was about to faint with the shock. Ruby was harder to read.

'And you're saying that you saw something about Paul's accident?' Rita asked.

'Yes. Yesterday, I saw Paul lying in the snow, bleeding. I tried to warn him that he was in danger. He just laughed when I told him.'

'And what about young Tommy? Did you have a dream about that too?' Joey asked looking confused.

'Not at first. It was only last night that I saw that he was with Paul, in the car.'

'I don't know what to think!' Rita said, sounding very hurt. 'Why have you never told any of us about this before?'

'I'm sorry, Rita; I was very worried about telling anyone. I didn't want to risk saying anything to you all in case you didn't believe me, and I couldn't have borne that.'

It didn't go unnoticed to James that so far nobody had made any comment one way or the other about believing her.

'You said you've had several dreams and that they'd come true. What else?' Ruby spoke for the first time.

Sarah took a deep breath; she wasn't sure what to tell them. She looked at Joey and wondered should she tell him about her vision of his future. Maybe later, but not right now.

She told them about Bridie and how she helped her a few days previously.

'Be the lord.' Joey exclaimed. 'That's some story.'

James couldn't help but laugh at the expression on his face.

'It all seems very farfetched.' Rita said. 'I don't know what to think if I'm honest.'

Sarah felt like crying. She wished with all her heart that Rita would have just stood up and taken her into her arms, saying that of course she believed her. If she said it was true, that was good enough for her. But it didn't look like that was going to happen.

'Have faith.' Edward said again to her.

'It must be a lot to take in.' Sarah acknowledged. 'I found it very hard to get my head around it all myself, so I understand that it must sound strange to you.'

'What else have you dreamt, Sarah.' Joey said with obvious curiosity.

'I've had dreams about Rachel Finch's murderer.' She replied quietly.

Joey made the sign of the cross on himself again. 'You've seen the murderer?'

'Yes. I dreamt about him and then when I was at the funeral I recognised him from my dreams.'

James sat down beside his sister. 'It was because of Sarah's dream that I looked into Mal Wickham as a possible murder suspect. And now he's in custody being questioned.'

'You said it was an anonymous tip off!' Ruby said to him. 'You never said it was Sarah.'

'It wasn't my secret to share.' James said. 'But I hated lying to you, honestly.'

'Ruby?' Sarah asked her friend who looked quite pale.

'I'm ok. Just taking it all in. You ever dream about me?'

'No never. But it was Edward who talked me into ringing you when I did. The best thing I've ever done.'

Ruby moved a step closer to Sarah, but still kept her distance.

'Well I've never heard the like of this before.' Rita interjected. She was definitely finding it hard to accept. 'Angels!'

'I've known you for years and you've never mentioned a guardian angel before.' Ruby said. Sarah could tell she was wondering if perhaps it was all made up, but couldn't work out why.

'I've never mentioned Edward to you because, as I said, until a couple of months ago I'd not seen him for years. You see when I told my parents about Edward they didn't believe he existed. They thought I simply had an imaginary friend and they did everything in their power to make me admit that.'

She shuddered at the memory.

'It was a horrible time for Sarah back then,' James said. 'My parents were relentless in their quest to get her to admit she was making it all up. They just wouldn't open their minds up for even a moment to contemplate that just maybe Sarah wasn't telling them lies. The more she was adamant that she was telling the truth the more angry they got.' He shook his head as he remembered that time. If he was ever lucky enough to have children of his own one day he vowed that he'd never not believe them if they swore something to be true, no matter how fantastical it sounded.

Sarah continued, 'They told me if I didn't admit I was lying that they would start taking away things from me. The first thing to go was the television. I wasn't allowed watch anything until I admitted I was lying.'

'That went on for nearly a month!' James remembered.

'Did you see this Edward guy, James?' Joey asked.

'No, I never saw him myself, but I knew he was there alright. I believed Sarah; we're twins, we always know if the other is lying. Plus she never lost a single game of hide and seek in all the years we played it. He always told her where I was!'

Sarah started to smile at the memory. 'That's true!'

James continued, 'When the TV ban didn't work they decided that they would take away all of Sarah's treats. No sweets, no cakes or biscuits, basically she was put on the bare rations for all her meals. And if I even tried to give anything to her, then Dad would go mental. It was cruel.'

'I'd say most children would have said they were lying, just to keep the peace.' Joey said.

'That's true.' James replied. 'But most people aren't Sarah.'

'And then finally the bible came out.' Sarah said. 'They kept making me swear on it that I was telling the truth. But when I swore that I wasn't making it up they got really angry, saying I was blaspheming by lying with a bible in my hand. I just couldn't win.

They brought the parish priest in, who in fairness tried to speak up for me, but they wouldn't listen to him either.'

Sarah felt a tear run down her face, as she remembered this time in her life that was very painful. 'I mean, I was brought up always to tell the truth and I wasn't lying, but by not lying I was getting in such trouble. And it was causing so much pain all around me. I could see that James was also getting it too, because the more he tried to stick up for me, the more mad they got with him too.'

'I should have done more.' James said with remorse. 'I've always felt guilty for not stopping them.'

'You did more than any ten year old should have to.' Sarah said in earnest. 'You couldn't have stopped them, nobody could. They were on a quest.'

Sarah had buried the memories so deep it was very painful dusting them off.

'Eventually they ran out of patience with me and brought me to see a doctor. I was referred to a psychiatrist and, to cut a very long story short, I was admitted to a hospital for psychiatric treatment.' Sarah could feel the tears pouring now. 'It was horrible there. The questions were endless. I was physically and emotionally at the end of my tether. And then they played their trump card, I was told that James wasn't allowed to visit me anymore. I was a bad influence on him and they felt it was safer for James if we didn't spend any time together in future. This was just the last straw for me. I was so scared all the time and so lonely. I loved Edward, but James is my twin. So I told them what they wanted to hear. I told them I'd made it all up and I begged Edward to go away and never come back.'

Rita stood up and walked over to Sarah. 'Ah Sarah, how dreadful for you. I always wondered why you and your parents have such a strained relationship.' She sat down on the other side of Sarah and gave her a hug. 'How could they not believe you? You're the most truthful person I know. If you say that this is true, then that's good enough for me.'

Sarah slumped into Rita's arms. She felt years and years of self-doubt and pain pour out of her and a hurt that had been hidden inside a part of her she'd not looked into for a long time, began to heal.

Joey was crying too. He'd grown awfully fond of the two women who were in such pain in front of him. Having spent years being on his own, with no family so to speak, he finally felt like he was part of something bigger than himself.

He walked over and said to Sarah, 'I believe you too. I always thought it was an angel that brought you into my life anyhow. When I think about how lonely I was before you came along… That was no accident was it? You knew how I was feeling?' He didn't finish the statement. James thumped him on the shoulder. He had a lump in his throat. He was watching Ruby closely. He needed her to believe Sarah, because if she didn't, he wasn't sure where that would leave them both for the future.

Ruby moved over to Sarah. 'I would have believed you.' She stated with such sincerity that Sarah was ashamed she hadn't trusted her years ago.

'Edward, is he here?' Joey asked.

'Yes. He says he never left me, but he just didn't show himself. He's here when I need him. Like right now.' She nodded in the direction of the sleeping children, where he was standing beside them, on guard.

Joey jumped and looked quickly over there. 'Is he standing there now?'

'Yes, as it happens he is.' Sarah answered.

For the third time made the sign of the cross and then genuflected for good measure!

'Edward says thank you Joey, but that's not necessary.' Sarah said smiling.

'I've never been in a room with an angel before,' he said. 'Wasn't sure what the protocol was!'

Sarah and Ruby started to giggle at this. Before long Rita and James joined in, followed soon by Joey too.

The highly charged emotions just passed fuelled their giggles, making everything seem alright for a minute.

Edward said to Sarah, 'I hate to say I told you so, but I told you so. I knew they'd believe you.'

It wasn't long before the laughter stopped and they all remembered the reason that triggered the recent heart to heart they had just shared.

'I tried my very best to make Paul believe me.' Sarah said to Rita earnestly. 'I even told him that I was psychic. And that was a hard thing for me to admit to, believe me. But he kept making fun of me, he didn't believe a word I said, I could tell. If only I had known that Tommy was in the car all that time.'

'You said that Thomas is here.' Rita replied, clasping Sarah's hand.

Edward walked over to Sarah and said. 'Tell Rita that Thomas says, do you remember Kenmare?'

Sarah turned to her mother and said, 'Rita, Thomas says to remember Kenmare.'

Rita paled and whispered, 'Thomas! You are here!'

'Yes.' Sarah replied gently. 'He's here for Paul and you too. Do you know what he means by Kenmare?'

Rita nodded. 'We went to Kenmare for our 30th wedding anniversary. Thomas was sick, but even so we had a great time. We talked for hours; it was like we were young again. I told him I was scared, didn't want to be on my own.'

She stood up and looked around the room wondering where her husband was. She held her hand up as if to caress the air in front of her.

'Thomas said to me that he'd always be here for me. That even death wouldn't keep him away from me if I needed him.'

'He kept his promise.' Sarah said, clasping her hand. 'He's here, as he said he would be.'

'I know.' Rita said between sobs. 'I can feel him. I've been sitting here praying for a sign, something to show me what we should do.'

'He was a good man, Rita.'

'So we have to say goodbye to Paul, let him go to his father?' Rita said.

Sarah nodded silently.

Edward said, 'Tell Rita this.'

Sarah listened then repeated his words, as he spoke, her eyes wide in wonder.

'Some good can come from this awful situation, Rita. If we donate Paul's organs, we're giving three people the chance of a better, healthier life. We can save their lives, and one will be a little boy who has been waiting a very long time for a donor.'

'I want to see Paul.' Rita said suddenly, standing up.

'I'll go with you.' Sarah said. 'James, when the children wake up, bring them in.'

Rita walked over to her son and stroked his head, 'You will be a hero, Paul. Three lives you will save. I'm so proud of you.'

'So our decision is made?' Sarah asked quietly.

'Yes.' Rita replied, never taking her eyes off her boy.

They sat, one on either side of him.

After a time, the door opened and the children walked in with the others.

'Is Daddy still sleeping?' Katie said to her Mammy, who nodded in response.

'What did the doctor say?' Tommy asked.

'Well we need to have a chat about that.' Sarah replied. 'Let's all sit down.'

Rita and Sarah sat on either side of Tommy and Katie. Ella was in her buggy fast asleep.

'The doctors have been doing lots of tests on Daddy.' Sarah said to them. 'And they have said that his brain is really badly hurt.'

'That doesn't sound very nice.' Katie said solemnly. 'Can they give him medicine to fix it?'

'I'm afraid that they can't, darling. Daddy was hurt so badly that he's not going to wake up again.'

Tommy and Katie looked really scared now.

Sarah took a deep breath and continued. 'You see that machine that Daddy is hooked up to?'

They both looked over at it and nodded.

'Well, that machine is helping Daddy to breath and helping his heart to beat, because they won't work any more on their own.'

Their eyes were wide with shock. Sarah was shaking. She could see them both trembling too.

'Do you remember Granddaddy Thomas?' Rita asked them both.

'Yes Nana.' Tommy answered. 'When we say our prayers, we always say God bless Granddaddy Thomas in Heaven.'

Rita smiled at her grandson. 'That's right pet. Well your Granddaddy Thomas wants your Daddy to come and be with him in Heaven.' Rita said. 'He's waiting for him now.'

Katie started to cry. 'But if Daddy goes to Heaven with Granddaddy we won't be able to see him.' Katie said.

'I know that darling. It's very scary to think that isn't it?' Sarah said to her.

Katie nodded.

'Is Daddy dead?' Tommy asked her. 'He doesn't look dead, Mammy.'

'I know. I thought that too. He looks so peaceful doesn't he? But that's because he's ready to go on and see Granddaddy Thomas now.'

'I don't want him to go.' Tommy said, crying now too. 'Make him stay with us instead.' He walked over to his father's bed and started to cry, 'Daddy, don't go. Stay here with us. You promised me you wouldn't leave me again. A promise is a promise, Daddy!' He finished sobbing. Sarah walked over and held her son in her arms. Katie was in her Nana's arms sobbing too.

'He didn't mean to break that promise.' Sarah said to him. 'It was an accident darling. Your Daddy would never have left you if he could have helped it. He loved you all so much.'

Ruby and James watched the scene unfold in front of them, powerless to do anything.

Joey walked over to Rita and put his arms around her as she held Katie in her own.

'We have to say our goodbyes now.' Sarah said to the children. 'You can take as long as you want.'

Joey walked over to Paul's bedside and said, 'I'll look after your Mam, Paul, I give you my word.' He touched him on his hand.

Ruby touched Paul's face gently and said, 'Have a G&T for me up there, Paul Lawler.' Then she walked back to Ella and started rocking the pram. Sarah lifted Katie up so that she was sitting on the side of Paul's bed.

'Can I snuggle him?' Katie asked.

'Yes my darling, of course you can.' Sarah answered.

Katie moved her little body in close to her Daddy's and put her arms around his neck. 'I love you Daddy. I'll see you in Chocolate Land in my dreams.' She whispered.

Then suddenly, she said, 'Mammy I want to go home. I don't want to be here anymore. Please Mammy.' She was very distressed. Sarah pulled her away from Paul and held her close. 'We're going home very soon, I promise you that.'

Joey walked over and took her into his arms, carrying her to one of the seats. 'There now. I've got you; you just cry it out.'

Tommy was just staring at his Daddy, never taking his eyes off him. Sarah watched him and said nothing. She didn't want to push him right now. He needed to do this in his own way.

He looked over to Katie and Ella, his Nana and finally his Mammy. 'Daddy I have to go now. Katie and Ella need me. Katie's getting scared and Ella is probably scared too, she's only a baby.' He leaned in and kissed his Daddy on his cheek. 'I know you didn't break your promise. I love you Daddy.'

He walked over to Katie and she jumped out of Joey's lap to go to him. They gave each other a hug. Thank God for brothers and sisters, Sarah thought. 'I have to take the children home,

Rita. I've got to think of them now. We can't be here for ...
You know....'

'You go home and put the children to bed in their own house.
It's what they need right now. They need their Mammy, just like
Paul needs me here. I'll stay with him until the end.'

Sarah nodded. She walked over to Paul and kissed him on his
lips. 'Thank you Paul for giving me our children, for loving me,
for the life we shared.' She touched him lightly on his forehead,
moving his hair to one side again. His fringe always flopped down.

'Come to us when you get home.' Sarah said to Rita, giving her
a hug. 'We'll be waiting for you.'

Joey got up and hugged Sarah too, saying gruffly. 'Drive carefully now. You're my family now.'

'I know Joey.' She said.

James took her hand and held it tightly. 'Let's go home.'

Chapter Thirty Five

It was 5am. The children were all asleep. They were exhausted from the previous day and had slept most of the journey home.

Ruby had curled into bed beside Sarah. She held her like she was a child and stroked her hair until she fell asleep crying.

Sarah needed to get out of the house; she felt that the walls were closing in on her. She had woken up thirty minutes before and felt so much tension bubbling up inside of her, she needed to scream and she thought that if she started, she'd never stop. She quickly wrote a note and stuck it on the fridge. Sticking on a pair of wellies and a coat, she walked out to her car. She didn't really know where she was going to go, but she knew that she needed to get out of the house.

Before she knew it she had arrived at Ballyaislinn beach. She parked the car in the car park. It was empty and beautiful there. Daylight was just breaking through the dark clouds of night and golden rays reflected on the crashing waves. She pulled her coat around her tight. It was bitterly cold, but she welcomed the feel of the sharp wind on her face. It made her feel alive and she needed to feel that way right now. She walked to the water's edge and felt saltwater tears wash her face.

The stress of the past few days finally exploded out of her and she started to scream, gut wrenching shrieks that bounced off the waves.

She screamed until her throat hurt. What use was the gift of a gift that didn't stop someone she cared about dying?

Edward stood beside her. 'You warned Paul, he chose not to listen to you. But think about the lives you have saved. Tommy, Joey, Bridie. And the lives you've changed for the better? Marie? Where would she be if you hadn't used your gift to uncover Malcolm?'

'I should have done more.' Sarah screamed again.

'You know that's not true, Sarah.' Edward replied calmly. 'You cannot control the actions of others. Paul was not going to listen to you no matter what you said.'

But all the months of change and turmoil had finally come to a head for Sarah. Edward stood there, watching over his friend. He watched her as she screamed and ranted at the sea, until she had no more to give.

'You must get sick of the sight of me crying,' she joked, then stopped suddenly as she felt the energy change around her. She was having another vision.

A little boy is sitting up in hospital, bandages around his face. His mother and father are standing by his bedside, in silent prayer. A doctor gently removes the bandages and urges the boy to take his time, let his new eyes become adjusted to the light.

And then, miraculously, he speaks, 'Mammy, You look pretty.'

He sees everything.

Sarah looks at Edward, who is smiling at her.

'Paul did that,' he states.

The boy is on a trampoline, jumping up and down, laughing with his friends.

Then, time flashes forward and Sarah sees him wearing a mortarboard and gown, his parents clapping and cheering him on at his graduation. Their little boy now a man.

She sees him at the top of an altar waiting for his bride on his wedding day, and he gasps as he sees her beauty.

He holds their firstborn, a boy, in his arms and has never seen a more beautiful sight. He closes his eyes and thanks God once again for the donor that changed his life.

'Paul did that.' Sarah repeats smiling.

'When the time is right, you can tell Rita and the children about that boy.'

Sarah nods in response, she still feels in awe at the vision she has just witnessed.

'Go home to your children.' Edward said gently.

'I can't bear the thought of them feeling even one fraction of how I feel right now, Edward.'

'They have you. That's all they need.' He reassured her.

Sarah lifted her top up and wiped her face which was wet from the sea and her tears.

The angel turned and waited for Sarah to head back to her car. She stopped suddenly, and they both felt the now familiar feeling of a shift in energy.

Edward watched as Sarah's hand flew to her mouth in surprise at what she was seeing in her vision.

He smiled.

'I was just going to look for you!' James said to her, as she returned home.

Ruby was standing behind him too. 'You can't do that, Sarah! Jeepers, our nerves!'

'Are the kids ok?' Sarah asked them.

'All fast asleep. I just checked.' Ruby answered. 'You look frozen. Come in, time for coffee.'

'Where have you been?' James asked.

'I needed to get out for a while. I went for a drive and ended up on Ballyaislinn beach but there's something I have to tell you.'

'You're giving me a heart attack here. You know I'm helping investigate a murder that happened there. Of all the places to go to, you decide to have a walk on fecking Ballyaislinn beach in the middle of the night!'

'Don't be cross with me. I can't take that right now. And the murderer is still locked up isn't he?' Sarah said.

He nodded in reply. 'So he wasn't going to hurt me and I reckon that we'd be very unlikely to have a second psychopath in our small village!' Sarah finished.

James said. 'I was just worried. I need you to be safe. I couldn't bear it if something happened to you.'

He was still shook up about Paul. 'That could have been you; I can't stop thinking of that.'

Sarah looked up at him, 'How so?'

'You slipped on the snow two days ago, what if you had cracked your head open like Paul did?' James said.

'I'm fine.' She answered him gently.

'Did the walk help at all?' Ruby asked Sarah.

'Yes, it did as it happens. I needed to shout and scream and I can't do that here. Here I'm Mammy and I have to be strong for the children. I mourned Paul once already when he left me; I never thought I'd have to do it for real. I'm not sure I can find the strength to do it a second time.'

'Oh sis.' James said giving her a hug. 'Remember you don't have to be strong for me. You can shout and scream to me anytime you like.'

'I just needed to be on my own.' Sarah whispered.

'I understand.' Ruby said, placing a hot steaming cup in front of her. 'We've all got to escape every now and then.'

'I wish the kids didn't have to go through this.' Sarah said.

'They're tough like their mother. They'll get through it.' James said.

Sarah put her hands around the hot drink and let the mug warm them. She was cold but remembered what she had seen before she got in her car. She had to tell James.

'When I was on Ballyaislinn beach, in the car park, I had a vision.' Sarah had decided to keep the vision about the little boy to herself for now. Rita should be the first to hear that. But James needed to know about this second one.

'I'm nearly afraid to ask.' James replied, excitement building inside him despite his comment to contrary.

'I saw a courier van called Arlen's in the car park, passing what looked like computers to another car parked there. Then the driver of the car hit the driver of the van to make it look like he'd been attacked. After the car left with the stolen computers, the van driver saw someone walking back from the beach with something that looked like large piece of driftwood. He remembered because it was such a strange thing to see someone carrying. He saw the man clearly, James. He saw Mal Wickham.'

'Oh Jaysus, this is huge!' James exclaimed. 'Let me get this straight. You're saying that there was somebody else in that car park that night, and they saw Mal?'

'Yes, that's exactly what I'm saying. Find that courier driver and you have your witness.'

'It's like watching a movie! Have you any idea how cool this psychic stuff is?' Ruby asked. 'I'm all ears to hear what's in store for me!'

Sarah smiled at her friend.

'I've got to go see Roger straight away with this information.' James stopped suddenly. 'I can't leave you though.'

'Yes you can.' Sarah replied. 'You have a job to do, so go do it. We'll all be here tonight when you're finished. Maybe you can bring a takeaway home with you as a treat for the kids.'

'I'm going to stick around here today too.' Ruby said to them both. 'That's if I'm not in the way.'

'You have made yourself pretty much indispensable to me, Rubes.' Sarah said to her.

'Well, I can't lie, I am pretty amazing,' her friend replied in mock seriousness. She was delighted that she had been able to make Sarah smile. Things were going to be so hard over the coming months and Ruby vowed to herself that she'd be there for Sarah every step of the way.

James was dressed and out the door in a few minutes. He called into his office as it was so early. He figured there was no point waking up Roger before six am. He turned on the computer and started looking for any reported incidents by courier companies in October. It was too easy really, as Sarah had given it to him on a plate. There it was in The Wexford Echo, a courier van was hijacked on its way to the depot, with over twenty computers taken. The driver sustained a broken nose during the attack with no possible suspects identified. Arlen Couriers were in Arklow, about thirty minutes away.

He drove to the industrial estate where the courier company was based and wandered around the back, into a big warehouse.

'Can I help you?'

'Sure can.' He flashed his badge. 'I'm looking for a guy who works here called Tony O'Connor.'

'You're in luck; he's on shift at the minute. Try the locker room.'

He pointed in the direction of the back of the warehouse. James walked quickly to the locker room and a few minutes later he was face to face with the bold Tony.

'You got a minute?' James said to him.

'Sure.'

'I want to talk to you about the hijacking on October 3rd.'

'I've told you lot everything I know.' He said. 'Not sure how I can help you?'

'Maybe you could start by telling me how long you have been ripping off your employers?' James asked bluntly.

'What the ...?' Tony spluttered.

'I know that you set up the hijacking, Tony, on Ballyaislinn beach and you were in on the whole thing.'

The man's face whitened with shock.

'That's a serious crime you committed there. You're going to spend a long time behind bars for that one.'

Tony was lost for words.

'You'll be relieved to hear that I'm not interested in what you were up to that night. I should be, but I have a bigger issue I need your help with. I want to know about the man you saw on the beach that night.' James continued.

'How do you know that?' Tony asked. He'd never told anyone that he'd seen a soul.

'That doesn't matter. I'm going to need you to come to the station with me now. I need to find out exactly what you saw.'

'I'm saying nothing.' He said, finally finding his voice.

'Then I'm going to charge you right now. Shall we do it here, or will I move us to the middle of the warehouse floor to ensure that everyone sees us?'

'Hey man, no need for that. I'll talk but only if I get something out of it.' Tony said.

'Come down the station and we'll work something out.' James said to him, sure that if he presented him to Roger, he'd make a deal, for the right information.

'I'm due on shift now.' He said trying one more time to dodge the bullet.

'I'm happy to arrest you, Tony. You're coming with me the easy or the hard way, you choose.'

Five minutes later they were on their way back to the station. James called Roger on the way and told him to meet him there.

'I've had an anonymous tip off earlier this morning.' He said to him when he arrived at the station. He quickly filled Roger in on the incident on Ballyaislinn beach.

Roger looked at him sceptically. 'I'm not buying this tip off story. But I don't really care how you found out about this O'Connor fella right now. I just want to get this case wrapped up.'

After taking a formal statement from Tony, Roger and Johnny walked into the interview room where Mal Wickham was sitting with his lawyer. She had arrived a few minutes ago and looked ready to do battle once again.

'Just how much longer do you intend to hold my client?' Elaine demanded. 'This is an outrageous infringement on my client's constitutional rights.'

Roger ignored her and turned to Mal saying, 'Malcolm Wickham, I am arresting you on suspicion of murdering Rachel

Finch on October 3rd 2012. You are not obliged to say anything unless you wish to do so, but whatever you say will be taken down in writing and may be given in evidence.'

Mal slumped down on the table.

Chapter Thirty Six

12 months later

Christmas Day

Sarah stood in the door of her dining room and looked around at her family and friends who were gathered side by side, waiting to dig into the Christmas dinner that was before them. Rita and Joey, James and Ruby and Mary were all there, right beside the children. She heard murmurs of appreciation from the group as they took in the feast that was laid before them. The only thing missing was the turkey which was ready and waiting to be carried in.

Sarah's eye drifted down to the bracelet she was wearing. One single charm hung from it, a small silver heart. She smiled as she remembered Art placing it on her wrist, his touch making the tiny hairs on her arm rise.

'Every year, I will add a new charm and when there are no more links left, I'll buy another bracelet and then another and another...'

'You plan on sticking around?' Sarah had teased.

'I'm not going anywhere. This is where I want to be.'

Only a year ago, she'd thought she'd blown any chance of a future with Art. She figured that whatever they had tentatively began, had ended on that night that Tommy and Paul went missing.

But the day after Paul died, Art called to see her and as soon as he saw her ashen face, he reached for her. Sarah stepped back from his embrace; she knew that if they had any chance to move on, now was the time to be honest. No more hiding.

'We have to talk. There are things I need to tell you.' She told him.

Sitting at her kitchen table she shared with him her relationship with Edward, finally telling him about Paul's death.

He said very little throughout it all, asking the odd question, understanding that he needed to let her speak and just listen. When she told him Paul had died, he pulled her towards him and held her as she cried.

'This is becoming a habit.' She whispered to him as she pointed to his shirt, now smudged with mascara.

She looked up to him earnestly, 'I understand, you know, if you can't get your head around all the Edward stuff.'

'For someone who claims to be psychic, you're not very good at seeing what's right in front of you,' he had replied gently. 'I've been dying to ask you out for ages, have had a stupid crush on you since you called up to the office to see me all those months ago and ruined my shirt!'

Sarah was stunned. She had no idea he felt that way about her for so long.

'I know that my timing is lousy but I need to tell you this. I'm pretty sure I'm in love with you Sarah.'

'You love me?' Sarah asked incredulous. 'You don't think I'm crazy?'

'Yes and Yes! Well, maybe only a little crazy, but the kind of crazy I can live with. Not having you in my life, that's something I can't live with.' He replied with a smile.

'I can't even think about another relationship right now though.' Sarah said sadly. 'I need to think about the children, they come first, they always will. And Paul... it's complicated.'

'I understand.' He said. 'But when the time is right, I just want you to know, that I'm claiming a date. I love you. In the meantime,

I'm here for you, as your friend. And when you want to talk, I'm here to listen. I'd really like to learn more about Edward and you.'

And with that he turned on his heel and walked away. But he came back every few days to visit, texting her at odd times with silly things that made her smile.

So between Ruby, James and him, they got her and the children through the dark days that followed Paul's funeral. And soon, they all began to move forward, small steps, but steps all the same.

Ruby and James insisted that they start a new tradition of going to Freddie's every Thursday night for a drink. Rita and Joey would babysit and Sarah would amble to the pub excited to see everyone. Art seemed to always arrive about an hour after they got there and would saunter over with a tray of drinks. Pretty soon it was expected that he would join them and Sarah would find herself looking forward to his arrival.

Finally, as the winter turned to spring, Art whispered to her, 'I know I said I'd wait, but Sarah, this is killing me! Would you please put me out of my misery and come to dinner?'

'I thought you'd never ask.' She answered, giving him a dazzling smile.

They went to Cistin Eile, a restaurant in Wexford town. The simple charm of the décor coupled with the amazing food was the perfect backdrop for a first date, allowing them to talk for hours about nothing and everything. And then as they waited for a taxi to take them home, Art leaned in and kissed her. Her body responded instantly to his touch and she whispered to him urgently, 'Can we go to your place?'

So now, a year after Paul's death, life was unrecognisable for them all. Last year on Christmas Day, it was a time filled with tears and sadness, but she was determined to make today far more memorable for them all.

Her reminiscing was interrupted as Art grabbed her by her waist and pulled her back into the kitchen, shouting, 'Hey woman, there's starving people out there! Are you going to serve that turkey or what?' Then he pulled her in close.

'The children!' Sarah half protested.

'Sshh.' He whispered. 'They are well used to us by now.' He leaned down and kissed her, tentatively at first, then as she began to respond to him, more passionately.

Sarah marvelled at how Art could still make her feel like a teenager every single time he touched her. She felt desire bubbling inside of her in response to his hand moving down her spine.

They pulled apart, both flushed.

'You're killing me!' Art joked, holding his chest.

'You always say that.' Sarah replied smiling at him. To feel desired by such a gorgeous man was a revelation for her. She had to keep pinching herself.

How had this happened? She thought her life was over but here she was on Christmas Day, feeling strong again, no longer drowning, no longer struggling to breathe.

'Mammy, where's the turkey? I'm starving!' Tommy's voice shouted.

'Coming!' Sarah shouted back. 'You go on in; I'll be there in a sec.'

She had no idea what the future would hold for her and Art, but that was ok, she was going to enjoy finding out.

She looked at the resplendent turkey, remembering Christmases for years where her father and then in turn Paul had carried it with great ceremony into the dining room. Always the man of the house taking the honour, she realised.

But this year she was doing it herself. Smiling, she walked into the dining room.

'I've never seen the like of this feast in all my life!' Joey declared. He couldn't believe that he was having a Christmas with people he loved. Benji was at his feet, happily waiting for a sneaky piece of meat.

'It looks heavenly.' Mary said eyeing up the roasted sweet potato.

'One of those legs has my name written all over it!' James said pointing to the turkey.

'The other has Tommy on it!' Tommy said, copying his uncle.

'Where's your name written?' Katie said. She looked puzzled. 'I don't see any name written there.' To which everyone laughed.

'The table looks so pretty.' Ruby complimented. 'You've gone to so much trouble.'

'I love the place names for everyone.' Mary added.

'I made those!' Katie said with pride.

Their eyes were all drawn towards the place setting she had made for her Daddy. He may not be there, but he would never be forgotten. The children had both good and bad days now and she knew that they would still have many more tough times ahead as they got used to life without him. But she would be right by their sides, helping them deal with it all.

'I have a joke about turkeys.' Tommy said. 'Why did the Gardaí arrest the turkey?'

He looked around the table as they all looked expectantly at him for the answer. 'They suspected it of "fowl" play!'

Sarah smiled as she listened to everyone laughing at Tommy's joke. At every battle she'd faced, these precious people were right by her side. They had all celebrated when Mal Wickham was finally convicted of murder and he was now serving a life sentence. Marie had sent James a Christmas card and seemed to be doing better. She was adamant that had Mal not been arrested when he was, she would be dead now. It felt good, that she had played a part in saving that life.

James and Ruby had surprised nobody when they got engaged during the summer and they were now planning their wedding. Sarah had never seen her brother look so happy; he never stopped smiling when they were together.

Angel Cupcakes had really taken off too and was a huge success. The demand had grown so much that Rita now worked with Sarah.

There was no denying that it had been a tough year, a year of change and loss, but also a year of wonderful new beginnings. She looked forward to the future and the many surprises that it had in store for her. Edward kept her on her toes, with premonitions coming at the oddest of times! But having acceptance from her loved ones, in turn helped her have peace about who she was for the first time in her life. It was also a lot more fun deciphering dreams, now that she had a gang of supporters who were all willing and able to help her and in turn help others. She knew that life would continue to offer up surprises to them all, but as long as she had the people in this room by her side, she'd muddle through it all.

She raised her glass to salute the people who kept her going this past year and whispered, 'Happy Christmas.'

She looked to the door where she knew Edward would be standing, watching over her as always. She smiled and raised her glass to him too.

'Mammy!' Tommy said to her, tugging her arm to get attention. 'I'm starving!'

'Well then, we'd better eat!' Sarah exclaimed.

Turn over for an exclusive look at Carmel's bestselling debut,
Beyond Grace's Rainbow.

BEYOND GRACE'S RAINBOW

Prologue

Friday 13th February 2012

Grace felt like she was floating up on the ceiling. Down below on the ground, she could see Dr Kennedy sitting in a battered old brown leather chair. He was leaning forward, earnestly, looking at somebody who looked very much like herself.

'That reminds me, I must get my roots done,' Grace thought as she looked down critically at herself. Sitting beside Grace was Sean, her friend. She knew that it was not possible to be in two places at once – she hadn't lost her marbles – yet. But at this very moment here she was up on the ceiling, watching the scene below. Grace knew it had to be her sitting below because she could actually feel Sean's hand gripping hers tightly. So the only logical explanation she could come up with was that she was having one of those 'out of body' experiences. The other possibility was that the shock of the news that had just been delivered stopped her heart and she had actually died.

Oh feck, that couldn't be true. Surely you wouldn't think about the state of your roots just after dying?

'Do you understand what I've just told you Grace?' Dr Kennedy's voice jolted Grace back to reality with a bump and a crash. She felt like she'd fallen from the ceiling and landed unceremoniously into the uncomfortable chair. So she was not dead then, Grace thought wryly. For a second she felt like complaining about the terrible chairs the patients had to sit on, while doctors had lovely comfortable leather ones. The injustice of it seemed unbearable. But maybe this wasn't the time.

'I want to go back up there.' Grace said instead, pointing to the ceiling.

'Grace, honey, you're not making any sense.' Sean said to her, he looked really worried. She knew he was probably thinking she'd gone mad. Maybe she had.

'Grace?' Dr Kennedy said gently. 'Do you understand what I've just told you?'

No more floating on the ceiling. No more analysis on the state of the chairs. She knew she had to answer him. She decided she'd have one more stab at dodging the truth.

'No I don't understand, Dr Kennedy. There's been some kind of stupid mistake and I'll be honest with you, it's not on. I'll be writing a strong letter to complain. I have a cold or maybe even proper flu. That's why I've had this bad pain in my back. You always get aches and pains when you have proper flu.' She turned triumphantly to Sean. As a GP himself he was always complaining about his patients coming in with the common cold saying they were in bits with the flu. As he often said, when you have the flu, you know it, you can't move, your body is aching so much. Unfortunately Sean just looked away from her. He couldn't look her in the eye. That wasn't good.

Grace looked at both of them with growing desperation. She knew that at this stage she was clutching at straws.

Dr Kennedy tried again, this time his tone sharper. 'Grace, you have a form of leukaemia, commonly known as AML – Acute Myelogenous Leukaemia. I know that it's a lot to take in and you must have many questions for me. I'll do my best to answer them as honestly as I can. But there's no doubt I'm afraid.'